DEBBIE IHLER RASMUSSEN

M.O.M.M.
PUBLISHING
Mysteries of My Mind

For information contact:
authordebbieihlerrasmussen@gmail.com
Website: authordebbieihlerrasmussen.com

Published by:
M.O.M.M. Publishing
"Mysteries of My Mind"

Cover Design:
Dee Loupeti • www.deegraphicdesign.com

Interior Design:
Francine Platt • Eden Graphics, Inc. • www.edengraphics.net

978-1-7334645-0-5   Paperback

978-1-7334645-3-6   ePub

Library of Congress Number: Pending

Second Edition
Manufactured in the United States of America
11 10 9 8 7 6 5 4 3 2

DEDICATION

To my parents, Richard Ihler and Faun Tella Allen Ihler,
who supported me throughout my life in everything I wanted to do.
Love you, Mom and Dad!

SPECIAL THANKS TO:

Dottie Wilde Ihler

Marie Stewart

Lanae Turley Trejo

Your willingness to read the rough pages of this work and to offer your encouragement and support has been a true blessing to me and I appreciate all of you so much!

My middle school English teacher, Miss Harlan; after reading my first handwritten book—a story about a young girl's visit to the White House during the presidency of John F. Kennedy—she encouraged me to continue writing, and said she hoped to see something of mine published in her lifetime (I have no idea if I accomplished that).

Dear Readers,

I AM SO EXCITED to finally release the second book in my *Mystic Trilogy MYSTIC LAKE!*

Volume One, *Mystic Angel,* found Jackson Allen moving his family of four from San Clemente, California to the small town of Sommerville, Tennessee, for the sole purpose of selling the family home on Mystic Lake. He had one motive—get in, get out, and get back to their life in Southern California.

But that was not to be. He had not anticipated his daughter, Aspen, to suddenly be thrown into the world of the paranormal—a world he had tried to deny existed since he was a child. The family's arrival in Sommerville, unleashed truths behind a crime laden past that put his great-grandfather Allen at the very core.

With the comradery of Aspen's brother Noah, and their new friends, Kiryn Whitaker and Gavin Fielden, one crazy fact after another begins to surface, bringing to life the legends and stories of the past. The foundation of Sommerville is shaken as the buried, twisted past rapidly develops into cold, hard reality, involving past government officials and private citizens of the quiet town.

As in the first volume, the story takes on a life of its own, with new characters and situations popping up when even I least expected them.

Thank you for joining me on this journey, and I hope you enjoy reading *Mystic Lake* as much as I have enjoyed writing it!

Sincerely,

Debbie

SOMETIMES WE RECEIVE LITTLE thoughts or inspirations. Some say it is intuition, and of course, we all have that.

Some respond to those promptings, and some choose to ignore. In most instances, ignoring them can be a negative thing. How many times have you said: "If only I had listened to my intuition." "I knew I shouldn't have." "Should have." "Gone there." "Done that?"

However, it can be a positive thing, as well: "I am so glad I listened to my intuition." "I knew it was the right thing to do" and so on and so on.

There are also some who hear, feel, dream, or otherwise, receive messages. Some would argue with that phenomena, but that is simply because they have chosen not to connect.

For those that do, the rewards—and challenges—can be infinite.

How do I know what I did not know? Among the possible explanations, one is that of Jung's theory of the "collective conscious," in which we inherit the wisdom of the experience of our ancestors without ourselves having the personal experience. While this kind of knowledge may seem bizarre to the scientific mind, strangely enough its existence is recognized in our common everyday language. Take the word "recognize" itself...The word says we "re-know" the concept, as if we knew it once upon a time, forgot it, but then recognized it as an old friend. It is as if all knowledge and all wisdom were contained in our minds, and when we learn "something new" we are only discovering something that existed in our self all along.

– DR. M. SCOTT PECK
from the book *The Road Less Traveled*, page 11

1

BONES

Before Rocky's truck rolled to a stop in front of the little house, Aspen and Noah emerged from the front door and loped down the steps. Orange rays of sunlight visible only through the tops of the trees reminded Aspen that it was barely five am. Still basking in the magic of two days earlier—Gavin's kiss—and finding the statue their great-grandfather had buried in the floorboards of his house, Aspen wasn't sure she was ready to stir everything up again.

But there was no stopping Gavin and Noah. More studying of the hand-drawn maps of Grandpa Allen's house had convinced both there was possibly another hall or tunnel on the other side of the house under the bedrooms. With just three and a half weeks before FBI agents Byron Coulsen and Larry Brimhall would want to meet with them again, Rocky agreed with the boys that they had better step-up their own investigation.

Arriving at the big house, they all bounced out of the truck, but Aspen hung back.

"What?" Kiryn stood beside her.

"I don't know. I feel kind of sad or something."

"Sad? Are you crazy? Why?"

"I don't know. I guess because even though we know what happened to Ronda, it's frustrating to know there are still so many unanswered questions."

"This may be a chance to find more clues," said Kiryn.

"I know, but—" Aspen paused. "Oh, actually, I don't know. Let's go." She grasped Kiryn's arm and pulled her onto the porch.

From the drawings in the notebook Gavin had found, Noah led him and Rocky right to the bedroom where he had felt someone touch his shoulder the first day he and Aspen had been in the house. They had concluded that with its outdated furnishing and yellowing curtains, this was most likely a room that had not been occupied by siblings of their dad.

Kiryn looked around, "Maybe this was Ronda's room."

Aspen nodded, "It would make sense, huh? Maybe they just left it as it was."

The boys had already removed two empty boxes—the only things in the closet—and were now pulling up the floorboards when Aspen and Kiryn walked in.

Kiryn leaned over Rocky, who was crouched in the open closet doorway. "Why are you guys so sure there is a hallway under that floor?"

Rocky held up the small book of drawings Gavin had found in the storage room. "We're not, but the drawings do show some sort of a tunnel under this side of the house and look, this drawing shows it is directly east of the shaft. Right where we are." He pointed to the wall where the baseboard should be. "And besides, all of the other closets have baseboards."

"How do you know that?"

Gavin looked up from his work and rolled his eyes at his sister, "We checked."

"Oh." Kiryn shrugged, and Aspen laughed.

Several boards later, the floor revealed a sunken handle.

"Holy cow!" Noah whistled, and he and Gavin quickly removed the rest of the boards.

Everyone backed out of the closet and Noah yanked on the handle. The hatch lifted.

"Geez, this thing is heavy."

Gavin grabbed the edge. They both lifted the hatch and leaned it against the wall. Gavin shined a flashlight down the opening.

"Another staircase. These guys—whoever that would be—were totally into hidden staircases."

Cold air rushed up at them, and they exchanged looks of apprehension.

Rocky checked the two-way radios to make sure they were on. "You kids be careful. I probably should go with you."

"Who would save us then, Dad?" Gavin grinned and put his hand on Rocky's shoulder. "We'll be fine."

"Famous last words," mumbled Kiryn.

Gavin rolled his eyes. "Seriously, Dad."

"We got this, Rocky. We need you up here. We won't do anything stupid," said Noah.

"Okay, but if you run into anything—you know, dangerous— just get out of there. I'll be right here."

"Okay, let's go." Noah started cautiously down the staircase, the other three following close behind. They each carried high-beam flashlights so they could easily see what was in front of them, and Gavin had the radio handset Rocky insisted they take.

"Okay, this is the weirdest yet," said Noah when he reached the bottom of the stairs. "This is a tunnel." He shined the beam of his light into the darkness, "A very long tunnel."

"Fourteen steps," said Kiryn. "And that was steep. We are down pretty deep."

"Obviously. It's so musty and damp in here," said Gavin. "I'll bet this goes over near the lake." He pushed the button on the handset, "Rocky, we are in a tunnel. It looks pretty long."

Rocky laughed, "You know I can still see you?"

They all looked back up the stairs where Rocky stood at the top. Gavin grinned, "I know, I was just testing."

"Okay. Keep me posted, and be careful."

"Will do," Gavin said into the handset and Noah, and he laughed.

Aspen and Kiryn did not find it so funny and were both grateful Rocky could hear Gavin.

Somehow this adventure scared Aspen. Maybe because now

they knew for sure murder had been committed nearby? Maybe because the one murdered was the girl Aspen could see—Ronda? She couldn't put her thoughts in order. Why did she feel so much apprehension now? She had been trying to shrug the feeling off since this morning, but it still lingered in the pit of her stomach.

"Hey, Gavin, why do you think this tunnel goes near the lake?" Kiryn's voice was quivering.

"Are you afraid?" asked Noah.

"As a matter of fact, I am. This is creepy."

Noah reached back and grasped her hand. "Here, stay by me."

Aspen grinned. She knew Kiryn really liked Noah, and she loved seeing him being so sweet to her.

Gavin stepped up behind Aspen and put one hand on her back, sending tingles down her spine. He hadn't been this close to her since their kiss. She breathed deeply to quiet her heart.

"I'm right here," he said softly. Then louder, he answered Kiryn, "Well, think of where this house is, and the direction the tunnel is going."

"Oh," mumbled Kiryn.

The tunnel was very long, and there were places they had to either duck or walk single file. It was dark, damp, and musty, and no one had much to say. They kept walking.

"This is scary down—" Aspen began, but was interrupted by Noah.

"Look at that!" he yelled and jumped back, almost knocking Kiryn to the ground.

Gavin stopped Kiryn from falling, and they all huddled close around Noah, all their lights pointing to a cave in the side of the tunnel.

"Are those bones?" whispered Noah.

"No! Those are dead people!" Kiryn shrieked. "Ahhh…let's get out of here!" She turned pushed past Gavin and Aspen, but stopped immediately. "It's pitch black!"

"No kidding," said Gavin. He grabbed Kiryn's shoulder and pulled her back, "We have to stay together."

"Who are they?" Aspen felt sick.

"I hate to even imagine," said Noah.

Gavin took a deep breath, "C'mon you guys, we can't have too much farther to go, we've been walking forever." He again clicked a button on the handset. "Rocky?"

"Yeah?" Rocky said something else, but they couldn't hear him for the static. "We found a sort of—I don't know, graveyard."

Kiryn leaned toward the handset. "Actually, it's a pile of bones!" she called.

"What? Maybe you kids had better come back out." Rocky's voice crackled through the speaker, but it sounded like he was yelling now, and they could hear him better.

"We're okay," Noah called. "They can't hurt us now."

"Oh, well, that's comforting," said Kiryn.

Noah winced, "C'mon, let's keep going."

Hugging the wall opposite the cave, the four trudged past the bones, cautiously shining their lights on them as they passed.

Aspen counted skulls but stopped at fifteen. It was just too depressing. "You don't suppose these could be those…those boys from the journal, do you?"

"They could be." Gavin was now in front of the group, as Noah had taken up the rear with Kiryn as they continued to make their way through the blackness.

Aspen shuddered. She kept glancing back and bumped into Gavin when he abruptly stopped.

"Look at this," he said.

The four scanned the area with their lights. They had arrived at a small square room with gray cinderblock walls. The room was empty, and on the opposite side from where they stood was a door.

Gavin crossed the floor and pulled on the door handle. It didn't open at first, but with a second jerk, the door moved.

"Aren't you the least bit concerned about what you might find in there?" asked Kiryn, but when the door opened, a faint beam of light came through she stopped talking.

"Looks like it may go outside," said Gavin. "There is a breeze.

Can you guys feel that?"

"Good! Let's hurry!" said Kiryn.

Aspen nodded, "I can hear water." Goosebumps pricked her arms and neck.

"Yeah, I can too," said Gavin. "I think I know what we are going to find."

"You do?" Aspen was puzzled.

"Yeah, we have walked a long way and remember my house is two houses from your grandpa's. There is a big cement culvert that comes up near the boat dock. It's old, and the opening is covered with a grate. I'll bet that is where this goes."

"But water would get in here, wouldn't it?"

"Maybe, but the lake is never more than two feet higher than it is right now. You can tell by the shoreline. The culvert sticks out of the ground about four feet."

They stepped into the tunnel that was now concrete instead of dirt. The tunnel began slanting upward, and as they walked, a faint light at the far end came into view.

"Looks like maybe fifty feet." Gavin guessed.

"I just think this is weird," said Kiryn, but no one responded to her comment.

The end of the tunnel was a solid concrete wall, and the light came from a cement pipe about five feet in diameter. It connected to the tunnel above their heads and could be accessed by an iron ladder fastened to the wall. The ladder stretched the entire length of the pipe and went straight up. There was a lot of debris on top, but they could still see the sky.

Gavin was right—a huge grate held in place by four large padlocks covered the entire opening. It was partially covered with debris, but not enough to block out the light completely.

"No one goes near this because there is a big danger sign on the other side," said Gavin.

"Yeah, danger, *bones ahead*," said Noah flatly.

"Do you think that's where Tygert put the bodies of those boys? In that pile?" Aspen's stomach was in knots.

"No." Noah quickly disagreed. "I think those are the ones who weren't lucky enough to make it to the root cellar."

"Lucky?" Aspen narrowed her eyes. "Are you kidding me, Noah?"

"Okay, not lucky, but you know what I mean. The ones in the root cellar are probably at least buried."

"Hopefully," said Kiryn.

"You mean if they are actually there," said Gavin.

"Maybe they just dumped them. Like those back there." Kiryn thrust her thumb over her shoulder.

"Yep, you're probably right—*if* he killed them—we still don't know that." Aspen sighed. "Can we get out of here?"

"Yeah, we better go. Rocky is probably wondering about us," said Noah.

Just then, Rocky's voice squawked through the handset, "Hey!"

Gavin brought it to his mouth. "We're here. We're looking straight up a concrete pipe to the outside. I'm going to climb up the ladder."

"What pipe?"

"It's a culvert, Dad. It was there when Mom and Doug bought the house."

"Stay away from that thing, Gavin. You kids need to get out of there."

"It's okay, Dad, I know where it goes. I'm just going to see if we can get out this way."

"Be careful, Gavin. The ladder may not be very secure." Rocky's voice was surprisingly clear.

"No worries." He handed the handset to Noah and began climbing the iron rungs while the other three watched.

Aspen kept looking back over her shoulder. The uneasiness wouldn't go away.

Gavin was back in minutes. "All I can see through the opening are trees, but I know this is that culvert by the boat dock. I'll show you when we get out."

Kiryn shuddered. "Oh, I hate that we have to walk past those bones again. I wish we could go out this way."

"Me too," Aspen agreed.

"Those are pretty big padlocks," said Noah. He looked at Gavin, "I don't suppose—"

Gavin shook his head. "There is no way. They are not only locked, but they have chains on them too. We're not getting through that."

Kiryn sighed, "Well, then let's go."

As they started back, Aspen said, "I wonder why no one went down in that culvert—you know, the city or something. They would have found the bones."

"That's easy," said Gavin. "The lake is private property."

"That's why no one has seen the mist people are always talking about, no one can use this lake except the people who live here," said Kiryn. "The mist is probably not even real."

They all passed through the cinderblock room, and Noah pushed the door shut. The darkness was dense until their eyes adjusted again, and with the help of their lights, they continued to make their way back through the tunnel.

They stopped again by the bones, and Noah pulled out his cell phone. "At least these are good for something down here." He snapped two pictures of the bones, and they continued. "Just in case they are gone when we come back down."

"What? Are they going to up and walk away?" asked Kiryn sarcastically, but the quiver in her voice confirmed she was still nervous.

"Yeah, why would they be gone? The people who put them there are probably dead," said Aspen. "And anyway, who says we are coming back down?"

"I just assumed—" began Noah.

"No, Noah is right. We need to show Rocky and probably the police at some point," said Gavin.

"It is real, by-the-way," said Aspen.

"What is?" Noah kept walking, and Kiryn followed, but Gavin pulled on Aspen's arm and turned her around.

"What's real, Aspen?"

Now Noah and Kiryn had stopped too, and both were listening.

"The—the mist. It's real, Kiryn."

"You've seen it?" Kiryn sounded shocked.

"Yes—" Aspen looked at Noah. "That day—at the lake—when we were leaving, I looked back, and there was a mist—"

Loud shrieking interrupted Aspen, and they all whirled, shining their lights down the dark tunnel.

Kiryn clung to Noah's shirt, "Let's just get out of her!"

"What is that?" asked Gavin.

The sound was getting louder, and they all began backing away.

Suddenly a small object flew directly at them, hitting Gavin in the chest, then another and another. They were coming fast; pelting all of them.

Kiryn, Noah, and Gavin turned and ran for the entrance, but Aspen froze as one flew directly into her light. It stopped just in front of her face its tiny black eyes, and sharp teeth seeming to threaten her very existence.

Aspen turned running while she screamed, "They're bats!"

She saw Kiryn and Noah disappear through the hatch. Gavin stood on the middle of the ladder, his arm outstretched, "Hurry, Aspen!"

Aspen ran as hard as she could, but within just a few feet of the ladder, she was suddenly pulled backward, and at the same instance, Gavin was propelled through the open hatch.

"Aspen!" Gavin yelled.

To her horror, the hatch slammed shut, leaving her in total darkness. The piercing shrieking seemed to consume her as she crashed to the dirt floor.

Aspen's pounding heart and anxious breathing were all she could hear as she inched slowly toward the ladder. Frantically groping at the darkness, she found only more dirt. She froze and listened—nothing.

"Noah?" she croaked.

She held her breath so that she could hear any little sound—still nothing. Pulling her knees to her chest, she wrapped her arms around them and shaking uncontrollably, she tried to call out to her brother and her friends.

"Noah! Gavin! Kiryn!" her voice cracked, and the sounds were nothing but whispers.

Blackness. Silence.

She was all alone. Inching backward until she found the corner, she pressed herself against the cool, damp dirt.

Images or experiences of things that are not really happening to you. Patrice's words popped into Aspen's thoughts.

But the others heard the screaming. This is not the same as the rats. The bats hit us.

Exasperated, she covered her face with her hands and whimpered, "Help me. Someone, please help me."

Aspen hadn't moved from the corner. There were no sounds in the tunnel, and she cautiously felt around for one of the flashlights. Her hand bumped something soft, and the image of a lifeless bat made her sick. She pulled away quickly and sank farther into the corner.

Think! What else did Patrice say? Her head was spinning. *Where did everyone go?*

She suddenly thought of the pile of bones not far from her, and she began to panic.

"I have to get out of here! Help! Someone help me!"

Thick blackness only loomed heavier.

How will I ever get out of here? Why is no one coming for me? She buried her face in her knees.

"Please, somebody—if there is a God—please…"

Deathly silence.

She slowly lifted her head. Someone or something was breathing.

Terrified of making any sound, she held her breath. The sound was coming closer.

"Is…is someone there?"

I DIDN'T SLAM THE DOOR!

"WHY DID YOU SLAM the door?" Noah leaped toward Gavin, and pushing him aside, he grabbed the handle and pulled. An invisible force pushed him backward, and he crashed into the wall.

Gavin glared at him and lunged for the handle himself. "I didn't slam the door!" he barked. He too jerked on the handle but was thrown backward.

"What is going on?" Kiryn screamed. "Where is Aspen?"

Rocky's head was still reeling from the scene he had just witnessed when the hatch flew open, and cold air had filled the tiny closet along with a piercing screeching sound. Noah and Kiryn scrambled out of the hole, but suddenly Gavin flew out of the opening, and the hatch slammed shut. The screeching had immediately stopped.

Now Rocky hurried past the two boys to join in the efforts to open the hatch. It simply would not budge.

Gavin and Noah each again tried the handle, but to no avail, and the three of them stood in silence sweating and breathing hard.

Frustrated Kiryn wailed, "Do something!"

Noah fell to his knees and pounded on the closed door, "Aspen, answer me!" He felt the hatch move, and he jumped away from it. "Did you—"

"Yes!" Gavin reached for the handle, and Noah grasped the edges of the heavy door.

WAIT!

ASPEN COWERED INTO THE corner.

She could see a faint light materializing way down the tunnel. It seemed to be coming toward her. She scanned the darkness for any sign of the bat that moments earlier had confronted her. Nothing.

The light moved closer.

Aspen wiped the tears from her eyes with the back of her hands, trying desperately to focus on the image inside the light.

There *was* an image, but it was shrouded behind a sort of veil—a curtain—or a cloth.

In the distance, she could hear water running. As the light moved closer, the sound grew louder.

Aspen jumped to her feet. *Was water coming down the tunnel?*

She groped the darkness, hoping to possibly find the ladder, but her efforts were in vain. She only clawed the dirt wall of the tunnel.

The image and the now brilliant light seemed to fill the entire tunnel, and the sound of rushing water was deafening.

Tears again spilled down Aspen's cheeks. "Who are you? What do you want?"

The sound stopped.

The light dimmed a little, and Aspen stared into it.

The veil was not cloth at all. It was a curtain of water—running water—like something she had seen in a fish restaurant. A huge wall of moving water locked between two glass partitions, only this was not behind glass. She could feel the light spray it created.

Now the sound became louder. The sound of a waterfall was unmistakable.

The image moved. She could not tell if she was looking at a girl or a boy. The image did not seem to have any features, and it moved seemingly with the movement of the water.

"Help."

Fear gripped Aspen, and she began shaking. Had she heard a voice? *Was it coming from the water? The image? Where?*

She could not keep from crying any longer, and she wailed, "Please don't do this. What do you want? Who are you?"

She had not taken her eyes from the image, and suddenly it seemed to pull away and move farther down the tunnel, but the water stayed.

With tears running freely down her cheeks, she huddled against the cold dirt and sank in a heap. She buried her face in her hands. "Why did everyone leave me here? Why is this happening to me?"

Thoughts tumbled over and over in her head. She tried to focus on just one—Ronda—she had helped Ronda, hadn't she? Was this someone that needed—

She suddenly thought of something else Patrice had said when Aspen told her about the lights in the lake.

"This is, I believe, someone trying to contact you for help."

Aspen jumped to her feet, "Wait!"

She clamped both hands over her mouth. *I can't believe I just did that!*

But it was too late. The image stopped. It turned and lifted an arm as if to acknowledge her.

In an instant, a flashlight clicked on. It was right at Aspen's feet. She grabbed it and shined it toward the wall of water, but all she could see was a dark tunnel. She whirled, and as she did, she bumped into the ladder.

The hatch above her head opened, and Gavin and Noah peered down at her.

"Aspen, what are you doing?" Noah sounded angry, but Aspen detected the concern in her brother's voice.

Gavin scrambled down the ladder, "Aspen, are you okay?"

"Well, don't just look at her, get her out!" Kiryn yelled.

Aspen looked up and locked eyes with Noah. Tears were leaking down his cheeks. Gavin wrapped his arms around her and pulled her to his chest, but Aspen still stared into Noah's eyes. "I'm…I'm okay." She said softly. She was overcome by the closeness she felt for her brother.

Gavin held her away from him and investigated her face. "Are you sure you're all right?"

Aspen nodded, and she buried her face in Gavin's shoulder. "Yes. I'm sorry. I couldn't reach you."

"Let's get her out of there, Gav." Rocky's commanding voice caused Gavin to release Aspen, and gently shove her toward the ladder.

He waited for her to ascend the rungs, while constantly looking back over his shoulder.

Aspen glanced down at him. "It's gone." She said softly.

Gavin's eyes widened, and he hurried up the ladder behind her. "What's gone?" he asked as he stepped from the ladder.

Noah hugged his sister. "Seriously, Aspen, don't do stuff like that."

Aspen looked puzzled. "I didn't *do* anything. You guys left me there."

"We didn't—"

Aspen held up one hand. "I know, I know you didn't."

It was then that Rocky must have noticed her dirty fingernails, and he took her hand, inspecting her fingers. They were bleeding. He turned questioning eyes in her direction.

Aspen shrugged. "I couldn't find the ladder."

Kiryn sighed heavily and pushed through all of them. She linked arms with Aspen and pulled her from the closet. "Can we just get out of here already? Do we need to dissect that whole thing standing in this little, tiny closet? She's out now let's go!"

Gavin, Noah, and Rocky exchanged a quick glance, but then they obediently followed Kiryn and Aspen.

Kiryn did not stop until she was outside on the back patio. She pushed Aspen to a lounge chair and then plopped on to one closest to her.

"What was that all about, Aspen? What happened?"

"I was running to the ladder, and then you weren't there anymore and the hatch closed." She furrowed her eyebrows. "Why did it close?"

Gavin shook his head. "I'm not sure, but I didn't close it."

Kiryn was shaking her head. "He didn't, Aspen."

"I know," said Aspen, and she looked at Kiryn who was staring at her. "It's all right," she whispered.

"Oh, I'm sure it is—with you anyway. You and your dead people." Kiryn rolled her eyes.

BEST FRIENDS

THEY DUSTED OFF THE patio furniture and pushed some chairs and lounges together.

Rocky lagged a little. When he finally joined them, he had ordered pizza and handed Aspen some wet towels to wash her hands.

Rocky started the conversation, "What happened down there?"

Aspen didn't answer at first, but then she asked again, "Why did the hatch close?"

"Now wait—" began Noah.

"I don't mean you guys closed it. Duh, Noah. I just mean what happened. It was all so strange."

Gavin explained, "No *one* actually threw me, but some*thing* did. I just felt a force, and I couldn't hold onto the ladder any longer. Then I was on the floor in the closet and the hatch closed—well, slammed."

Noah shrugged, "That's pretty much it, Aspen. We couldn't get the door open again. No matter how hard we tried, we couldn't budge it."

"But then Noah was pounding on it, and it just moved, and then they opened it," said Rocky.

"Could you hear us yelling at you?" asked Gavin.

Aspen shook her head. "No. At first, all I could hear was that loud shrieking." She looked at all of them. "You guys heard that, right?"

"Did we ever!" said Kiryn. "That's why I wanted to get out."

"How did you know it was bats?" asked Noah.

"One stopped right in my light—it was ugly too—little, but ugly. It just stared at me, but then I tried to get away, and I could only get to the corner. I couldn't find the ladder or a light." She paused. "But I guess they were there all the time."

Rocky looked puzzled. "Why bats?"

"I don't know. Why rats before? Seems like there must be some connection, but I don't know what it would be. How long was I down there?"

"Five, maybe ten minutes," said Noah.

"That's it?! A lot happened in that short of time."

"What happened, Aspen? What's going on?" Gavin leaned on his elbows. "Was there someone—*something*—down there?"

Aspen took a deep breath. "Yes, at least I think so. The shrieking stopped, and it was quiet for a long time—longer than five or ten minutes—I'm positive. Then, I could hear breathing, and I saw a light, but I could hear water, and I saw a waterfall. Then I saw an image—"

"Was it another girl?" asked Noah.

"I don't know. It didn't seem like a person. It was weird."

Kiryn sighed noticeably. "Oh, great. A non-person who is dead."

"Well, we don't know that," said Gavin.

"Perfect. So, this non-person could be alive?"

Rocky pumped the air with one hand. "Relax Kiryn. We don't know what this is. What we do know, is that—again—someone is trying to reach out to Aspen."

"It scared me to death until…well, until I asked what it wanted, and why it was doing this. Then it started to fade away, but it came back. Well, at least it stopped."

"Why did it—"

Aspen interrupted Kiryn. "Because I told it to wait."

You WHAT?" Are you crazy?" Kiryn jumped to her feet. "Actually, are we ALL crazy?! Am I the only one in this group who finds it odd that there are bones under the house, bats flying at us and… and waterfalls in a dirt tunnel?!"

The other four stared at her.

Then Noah confronted her. "Kiryn, have you been hurt in any way through all of this?"

Kiryn continued to stand with her hands on her hips. "No. Not yet."

"Well then, why are you so upset?"

Kiryn looked at Noah for a long time before she said anything. "I guess I was just hoping for a normal friend with school starting and all."

"Normal?" Aspen glared at her.

"Not normal meaning you *normal*. Normal meaning life normal." Kiryn sank into her chair. "I'm sorry, Aspen. I just thought it was over."

"Who is the one who encouraged me this morning? *Like we might find some more clues?*"

Kiryn rolled her eyes, at the same time shaking her head. "That would be me," she confessed.

"Well then, what's up with you?" It was Gavin's turn to question her.

Kiryn was silent.

"Kiryn?" Rocky gently reached over and patted his daughter's knee.

"It was scary, Dad, there are bones down there, and then the loud shrieking, and bats hitting us. Then Aspen got locked in. I guess I am just afraid we are pushing too far. I guess I didn't expect anything so soon after finding—finding Ronda."

Gavin leaned back in his chair and laced his fingers together. "I have been thinking about that. We didn't find Ronda. We found a statue. We found out what happened to Ronda, but I'm thinking there is more to this story."

"And then there are the boys—" added Noah.

They all looked at each other, but no one said anything for several minutes.

Rocky left for a minute and met the pizza guy out front. When he returned, he placed pizza, breadsticks, and water on the table.

Aspen helped herself to a breadstick and took a bite. "Then there's Dad. I don't know, Noah, I just think there is a connection somewhere."

"To Ronda?"

"To something." She looked up at the Mansion House. "To this place, and the lake. It all has to be intertwined somehow."

"You're probably right," said Noah. "But I don't know if Dad is ready for all of this."

"Yeah, me either. Then there's Mom. She seems to be a little more normal now. Maybe we should just let it go."

Rocky leaned forward with both elbows on his knees. "I'm going to tell all of you something. This can't be pushed under the rug any longer. Jackson needed to come back here for a reason. I'm not sure what that is yet, but there is a reason. And you, Gavin, you have learned about who you really are, and Aspen and Noah, you have just touched the tip of the iceberg of your family's history. There is too much at stake. We have uncovered a lot of things that have been buried in this town for a long time—literally, it seems—and we need to continue. We need to finish what we started."

"But where could it be going?" asked Noah.

Rocky shrugged. "I don't know, but I do know that your family's arrival here has caused an upheaval, and brought things to the forefront—things that no one has wanted to talk about for a long, long time."

"What about me?" asked Kiryn quietly, "What good am I?"

"What?" Aspen leaped to her feet, crossed the patio, and plopped onto Kiryn's lap. "You are my best friend!"

As she said those words, she felt a tug in her heart, and she caught the look in Noah's eyes. He smiled, and she knew it was okay. Kiryn *was* her best friend, and Krista would be her best friend—forever—however long forever might be.

5

LIGHTS IN THE WINDOW

ASPEN ROLLED TO HER side, and her feet dropped to the floor. She leaned back on her bed so she could see the clock. The red numbers glared at her. *Two AM. I am so sick of not sleeping all night.* She rubbed her eyes with her fists and picked up her water bottle from the floor. Scooting back on her bed, she crossed her legs, slowly twisted the cap, and stared through the partially open blind. Exasperated, she rubbed her eyes again, drank the rest of the water, and dropped the empty bottle on her bed.

A week had gone by since they had found the tunnel under the house. The image she had seen behind the water would not go away. It was fixed in her mind like an actual picture had been embedded there. She wanted so badly to talk to her dad, but he had only been home two days and was still working with a psychologist to help him sort out whatever was going on in his head. The whole thing frustrated Aspen. She wondered what he could have possibly gone through that would have scared him to the point that he would have locked it away all these years.

This past week, all of them had been busy getting ready for school to start—only two more days. Aspen couldn't bring herself to dwell on it. It was Noah's senior year. He would have been on the San Clemente High surfing team, and probably would be heading to San Diego State the following year. It made her sad for him, although to her surprise, he had not even mentioned it.

After the incident in the tunnel, and more conversation with Rocky, Noah, Gavin, and Kiryn, they concluded it was about time to bring Aspen and Noah's parents up to speed as to what had been going on over the summer, but when and how, was another subject entirely. Although they all knew it would be impossible to keep all this quiet much longer.

Mr. Weston had already called Rocky twice about releasing the findings in the painting in the Mansion House. He felt it was wrong for all of this to be kept secret.

Seeing no other options right then, Rocky stepped out of his comfort zone and talked to Gavin's step-dad, Doug. He asked Doug to loan him some money so he could give to Mr. Weston to keep the story quiet until the Allen family decided to release it. He had not given Doug and Sara full details however but asked that they trust his judgment until Jackson Allen was well. They had agreed, and Rocky swore—or rather bribed—Mr. Weston to secrecy.

The next obstacle, was that the only two Allen's who knew anything about the findings were teenagers—Aspen and Noah—and the people who actually needed to make this decision were their dad, Jackson Allen, who knew nothing about what had been happening, and his sister Dana, who lived in Oregon, and also knew nothing of the events.

Rocky had talked to Mom about the will belonging to Noah and Aspen's great-grandfather, and the fact that it seemed to have disappeared. He asked her if it would be possible to meet with the attorney the Allen's hired to find the will, but Mom had emphatically said no. She would not go behind Jackson's back, which made Rocky even more passionate about bringing Jackson and Suzann into the entire menagerie, mystery, or "mess," as Kiryn called it.

On top of everything else, Drew and Dylan Dixon had been pressing Rocky for more information as well. They had pretty much backed off for a while, but now they wanted to know if there was anything they could do to help. After learning that their grandfather had been involved in the murder of Ronda Allen, they wanted to find out as much as they could about their family's past, and they hadn't lost hope of finding the document their aunt had told them about which supposedly included them in the Allen inheritance.

As always happened when Aspen let her mind dwell on all of this, she ended up feeling confused, and with a headache. She shuffled to the kitchen to get some more water, and something to relieve the pain. Her parents and Noah were sleeping—of course—it wasn't even three am yet.

Just as Aspen stepped into the kitchen, a bright light flashed outside the window. For a second, she froze. There was nothing in the backyard that could have caused a light like that. Cautiously, she moved closer to the window but stopped. There was no sound, and the light was no longer there.

Her heart racing, she waited a few seconds for it to calm, and then she crept next to the window and parted the blind with her fingers. Except for the dim glow of the yard light, there was only blackness. She shrugged.

How much of this is my imagination?

But somehow, she was compelled to stay by the window. Parting the blind further, she leaned closer to the glass and tried to see beyond the yard light. The trees cast tall shadows across the grass, but there was no wind, and the shadows were still. She wanted to open the door to see more clearly, but her better judgment told her not to, and she held her vantage point where she was.

She sighed and glanced at the clock on the microwave. It was nearly three-thirty. She had been standing there for over half an hour. *How could that be?*

Aspen breathed deeply and realizing her headache was gone, decided to go back to bed. She turned just as a blinding light flashed in the window, and whirled around.

Frozen with fear, she watched through the open blind as the bright light slowly dimmed, and seemed to move away from the house. She wanted to cry out. To call Noah or her parents, but she could not make any sound. Paralyzed, she stared at the light that had now become an amber glow. It seemed to have settled at the far back part of the yard.

The shed.

"Aspen?"

Aspen threw her hands to her mouth to muffle her scream as she whirled around. Noah was walking toward her from the hallway.

"You scared me to death, Noah!" She turned back around and pointed to the window.

"What?" Noah continued toward her. "What are you doing? You look like you just saw a ghost." He paused, eyeing her and added slowly, "Did you?"

Aspen shook her head. "A li...there's a li... There is a light."

Noah was beside her now. He took her elbow and slowly turned her around.

They both stopped. The glow was still there.

"What the?" Noah yanked on the cord, and the blind opened. "What is that?"

"It was really bright at first. Just outside the window."

"It looks like it might be in the shed."

"Should we go get Mom and Dad?"

"No," said Noah flatly. "I don't think that's a good idea." Then he paused and looked at her. "Do you?"

Aspen noticed the deep furrow in Noah's brow and suspected hers looked the same. "No, probably not. What should we do?"

"Nothing."

"Nothing?"

Still holding her arm, Noah quickly closed the blind, "C'mon."

They walked to his room, slowing down when they passed the hallway to their parent's room.

"They're still asleep."

Aspen nodded, and they continued to Noah's room, where he quietly closed his door.

Noah didn't say anything at first, and Aspen stood motionless by the door.

"Let's wait till morning, and then we can see what it is."

Aspen scrunched her face. "I don't know if I want to know."

"Well, it's something, Aspen. What I can't figure out is why I can see and hear this stuff suddenly. Kiryn, too. The bats and the shrieking, for example."

Aspen shrugged. "I don't know. But I'm kind of glad. I wish you could see the people too."

"That's okay. I'm good not seeing those." He plopped on his bed. "We should probably get some sleep."

"Are you kidding me? I can't go to sleep."

Noah chuckled. "Me either." He picked up his phone. "Wonder if Gavin and Kiryn want to go to breakfast in the morning. Like really early." He smiled and sent Gavin a text.

"So you don't want to check it out alone?"

Noah chuckled again. "Naw. The more, the merrier."

"Agreed," said Aspen, and she sank down on the bed next to Noah.

Mom walked into the kitchen. "How long have you kids been up?"

"Not too long," Noah lied. "Gavin and Kiryn are coming over, and we are going to breakfast. Want us to bring something back for you and Dad?"

Mom shook her head. "No thanks. Dad's still sleeping. I'll fix something for us later. What do you kids have planned for your last Saturday of the summer?"

"Same ole, same ole," said Aspen. "We're just going to figure it out as we go along."

Mom laughed. "Okay. I'll see you later. I'm going to take a shower."

"K, Mom. See you later." Aspen gulped down a glass of chocolate milk.

Noah scowled, "How do you drink that stuff so fast?"

Aspen wiped her mouth, rinsed the glass, and placed it in the dishwasher. "I love it." She laughed.

"Hey." The front door opened and Kiryn poked her head inside. "You guys ready?"

"Ready!" called Aspen, and she and Noah joined Kiryn on the front porch.

Gavin was still inside the truck and held up his phone. "So what is this text at 4 am? What light?"

"Yeah, shut the engine off and come back here with us." Noah started through the breezeway, and the three followed. As they walked, he asked Aspen to describe what she had seen the night before, and then he added what he had seen.

"Okay. This is new," said Gavin.

"I know. Never seen anything like this before," said Noah.

"This is a pretty backyard," said Kiryn. "Who takes care of the grass and garden?"

Noah shrugged, "Some gardener. We have never seen whoever it is. He always comes when we aren't home."

"That's because we are never home," said Aspen, suddenly realizing she had never even thought about who took care of the yard at the little house. It just always looked nice.

"That's true," said Noah.

The four walked along the cobblestone path that neither Aspen nor Noah had set foot on since that first day in Sommerville. Neither had a desire to go in the backyard after the first incident and with so much that had happened, they really had not given it any consideration.

Aspen noticed the vegetables in the garden had matured and were free of weeds. It was obvious many had been picked, but there was still plenty left to harvest.

The path turned, and goosebumps formed immediately on Aspen's neck and arms.

Gavin put his hand on the small of her back. "Are you okay?"

She nodded. "Yes, just a strange feeling."

The shed came into view, and they all stopped.

Noah took a deep breath. "C'mon, let's go check it out."

"Wait, is this where those rats were?" Kiryn pulled back.

Aspen nodded, and at the same time, grabbed her brother's arm. "Noah the door is open."

It *was* open about four inches. Noah stopped. After a few seconds, he said, "Well, the gardener does use the shed, Aspen."

"I know but—"

Noah turned to her, "Let's just take a look."

He turned back and started toward the shed, and Gavin followed. Aspen stayed where she was, and Kiryn joined her.

A slight breeze picked up, and the two girls turned when they heard a creaking sound coming from the trees.

"That's odd," said Aspen.

"I've heard that sound before. Rocky said it's usually a weak branch," said Kiryn.

Noah stood near the open door of the shed, "There is nothing in here except tools, just like before."

Gavin opened the door wider and peered inside. "Nothing unusual. Hey, Noah did you notice there is no light bulb in the socket."

He flipped the switch anyway. "So, then what caused the glow from the shed?"

Noah was almost back by Aspen and Kiryn. "I don't—"

A loud creaking and then breaking sound distracted Noah, and he looked up at the trees just as one of them snapped like a toothpick, and a massive branch headed straight for Aspen and Kiryn.

"Look out!" Gavin yelled, and both he and Noah leaped toward their sisters crashing into them, and pushing them out of the path of the falling tree.

The girls tumbled across the grass, and Noah slid into them, but Gavin did not get out of the way in time, and the huge branch crashed into him, knocking him to the ground.

Gavin wailed in pain as he landed on his back.

Noah scrambled over the fallen tree to his friend. His stomach wretched when he saw the damage the tree had done. "Aspen call 911 NOW!"

Gavin's face was scratched, and bleeding and his natural dark complexion looked pale, as blood gushed from a long gash in his arm. The limb had impaled Gavin and still protruded from his arm. It appeared to have gone all the way through, pinning his arm to the ground.

Noah knew immediately by the bright red color of the blood that an artery had been cut and he pulled his T-shirt off and wrapped it tightly around Gavin's bicep just above the wound. Another thick piece of wood was sticking out of his shoulder.

Gavin wasn't moving.

"Gavin!" Kiryn screamed, and she started toward him, but suddenly turned around and ran up the path. "I'll get your mom!"

Aspen's hands shook as she pulled her phone from her pocket and punched in the numbers. "Please send an ambulance! We—we are at the Allen Manor—well not actually there—at the house at the bottom of the hill." Aspen was crying now, and the women's voice spoke sternly. "Miss, miss—what is your name?"

"Please hurry, we are—"

"I know *where* you are." Came the voice through the speaker. "An ambulance is on its way. I need to know *who* you are."

"Aspen. Aspen Allen." She turned to look at Gavin.

"Gavin, Gavin!' Noah yelled directly in Gavin's face. "He passed out!"

Noah looked up when he heard someone running. "Mom!"

Suzann and Kiryn ran toward them, each carrying blankets and towels.

Mom fell on her knees next to Gavin. "I can hear the sirens Noah; they're coming." She quickly covered Gavin with the blankets and mopped his forehead and neck with a towel. She piled more towels on the wound, as Noah's t-shirt was saturated in blood.

Kiryn threw her arms around Aspen and wept bitterly. "He isn't dead, is he?"

Mom looked up. "No Kiryn, he is not dead. He is in shock. He will be okay but—"

"But what?"

"Nothing, he will be okay. Noah helped the bleeding with his shirt." She looked at her son whose face was streaked with tears, and then called over her shoulder, "Kiryn, call Rocky and have him meet us at the hospital."

The sirens screamed down the long driveway, and in seconds two paramedics were at Gavin's side. Mom stood and pulled Noah to his feet. She wrapped her arm around his waist and moved him back next to Kiryn and Aspen.

"Yes, Dad," wailed Kiryn into her cell phone. "A tree fell on him. He's unconscious."

Suzann took the phone from Kiryn. "Rocky, meet us at the hospital. He is going to be okay. The paramedics are here and—" she stopped talking.

Two firefighters hurried past them carrying chain saws, and Mom pulled the three kids out of the way, before speaking into the phone again. "Rocky, maybe you had better come here." She turned to Kiryn and hugged her shoulders. "He's on his way."

"Suzann?"

They all looked up. Dad was standing on the path, and Mom rushed to his side. "There was an accident, Jackson. A tree—I guess a tree broke, and a branch hit Gavin."

Aspen ran to her dad, and threw her arms around him, crying uncontrollably. Dad hugged her but said nothing. He stared up at the ragged trunk of the broken tree.

A third firefighter approached them. "Folks, I'm sorry, could we get all of you to move back out of the way."

Dad and Mom ushered the kids down the path toward the house, just as Rocky's truck screeched to a stop behind the fire truck. He leaped out and crossed the grass in seconds.

"Rocky!" called one of the firefighters, and just then, Aspen heard the chain saw. She buried her face in her dad's shoulder.

"He's lost a lot of blood," she heard the firefighter say, as he guided Rocky to where Gavin lay.

Rocky looked back over his shoulder and yelled to Kiryn. "I called Sara and Doug."

Kiryn nodded absently through her tears. She had her arm through Noah's, who was also crying.

A feeling of absolute helplessness engulfed Aspen as the chocolate milk churned in her stomach, and nausea overtook her. She sank onto the grass weeping, the wailing of chainsaws piercing her senses.

One of the paramedics recognized Dad. He had been in the crew that transported Dad to the hospital when he had his heart attack. He advised Dad to stay home, but he refused. Mom convinced him to eat something first, so Rocky drove Noah, Kiryn, and Aspen to the hospital where Sara and Doug were waiting in the emergency entrance.

Aspen watched as they pulled the gurney from the ambulance, and wheeled Gavin through the open glass doors. Tubes protruded from his nose and uninjured arm. The huge red emergency sign loomed above the ambulance as she and Noah passed under it.

Gavin was wheeled into a room, followed by Rocky and Sara, but Doug stayed in the waiting room with the three teenagers.

No one was crying now. Aspen had no tears left, and both Noah and Kiryn's faces were pale and drawn.

"You kids must be starving," Doug said.

Aspen looked up and nodded. "I can't eat right now."

"Me either," said Noah, and Kiryn nodded absently.

None of them said anything more. The emergency waiting room felt cold and empty to Aspen. Much like the day Dad had been brought in with a heart attack.

Aspen looked around. Except for two nurses and the paramedics who had now emerged from the double doors they had taken Gavin through, the waiting room was empty.

Doug jumped to his feet and approached the paramedics. "How is he?"

"They have him stabilized for now. They will have to do surgery on his arm right away to get it cleaned out." The paramedics were Connor and Trent, Kiryn had explained, and Doug was talking to Connor.

Trent walked over to the three teenagers. He stretched his hand out to Noah. "You did a good thing back there—" he paused.

"He's Noah," said Kiryn.

Trent continued, "Noah. You probably saved his life, if the truth be known. The limb nicked an artery. Without that pressure you applied, and the tourniquet, he might have bled to death before we got there."

The color drained from Noah's face, and he suddenly seemed to become aware of the blood all over his arms, chest, and jeans. "I didn't—"

"Yes, you did," said Trent. "I'm not sure most kids would have thought that fast."

"He's…he's a lifeguard," said Kiryn.

Trent looked thoughtful. "Good training," he said and released Noah's hand. "Gavin is lucky you were there."

Tears welled up in Noah's eyes. "Gavin wouldn't have been there if it wasn't for me. I took him back there."

Trent knelt in front of Noah. "Life happens, Noah. The chances of that tree falling was one in a million. Those threes have been pruned regularly. The firefighters checked them. This was just a freak accident."

Noah nodded. "I guess."

"It's true. The wind wasn't even blowing. I could see it if maybe we were having a storm or something, but this was— Well, this was just an accident. No one could have seen this coming."

The double doors opened again, and Sara and Rocky emerged. Sara walked right up to Connor and Trent and gave them each a hug. It was obvious she knew them. Of course, she did. Aspen was getting used to everyone knowing everyone else in Sommerville— except for her family, but that too would soon be remedied. With all the strange things happening since they arrived, it was a wonder they weren't household names by now.

Rocky reached for Noah's hand and pulled him to his feet. He enveloped him in both arms and hugged him to his chest. "Thank you, Noah," he choked.

Noah cried. "I'm sorry, Rocky. We were just going to show him, and Kiryn something, and then we were going to breakfast. I'm sorry."

Rocky patted his back. "Don't talk that way, Noah. He's going to be okay. It will take a little time, that's all."

"Guess it's good water skiing season is almost over," said Noah.

"Yeah, and it doesn't look good for basketball season," said Connor.

Noah's head jerked up. "Gavin plays basketball?

"He's the center. Darn good one, too." Connor looked puzzled. "Wait, you didn't know that?"

Noah shook his head. "He, he never mentioned it." He looked at Rocky. "None of you did."

"It just didn't come up, Noah. That's all." Rocky patted his shoulder and then joined Sara and Doug.

Noah sank back onto his chair and buried his face in his hands. He turned and looked sideways at Aspen, and she could read the agony on his face. She knew he felt the same thing she did, and she was painfully aware that Sara had not approached either of them.

Why should she? The Allen's family arrival was the cause of Rocky getting beat up, their own Dad's heart attack, and now Gavin was severely injured. That was just the physical injuries. There had also been a lot of hurt surface in more than one family. The image of Dylan Dixon sobbing flashed through her mind.

Noah buried his face in his hands again, and Aspen looked down at the floor. She was afraid to look at Kiryn. She wondered if their friendship would last through this one. Kiryn idolized her brother, but even more than Kiryn, what would become of her relationship with Gavin?

Aspen realized more than anything right now, this entire summer's focus had been on her and her family. Apparently, everyone else—especially Kiryn and Gavin, and maybe even Rocky—had set aside their own lives.

Aspen's heart ached, and a part of her suddenly wished she had never heard of Sommerville, Tennessee.

6

COLD SHOULDER

ASPEN AND NOAH WERE at the hospital until early evening after Gavin was moved to a room. Coaxing from Mom could not convince them to leave until they knew Gavin was okay, so Mom brought Noah some clean clothes and took her kids to the cafeteria for lunch where they barely touched their soup and sandwiches. Mom gave in and went back home to be with Dad, and Aspen and Noah held their vigil in the same room where they had waited while Dad was in surgery.

After a while, Mom and Dad both came back to the hospital to be with their two children.

Over an hour passed before anyone came to talk to them and that person was Rocky. Aspen anticipated Kiryn to come as well, but she never showed up.

Rocky hugged them both and assured them this was not their fault, but Noah was inconsolable and wanted desperately to talk to Sara and Kiryn. Rocky suggested maybe a later time would be better. He seemed evasive—in a strange sort of way—and Aspen felt a distance from this man who had just yesterday been their greatest confidant.

Rocky explained to Aspen, Noah, Mom, and Dad that the surgery had taken just under four hours. The broken trunk that impelled Gavin's arm was nearly six inches in diameter. A chunk of wood not only went completely thorough his arm, pinning it to the ground, but the weight had crushed all the bones between his shoulder and hand. He explained that just above his elbow, the brachial artery had been nicked, and the jagged wood tore a five-inch gash from just above his wrist into his bicep. The future use of his arm was still in question and the worst part—Gavin had no clue. He was in intensive care and would be for a couple of days. He was sleeping, and no one could visit him except Rocky, Sara, Doug, and Kiryn. Rocky suggested that everyone just needed a little time. It had been a long, grueling day.

Aspen, Noah, and their parents trudged from the hospital. This was an all too familiar scene for them, but this time, the feelings of isolation were unbearable. Neither of them said anything on the drive home. When they arrived, Mom and Dad asked them to come into the living room. Dad still looked gaunt and thin. He had lost a lot of weight and had not gained back much of his strength.

Mom's face was pale, and the worry lines on her forehead and between her eyebrows were deeper than ever.

The two teenagers collapsed on the sofa, while their parents tried to console them, but their efforts seemed useless.

Mom had spoken with Rocky a couple of times throughout the day, and she had agreed maybe Kiryn, and Gavin and their family just needed a little space right now.

Noah's head lay back on the couch, and he stared blankly at the ceiling, contributing nothing to the conversation.

Dad was quiet, but when Aspen looked directly at him, she saw a distant look in his eyes. Not quite like the look she had seen for the past few months, and not that look of fear she had spotted on a few occasions, but more a look of contemplation, and she couldn't help but wonder what was on his mind.

However, she was too exhausted to address it and took the first turn in the shower. The warm water that usually soothed her sore muscles did nothing to calm her aching heart, and she soon found herself curled between her sheets with Sprinkle wrapped tightly in her arms. She stared at nothing. The feelings of emptiness consuming her and finally giving way to wrenching sobs until she was lost in restless sleep.

Dripping wet from his shower, Noah wrapped a towel around his waist. He ran his hand through his hair and then leaned both hands on the sink.

If only we had not gone into the backyard. We should have just gone to breakfast; the tree would have fallen when no one was back there.

He lifted his head and stared at his reflection in the mirror. He used to have a plan—daily—a plan of exactly what he was going to do, and he did it. Get up go surfing, go to work or school, do homework, surf some more and make plans for college. He wanted to attend San Diego State as his parents had. He had good grades at San Clemente High, and in his junior year, had been awarded a scholarship if his senior year was as productive. He was going to room with Derrick and hopefully be dating Krista.

The mirror fogged from his labored breathing, and he suddenly sobered more when unsettling thoughts tumbled over and over in his mind.

Krista was dead. He was now attending his senior year in a small town that seemed like a million miles from San Clemente, California. His crazy sister was cavorting with dead people. His mom and dad, who had in the past week shown some semblance of normalcy, would probably now retreat back to the same distant parents he and Aspen had become accustomed to this summer. The only people who made him feel like this move was somewhat worth it, was now isolating his sister and him from their family, and the very worst—at least for today, because there had been a lot of competition for worst these past few months—Gavin—his one and only friend in this stupid state—was lying in a hospital bed with an injured arm that might be useless to him for the rest of his life, for which Noah felt totally responsible.

Noah lifted his hand and wiped the mirror, making a small circle where he could see his face. He stared into his eyes.

And I really like Kiryn.

Tears leaked down his cheeks and soon ran freely. His chest hurt as sobs overtook him, and with slumped shoulders, he grabbed another towel and slowly walked to his room.

Mom was standing by his door, and as he approached, she reached for him. Even though he towered above her, he welcomed her comforting arms around him.

"I love you, Noah." She whispered.

Noah choked between sobs. "Everything is a total mess, Mom. I don't know if I can do this anymore. I can't stand the thought of starting school Monday."

Mom stroked his wet hair. "I know, I know. We will just have to take this one day at a time."

"Maybe we should just go home."

Mom nodded. "Maybe." She released him and put both hands on his shoulders, looking directly into his eyes. "We will talk about it tomorrow. I mentioned it to Dad, but he didn't have much to say. I think he may be giving it some thought, though. I really believe he will heal better if we are home, but it's a little early to make that decision."

Noah assumed that Mom was talking about his heart attack. "They have doctors in California, too, Mom."

Mom smiled. "I know they do, but I'm not sure that is the kind of healing your dad needs." She leaned forward and kissed his forehead. "You must be freezing. Go to bed. It's been a long day. We'll talk tomorrow."

Noah nodded. "Okay, night, Mom."

"Night Noah." She pulled his door closed and stood quietly leaning against the wall.

⁓

Suzann was not sure what to do right at this moment. The realization of her children's feelings for Gavin and Aspen had literally slapped her in the face today. How could she have been so insensitive to them these past few weeks—months? Caught up in her anxiety about Jackson, she had ignored their cries for attention, and now she was paying for that. They had gravitated toward Rocky and—she believed—they really loved him, but now it seemed he too, was setting them aside, and it hurt her heart to see the pain they were feeling.

Rocky had taken her children under his wing and helped them through some very difficult times, and she feared for their hearts if he simply decided it had been too much. Who could blame him? The Allen's arrival had brought turmoil to the very core of Sommerville, and Rocky and his kids were right smack in the middle of it.

She sighed and started for her bedroom.

It's only been one day. Rocky just needs some time. This has not been a good day for them.

She was still trying to convince herself when she climbed into bed next to her sleeping husband. So as not to awaken him, she rolled to her side away from him and scooted to the edge of the bed.

Her heavy eyelids soon closed but were startled open when she was pulled gently into the arms of her husband. He softly kissed the back of her head, as tears leaked from the corners of her eyes.

"I love you, Suzann Allen."

Suzann could only nod. She closed her eyes again, relishing in the security of Jackson's warm embrace. Maybe there was hope for her relationship with this man she had loved intensely for nearly three decades.

7

I Think I Hate You

The first day of school kicked off with a pep rally in the gym—the very last place Aspen wanted to be. She and Noah slumped against the wall on the back row of bleachers. She had texted Kiryn since she had not heard from her all day Sunday, and Kiryn answered that she and Rocky would not be at school the first week. Noah and Aspen had reluctantly driven to school and found their way into the gym.

Aspen watched as annoying student body president, Cassie Garrett, snatched the microphone from the principal and squealed into it.

She so bugs me.

"Hi, Panthers! Soooo good to be back at Sommerville High!" to which the student body cheered and clapped.

Noah looked at Aspen, and rolled his eyes and she returned the gesture.

"We have a great year ahead, and we are starting with our first football game this Friday night! I hope all of you will be out there supporting our mighty Panthers and cheering them onto victory!"

With that, the band began playing, and six cheerleaders—three girls and three boys—charged onto the gym floor doing an assortment of flips, back handsprings, and cartwheels. The entire student body joined in a unanimous yell, "PANTHERS!" *Clap, clap.* "PANTHERS!" *Clap, clap.* It continued until Cassie cooed into the microphone. "Okay, guys, okay! Love the enthusiasm! A couple of things we need to announce," and the audience quieted.

"First of all, Coach Ryner and his wife had a new baby boy over the summer. They named him Justin. So cool, huh?" and the audience clapped and cheered.

Cassie continued, and as you all know, our incredible center of the basketball team was injured in an unusual accident just this past Saturday. He is in the hospital and may not have the use of his arm for a long time, if ever," she choked. "And you *all* know how I feel about Gavin Fielden."

There were a few random claps, and a girl in front of Noah whispered to the girl next to her, "I thought they broke up."

The girl responded, "I heard he was dating that new girl from California, but I don't know how serious it is, and anyway, when have you ever known anything to deter Cassie?"

"No kidding."

Aspen bristled and Noah, who had been leaning forward, his head in his hands, turned to look at her. He patted her knee but said nothing.

"Well anyway," Cassie was saying. "Just keep him in your thoughts, if you could. We are hoping for the best. I have talked to his mom several times since it happened, and she said he is still in intensive care, so visits to the hospital will have to wait a week or two. Except for me, of course." And she giggled.

Aspen thought she was going to throw up. Sweat immediately ran down her face and neck, and she jumped up, tripping over Noah trying to get to the isle. She grasped the railing and stumbled down the bleachers, not making eye contact with anyone, but she could feel piercing eyes staring at her.

Climbing over two boys who were sitting on the floor at the bottom of the steps, she bolted for the double doors.

A teacher stepped in front of her, but when he looked at Aspen's face, he stepped aside and pushed the doors open for her.

"I'm with her."

She hadn't realized Noah was behind her.

Not looking back, she ran down the hall and pushed through two sets of double glass doors emerging into the parking lot. Reaching some bushes, she bent over, wrapping her arms around her waist and sobs wrenched from her throat.

"Aspen." Noah came up behind her.

"Please take me home!" she wailed. "Please, Noah!"

Noah reached for her arm. "Okay, but—"

"Give me the keys or take me home!"

Noah raised his eyebrows and mumbled as he opened the car doors. "Uh, that will not be happening."

Mom and Dad were sitting on the front porch, and there were two trucks in the driveway, both had "JB's Tree Service" printed on the doors.

Aspen leaped from the car the second Noah put it in park. She ran up the steps, "I'm going back to California whether you guys come or not!' and she stormed through the door.

Noah sauntered toward his parents. "I don't think this is going to work."

The tree cutters worked for about two hours to finish cutting the broken tree, and chop the branches on the ground into chunks that would fit in the wood chipper, and then they cleared the rest of the limbs from the grass and path.

Aspen watched from a spot just beyond the garden where she could see the men work when they were up in the tree. Then she could only hear them until they walked by her, carrying the doomed limbs.

"I can't believe that happened. We just trimmed those trees a month ago," one of them said.

The other shook his head. "More like an act of God or—"

The first man interrupted him, "The devil. That was just weird."

"Yeah, this family has always been a little—" The first man glanced at Aspen, and stopped talking. Both men disappeared around the corner of the house.

Aspen cringed, and the familiar panic enveloped her entire body. *Could it be—*

She heard the trucks drive away, and Dad joined her on the grass.

"So, what happened at school?" he asked and draped his arm around her shoulders.

"Nothing. I just don't want to go back to school here. I was thinking I could finish high school online."

Dad scowled. "Aspen, you love school."

"No, Dad, I don't. Not here."

They sat in silence for a long time.

"I'm sorry I haven't been there for you kids, Aspen."

"It's okay, Dad. You have things to do. Right now, you just need to get better.'

The backdoor opened. "Lunch is ready?"

"I'm not hungry," snapped Aspen.

"Actually, it wasn't a question. Lunch is ready."

Aspen looked up at her mother, who had not budged.

"Now."

Aspen rolled her eyes at her dad, and they both stood and followed Mom into the kitchen.

Aspen plopped into a chair, "Where's Noah?"

"He went to school." Mom placed a bowl of fruit on the table.

"Good for him," said Aspen dripping with sarcasm.

"You can stay home today, Aspen, but tomorrow you need to go back."

"I said I'm not going to school. I can finish online. I hate that school."

Dad took a bite of his sandwich. "Why don't we let it go right now, Suzann? We can talk about it later."

Mom sighed. "You left your phone home, Aspen. Did you realize that?"

Aspen hadn't noticed. She had been so consumed with the depressing idea of going to school without Kiryn and Gavin she had absently left it on her dresser.

"You were getting texts from someone—several texts. You might want to check it."

Aspen jumped from the table and ran into her room. She scrolled the screen to unlock it, seeing that she had five texts. She touched the little folder, and the texts opened. Aspen's heart leaped when she saw that they were all from Kiryn.

Without reading them, she punched Kiryn's number and waited.

"Hey," came Kiryn's voice from the speaker.

"Hey! I got your texts. What's…what's up? How's Gavin?"

"Umm, he's not so good, but it's only been a day since his surgery. Dad said that's to be expected," she paused. *"So, Aspen, can we talk?"*

"Sure. When?"

"Can you meet me after school?"

"Well, actually, I am not at school. Do you want me to come over?"

"No…no. Why…why aren't you at school?"

"Long story."

"Oh. Well, why don't I come and get you? Maybe we could drive to Memphis and get a shake or something. Rocky said I can use the truck."

"O…okay. Why do we need to go to Memphis to get a shake?"

"Just want to talk to you, that's all."

An anxious ache welled up inside Aspen's chest. "Okay. When?"

"I'll come now."

The two girls rode mostly in silence for the first twenty minutes of the drive. Kiryn reported on Gavin's progress, which wasn't much more than she had told her on the phone.

Aspen's stomach ached, and she wished she had finished her lunch. "When are we going to *talk*?"

Kiryn sigh was labored. "Aspen I…I think we had better not see you and Noah for a while."

Aspen's heart felt as though it would break. "Okay…why?"

"It's just gotten so hard, you know, so much stuff to deal with. We had a pretty normal life until you guys showed up."

"Well, I'm sorry. No one forced you to be our friends."

"Nope, you're right about that." Kiryn paused. She turned the truck into the same fast-food parking lot the four had come to the first day Gavin wanted to ride in the Iroc. She turned off the engine and leaned back in the seat. Then she turned to look directly at Aspen.

"The thing is—first Dad and now Gavin, and yeah, Dad healed up okay, but honestly, Aspen this thing with Gavin's arm could change his whole life.

Aspen blurted, "Why didn't any of you tell us he played basketball?"

Kiryn shrugged, "It didn't seem relevant, and besides you never asked."

"Why would I ask if he played basketball?"

"You never asked much about us at all."

Kiryn's words stung, and Aspen winced. "I guess I…I thought we knew you pretty well. I guess— I guess it didn't occur to me there was more."

"Oh, well thanks. Just plain country folk to you California kids, I guess."

"That's not what I mean, and you know it."

"Well, what exactly do you mean? This whole summer has been about you guys. I haven't even spent any time with my other friends and Gavin and Cassie—well—I think he still cares for her."

Aspen fought back the tears. "What about you and Noah?"

"What about Noah? He is still hung up on your dead best friend."

Aspen whirled to face Kiryn. "What did you say?"

"You heard me. Krista. Noah is still hung up on Krista. You don't think I noticed that?"

"You never…you never mentioned it."

"Guess I didn't want to know."

The two were silent for several minutes.

Kiryn traced the steering wheel with her finger staring through the windshield. "Look, Aspen, it's Sara. Gavin is her whole world. She is pretty upset about this and she and Cassie, well they are kind of alike. She really likes Cassie—not that she doesn't like you—but she told Rocky she just thinks you will break Gavin's heart anyway once the newness wears off. She told him she has been trying to cope with all this stuff—Gavin's gift, Rocky getting beat up. She doesn't hate Rocky. They are just different; Doug is more her type."

Aspen wasn't sure why Kiryn felt the need to clarify how Sara felt about Rocky.

Kiryn continued. "She told Rocky she wants Gavin to come live with her and Doug when he gets out of the hospital and if he doesn't keep you guys away from him—at least most of the time—she will move him to Memphis to finish high school." Kiryn looked over at Aspen. "That would kill Rocky, Aspen. It really would. Especially after how close they have gotten this summer."

"And you don't think Noah and I had anything to do with that?"

"I think you had everything to do with that, but Sara doesn't see it that way. She has even decided she doesn't want Gavin to meet with Patrice anymore."

"What does Gavin say about all of this?"

"Gavin doesn't know any of it, but what can he say? Sara is his mother, and he is still in high school."

Kiryn reached over and touched Aspen's arm, but Aspen pulled away. "Can we go home now?"

Kiryn quickly pulled her hand back and started the engine. "I hoped you would understand. Or at least *try* to."

Aspen couldn't hold the tears back any longer. "Well, I don't understand, okay? I really don't. Your family is two-faced and insincere. How do you just decide not to be friends with people who thought you loved them—especially when you know those friends love you?!"

Kiryn wiped the tears that were now trickling down her cheeks. "It's going to be for the best. You guys will go back to California and forget we even existed. You watch. That's what Sara and Doug said, and I think maybe they are right."

"Some friend you turned out to be."

"What? Whatever."

Again, they rode in silence, Aspen crying and silent tears streaking Kiryn's face.

Kiryn pulled the truck up in front of Aspen's house. No one was in the yard, but the Iroc was in the driveway.

Aspen opened the door and stepped out. Turning back to face Kiryn, she said, "I think I kind of hate you right now."

Kiryn stared straight ahead and nodded slightly. "Yeah, that's what Sara said would happen."

Aspen stomped into the house and slammed the door.

Kiryn put the truck in reverse, backed up, turned around and then drove away. Her tears flowed freely now, and through the rearview mirror, she saw Noah step out onto the front porch. When she reached the main road and knew she was out of Aspen and Noah's sight, she put the truck in park, lay her head on the steering wheel and sobbed.

Two weeks had gone by, and Aspen and Noah had fallen into a routine. Aspen was doing studies online, and Noah went to school. He didn't see much of Kiryn and had asked to be transferred out of Rocky's class. Noah saw Rocky occasionally, but he always seemed preoccupied. He was kind to Noah, making small talk, but he didn't make any effort to really interact.

Noah had become friends with a couple of the guys from summer school and hung out with them occasionally. Joseph had tried to talk to him a few times, but Noah blew him off, making Aspen feel sorry for Joseph. Not sorry enough to bring him back into her life. She was finally sleeping through the night, and that was something in and of itself. She was afraid opening the door to Joseph, and his family's connection to everything would ruin even that.

Aspen and Noah remained close, but there was an awkward distance. They both felt it and tried to side-step it every day. Aspen was becoming more and more withdrawn, and Noah just seemed to be getting by day-to-day. He didn't laugh as much as he had when they were spending time with Gavin and Kiryn.

They had heard that Gavin had gone home, but then developed an infection and was back in the hospital.

Dad was seeing a psychologist regularly and had started meeting with his attorney again regarding the Allen will. Mom had contacted an appraiser for the big house as well as an appraiser for the gun collection. She was pretty much handling all of that.

The two FBI agents, Byron Coulsen and Larry Brimhall, had left several messages for her and Noah, but neither of them had responded.

None of the family had set foot in the big house.

Occasionally, Noah and Aspen talked about all the stuff they had been involved in that they had not told their parents. They agreed that they knew they needed to, but they were not sure when the time would be right. They now realized how much they had relied on Rocky's adult guidance through all of this and longed for that friendship again, but it didn't seem likely.

Noah and Aspen talked to their parents about possibly returning to San Clemente High School, staying with friends during the week and living with Grandma in San Diego on the weekends. Jackson and Suzann were not exactly against it but didn't want to consider it until after the holidays. That suggestion put a lot of stress on Noah because he wasn't sure his credits would transfer, possibly making him ineligible for a scholarship.

Patrice had texted Aspen several times, but she had not answered. She had abruptly put the big house, Ronda, the painting, the tunnel and the Dixon's behind her. She didn't want to reopen that can of worms again. All the excitement and mystery had left her. And interestingly enough, all the contact she seemed to have with the unseen world, had left her as well. She couldn't help but wonder about the correlation. She was sure there was something.

The hole in her heart left by Gavin and Kiryn simply would not heal, and she had difficulty with it every day. She often compared it to her feelings when Krista had died, but this seemed worse—they were still alive and wanted nothing to do with her. The feeling of helplessness was endless, and it tormented her every minute.

It was on a particularly difficult morning that Aspen got a text from Rocky. Noah had already gone to school.

The text read, "*Gavin wants to see you. If you have a minute to stop by the hospital, that would be good. He is in room 322. Go right after school because his mother always goes in the morning, so his friends can have time with him after school, and I go around six and have dinner with him. He will most likely come home the first of next week.*"

Aspen stared at the text for a long time. It read like a newspaper report. Straight and to the facts. This did not seem like Rocky at all, which confused Aspen. Maybe he didn't want her to see his son, but had he completely turned off his feelings toward her and Noah? It certainly seemed like it, but she wasn't sure how that was possible.

Finally, she responded to Rocky with a simple, "Okay, thanks."

Aspen resolved to borrow her mom's BMW, and leave before Noah got home. She really wanted to talk to Gavin alone, and she didn't want to have to explain that to Noah.

Apprehensively, Aspen pulled into a space in the hospital parking lot. School would not be out for another fifteen minutes, so she was certain she would have time with Gavin alone before any of his friends dropped by. She picked up the chocolate shake she had purchased and pulled the card from her backpack.

She had agonized over what to write in it and finally concluded with, *Get Well Really Soon—your good friend, Aspen.*

It seemed kind of cold and impersonal, but that's how this whole time apart had been, so anything else seemed inappropriate.

Aspen wiped her sweaty palms on her jeans as she stepped out of the elevator on the third floor. She followed the room numbers past the nurses' station and stopped. Room 322 was at the end of the hall—she could see it from where she stood.

As she approached the room, she could hear two unfamiliar male voices. She hesitated and then stepped inside the room. She barely noticed the two guys sitting in chairs next to the window because her eyes were fixed on Cassie who was just bending over to kiss Gavin. Cassie touched his hand, but then seemed to notice the two boys looking in Aspen's direction and whirled around.

It was then that Gavin saw her.

"Aspen!"

Aspen heard Gavin say her name, but she couldn't move. She looked again at the two boys and realized they looked exactly alike. They must be Gavin's older twin step-brothers.

Finally, able to make her feet move, she stepped near a table next to the door and set the shake down. She smiled weakly. "I'm…I'm sorry…I didn't—" She began backing out of the room.

She glanced from Gavin to Cassie and back to Gavin. Cassie was holding Gavin's good hand. His other arm was wrapped and elevated. His fingers were an ugly mixture of red and blue. Her eyes darted back to his face, which now looked somewhat distorted.

"Aspen it's so—"

"Bye, Gavin. I— See ya."

Aspen turned and walked briskly away.

"She's a strange girl," she heard Cassie say.

Aspen broke into a dead run and jumped into an open elevator. It started to close, but then a hand jutted between the doors, and as they opened again, she found herself face-to-face with Cassie.

Cassie held the elevator door opened and blocked the entrance.

"Maybe, Miss California, maybe you should just realize you don't fit in around here and leave. Look at what you have done to one of the most popular and sweetest guys in Sommerville. *You have ruined his life. You and your stupid brother need to leave. You need to get that you have been beaten—that you're not wanted— you were just a summer fling for Gavin while I was gone. I am* going to marry him, Miss California, *deal* with it."

Cassie's condescending tone cut right through Aspen, and she found herself speechless.

Suddenly, she ducked under Cassie's arm, darted from the elevator, passed the remaining closed elevator doors, and pushed through the doorway to the stairs. She couldn't get out of the hospital fast enough. She ran through the lobby, quickly depositing the card in the nearest trash can, and continued running until she reached the car.

Pushing all the wrong buttons, she opened the trunk and set off the car alarm. She finally found the right button to unlock the doors, closed the trunk, and quickly climbed into the security of the car. Grateful the windows were tinted, she sprawled across the seat sobbing until she thought her heart would burst from her chest.

8

GOT ALONG WITHOUT YOU

WHEN ASPEN GOT HOME, she went straight to her room. She fell asleep lying across her bed, and when she woke up, it was just getting dark.

"Aspen?'

She sat up, making no effort to wipe off her face or fuss with her hair. "What do you want, Noah?"

"I'm coming in, okay?"

"Fine."

The door opened, and Noah stepped inside. He plopped a bag of cookies and a Coke on her dresser. "You should probably eat something."

Aspen raised her eyebrows. "Umm, thanks. Very nutritious."

Noah shrugged and sat down next to her. "Can we talk, Aspen?"

She nodded. "Why not?"

Noah fiddled with the corner of her comforter, twisting it between his fingers. "I have been thinking. I know how miserable you are because I'm just as miserable. I had kind of started to like Sommerville and figured we would have a good school year. But now—"

"Now you feel like your heart has been cut out," said Aspen flatly.

Noah nodded, and then he choked when he tried to talk again. "This is almost worse than I felt when we left California. School is no fun. It's boring and depressing, and I really don't fit in there."

"Why don't you do online school with me. It's great. You don't have to actually—" her voice caught, "actually see anybody."

"I guess."

"Look, Noah, I appreciate you coming in here, but everything has changed. I really hate it here."

"Yeah me too, I—"

"Have you tried to see Gavin?"

Noah shook his head, and pulling his phone out of his pocket, he scrolled the screen, clicked it a couple of times and handed it to Aspen.

Aspen read the text he had pulled up for her.

"So, Noah, I talked to Aspen—I don't know if she told you or not—but Sara has forbidden Gavin to have anything to do with you guys and on top of that, she is threatening to move Gavin to Memphis if Rocky doesn't comply with her request. So, I can't see you either. I'm sorry. I really feel bad, but Doug and Sara have a lot of money. Rocky doesn't, so he is not willing to risk losing the chance to be a part of his only son's last year of high school. I'm dreading seeing you when I come back to school. It was hard enough to talk to Aspen, that's why I'm texting you. It's been fun, but I guess it was one of those summer things. Now life must get back to normal. So... bye."

Aspen stared at the screen, blurry now through water-filled eyes. "I hate her."

"No, you don't."

"Yes, I do, Noah. I can't believe—" but then she threw herself on her bed and wailed, "I don't hate her! I love all of them, and that's why this hurts so much! I just want to go home."

Noah leaned forward, resting his elbows on his knees and rubbed his face with his hands. "That's not going to be normal either, Aspen. Krista is not there."

"But all of our other friends are."

"It will be the same empty feeling we have here, Aspen. Face it, that's part of why it was so easy to like this place because everything at home had changed. Not to mention Mom and Dad."

Aspen twisted around on her bed so that she was facing the same direction as Noah. She rolled onto her stomach, propped her elbows on the bed and rested her chin in her hands. "What should we do?"

"Well, what do you think about Mom and Dad?"

"What do you mean?"

"I mean, do you think they are going to be okay?"

Aspen took a deep breath. "No."

That seemed to surprise Noah, and he turned to look at his sister. "No?"

"Seriously, Noah, nothing has changed for them either. They still have to deal with the will. With whatever in the heck is bothering Dad, *and* there is still Dylan and Drew. The house is not sold, *and* they don't even know about the tunnel—the shaft—the secret doors in the bedroom closet—all the crap surrounding the Dixon's—" She scooted to a sitting position and glared at her brother. "*And* the painting! What about that? Do we just pretend like none of it exists?"

"Well, they don't know about it—"

Aspen's eyes narrowed, "I guarantee Dad does."

"What?"

"Dad. I don't mean he knows all of it, but there is something he knows, and he is not admitting it. *That* is why he has been such a mess. He doesn't want to know about any of it. I think he was hoping to sell the stupid house and go back to California like nothing ever happened."

Noah raised his eyebrows, "You're right, but I'm not sure Mom even wants to know."

"Too bad, so sad."

"What? Geez, you're sarcastic right now."

"You know what, Noah? I'm just tired of all of this. We have been caught in the middle of some huge thing that we couldn't even talk to our own parents about because we didn't want Dad to die. Well, maybe he shouldn't have been so secretive all these years. Maybe he shouldn't have lied to Mom. Maybe he should have talked to his parents occasionally. Maybe we wouldn't be in this stupid mess if Dad wouldn't have been such a chicken about his poor rich childhood!"

Noah stared at his sister. "Aspen, you are losing it."

"Am I? Don't say you don't agree, Noah because I know you do. Don't defend him. I got this gift—curse—from somewhere. It must be Dad. Where else?"

Noah still stared at her. "I'm not sure what to think right now. You sound like you hate Dad."

"Oh, Noah, I don't hate Dad, but think how this whole thing has played out this summer. Look at all the crap we have dealt with and we couldn't even confide in them. Doesn't that make you mad?"

"Are you mad at Dad, or are you mad at Kiryn and Gavin?"

Aspen's mouth clamped shut, and she stared at Noah through hurt and tortured eyes and then began weeping again. "I don't know who I'm mad at. I just feel so awful. I don't want to feel like this anymore. I just don't want to hurt anymore, Noah, and I don't know what to do."

Noah turned and pulled his sister into his arms. He patted the back of her head. "I know, Aspen, I feel the same way."

He held her until her crying subsided and then he pulled away and stood up. He walked to her dresser, picked up the bag of cookies, opened it, and promptly ate two.

Aspen laughed. "That's your answer. Eating cookies."

"No need to starve *and* be miserable." Noah smiled. "You going to drink this Coke? 'Cause if you're not, I am."

Aspen waved her hand at him. "Drink it. I would hate for you to starve to death *and* die of thirst."

Neither of them said anything for several minutes. Noah downed most of the soda and ate half of the cookies, and Aspen just stared at the wall.

Finally, Noah spoke up. "The way I see it, we have two choices."

Aspen looked up at him. "And they are?"

"Tell—well ask—Mom and Dad if we can go home and live

with Grandma while they sort through all of this—"

Aspen interrupted him. "I've been thinking about that. Why can't Grandma come and live at our house in San Clemente and then we can be home. We wouldn't have to stay with friends?"

"Do you think that's fair to Grandma?"

Aspen shrugged, "I hadn't thought about fair."

"Exactly. Anyway, as I was saying, or... we could stay here and go see Patrice, talk to Mr. Weston about the painting—you know—finish what we started."

Aspen dropped her head. "I'm not sure I want to without—"

"Gavin?"

"Not just Gavin. Kiryn and Rocky too."

"Yeah, I thought about that but what's that little song thing Grandma used to sing to us? Remember when you had that mad crush on Randy Winkle in the sixth grade?"

"Are you kidding me right now? Randy Winkle?"

"Yeah, remember you were pretty sure you were going to die, and Grandma was over for dinner and sang this little song to you—"

The corners of Aspen's mouth turned up, and her eyes suddenly twinkled, "Got along without ya—"

"Before I met ya, gonna get along without you now." Noah finished it.

They both laughed and sang it again this time together, "Got along without ya before I met ya, gonna get along without you now."

They laughed together until suddenly Aspen began crying again. "I don't want to get along without them, Noah."

Noah sighed. "Me either."

9

FAMILY CONFLICT

Jackson knew he needed to move away from the door, but he couldn't. Liar? Chicken? He had heard it all.

Suzann had left to pick up take out for dinner, and he had come to Aspen's bedroom to talk to her, but instead, he was privy to the conversation between his two kids, and now his tormented heart wracked inside his chest with new wounds—new pain—the worst pain ever. His own kids thought he was a liar and a coward.

Jackson plodded from the house and into the backyard. He stood silently, searching the backyard of the little house. After several minutes, he slowly made his way along the cobblestone path. When it curved, he found himself beyond the garden and between the newly cut tree and the shed. He looked down. He could still see smudges of Gavin's blood on the path. He thought the sprinklers would have washed the remnants away by now.

It sickened him, and he looked away, turning his gaze toward the trees.

Suddenly he was six years old.

"I want you to quit telling your mother these ridiculous stories do you hear me, Jackson?!"

Jackson coward in the shadow of David Allen as he loomed above him.

"I am not telling stories, Dad. The girl was in my room again, and I saw the light—"

David Allen snatched his son by the arm, dragged him up the stairs of his grandparent's home, and tossed him like a rag doll into the storage. He pulled the door shut and Jackson heard the key turn in the lock. It was dark in the storage room. He knew she would come.

Jackson crawled to the door, and standing, he fumbled for the light switch. He clicked it. Nothing. He clicked it again and again. Nothing.

Jackson sank to the floor in a heap. He wrapped his arms around his legs and buried his face in his knees.

He waited.

For a second Jackson snapped back to the present, but quickly he was back in his childhood.

"Jackson!"

Jackson whirled to see his dad stomping down the cobblestone path.

He had just celebrated his tenth birthday with a party at the lake. The lights were there again, but when he tried to confide in his older sister, his dad stopped him cold, telling him to quit lying to people.

Jackson ran away from the lake, through the trees, across the lawn of his grandparent's house and down the long steep stairs crossing the driveway of the servants' quarters. He kept running into the backyard until he reached the shed, but the door was locked.

Panting heavily, he ran across the lawn, and into the trees at the back of the yard. He huddled between two stout trunks, hoping his dad would not pursue him, but he knew his dad too well for that.

He decided to crawl out of the trees and make his way to the back of the shed. There were some tall bushes there. He could stay until his dad calmed down, but then heard his dad's heavy breathing right behind him.

Jackson turned to face him, "Dad, I—"'

David Allen grabbed the back of his son's neck. He marched him across the grass toward the trees. "Is this where you have been hiding from me?"

But Jackson did not have time to answer.

A loud cracking sound from the trees caught their attention, and Dad stopped in his tracks forcing Jackson to stop with him.

"DAD!" Jackson jerked away from his dad as a huge branch crashed to the ground between them, sending chips of wood and splinters in every direction.

Jackson stared across the fallen branch into the tortured eyes of his father, who turned and walked deliberately away from his son.

Suddenly, he turned and called over his shoulder. "This is your fault, Jackson! You are a menace to this family!"

〰

"Dad?"

Jackson slowly opened his eyes. The sun peered through the trees, making it hard to see his son's face. He closed his eyes and then opened them again.

"Noah?"

"Dad are you okay?"

Jackson extended his hand, and Noah took hold of it, helping his dad to his feet.

Jackson rubbed his face with the other hand, suddenly aware of the wetness on his cheeks.

"Why were you laying on the grass? You scared me, I thought you…well anyway, are you all right?"

Jackson nodded. "I'm fine, Noah. I'm fine."

Jackson put his hand on Noah's shoulder, and the two started to walk back toward the house.

Dad said, "What were you doing out here?"

Noah shrugged. "I don't know. I haven't been out here since Gavin got hurt. Guess I just—"

Dad patted Noah's shoulder. "I know." And father and son walked silently to the house.

When they got into the kitchen, Dad went directly to the sink, filled a glass with water, and drank it straight down.

Noah found that odd since their dad never drank water from the faucet. He always drank the filtered water from the fridge.

After Dad downed nearly all of a second glass, he turned and walked from the kitchen. "I'm going to go lie down for a while."

"Okay." Noah watched him until he disappeared down the hall, and then he turned to look out of the window.

"What's up?" Aspen startled her brother, and he turned quickly in her direction.

"I don't know, Aspen. I just found Dad laying in the grass under those trees out back, and he was crying, and mumbling."

"Mumbling? What was he saying?"

Noah's voice caught, "He was saying, 'Please don't, Dad,' over and over."

Aspen stared at her brother.

"Hey!'

Both kids turned to the sound of their mother's voice.

She plopped two sacks on the table both labeled "Bill and Nada's."

A stab pierced Aspen's heart at the sight of the sacks. "I didn't know you liked Bill and Nada's, Mom."

"I don't know if I do. Sara told me about it when she picked me up from the airport. I just thought I would try it. Have you kids eaten there?"

"A...a couple of times," said Noah, but Aspen said nothing.

Mom didn't seem to notice their apprehension, and she continued, "Well, good, then it was the right choice. Where's your dad?"

"He's resting," said Noah.

Mom looked surprised. "Resting? He had just gotten dressed when I left. Is he okay?"

Noah and Aspen exchanged a quick look, but neither of them volunteered any information.

Mom's pleasant demeanor now turned to sudden exasperation. She looked first at Noah, then Aspen, and then back to Noah. "What is going on?"

"Mom, I found Dad lying in the grass out back, under the trees that fell on Gavin."

Now Mom looked confused.

"He was crying, Mom," said Aspen.

"Not just crying. He was saying 'Please don't, Dad.'" Noah winced. "What does that mean, Mom?"

Mom pulled a chair away from the table and sank into it. She slowly shook her head. "I'm not sure, but there has to have been some issues with his dad while growing up. The doctors tell me the same thing. Since his heart attack, he talks about his dad in his sleep, but nothing ever makes sense, and when they try to get more information out of him, he just clams up."

Mom dabbed at tiny tears forming in the corners of her eyes. "When they hypnotized him, he cried and called out to his dad, but he never says anything coherent."

"Have you heard him talk in his sleep, Mom?"

She raised her eyebrows when she looked at Noah, "Actually, no."

"Well, I think he's a jerk." Aspen snapped.

"Aspen!" Mom jumped to her feet.

"Well, he is, Mom. It's his fault we are here and dealing with all of the crap we have gone through this summer."

"Oh, well, forgive him for having a heart attack! Sorry to have put you out!" Mom's exasperation now turned to anger, but Aspen did not back down.

"Really, Mom? *Really*? And what about us? What about you and the Drew mess? What about the stuff Noah and I—and—and Gavin, Kiryn, and Rocky have been doing?"

Noah lifted his hand to stop her, but Aspen just glared at him and pushed it away. "Don't Noah! I am so sick of all this! Mom, you and Dad have practically ruined our lives dragging us here, and then keeping so many secrets from us!"

"Secrets!? What secrets? If you're talking about Drew, that was really none of your business! I could have handled that myself!"

"Yeah, Mom you were doing so well at that!"

Noah stepped towards his sister, "Aspen, is this really—"

"SHUT UP NOAH!" Aspen screamed. She turned on her mother again. "We used to be a family. Dad used to be honest with us—or so we thought! Now we know he is just a liar and he's a coward, too, Mom! He never even came home to see his mother! What kid does that?"

"Aspen!" again Noah tried to intervene, but this time Aspen shoved him away.

"Mom! Do you know that I see spirits? Did you know that Drew and Dylan's grandpa killed Dad's Aunt Ronda? Did you know that he may have killed a bunch of guys that worked for Great-Grandpa and him? Did you know there are tunnels and rooms and all kinds of stuff in that stupid *Allen Manor* that Dad *must* have known about? Did you, Mom? No, you didn't because you don't even know the man you have been married to for all these years! He's a liar, Mom, and he has been mean to you and us ever since he got that stupid letter from Aunt Dana—whoever she is—we don't even know Dad's relatives! They are probably all crooks and cheats and liars like him!"

Suddenly Mom slapped Aspen hard across the face, causing her daughters head to jerk to one side.

Aspen's hand shot to her wounded cheek.

Her mother, nor her father had ever raised a hand to her or Noah, and she was stunned for a few seconds, but she snapped back quickly. "Perfect, Mom! See what I mean! We are a bunch of stupid misfits just like the rest of this idiotic family! You would never have done that before we came to this godforsaken place!"

Noah grabbed his sister from behind, wrapping both arms around her waist. "Aspen, you are losing it! You have said enough!"

Aspen broke free of his grip and punched both hands into his chest, pushing him off balance. "I am not losing it, Noah! You feel the same way I do, so don't act all high and mighty right now! I wish Dad would have died when he had that heart attack, and we could have gone home!"

Noah and Mom were staring at Aspen, both wide-eyed and mouths gaping, but Aspen didn't care. She knew in her heart she didn't mean what she had just said about her dad, but right now she didn't care about that either.

"I'm going home to live with Grandma whether I have your

permission or not! I will take some money out of my college fund and buy my own ticket. I hate this place, and I am *not* staying here another day!"

Aspen turned to run from the room and came face to face with Dad. She did not know how long he had been standing in the doorway.

For a split second, their eyes locked and Aspen saw that same look of fear she had seen in Dad's eyes at least twice before, only this time, she also saw pain.

That didn't stop her. She glared back at him, darted around him and ran out the front door.

10

HELP!

Pure adrenalin took Aspen from the house, up the steep stairs, across the massive lawn of the big house, and through the trees to the lake, but now she collapsed on the dock.

She could barely see the lake through tears, and sweat pouring down her face. Sobbing gave way to choking, and she sat up and put her head down to catch her breath, then she rolled onto her back. Tears were running like rivers into her ears, but she didn't attempt to stop them. She laid still until her chest stopped heaving, and her tears subsided. Her insides felt like they were on fire and the throbbing in her chest was so painful she could hardly stand it.

Maybe I am just a spoiled little rich kid. Her Grandma had told her once that she and Noah had things so much better than most kids. She didn't completely understand that. Most of her friends seemed to live the same life she did. She had never thought of herself as spoiled, but maybe she was.

She had never thought of Kiryn and Gavin as being *country folk,* as Kiryn had put it, but maybe to others, it seemed like she did. All she knew right now is that she felt totally alone. Up until an hour ago, she and Noah had been comrades, but now after all the mean things she had just said about Dad, she figured Noah would write her off too, and she was quite sure Mom would never forgive her, after all, she had slapped her face.

Aspen focused on billowy clouds that danced across the sky, and her thoughts drifted to the dream when she saw her Great-Grand-father. In the dream, he had shown her the little box that led to finding the statue he had buried in honor of his daughter, Ronda. She closed her eyes and allowed her thoughts to go to the dream—to relive it—not the dream actually, but the feeling she had in the dream.

When her Grandpa stood before her, she had felt peace—abso-lute and total peace.

Is that what being dead felt like? Maybe and maybe not. She had not felt much peace around Ronda or Krista—well maybe Krista—but still, there was an unsettling. With all the other spirits she had encountered, none had given her that same feeling of peace her Great-Grandpa had.

Aspen thought about Joseph and how she had felt so uncom-fortable around him, but then how she realized he was just hurt-ing—much like his Uncle Dylan—and he just needed a friend. She pushed him out of her mind. She didn't have the energy to be his friend.

Then there was Cassie. Perfect Cassie. Miss Kiss-butt to Gavin's mom so she could get close to Gavin. Ugh—how she despised that dancer-student-body-president-person. She would love to just smack her little face.

Still, another knife seemed to stab through her heart. She was jealous of Cassie, and she had never been jealous of anyone in her entire life. Not really, but this was sincere, painful, hurtful jealousy and she hated it.

She thought about Rocky and how he had literally replaced Mom and Dad for her and Noah these past few months. She real-ized they had both been fools. Families are the only people that really love you and, she supposed, she had screwed that up too.

Still, she loved and admired Rocky and had trusted him, even though she now felt apprehensive. She would probably be sorry for those feelings too—at some point.

Thinking about Kiryn just made her mad. Kiryn was supposed to be her best friend. Wow, she had learned some hard lessons about best friends this past summer. If they don't die, they just quit being your friend. Aspen narrowed her eyes, and she felt a deep scowl spread across her face.

Who needs them anyway?

Aspen sighed. She figured she and Noah would probably make up at some point and maybe her parents would like her again, although she didn't expect Dad to forgive her. How horrible to wish one of your parents dead? She didn't deserve to be forgiven, so she would not expect it.

Aspen tried to force her thoughts back to the billowy clouds and Great-Grandpa Allen, but she couldn't. The one thought she had been side-stepping this whole time simply engulfed her and wracked her body with more painful sobs.

Gavin.

She really truly loved him, and she had messed it up, or she guessed she had. She didn't cause the tree to fall on him, but Noah was right if they wouldn't have taken him back there, if she wouldn't have pointed the light out to Noah, if she hadn't gone into the kitchen that night she would never have seen the light, and if she could just sleep she wouldn't have woken up in the first place!

Shoulda-woulda-coulda. What's done is done, so I might as well accept it. I don't know what use I am to anybody now.

She cried harder.

Aspen wasn't sure how long she lay there. She must have fallen asleep, or maybe she had just zoned out. Whatever state she had been in, she was now startled by the sound of waves lapping against the poles underneath the dock.

She quickly rose to her elbows and scanned the water. Aspen's eyes widened, and she slowly pulled herself into a sitting position.

She thought of running away, but somehow, the water beckoned her, and she simply stared.

The water in the lake was churning, slowly causing the waves to hit not only against the poles under the dock but to splash onto the dock. The spray wetted her face, and she suddenly thought of the tunnel, the wall of water, and the spray on her face.

Now it *was* time to get away from here! She jumped to her feet, but when she did, she saw something that made her stop.

The mist—in the middle of the lake—that same mist she had seen before. It swirled upward from the center of the lake but then began to spread across the water until the mist seemed to come from everywhere.

Aspen was mesmerized by it.

Slowly from the center of the mist, a dim glow. The same type of glow she had seen from the kitchen window. It grew brighter and brighter until she had to shield her eyes.

The light continued to spread across the face of the water until the entire lake glistened as though a huge light were shining from beneath the surface.

"Help."

Aspen froze.

It was only a whisper, but somehow it pierced the air.

Aspen held her breath. She thought again of running, but it was as though she was being held there. She could not move from that spot.

"Help."

The same piercing whisper.

Aspen now involuntarily walked to the edge of the dock. She tried to turn and walk back, but she did not have control of her legs.

She stood silently on the dock, the toes of her tennis shoes hanging over the edge.

"Help."

The voice came again. Aspen felt numb and somehow detached from her body.

Her eyes had adjusted to the light, and she stared across the water, looking for the source of the voice.

She saw nothing, but she now had no desire to leave. If anything, she wanted to be a part of the light—to find the voice.
She gently closed her eyes and stepped off the dock.

11

HOPELESS SEARCH

JACKSON WAS INCONSOLABLE, AND Suzann wanted him to call his doctor.

"No, do not call the doctor." Dad wiped the tears from his eyes.

"But, Dad, you need—"

"I *need* to face my fears, Noah. Your sister was right. I need to face my past."

"But your heart—"

"My heart is fine, Noah." He tapped his head, "My problems are up here."

Suzann took her husband's hand, "Not right now, Jackson, there is plenty of time for that."

"Plenty of time? I don't think so. I have a daughter who has decided I am worthless in her life, and most likely, a son feels that way, too." He turned to look at Noah, but Noah did not allow his eyes to meet his dad's.

Jackson leaned forward so he could look up into his son's face. "Noah?"

Noah shrugged, "I don't know, Dad, I don't want you dead, and neither does Aspen, but—"

"Jackson is this necessary right now? Maybe we should be looking for Aspen." Mom's concern did not deter her husband.

He held one hand up to stop her. "Suzann, this is long overdue. The kids are right." He turned back to Noah, "But what?"

Noah hesitated, and then he spoke slowly, "Dad, we have really been going through a lot this summer, and…and…actually, I do agree with Aspen. You and Mom just haven't been here—not really. After you had your heart attack, we didn't dare burden either of you with anything, so, we just—well we just figured it out." He paused for a few seconds. "Well, we had Rocky's help as well as Gavin and Kiryn's."

"And now?"

"Now Gavin is hurt really bad, and his mom won't let him see Aspen and me."

"I know; I have spoken to his mother."

Noah's head jerked up, "You have?"

Dad nodded, and Noah turned to his mother. "Did you know about this?"

"Yes, Noah, I called her. You're right. She wants—for the time being—us out of her son's life. He may never have the use of his arm again—at least not like before—and she said he was depending on a basketball scholarship."

"He never even mentioned basketball to us, Mom, not once. None of them did. I just wonder—"

Mom touched his arm, "What?"

"I just wonder if it was all that important to him. He hung out with us all summer. And…Aspen is in love with him—she really is."

"Well, I knew she liked him—"

"No, Mom, she loves him. This has been a tough summer, but we still had fun—*because* of Kiryn and Gavin."

"And Rocky?" Dad tipped his head to one side and studied Noah.

After several seconds Noah finally nodded. "And Rocky."

Dad sighed. "Maybe you need to tell us what has been going on. Seems the Allen's have a lot of loose ends to tie up."

"You have no idea." Noah sighed too, but then glanced toward the door. "I'm kind of worried about Aspen though. Maybe I should go look for her."

"She probably just needs some time," said Mom. "Noah is all of it true, what Aspen was saying?"

"Yes, Mom, and you're probably right that she needs some time, but this thing about spirits, it's true, and more than once, she has had some pretty scary experiences."

Dad had been looking at his hands, but now he raised his head. "Has she said what—or who?"

Noah stood now. "Yes, Dad, that's what I'm trying to tell you. This is a real thing, and it has put her through a lot all summer."

Suddenly Noah felt anxious and again glanced toward the door. "I'm—she—well, we talked to this lady, Patrice, she seems to be of some help."

"What's her last name?" Dad's eyes narrowed.

Noah noticed, but he didn't want to acknowledge it right now. "Uh, Munoa—I think. Yeah, Munoa." He started toward the door. "I'm going to see if I can find Aspen. I would rather we both told you about all of this—you know, together."

Noah didn't wait for his parents to respond, he darted out the front door and started down the driveway toward his car but stopped. He slowly turned toward the path that led to the big house. He had the strangest feeling Aspen had gone there, and almost as if he was pulled in that direction, he jogged across the driveway and headed up the path.

The thought crossed his mind to check the backyard. Maybe she would want to go to where Gavin was hurt as he had, but again, a strong prompting urged him to keep going. He was to the steps now and with the help of the rails, took them two at a time.

When he reached the top, he scanned the backyard and the patio of the Mansion House. No sign of her. He didn't think it was necessary to go into the house. He didn't want to anyway, and he was pretty sure Aspen wouldn't go in there alone.

He ran across the grass and onto the path on the other side.

Noah suddenly realized he hadn't even tried to call Aspen. He stopped for a second, found her number on speed dial, and pushed send.

It immediately went to voicemail. *"Hey, it's Aspen. Leave a message."*

Noah pushed end, jammed the phone in his back pocket, and continued running toward the lake. Except for his footsteps, he couldn't hear any other sounds.

He rounded the last bend in the path where it opened, bringing the lake into full view.

She was there. Standing on the dock.

"Aspen!"

She didn't turn. He was sure he was close enough for her to hear him.

He kept running and yelled again, "Aspen!"

She still didn't turn and then—it seemed to him—Aspen purposely stepped off the dock.

"What the— Aspen! What are you doing?"

Fine time to take a swim!

Noah closed the distance to the dock, jumped up onto it and jogged deliberately to the end, fully expecting to see his sister in the water.

He abruptly stopped.

There was no sign of Aspen. The water was not even moving, but he was sure he had seen her step off the dock!

"Aspen!" He fell onto his stomach and leaned over the edge of the dock so he could see underneath it.

His movement had caused the dock to sway gently, the water lapping against the poles, but other than that—nothing.

Noah jumped to his feet. Suddenly panicked, he pulled his cell from his pocket and punched in Mom's number.

"Noah, did you find her?"

"No, Mom! I saw her step, or fall, or something into the lake, but she is not here! Call for help!"

"Dad and I will come."

"No, Mom. I mean yes come, but we need some help if she has fallen in the lake. I'll be looking. Oh, and, Mom, drive Dad up here. The steps are too steep."

Noah pulled off his shirt, shoes, and socks, and tossed his cell phone on top of his clothes. He scanned the lake one more time.

Still seeing no sign of his sister—or any other movement—he dived in.

Noah was exhausted. He had gone under the water, searched, come up for air, and repeated over and over, but to no avail. Aspen was nowhere to be found. Hearing sirens in the distance, he trudged out of the water and sat on the shore of the lake.

"Noah?"

He heard his mom call his name, but he didn't look up. He couldn't. His muscles ached, but his heart felt like it would break at the thought of losing his sister.

There was no way to drive into Mystic Lake, and soon firefighters and police officers were swarming from the path that led to the big house. A lot of other people were coming too, but Noah didn't bother to look at them.

He was bombarded by what seemed like a dozen questions but always with the same answer. He had witnessed Aspen step off the dock. She did not jump or dive, she simply stepped off, and that was the last he had seen of her.

A team of scuba divers started a search of the lake. When they emerged, more than two hours later, they too had nothing to report.

Noah stared at the lake. He was praying desperately for someone to find his sister. His parents sat on either side of him.

He looked over at his dad. Jackson Allen was a handsome man; even Noah saw that. His dark hair mussed right now, was straight like his and Aspen's and a little long for a guy his age, but he had always worn it like that. He had little wisps of gray at his temples. Typically tan from being on the beach so much, his skin looked pale and drawn, but Noah credited that not only to no sun but the fact that his dad had suffered a heart attack just weeks earlier. He had lost some weight, but Noah knew he would gain that back. His dad exercised regularly. Both he and Suzann had been running marathons for years, just not since they had come to Sommerville.

They hadn't done anything they had done in their regular life in San Clemente.

Dad was not crying. He just stared across the water. It didn't appear he was looking at anything in particular.

Mom, on the other hand, had not stopped crying, and Noah thought that was a good thing. She had been so distant most of the summer, letting her emotions through occasionally, but not that often. He figured she needed to cry.

Noah had always thought that Mom was a pretty lady. Her long brown hair hung loosely around her shoulders. She always complained about it because it was wavy and she hated that, but Noah had always thought it looked nice. Mom, too, had lost color she usually had from the sun. In San Clemente, she and Dad regularly surfed too, and he had always thought their activity, and being in the sun kept them looking youthful. Mom showed no signs of gray hair, he suddenly wondered if she dyed it, and then he realized that was an odd thought at this crucial time. He was surprised at his entire train of thought right then.

Two firefighters were walking towards them, and suddenly Noah reached down and took hold of his parent's hands.

Dad started to stand, but the one firefighter, who introduced himself as Troy, motioned for him to stay where he was, and instead sat down on the ground next to him.

"Mr. Allen—"

"Jackson."

"Jackson. I'm sorry we have no good news right now, but I want Chet to explain to you what they found down there."

"Chet?"

Right then, Noah noticed a man in a wet suit walking in their direction.

"Yes, he is one of our divers."

Chet walked directly up to Dad, shook his hand, and nodded in Mom's direction.

"Mr. and Mrs. Allen?"

Dad nodded, and this time, he did not offer his first name.

Chet continued, "I have never dived—actually none of us have ever dived this lake—it's not that big, and the fact that it was man-made, usually makes it a lot easier to search, but in this case, we have located an underground channel of some sort, and it seems to go on for a long time. It's narrow and has a lot of jagged rocks. It must have formed over the years. I'm not sure, but we think maybe your daughter has slipped into that channel. It has a pretty strong current, which is also unusual. This came as a complete surprise to all of us."

That news turned Mom's cries into sobs, and immediately, Dad stood and walked around Noah. He pulled Mom to her feet and pulled her into his arms.

"Oh, Jackson—" Mom sobbed. "This is unbearable! I don't think I can live if we lose Aspen."

Dad said nothing. He buried his face in Mom's hair and wept.

It was starting to get dark, and the rescue team called off the search until morning. They had concluded they would be searching for a body. They didn't leave much hope of finding Aspen alive.

"Noah?"

He looked up when he heard Rocky's voice.

Rocky extended his hand and pulled Noah to his feet. Kiryn was with him.

She was crying, and when Rocky hugged Noah, she hugged them both.

Noah buried his face in Rocky's shoulder.

"We came as soon as we heard."

"This is so messed up, Rocky, she was standing right over there and then she was gone."

"I...I don't even know what to say." Rocky's voice cracked.

"I was so mean to her." Kiryn sobbed.

Noah didn't respond to Kiryn's comment. He didn't see a need to. He felt unsure about her sincerity, even though he genuinely believed they were all just trying to protect Gavin.

"How's...how's Gavin?" Noah pulled away from Rocky and turned the conversation in a different direction.

"He's in Memphis with his mom. He's doing okay, but it will be a while," said Rocky.

"Is he going to stay there?"

"No, he wants to come back to school. It will just be a few weeks."

"He asks about Aspen all the time, but Sara is not budging. She—"

Noah interrupted Kiryn, "Blames us."

Kiryn nodded, "Yeah, I guess so, but not so much you guys as the circumstances. You know, that you moved here and all."

Noah scoffed, "Yeah, well, that's our fault." His sarcasm was unmistakable. "Anyway, it doesn't matter. What matters is that my sister is lost."

Kiryn ducked her head and nodded.

Noah knew she must feel uncomfortable, but he didn't care.

"Do you think she could have gotten out of the water without you seeing her?" asked Rocky.

"I don't see how. I was on the dock in minutes after I saw her go in, and anyway, where would she go?"

"Maybe into the trees? Your mom told the police she was mad when she left the house."

"She was, but this is not like Aspen. She wouldn't let the entire town search for her if she were just trying to hide from Mom and Dad, and besides, she wouldn't put *us* through this."

Rocky's eyes narrowed. "I just had a thought."

Kiryn asked, "About what?"

Rocky seemed to backpedal as though he wished he hadn't said anything.

"About what, Rocky?" Noah pressed him.

"About something Dixon's journal said. That the bodies of Ronda and her boyfriend were not there when he and Tygert came back the next day."

"You mean the channel—or whatever it is?" asked Noah.

Rocky seemed hesitant, "Uh—probably not."

Noah sighed. "I don't know. All I know is that Aspen is gone." Tears filled his already swollen eyes.

Rocky put his arm across Noah's shoulders. "They will find her."

The three of them walked towards Jackson and Suzann.

Mom was saying to Dad, "I can't leave here, Jackson, not without knowing where she is."

"It could be days."

"I don't care. I can't leave her here."

Dad rubbed his face with both hands. "So, what do you want to do?"

"I'll stay here."

"Alone. All night?"

"I'll stay with her, Dad," said Noah.

Rocky shook Dad's hand and patted Mom's arm. "I have a better idea."

"What's that?"

"Kiryn and I will get some chairs and blankets. We can build a fire, and we will all stay. The rescue team will be back at first light, and that way, you will be here."

Dad looked at Mom, and she nodded. "Okay…okay thanks, Rocky."

Kiryn turned to Noah. "Want to go with me to get some food. You guys must be hungry."

"We…we never ate that food I brought home for dinner."

"No worries, Mom. We'll go get something."

The firefighter named Troy was standing close by. "I'll get some of my guys to bring up some chairs." He motioned to a pile of wood that Noah had not noticed. "They already brought some wood. A few of us will stay with you."

Mom and Dad both nodded, but neither said anything. The looks on their faces made Noah sad. Now there may be no hope for their family to heal from all of this. How he wished they had never come here, but he had wished that before, and nothing had changed. Instead, things just kept getting worse.

Troy was talking with Rocky. "We'll send down for some food. You all just stay here together."

Rocky nodded. "Okay."

Noah walked over to the dock, and Kiryn followed. They stood in silence as the moon cast a bright light across the water. On any other night, it would have looked pretty, but tonight it loomed over them permeating the feelings of dread that filled the air.

Kiryn put her arm around his waist, but he didn't respond.

Shoulders drooping and head bowed Noah stared into the water, silently praying for a miracle.

12

MAX

The first thing Aspen noticed was how warm the water was. She had not expected that. *Maybe it's the lights that make it warm.*

Against her will, she was being pulled deeper into the lake. She looked up. Looking through the water was weird. It was wavy, but she could see the blue sky and the same billowy clouds she had been looking at from the dock.

The thought occurred to her that she would need to get out soon because even though she was good at holding her breath, she couldn't do it indefinitely. She was surprised at how casually that thought came and went.

Aspen turned back to the direction she was going and immediately started to backpedal when she saw a figure coming toward her. It seemed to glide, not swim. Her desperate attempt to get away did nothing. She just kept moving forward, toward the figure.

In seconds, the figure was next to her, and she realized it was a boy. He took her hand, turned, and pulled her along.

Aspen started to feel anxious. She could not hold her breath any longer, and she began fighting to get her hand free.

The boy seemed to slow down. He turned to her, and with his finger, he briefly touched first her mouth and then her chest at the top of her rib cage.

A cool sensation filled Aspen's lungs. Her startled, wide eyes stared at the boy.

"Relax."

She heard the word, but she was not sure where it came from. The boy was smiling as he slowly nodded.

"Relax."

She realized he was communicating with her through thought.

Aspen hesitated, still holding her breath.

"Breathe."

The word came almost as a command.

Aspen started shaking her head and tried pulling away, but she was still held there. Now she was getting scared. She *had* to get some air.

"Just breathe. I promise it will be okay."

Aspen stopped fighting and stared at the boy. He nodded, ever so slightly.

Slowly, Aspen allowed a little water into her nostrils, but then she held her breath again. She was surprised it didn't hurt. She had experienced water in her nose many times, but it always hurt. This time, it simply felt like air.

This isn't possible.

"Apparently it is," and the boy began swimming again, still holding her hand, he continued to pull her with him.

Aspen's chest hurt, so she finally closed her eyes and allowed the water to completely fill her nose and throat. She felt the coolness spread through her lungs.

It was as though she didn't need to breathe. She was gliding through the water, and there was no pain in her chest. The warm water seemed to cocoon around her, and her fear now turned to curiosity.

I wonder where he is taking me.

"There."

Can you read my mind?

"I can."

Okay, where are we going?

"I told you, there," and he pointed ahead.

Am I dead?

She thought she heard him laugh.

"No."

They entered a cave. The water was clear and light all around her lit up the entire space. The walls of the cave appeared red and made Aspen think of Southern Utah where their family had vacationed at some national parks. She couldn't remember the names of the parks, but she did remember the red dirt.

Still holding her hand, the boy floated next to her, facing the wall opposite the cave entrance. He then raised his other hand and passed it before his face as though he were slowly waving to someone.

Instantly, the entire wall of the cave became a waterfall. She could see the waterfall, and even more profound; she could *hear* the waterfall. It was just like in the tunnel.

The boy did not move. He held her hand, and they stayed still as if they were not floating at all, but standing on the ground.

What is this?

The boy lifted a finger to his lips.

You want me to be quiet? Why? The waterfall is so loud!

He looked at her sideways and then he scowled.

Aspen looked away. *Who is this guy anyway and why does it seem so normal to be* under *the water? I must be dead.*

"I am Max, and I assure you; you're not dead."

Are you *dead?*

He appeared to chuckle. "Not exactly."

What does that mean, "not exactly?" You're either dead, or you're not! I know a few dead people, and you seem quite dead.

She shook her head as though to clear her thoughts. *Well, you sort of seem dead. I can see you clearly, though.*

This time, he did not just scowl, but his eyes narrowed. Aspen took a second to size him up.

Max was almost the same height as her. He wore a tunic of sorts that clung to his broad shoulders but hung loose to his mid-thighs. It didn't have any sleeves. Aspen was surprised that he was wearing jeans, and his feet were bare. His red, almost orange hair, was nearly as long as hers. From what she could tell, his eyes appeared green. His ruddy complexion complimented his hair and eyes, and he had a playfulness about him that made him easy to be around.

What is wrong with me? This guy is either a dream, or I am indeed dead.

She expected to "hear" a response from Max, but none came, and it suddenly occurred to her that he had never opened his mouth to talk.

Aspen's thoughts were distracted by movement coming from the waterfall.

"It's time."

For what?

She had barely thought the words when suddenly she was on the other side of the waterfall. Max was still standing next to her, still holding her hand. She had not felt any movement, but now they were in a different place. The waterfall was behind them.

No water. Aspen looked back. The waterfall *was* still behind them, but she could not hear it anymore. They were now inside a room which was filled with a mist or sort of fog, except for right where she and Max were standing. It wasn't a dense mist, but it was there.

Maybe it wasn't really a room because she could not see any walls. She looked all around. The quiet waterfall behind them and a light mist surrounded them. She was surprised that without any trouble at all, she seemed to be breathing air again.

Aspen attempted to speak, but she could not make any sounds. Instead, she asked her question with her thoughts.

Where are we now, Max?

No response and he had not looked at her. He was staring directly in front of them.

From the corner of her eye, Aspen saw movement, and she quickly turned to look in the same direction as Max.

There were people in that mist. Aspen squinted. A lot of people!

She gasped and jerked away from Max as both of her hands shot to her mouth. She backed away, but when she did, she began to fall backward into thick blackness. She gasped as she felt the air sucked out of her.

Max grabbed her hand and pulled her back to her feet. "Do *not* let go of my hand!"

She took a deep breath as she was pulled up. Now fearful of falling into the blackness again, she desperately clung tightly to Max's hand. She once again looked ahead of them, and her eyes widened.

Those are—those are boys!

Max nodded. "They are."

13

MISSING

Noah plopped down on a blanket. The air wasn't cold, but he felt cold. Mom and Dad were each wrapped in blankets and lying on the lounge chairs that Troy and his men had carried over from the big house. The night was pitch black except for the light from the flickering fire, and Noah wondered where the moon had gone. He could not see his parent's faces.

Troy had also sent for food. Noah learned that Bill and Nada provided the food free of charge. He felt like he should eat more of it, but his stomach was tied in knots. He assumed everyone else felt the same way because most of the chicken and French fries lay untouched, but several empty plastic water bottles protruded from a paper sack.

Noah was tired. He rubbed his face with both hands and lay back on the blanket.

Mom said quietly, "How are you, Noah?"

"I'm okay, Mom. How are you and Dad?"

"Dad's asleep."

"That's good," Noah mumbled, but then he heard his mother's muffled cry, and he immediately got to his feet and walked over to her.

When he was close, she reached for his hand and pulled him down next to her on the lounge. "Noah, what if we have lost her?"

Noah's head throbbed. He couldn't think of anything positive to say. Aspen had been missing since about 5:30 yesterday afternoon and it was now nearly four am. Noah seriously doubted there was any chance she was still alive, but he could not make himself say the words, so he just leaned over and hugged his mother. "They'll find her, Mom." But his voice cracked, and he began to cry.

Mom hugged him tighter, and for several minutes, they both wept, saying nothing.

"Excuse me, could I get you folks anything?"

Noah hadn't noticed Troy approach them. As he stood, he squeezed his mom's hand. "No, nothing for me," he said and walked back to his blanket and laid down. He closed his eyes tight, trying to block out the possibility of his sister being dead, but he couldn't dispel the thought, and tears rolled silently down his cheeks.

He was clearly aware of Kiryn sitting alone directly across the fire from him. She had not said anything to him since they walked back from the dock in silence. He knew she was probably tormented for the things she had said to Aspen, but somehow he couldn't bring himself to console her. He was kind of angry with her.

He didn't know where Rocky had wandered off to, but he hadn't seen him for over an hour. He wasn't sure he cared about that either. All he wanted right now is for Aspen to be okay, and as the minutes and hours ticked away, he was losing all hope of that reality.

He had just drifted to sleep when his buzzing cell phone woke him abruptly. He pulled it from his back pocket, quickly silencing it before it woke his dad.

He scrolled the front and pushed on the tiny envelope to open the text. It surprised him to see that it was from Gavin.

"Noah, what's happening? Where is Aspen?"

Surprised and a little annoyed, Noah sat up and stared at his phone. A part of him didn't want to answer Gavin, but he also knew that Gavin's not seeing Aspen was not his fault. He glanced over at Kiryn. Her head was down, and it looked as though she might be sleeping. He looked back at his phone.

Suddenly, the thought occurred to Noah that maybe Gavin really didn't know what had happened today. After all, he was in

Memphis, and even if Rocky told Sara, which he most likely did, Sara might not have told Gavin.

Noah continued to stare at his phone. Finally, he answered. "Why?"

The text from Gavin came back immediately.

"I just got my phone back from Mom. I have been texting Aspen all day, and tried to call her twice."

"She's—"

But the next text from Gavin appeared on Noah's screen before he could finish typing his answer.

"She's in water, Noah. Are you guys at the lake? I have a— Is everything okay?"

Noah was anxious now, and he frantically began typing. "What do you see her doing? Is she—"

But another text appeared, *"It's Sara. This is exactly why I have not given Gavin his phone. Please leave him alone."*

A chill crept from Noah's neck all the way down his back and onto his arms. Sara's text sounded so cold. Could she possibly not know that Aspen was missing? If she did, could she be so mad at the Allen's that she wouldn't even communicate with their family at a time like this? She didn't seem like that type of person, but how was he to know how parents act when they believe they are protecting their kids.

He mulled Gavin's words over and over. *"She's in water."*

Noah knew that much, but what stood out to him is that Gavin did *not* say that Aspen was dead. He said she's in water.

Noah understood he was grasping at straws, but even this tiny flicker of hope was something to hang on to. It was all he had. It was all any of them had, but he didn't dare share it with Mom and Dad. He wasn't sure how to explain right at this moment, how Gavin may know that Aspen was in water.

Commotion coming from the direction of the path to the big house caught Noah's attention. It appeared a fresh diving crew was arriving. The sun had not even peeked over the trees yet, but they were already setting up their gear.

He looked over at his parents. He was surprised they were both sleeping, but seconds later he knew why.

Rocky had reappeared, and when he caught Noah's eye, he motioned to Mom and Dad and then winked. Somehow Noah knew Rocky had convinced them to take something to help them sleep. Maybe the something he had given Aspen.

His thoughts drifted.

"Want some orange juice?"

Noah had fallen asleep himself, and Kiryn woke him when she sat down next to him.

"Your neck is going to hurt sleeping like that."

She was right. Noah lifted his head, slowly stretching it from side-to-side to work the kinks out. Rubbing the sleep from his eyes, he took the small carton of juice from Kiryn. "Thanks."

Kiryn nodded. "Looks like they are ready to dive again."

The sun glistened over the tops of the trees and danced across the water. Noah looked to where Mom and Dad had been sleeping, but they were not there.

Kiryn pointed, "They are over there. The divers are going in from that side of the lake this time."

Noah stood, and Kiryn followed.

He tossed the empty juice carton into the glowing embers of the fire and began jogging toward his parents. He didn't notice if Kiryn followed.

She hadn't. When he reached his parents, he glanced back to see her standing next to the fire with Rocky.

Right that second, Noah felt detached from everything. He was standing next to his parents whom he had avoided all summer, waiting anxiously for news about his only sibling who could very possibly be dead, two of the people he loved and shared the entire summer with now seemed uncomfortable around him, and the one person he had let in to be his friend was in another city seemingly unaware of the drama that had unfolded at Mystic Lake.

Everything had changed. *Nothing stays the same but change.* Derrick used to say that about the ocean and right now at least, Noah found his friend's observance to be true. Change is the only thing a person can really depend upon.

Everything seemed surreal to Noah, and the hole in his heart throbbed. At least that's what it felt like. An empty gaping hole that insisted on needling him with constant burning and unexpected jabs of excruciating pain.

Noah walked over to his parents, slipped in between them, and put an arm around each of their shoulders.

This really may be all there is. Just us. The...thr...three of us.

And the pain jabbed deeper.

14

NO ACCIDENT

"Mom! You can't keep me from my friends forever!"

"Gavin, we are not going to discuss this. You need to recover before you go back in for your next surgery. I am not going to have you upset because of—"

"My friends, Mom? They don't upset me. *You* upset me! I get that you want me to get well, and I really appreciate it, but Mom, you can't blame Aspen and Noah for this. It wasn't their fault."

"Gavin, don't you see? Everything is lost! No scholarship, no more basketball! All that you have worked and planned for!" Sara fidgeted with her hands. "And—"

"And what, Mom?"

"You have barely spoken to Cassie all summer, and she really cares about you."

Gavin sighed. "Mom, leave Cassie out of this. You have *never* tried to take over my life. Why suddenly—"

"I should have stepped in a lot sooner. That day we went to Patrice's—I knew things would get out of hand after that. I should have never let Rocky talk me into letting you go over there."

"What is that supposed to mean? Mom, she is your aunt. Are you mad because I know who my birth mother is and you don't like the possibilities of that?"

"Of what?"

"That I may have her gift."

Sara turned and moved from the window where she had been peering through the blinds. She walked slowly over to Gavin's bed and sank into a nearby chair.

"Gavin, I am not afraid for our relationship. I think we both know that, but I am afraid for you. For how all of this—the gift I mean—may affect your life."

"Why blame the Allen's? If I have the gift, I have it despite them. It came from *your* sister." He fell back against his pillows and winced as pain shot through his arm.

"Not in spite of them, Gavin, because of them," Sara spoke softly.

Gavin lay, his good arm across his forehead. "Mom, I don't understand what you are talking about."

Sara's eyes had been fixed on the wall behind Gavin, but now she looked directly at him. He was surprised to see her eyes brimming with tears.

"Gavin, that tree falling on you was no accident."

"What?"

"I mean, it seemed like an accident, but the truth is there are powers stronger than any of us that are involved here. Powers that do not want you kids or anyone else to uncover the truth surrounding the Dixons and Tygerts. You kids have gotten too close."

"It's a little late for that." Gavin sighed. "So, you think someone caused that tree to fall on me. That's crazy, Mom, there was no one there."

"Not someone. Maybe something."

Gavin stared at his mother. "I guess I don't understand what you're trying to say, Mom. Too close to what?"

"Gavin, I—" Mom's eyes suddenly averted to the door, and Gavin turned to see what she was looking at.

Doug, Gavin's step-dad, was standing in the doorway.

15

SHE'S GOING TO DIE

TWELVE HOURS AND TWO diving teams later, still no sign of Aspen.

Dad had been sitting by the cold fire for over two hours. He had not said a single word.

Mom was still holding vigil on the dirt near the edge of the lake, staring at the water as though if she did, Aspen might just walk out.

Noah couldn't sit still and had walked around the lake several times during the day. He stopped at lunch to make sure his parents ate something. Dad's doctor had even come to Mystic Lake to check on him and suggested to Noah that both parents—especially his dad—needed to eat something to keep their strength up.

At Noah's request, Kiryn had gone to the little house and made grilled cheese sandwiches and tomato soup, one of Mom and Dad's go-to lunches when they couldn't think of anything else to eat. He and Aspen had always teased their parents that with all their other expensive tastes in food, that simple lunch seemed to satisfy them whenever nothing else could.

It worked. Both Mom and Dad had eaten, and Noah felt like he had completed at least one positive task for the day.

The sun was getting low in the sky as Noah walked in silence. Suddenly, he stopped. The culvert Gavin had pointed out to him, and the girls protruded from the water about ten feet from shore. Why hadn't he noticed this before? Maybe he was just not looking in that direction when he passed it earlier, but every time he passed it? Seemed unlikely.

Noah pulled off his shoes and socks and waded into the waist-deep water. When he reached the culvert opening, he grasped the edge and pulled himself up. Bracing against the cement, he peered through the grate. The ladder Gavin had climbed was in full view but disappeared into darkness farther down. Noah could not see the bottom where he, Gavin, Kiryn, and Aspen had been standing not even two weeks earlier.

Bracing his feet against the side of the culvert Noah pried on one of the locks. It didn't budge. He was hoping, since it was so rusty, it may pull free, but no luck.

A low gurgling sound startled Noah, and he jerked around in the direction of the sound. He gasped when the water began spinning around him. Wrapping his fingers around the rebar, he clung to the grate, but the force of the water pulled him off, and he was thrown from the culvert, and hurled through the air, landing on his back in the dirt onshore.

Noah scrambled to his feet, backing away from the water as fast as he could. His heart pounded against his ribs, and he was panting so hard he couldn't catch his breath.

What just happened?

He quickly scanned his body as if to see if he had all the original parts. He was so shaken, he couldn't stand any longer, and he collapsed on the ground. He stared at the silent water. Not even a slight disturbance. Not even a wave lapping at the shore.

It was a whirlpool, like the one we jumped in when we were in Hawaii.

Aspen's words rushed through his head as he recalled the day she fell off the tire swing. He quickly glanced at the dock. The tire swing hung limp at the end of the rope.

Now Noah stood and ran as fast as he could toward his parents and the rescue party. Afraid of being followed—by what, or whom he had no idea—he kept glancing over his shoulder.

"Noah?" Troy called as Noah approached.

Mom was talking to Troy and one of the divers, but their conversation stopped when they saw Noah.

"What's the matter, Noah? You look like you have seen a ghost."

"I...I—" he looked from Troy to his mother, and then at the diver who was a tall, muscular African-American. He turned back to his mother, "Where is Rocky?"

"He and Kiryn will be right back," said Mom. She reached for her son's hand. "Noah, they are going to call off the search."

"What? No! They can't do that! Mom, I need to talk with Rocky!" Tears spilled from Mom's eyes.

Noah turned to the diver. "Why are you calling off the search?"

Troy intervened, "Noah this is Kendall Washington. These are his diving teams."

Kendall's sympathetic eyes locked with Noah's for a few seconds. When he spoke, he seemed to choose his words carefully.

"We have searched every inch of this lake, Noah. There is only one place her bod— Aspen could be at this point, and it is just too dangerous for us to go any deeper."

"Where? What do you mean?"

Troy put his hand on Noah's shoulder, "They went into that channel. It's actually a narrow tunnel and seems to go on indefinitely. It has a lot of rocks and gets pretty narrow in some places, but the biggest concern is the current."

"Why?" Noah asked absently.

"It's strong, Noah. I can't in good judgment, let my guys go any deeper. Once we got into the cave, maybe a hundred yards or so, the current was extremely hard to swim against making it very difficult to get back out." Kendall seemed to be apologizing to the family.

Noah dropped his head, and his chest wracked with sobs. "So you are just going to leave her there?"

Kendall put his arm around Noah, and he didn't pull away.

Mom reached for his hand, but Noah lunged toward her throwing his arms around her shoulders. "No, Mom, no this can't be happening."

Suzann Allen held her sobbing son in her arms. Her head spun with the reality that she had experienced this same scene with her daughter just a few months ago when Aspen's best friend, Krista was killed in a surfing accident. Her head throbbed, and her heart ached so much she was not sure she could contain her emotions for her son as she had for her daughter. This time, it was different. It was her own daughter that had been swallowed up by the water, and the reality was just starting to sink in.

Suddenly Noah pulled away and almost frantically asked, "Where is Dad?"

Mom motioned toward the lake, and Noah saw Dad sitting on the edge of the dock, his legs dangling over the edge.

Noah's eyes widened, "No! Dad get away from there!"

He broke free from his mother and ran as hard as he could toward the dock. He leaped onto the wooden platform, feeling it move under his weight.

Dad looked up but said nothing. His face and eyes were swollen, and Noah's first thought was that his father suddenly looked old.

Noah hurried to his Dad and, putting both hands under his dad's arms, he pulled him to his feet.

"Noah, what is it?"

"Dad, just c'mon, please. Let's get off the dock."

Dad didn't fight his son but allowed him to lead him to the other side of the dock, down the steps, and onto the worn dirt path. They walked in silence except for soft crying from both.

Finally, Noah spoke, "They're leaving her down there, Dad." His crying turned once again to tortured sobs.

Dad stopped, put his arms around his son's shoulders, and pulled him to his chest, hugging him tightly as they cried together.

***

"Kendall! Troy!"

The yelling caught Noah and his parent's attention, and they all turned in the direction it was coming from.

The last diving team were still cleaning up their equipment near some trees, the only place on the lake that the trees were so close to the water and near the path that led from Sara and Doug's house.

Both Kendall and Troy ran past them with Noah on their heels.

Noah's phone had buzzed three times, but he didn't take the time to look at it.

Kendall reached the divers first. "What's going on?"

"Can't believe this—she's right over there." One of the divers pointed to the bushes near the trees. "She just floated to the surface while we were all right there in the water. It's—it's crazy."

"Aspen?!" Noah yelled, and he darted around Kendall and the diver, but Troy caught his arm and stopped him.

Troy said quietly, "Let us check her first, Noah."

Noah turned and yelled to his parents, "Mom! Dad! It's Aspen!" He could not contain his emotions, and he choked the words, "Is…is she dead, Troy?"

Two EMT's with the diving team were crouched on the ground their backs to Noah. One of them must have heard Noah and briefly turned.

"She has a pulse."

Mom, Dad, Rocky, and Kiryn had reached Noah and Troy.

Mom whispered, "She's alive?"

"Yes." Came the flat reply from Kendall. He didn't volunteer any more information. It was several minutes before they carried Aspen past her family.

Noah's stomach was tied in knots, and he realized he was squeezing someone's hand. He glanced to his right. It was Kiryn's.

His parents, Rocky and Kiryn, and Noah stared at Aspen.

From what Noah had told Troy, they determined that Aspen had been in the water for approximately twenty-six hours.

Pasty white skin except for the blue around her mouth, her eyes were closed and her face and hair matted with mud. Tubes taped to both arms and oxygen tubes protruding from her nose. She looked awful.

Noah's eyes closed, and then he slowly opened them. The diver,

Kendall, stood directly on the other side of Aspen. He and Noah locked eyes, and for a brief second, Noah noticed a questioning look in Kendall's dark eyes, but he dismissed it immediately and turned back to his sister. She appeared lifeless on the blue stretcher, and a horrible reality hit him.

She's going to die.

16

SILENT WORLD

NOAH COULD NOT BELIEVE he was in the same hospital emergency room again. He had no more tears and no more energy. He stared at his feet.

Mom and Dad were in the room with Aspen and the doctors. No one had volunteered any information, so Noah just waited.

Kiryn and Rocky stayed with him, but they too sat in silence. Everything was surreal, and Noah's head was in a fog.

Noah's phone buzzed and so did Kiryn's.

They glanced at each other and then turned back to their phones.

The text was from Gavin. There were three other texts from Gavin, and Noah remembered the texts coming through at the lake. He scrolled the screen and read the previous texts first.

"Noah?" was all it said.

The second text, *"Noah, answer me."*

And the third text, *"Noah, Aspen is not in the water anymore."*

Noah could almost hear Gavin yelling in the third newest message, *"Mom does not know I have my phone. Answer me!"*

Kiryn looked up, "Did you get the text from Gavin?"

"Yeah." He turned to look at Kiryn. "He said he knows Aspen is not in the water."

Kiryn nodded, and her eyes widened. She looked like she was going to say something, but the doors to the emergency room opened, and Mom and Dad emerged. Noah jumped to his feet and quickly hurried to their sides. "What?"

Dad's sigh was labored. "She's in a coma, Noah."

"Will…will she wake up?"

Dad looked at his son, "They are hoping, but still trying to determine how long she has been like this. They don't know if there is brain damage, and they won't know that for a while."

At that statement, Mom gasped and began crying. Dad put his arm around her and turned again to Noah. "We are exhausted, Noah, and you must be too. We all need to get some sleep."

Noah had to admit he was so tired; he was dizzy. Both of his parents looked like they were completely out of energy, and he wondered just how much more they could take.

A nurse, whose name tag said Renee, appeared from behind a closed door. "Mr. and Mrs. Allen, we have an empty room down the hall. Would you folks like to stay here tonight?"

"That would be nice." The words barely escaped Mom's lips as she and Dad started to follow the nurse.

Dad stopped, "Would it be okay if our son stays as well?"

Renee smiled, "Of course," and she continued walking.

Noah turned to face Rocky and Kiryn. "Thanks you guys."

Rocky reached for Noah and hugged him. "No problem, Noah."

Kiryn started to wave her hand, but then quickly stepped up to Noah and gave him a quick hug. "Bye," she said lightly.

Noah nodded briefly and then turned and followed his parents and Renee.

The room had two beds, and a roll-away had been brought in.

He went into the bathroom. When he came out, the lights were out. The room was dark except for the moonlight peering through the window. He stopped just outside the bathroom door.

Mom and Dad were on their knees next to one of the beds—praying—and they were holding hands. He hadn't seen that for a long, long time.

He stood for a few seconds, thinking, and then quietly crept to the extra bed, knelt and silently poured his heart out. As he did, he wished he had made this more of a regular practice.

Where am I, now? Aspen looked around for Max, but he was nowhere to be found.

I am tired of these disappearing acts around here.

Around where? She seemed to be in a fog—not a mist any longer—an actual fog. There were no discernible objects. Nothing. Just fog.

"Max?" Aspen was startled to hear her own voice again.

Nothing.

She hesitated, but then whispered, "Krista? Ronda?"

No response.

Well, if I am dead, at least I don't hurt, but this is so weird. Not at all like I pictured it.

Her eyes suddenly heavy, she gave in to the urge to simply let them close.

The sound of familiar voices woke Aspen.

"Mom? Dad?" Aspen could hear her own voice, but Mom and Dad continued to talk to each other, neither acknowledging her. Now there was a third voice.

"There does not seem to be any brain damage, at least from the tests we have run so far," said the unfamiliar voice.

"But will she wake up?" That was Mom.

"We hope so, but it could take some time. Comas are funny things. Her brainwaves are responsive, her vitals are all good, but for some reason—and we are not sure why this happens—her mind just doesn't connect. It does not receive the signals to wake up."

"Can she hear us?" that was Dad.

Of course, I can hear you! Aspen almost screamed.

But the unfamiliar voice continued talking, "There are a lot of theories on that as well. Many people who have been in this state and wake up, claim they could hear everything while in the coma, so I choose to believe that she can."

"But not everyone?"

"Why is that?" asked Mom.

The other voice seemed to hesitate, but then he finally said, "Well, we can only ask the ones who wake up."

Mom gasped and started to cry.

Aspen felt pressure on her hand, and she knew her mother was stroking it with her thumb.

Then she felt Dad envelop her other hand with his bigger one.

"Aspen, it's Dad. Mom and I are right here with you. There was an accident, honey. You were in the lake."

The lake! That's right! The water where Max was. Did I—wait—I just walked into that stupid lake. What an idiot!

"Please come back to us, Aspen." Mom was crying.

But I'm here. I'm right here. It hurt her to hear her mother crying for no reason. She sobered. Well, maybe there was a reason.

Aspen was exasperated. She wanted to squeeze her parents' hands or say something or cry out, but she couldn't move, and all she could see was the persistent fog.

"Aspen, we will get things worked out. Please wake up." She felt a kiss on her forehead, and she knew it was Dad because he kissed the side of her face where he held her hand. Besides, it was Dad's kiss.

"Mom, Dad?"

Noah!

Dad let go of her hand.

"How is she?"

"The same," said Dad. "But the doctor tells us he thinks she can possibly hear us talking to her."

"Really? Is there any way to tell?"

Aspen felt Noah awkwardly grab the hand Dad had been holding. "It doesn't seem like she can hear anything. She's so limp."

Take advantage of this, Noah, I'll be back. Aspen joked, but then realized she was the only one privy to her joke.

"She doesn't have any control of her body, Noah. It's like she is in a deep sleep. We are hoping her brain is awake, that's all."

There was silence.

Hey, are you guys still there?

But then she heard Noah, "Wake up. We have a lot to do, and I'm not doing all of it by myself."

Just like Noah—not wake up so you will be okay, Aspen—but wake because he needs my help! Maybe I should let him suffer.

But then she stopped making jokes, the realization that she had no control was the cold truth, and she wondered how long she could lay in this silent world.

17

MEETING

ROCKY STEERED HIS TRUCK onto the highway. Blinding rain made visibility difficult as raindrops ricocheted off the road. After two hours of exhausting talk with Sara and Doug, no agreements had been reached. Sara was still holding firm to her demand that Gavin have no contact with the Allen's, and Rocky couldn't believe she could be so difficult—well he could believe that about Sara—but not in this case. No amount of reasoning made Sara budge. Even advising her that Aspen may not wake up from her coma didn't sway Sara. Instead, she used that as another reason, Gavin did not need the trauma.

Finally relenting, for now, Rocky had left Kiryn to hang out with Gavin for the day and then headed toward Sommerville in response to a request from Jackson. The text message he received simply said, *"Rocky, I have to talk to you. Today if possible. It is important."*

Rocky had agreed to meet with Jackson around one o'clock. He glanced at his dash clock. It was just past noon. He had plenty of time even on this dark rainy October day. Temperatures had cooled the last couple of days, and the leaves were just starting to turn. Rocky loved this time of year in Tennessee, but he hardly had time to think about autumn leaves, Halloween, or anything else he normally thought of.

Instead, his head was crowded with frustration and fear. If he was completely honest with himself, fear was his deepest emotion right now. Not for himself, although there was an element of that, but for his son, possibly for his daughter, and without question for Aspen Allen, and her brother, Noah.

There was very little traffic on this early Sunday afternoon, and even though pelting raindrops kept the windshield wipers busy, Rocky instinctively traveled the familiar highway while his mind recalled the events of the past few months which had thrown his family into adventure and now, turmoil.

He smiled at the awkwardness on the first day of summer school when Noah and Aspen Allen entered all their lives. How out of place they both seemed with their dark tans and California casualness. Aspen making every effort to fit in, and Noah trying his best not to, but Kiryn had seen right through their façade and immediately connected with Aspen. It had taken Gavin a little longer to break through Noah's tough shell, but soon, the four of them were inseparable, and he may be what the kids considered old, but it was impossible not to notice the attraction between Gavin and Aspen, especially after that kiss. He wasn't sure about Noah and Kiryn, although there seemed to be something a little more than friendship.

When the kids first confided in Rocky about the things that were going on at the Allen Manor involving Aspen, his curiosity piqued, and he willingly volunteered his help, not expecting the gravity of what they would uncover.

The carefully guarded mysteries of the legendary Allen Family could no longer be contained with the arrival of this innocent teenager, and once unlocked, it seemed as though every facet of the past was begging to be heard. Rocky had soon realized there was no stopping the unexplainable, the incomprehensible, and yes, the supernatural that surrounded the Allen Manor, Mystic Lake and the two most prominent founders of Sommerville—Lloyd Dixon and Jackson Humphrey Allen.

The past began to unravel at breakneck speed and soon Rocky's only goal was to slow it all down in an effort to uncover every detail so that once and for all maybe their sleepy little town could put the past where it belonged—in the past—and the families that had been so deeply affected would be allowed to heal. Even though he was very familiar with the news articles and some of the accusations against the two families, he honestly had not expected the component of Jackson Allen to play such a huge role.

However, fully aware that the only living son of David Jackson Allen had not set foot in this town since he was eighteen years old, Rocky should have realized the significance of his return, but he hadn't. Even though he had studied the town's history and knew more of the facts than most, somehow he felt it was just a myth that had been told and retold over the years until it had grown into something so unbelievable that it could not be real.

An involuntary shudder rippled through Rocky, and he unconsciously turned the heater on. Rain now accompanied by cracking thunder continued to pound the truck as he turned onto the country road surrounding the pricey Mystic Lake homes.

His thoughts raced. His only son was facing his third surgery after a random accident in the Allen's backyard and—

Rocky slammed on his brakes, sliding to a stop on the wet asphalt.

Random? And now Aspen is in a coma? Is it possible that all of this is not so coincidental?

The thought caused real fear to course through his body. Slowly he rolled the truck forward again, and soon found himself parked in front of the Allen's "little house," as the kids called it. There was a black SUV already there. Jackson's truck was parked in front of the closed garage door. He assumed Noah's Iroc and Suzann's BMW were inside, or maybe the two of them had gone to the hospital to visit Aspen.

Aspen had been in a coma for three days now, and through conversation with Suzann and Jackson, he knew their hopes of her waking up were starting to fade.

Kiryn however, remained valiant that Aspen would fully recover, but she had not expressed that same confidence in the possibility of

Gavin having full use of his arm again.

Rocky sighed as the rain pelted the windows of his truck. He never carried an umbrella and knew he would be soaking wet when he reached the cover of the front porch. He threw the door open and leaped out.

The little house was just that, little. Immediately upon stepping inside, he was in the living room. His heart sank when he recognized the occupants of the SUV: Byron Coulsen and Larry Brimhall, the two FBI agents who had been assigned to the case. Hank was there too, and he immediately stood and reached for Rocky's hand.

Rocky suddenly realized he hadn't seen Hank in a few weeks. "Good to see you, Hank, where have you been?"

"You too, Rocky. So sorry to hear about Gavin. Byron and Larry filled me in on the way over here. To answer your question, we were notified that my wife's mother was dying of cancer and with only a few weeks to live, I took a leave of absence so we could go to upstate New York to be with her."

"Is she—"

"She passed. Her funeral was a week ago, and we just got back on Friday." He motioned to the two agents. "I had been keeping in contact with these two. They promised to wait until I got back to approach Jackson."

Jackson entered from the kitchen carrying two towels, which he handed to Rocky, and then invited all of them to sit down.

Byron added, "We did try to get ahold of Aspen and Noah, but they didn't answer our texts, so we left it alone. When we learned what had happened to Gavin, we decided the entire thing could wait a little longer, but then with the news of Aspen—well—we just couldn't. So, we called Jackson."

Rocky looked over at Jackson, who seemed to be scrutinizing him. "How much do you know, Jackson?"

"Probably not enough. I was hoping you could enlighten me."

Rocky hesitated, but then asked, "Is Noah home?"

Jackson shook his head, "He and Suzann went to the hospital. I didn't want Suzann here and—"

That irritated Rocky. "Don't you think there have been enough secrets?"

"I don't know, Rocky, you tell me."

Hank quickly intervened. "Okay, this is not the way to start this meeting." He turned to Jackson. "You can't expect to know all that your kids have been involved in these last few months, Jackson. You have not exactly been available. In Rocky's defense, your kids were lucky he has been on board with all of this or your kids may have gotten hurt at some point."

Jackson sank back into the overstuffed chair. He rubbed his temples with one hand. "You're right, Hank. I'm sorry Rocky."

Rocky didn't respond. He felt sincere apprehension about talking to the agents, Hank, or Jackson without the consent of the four teenagers who had been involved in, and basically the victims of the whole mess. When he spoke, he did so cautiously, "What exactly do you want to know?"

"What has been going on? What have my kids—and your kids—been involved in that I don't know about?"

Larry spoke up, "We need to open the investigation into the house, but we can't do that without permission from you, Jackson."

"Well, technically we can," said Byron.

Hank nodded, "Yes, you can, but is it absolutely necessary? Would it be so bad to wait a week or so? See how Gavin is doing and—" his voice trailed off.

Larry didn't respond.

Jackson sighed, and when he spoke, his voice was now labored, "We may not be able to wait on Aspen."

The uncomfortable silence lasted several minutes.

"Dad?"

The five startled men turned in the direction of the kitchen where Noah stood in the doorway.

Jackson looked shocked. "I thought you were with your mother."

"I know you did." Noah did not move from where he stood, but continued, "Dad, you can't do this. None of you can. Everything started with Aspen, and we at least have to wait to see if there is a chance that she can explain—to maybe wake up and—" Noah's voice caught.

"What if she doesn't—"

Noah turned on Hank. "That is *not* a possibility. She will wake up, and all of you need to give her time to do that, She is the one who is being contacted, not me, or Mom, or *you*, Dad. It has been Aspen. We can't secretly go behind her back just because she isn't here. She *will* be here!"

Rocky sighed. He felt he should say something, and when he looked at Noah, he knew that was his expectation as well. He took a deep breath. "He's right, you know. This has all been about Aspen, and for whatever reason, she is the one who has been injured in this."

"And Gavin," said Noah. "He has been a big part of this, too, Dad. He and Aspen have some kind of gift or something—"

"I don't want to discuss *gifts*," snapped Jackson.

Noah crossed the room immediately and stood before his father. "Too bad, Dad!"

Jackson glared at his son.

"I'm sorry, Dad, I know I am being disrespectful right now so I will apologize to all of you for that, but the reality is, *you* know more than you have let on! Aspen said that herself!"

Jackson had turned his gaze to the floor, but now his head jerked up. "What is that supposed to mean?"

Noah dropped to his knees in front of Jackson. "Dad, she knows you must have the same gift. Patrice—Patrice told us it runs in families." He motioned to Rocky, "And Gavin got his gift from his mother."

Now everyone, but Rocky stared at Noah in disbelief and Jackson averted his eyes from his son's, but Noah did not turn away. "Dad?" he said softly.

When Jackson lifted his head, Rocky felt immediate concern for him. His eyes brimmed with tears and his face twisted in agony. "I don't— I'm not sure I can, Noah."

"Dad, whatever it is, we can face this together—as a family. We must, Dad. This whole thing has practically ripped us apart, and it seems like—"

"Like what?" Dad barely whispered.

"Like you have let it," Noah mumbled.

To Rocky's surprise, Jackson did not react the way he expected him to. He simply nodded, and again, he looked down.

Rocky realized Jackson must have had an agenda when he called this meeting. He must have hoped to get information from Hank, Rocky, and the two FBI agents. Maybe he had hoped to bring everything to a close—to simply end it, but he obviously had not anticipated his son's intervention.

"We have all been holding back feelings, Dad, you can see that. Our family has been hurt, it's like who we used to be is just seeping into the cracks, and we are not the same people. Please, Dad, please, let this wait for Aspen—and for Gavin, too. He, Kiryn, Rocky, and I have seen a lot this past summer. We *want* to include you but, Dad, I *won't* let you exclude us."

Noah stood now and walked back into the kitchen.

Rocky heard the fridge open, and he smiled when he heard the familiar pop-top of a soda can. He knew Noah was drinking a Coke.

"Well—" began Hank.

Byron opened his briefcase and pulled out a pad of paper and a pen. The others stared at him.

Seeming to notice their questioning looks, Byron smiled, "I'm old school, partial to actual notes."

Larry nodded, "Yeah, he drives me nuts. He has an iPad, but he insists on using paper. Cracks me up." He turned to his partner, "What are you thinking?"

"Well, I know that Mr. Allen is having some issues locating a will of sorts. I was thinking maybe we could help."

Jackson looked up, and the sign of relief on his face was unmistakable. "That would be a good place to start."

Rocky glanced past Jackson to where Noah was standing in the kitchen. He watched as he took a long swig of his soda and then caught his eye. Noah smiled and nodded, and Rocky nodded back.

He had gained a great deal of respect for this young man who had shouldered adult responsibilities almost since the first day he had met him. Watching him with his dad today had only confirmed that the respect was well-earned.

18

A GLIMPSE

Aspen seemed to wake up, but how could she wake up when she couldn't see anything, and she couldn't move. She had spent a lot of time alone, and she could now distinguish the sounds of the heart monitor and the oxygen machine. It was usually very quiet unless her parents or Noah were there. She wasn't sure Kiryn had come, but she really didn't expect her to, and she knew for sure Gavin wouldn't be by. Then she realized that she must be in intensive care. No one would be able to come in, except family. She didn't want anyone to see her laying there doing nothing anyway. She had overheard her parents talking about flying Grandma out, in case she died.

Well, that was a fine thing. She would show them. She had no intention of dying. She just wasn't sure how to get out of this blackness.

She lay quietly. She did not have any idea how to lay any other way than quietly. She couldn't make any sound. This was so confining.

In the distance, she heard the low rumble of thunder, and she wished she could be there to experience it. She loved to watch the lightning. She wondered if it was day or night. Mom had been there a long time today, but the nurse they called Marie, had suggested she go home. Mom protested, and she heard the nurse tell her she would get her some blankets.

Aspen sighed. Poor Mom. If only she could tell her she was okay.

Hmm. How okay am I? I am stuck in the dark. This sucks. I wonder who thought of comas.

"Aspen?"

Aspen's heart leaped at the sound of Max's voice. *Where have you been?* Aspen was thrilled to see the only person whom she had communicated with since she had stepped into Mystic Lake.

"I have something to show you. Come."

He totally ignored my question, and why can't I talk when he is around?

"I did not ignore your question, I simply haven't answered it, and you are talking. Your mind knows when you need to use your mouth."

Aspen was pretty sure she should be offended by that remark, but she decided to ignore it. After all, she didn't have much control in this world, and Max was taking her someplace, although she couldn't imagine where, because they were still in the fog.

Almost with that thought, Max and Aspen emerged from the fog. They were on a sort of balcony—a very high balcony that over-looked a spacious, beautiful garden that was filled with people.

Who are all these people, Max? She didn't wait for an answer when something way on the other side of the garden caught her eye.

Max! There are those boys again. Who are they?

The boys seemed to be the same boys she had seen in the water, and there were a lot of them. At least a hundred she thought, maybe even two hundred. Her eyes widened, and she turned to Max. *Are they—*

"I am giving you glimpses, Aspen, pay close attention."

I am.

But Max gave her a wary look. 'Closer attention. I realize it is hard not to get caught up in all of this, but I am giving you valuable information."

What am I going to do with it? I can't talk, I can't move, I can't—

"Will you shush? Be patient."

Aspen's eyes narrowed. *Okay, fine.*

"Good. Now look."

Max turned her attention to a glistening pond of water. Huge lily pads floated aimlessly on top of the pond and on one of those lily pads, sat a young boy.

Why doesn't he sink?

"I have actually wondered that myself, but he doesn't, so that's all we need to be concerned with."

Aspen shrugged.

"Do you recognize anyone?"

Am I supposed to?

Without answering, Max turned back toward the people, and Aspen assumed he expected her to do the same, so she did.

The colors were brilliant, and there were colors she was sure she had never seen before. It seemed there was every kind of tree and it struck Aspen that palm trees and pine trees were never in the same place at the same time on— On earth?

It seemed every season was represented as well. Some trees were green, some had snow on them, others seemed to be turning fall colors, and still, others even had new buds. The pathways the people were walking on appeared to be cement, but at the same time, they glistened, like gold. Velvety grass covered every inch of ground which was not already covered with flowers or paths.

Another thing that struck Aspen was the difference in people. There were children and older people and everyone in between, and every race she had ever imagined. It was beautiful! Everything was so beautiful!

Max still stood alongside Aspen, but he had not spoken. She was frustrated because she was not sure what he expected her to see.

Aspen turned her eyes back to the pond and the little boy. The lily pad turned, allowing her to see his face.

That little boy? Is that? My dad? Aspen's scrunched her face. *Are you sure, Max?*

No sooner had she thought the words, than the little boy was gone. The balcony she and Max were standing on was very high, giving Aspen full vision of the expansive garden, but there were so many people she could not see where the boy had disappeared to.

A young couple now caught her eye. They were walking in her direction, but they were not looking at her. Something about the girl was familiar, and as they got closer, Aspen realized it was Ronda. *That must be her boyfriend, the one she was killed with.*

Again, Max did not respond.

This time it was an elderly man who caught Aspen's attention, and he too moved toward her. As he got closer, she knew immediately it was her Great-Grandpa Allen, the same grandpa she had seen in her dream.

Max?

"Aspen?"

His response made her chuckle.

I am confused, Max. My great-grandpa and Ronda are dead, but my dad is not. How come I can see him here too? And you said this is not heaven, but where is this?

"As I explained before, you have jumped to another dimension. There are many of them throughout the universe. This one is where I can most easily show you the people that need your help. That is why I have brought you here.'

Didn't we already help Ronda? We know she was murdered.

"Yes, but there is more. You helped your great-grandfather Allen in finding the statue, but Ronda needs a different kind of help. So does her boyfriend. You can help them both.'

Does her boyfriend have a name? We never found his name.

'Thomas.'

Oh, nice name.

Max looked directly at her, smiled, and shook his head. "You're a strange girl, Aspen Allen."

Look who's talking!

And they both laughed.

Aspen thought for a few minutes, and Max did not interrupt her. It was then that she realized Max could hear all her thoughts but seemed to respond only when her thoughts were relevant to him or his mission she guessed. She looked at Max. He still didn't respond, but she knew she was right.

Aspen kind of understood what was expected of her where Ronda and Thomas were concerned, but she was not sure how she could help her grandpa, and she was totally in the dark about how to help her own father.

"As you and your friends continue your search, you will see what your grandfather needs, I can't tell you that. It will also be clear what Ronda and Thomas need. Do you still see the boys?'

Aspen turned her attention to the other side of the garden again, to where the many boys milled about. They seemed as though they could not cross a wide road which stood between them, and the rest of the garden, but then beyond the boys was more garden.

"They can't. Well, they can, but they won't. Each of those boys has a very real concern and it something you can help them with."

Aspen felt anxious. *Max! I don't think I can do all of this!*

"Of course you can. You have your friends to help you."

Aspen suddenly thought of Gavin and Kiryn. *You must not know everything. Gavin's mother won't let him even see us.*

"You worry too much." Was all Max said, and he turned his attention back to the boys. "They are all looking for the same thing."

What?!

Max only smiled, and his eyes twinkled.

Aspen's eyes narrowed, but even as she gave Max an uncertain scowl, she was suddenly filled with fear. She had no idea what she was supposed to do.

Aspen's hands rested on the railing of the balcony, and Max still held one of them. With his other hand, he patted the hand he held. "You will be okay, Aspen Allen."

With that, the colors of the garden seemed to fade into one, and all that she could see now was a colorful mist. The people were gone.

Aspen turned to Max but was surprised to see him smiling. He was looking past her to something else.

Aspen turned around and was stunned to see Krista standing before her. She gasped, and Aspen reached for her lifelong friend.

Krista reached for Aspen too, and the girls fell into each other's arms.

Aspen wept. The familiar hug of her best friend warmed her entire being.

Oh, Krista, I have missed you so much.

"Me too, Aspen, but I have been with you all along." She stood back and looked at her friend. "Many of us have."

Really? I wish you wouldn't have died. I hate that you're gone. And Aspen cried even harder.

"None of us are as far away as you think, Aspen. We are just sort of divided. We all exist in the same space, just, as Max explained, in different dimensions."

You know Max?

Krista laughed, and the sound of it was like music to Aspen's ears. She nodded, "Yes, I know Max."

Suddenly Aspen sobered. *Noah misses you.*

"I miss him too. I miss all of you. I love you, Aspen."

I love you, Krista.

"I have to tell you, this is all pretty crazy. There is an ocean and everything! Just like me, you will remember it all when it's your turn, but right now, I have to go."

No! Don't go! I want to go with you! She turned to Max. Please don't make her go!

Krista laughed. "He is not making me go. It is really you that has to go back."

I don't want to go back. I would rather stay here.

"No, you wouldn't. Your parents need you. Lots of people need you. I'll be here waiting for you."

Again, Aspen threw her arms around Krista and hugged her as tight as she could.

Krista laughed, "I love you, Sand Buddy! Oh, and Aspen, that Gavin guy is totally hot!" And with that, she turned and disappeared into the mist, but Aspen heard her call, "Now go back, you're burnin' daylight!"

Tears still trickled down Aspen's face, but she now started to laugh and turned to Max. *Are spirits supposed to say stuff like that?*

"Well, she's still Krista!"

Aspen raised her eyebrows. *That is so cool, Max!* But then she became serious again. *Am I supposed to help her too?*

"No, she will be helping you. She has chosen to do that, and yes, it is totally cool." Max grinned.

So, is she like my guardian angel? Aspen took the tissue Max miraculously produced and wiped her nose.

"Not exactly."

Oh. Suddenly Aspen had a question. *Max, I thought spirits didn't have a body.*

"We don't."

Then how come I can touch you and Krista?

Max smiled. "A glimpse."

They began walking again, and almost immediately, Aspen felt Max was slipping away from her.

Max! Before you go.

Before I go, what?

Am I supposed to help my dad find something, too?

"Himself, Aspen. Help him find himself."

But—

19

PLEASE WAKE UP

SUZANN WATCHED THE PHYSICAL therapist exercise Aspen's legs. Suddenly, she jumped up from her chair, "Here, I can do that."

The therapist turned around, "You don't have to Mrs. Allen, I'm okay."

Suzann smiled, "Please, I want to do it."

The young therapist stepped aside and allowed Suzann to take over. She watched for a few minutes, and then Suzann assumed she felt okay about letting her help her daughter, and she left the room.

Suzann massaged Aspen's calves and thighs and rubbed her feet. Surprisingly, Aspen had not lost much weight, even though she had been laying in a coma for five days.

"I guess it's not that long in the grand scheme of things," Suzann said out loud. "Then why does it seem like forever?" She stroked her daughter's hand. "Aspen, please wake up. Please, please wake up."

Suzann took one of Aspen's legs and stretched it straight up, so her foot pointed to the ceiling, then she bent her knee and then straightened it out again. Repeating it three more times, she then changed to the other leg. She carefully did the same with each of Aspen's arms, and then softly massaged those muscles as well.

Suzann was glad to have this time alone with her daughter. She had finally convinced Jackson to ride into Memphis with Larry and Byron. They were doing some investigating on the Jackson

Humphrey Allen will that seemed to have grown legs and walked away from all filing cabinets or computer files in the entire city of Memphis. Larry and Byron felt strongly the will still existed, but had been purposely misplaced and they had launched a full investigation to that effect.

It was a relief to Suzann to see her husband get involved, and it was also a good distraction from Aspen. He needed that right now, and Suzann needed him to have something else to do. It seemed silly for the two of them to sit and watch Aspen all day, but Suzann was afraid she might wake up, and no one would be there.

Noah, too. He would sit there all day as well, but Rocky had suggested Noah help him with some of the things he was working on and Noah reluctantly agreed. He wasn't against working with Rocky, but he was still uncomfortable around Kiryn, and he still had not actually spoken to Gavin. To alleviate the problem, Rocky took a leave of absence, and he and Noah worked on their end during the day while Kiryn was at school. By the time Kiryn got home, Noah had left.

Suzann and Jackson were against Rocky interrupting his work to help them, but Rocky insisted it would not even affect his pay. He had enough tenure to take a twelve-week leave of absence and still collect his regular pay. The teacher who took over for him would be filling another vacancy at the middle school the first of the year, so it worked out well for all concerned.

Suzann finished Aspen's exercises, tucked her blankets around her, and then sank into a chair next to the bed.

Her mother was flying into Memphis this afternoon and Jackson, Larry, and Byron would pick her up at the airport. Jackson was a little perturbed that he was not driving his own truck, but the two agents had convinced him they needed the travel time to talk, and that had made Suzann feel more comfortable. Not that he couldn't drive. She was simply worried about his mental state. He was still struggling with who knows what. Noah's confrontation had seemed to sink it, but after the fact, Jackson crawled back inside his own head and refused to address it.

He had told Suzann his main concern was Aspen and when they were sure she was okay, he would then revisit his own problems. Suzann was tired of arguing with him, so she had reluctantly agreed, just to keep the peace.

She turned her attention back to her sleeping daughter. "Aspen, please wake up. We can go home if you want to. Or just you and Noah can go home. I am trying to figure out why you jumped into the lake in the first place. The water is cold. What were you trying to do?"

Suzann realized she was rambling and so she stopped talking and quietly stared at Aspen's silent face. She gazed at her for a long time and then almost without thinking, she began singing a song she used to sing to Noah and Aspen at bedtime when they were little:

"Whenever I hear the song of a bird…"

In the silence, Aspen smiled, her mother was singing to her.

Noah pulled the Iroc to a stop in front of the house and shut the engine off. Neither of his parents were home. He had stopped by the hospital and sat with Mom for about an hour, and then he came home so he would be here when Grandma and Dad got back. They planned to go to the hospital this evening and have dinner with Mom.

He looked across at the tattered journal laying on the passenger seat. Rocky had borrowed it from Aspen, and now Rocky had given it to Noah to take home. He picked it up and flipped through the pages.

"What do you mean she's in a coma? What happened?"

Kiryn glanced over her shoulder, making sure she and Gavin were alone.

"Your mom will kill me for telling you this, Gavin." Kiryn hesitated.

"*What?*"

"She fell in the lake. Mystic Lake."

"What do you mean she fell in? She can swim."

"You would think, right? But Noah said he saw her step off the dock and when he got to her she wasn't there, anywhere. It was like she just disappeared."

"That doesn't make any sense!"

"Get real, Gavin, what does make sense with Aspen?"

Gavin glared at his sister, "Why did you say that?"

Kiryn shrugged, "I don't know. I just—" She couldn't stop the tears from trickling down her cheeks. "I hate this."

Gavin stared past Kiryn. "What the heck happened to all of us?"

"Your mom thinks it is because the Allen family came here. She acts like there is some sort of a curse or something, and she is worried about you being involved. She is dead serious, too, Gavin."

"She can't keep me away from them."

Kiryn rolled her eyes. She first looked at Gavin's arm then she looked around his room and then back to his face. "Really?" she said sarcastically. "*Who* is in the hospital—in *Memphis?*"

Gavin sighed. He shifted his weight but winced in pain at the same time.

"Do you need something?"

"*Yes*! I need for my stupid arm to stop hurting and I *need* for this never to have happened, and I *need* Mom to stop treating me like I'm five years old and I *need*—"

"You need Aspen."

Gavin sighed. "Yeah, I guess I do. I really miss her."

Neither of them spoke for several minutes. Finally, Kiryn said, "Gavin, the reality is, she may never wake up."

"That is not reality to me."

"Sara said we might have to face that."

Gavin scoffed, "Mom says a lot of things. I never thought I could be so mad at her."

"She is just trying to protect you, Gavin."

"From *what*? From Aspen and Noah? Admit it, Kiryn, we have never had so much fun."

Kiryn nodded, but she seemed unwilling to agree. "The thing is, we may never have that again."

Gavin sobered. "She's going to wake up."

"I hope so."

"Do you?"

Kiryn's head snapped up, "Of course, I do! But I also want everything to be the same as it was a month ago. Before your arm was all jacked, and before Aspen decided to freakin' disappear in the lake!" Kiryn clenched her fists, and her jaw tightened. "Any lake, but Mystic Lake. There is something weird out there."

Gavin chose to ignore the obvious. He turned and looked out the window, and his eyes narrowed. "You need to get me out of here."

Kiryn stood immediately, holding both hands in front of her. "Oh, no, Gavin. I am not tangling with your mom and Doug, and besides, she is mad enough to keep you from Rocky. She is threatening to make you finish school in Memphis if Rocky lets you see Aspen and Gavin."

Gavin's face twisted. "What the— What is wrong with her?"

"Well, look at you? What are you going to do about it?"

Gavin slumped back against his pillows. "I'm not sure."

Kiryn studied him for a few seconds. "Gavin, what about basketball?"

"Humph. I couldn't care less."

"Are you serious?"

"Totally. I thought it was what I wanted, but it really isn't. I don't want to be a professional athlete. I want to do something else, something meaningful."

"But your scholarship?"

He motioned to his damaged arm. "Well, that's pretty much water under the bridge, don't you think?"

Kiryn sighed. "Yes, I guess it is."

"Besides, I have good enough grades to get an academic scholarship."

"Okay," said Kiryn absently.

"I just don't want to think about it right now. I don't want to think about anything right now."

"But Aspen."

"Yeah, and Mom keeps bringing up Cassie. So annoying."

Kiryn pulled a face. "I know. I mean, I kinda know."

"It's stupid. I don't like Cassie." Gavin looked directly into Kiryn's eyes. "I don't know what I'll do if Aspen dies."

"More like if she sleeps forever. Apparently, her brain activity is fine."

Gavin's face lit up. "Well, then that's it! We just need to wake her up."

Kiryn rolled her eyes and plopped back down in the chair. "Oh, brother, Gavin. What is wrong with you? Even the doctors can't wake her up."

His eyes twinkled, "Well, maybe we could."

Now Kiryn's eyes narrowed. "I'm not sure I like where this is going."

"That's because I'm not *sure* where it's going…yet."

"You can't do anything—"

"Kiryn, I saw her."

"What do you mean 'you saw her'?"

"In the water. I knew she was in the water. No one told me. I just knew."

Kiryn swallowed hard. "Are you saying—"

Gavin nodded. "I'm saying I saw her—in the water."

"Well, what was she doing?"

"Nothing. I mean, I just saw her, and I knew she was surrounded by water. That's all. The images are not really clear, and I felt kind of— I don't know, a depressing feeling. I felt like something was wrong. Like she was in trouble."

"But not dead?"

"No, not dead."

Kiryn raised her eyebrows. "Well, you were right on both accounts but—"

"I want to talk to Patrice."

"Good luck with that."

Gavin scowled, "What's that supposed to mean?"

"Sara won't hear of it."

Anger suddenly rushed through Gavin, and he punched the bed with his good hand. "It is not Mom's choice!"

Pain shot through his shoulder, and he clenched his jaw until it subsided. When he turned to Kiryn, his eyes were brimming with tears. "What should we do?"

Kiryn shook her head, "I don't know, Gavin. I really don't."

Gavin's heart ached as a feeling of helplessness overwhelmed him.

"Don't what?"

Kiryn and Gavin both looked up. Rocky was standing in the doorway.

20

NIGHTMARE—FULLY AWAKE

JACKSON WINCED WHEN THE elevator doors opened, and he found himself standing at the door of the attorney's office where he had been a few months ago with Suzann.

Only this time, Larry and Byron—the two FBI agents—were with him. The three had just sat down when the receptionist who had left to announce their arrival reappeared. "It will be just a few minutes."

Jackson stared at the floor.

None of this will matter anyway if we lose Aspen. How could things have gone so wrong? Why didn't I confront all of this when I first came here? Why am I still so afraid? How could I be so stupid to let the kids get so involved, and not be there for them? I am such an idiot to think I could hide.

He paused for a second. *I have always hidden. I am exactly what Aspen said, a coward.*

The heaviness in Jackson's heart was unbearable, and he quickly brushed a tear from the corner of his eye.

"Are you okay, Mr. Allen?"

Jackson realized Byron was talking to him, and he quickly nodded. "I'm fine. Just thinking."

Byron nodded. Larry turned to look at him but said nothing.

Jackson stood and walked to the window. It had been raining, and the fall leaves in Memphis were beautiful. Jackson had forgotten how incredible the colors were. They didn't have this type of fall in San Clemente.

The wind picked up, and he noticed an unusually large leaf break free of a branch and slowly dance through the air. The leaf seemed to hover, but then it took flight again. Jackson was mesmerized by the dark red leaf. He continued to watch it as it flew this way and that. A gust of wind caught it, and the leaf flew straight at the window plastering itself against the glass right in front of Jackson.

"That was weird." It was Larry. "He can see us now."

Jackson stared at the leaf. He knew it was ridiculous to think the leaf did that on purpose—completely ridiculous—and yet he could not dismiss the thought.

He shrugged and turned away from the window and started to follow Larry, but suddenly, he looked back. The leaf was still there. No other leaves, just that one.

Jackson whirled and stepped back to the window. He studied the leaf and then his eyes slowly drifted to the street below. Near the tree where the leaf had been attached, stood a teenage boy who seemed out of place.

Jackson stared down at him. Slowly, the boy looked up and locked eyes with Jackson.

Jackson swallowed hard, and beads of sweat immediately formed on his neck and forehead.

That can't be. He's…he's—

"Jackson?"

Startled, Jackson turned around, "What?"

Larry was standing in the open doorway to Corey Baker's office. "You coming?"

"Yes—" Jackson wiped his forehead with the back of his sleeve and turned back to the window. The boy was gone. So was the leaf. Jackson could not move. He turned, put both hands on the window and stood still, bracing himself, and hoping Larry would not walk over to him. He just needed a minute to collect his thoughts.

He closed his eyes and searched his memory, allowing it to race back in time.

"So, Allen, you in or not?"'

Jackson could see the three boys as clearly as though it was twenty-eight years earlier, and the smell of damp dirt just as strong as it was then.

"Mr. Allen?"

Why did Byron always call him Mr. Allen and Larry called him Jackson?

Jackson stared at the spot where the boy had stood. Saying nothing, he slowly turned and walked directly to the office, and past Byron who closed the door behind them.

Corey Baker extended his hand.

Their last encounter had ended badly. Jackson had been hard on the nervous attorney a few months ago. He wondered how today would go.

Jackson briefly shook the attorney's sweaty hand. "Corey," he said flatly and sat in the only empty chair on this side of the desk.

Noah placed the open journal on the coffee table. He was home alone.

He took a bite of his peanut butter and jelly sandwich, and then gulped half a bottle of water to wash it down. Leaning over the journal, he started at the very first page. He had no idea what he was looking for. He figured he would know when he found it.

A text interrupted his thoughts, and he fished in his back pocket for his phone.

It was from Mr. Weston. Noah scrolled his screen. "What have you folks decided about the painting? I am not trying to pressure you, but I do have some information that may be helpful."

Noah thought for a second, then he typed, "A lot going on here with Aspen and Gavin. I will ask Rocky to contact you." He pushed send and waited.

Almost immediately, a text came back. "Okay, but tell him ASAP."

I wonder what that's all about. "Okay." Noah pushed send again and dropped his phone on the sofa next to him. He turned back to the journal and picked it up. He ran his fingers over the worn initials on the front of the battered suede cover. JHA.

"'Jackson Humphrey Allen. What are you hiding from us great-grandpa?'

Noah turned the journal back over and began scanning the pages. Nothing seemed to jump out at him. He kept reading and suddenly stopped. The entry was one they had read before from May 11, 1996. It talked about finding replacements to take care of Nina and the long years she had spent in an asylum.

Where? He never mentions anything about her death.

Noah wondered if Rocky still had Joseph's Grandpa Dixon's journal which Joseph had given them. There was something in that journal about a hospital—or two hospitals—or something like that.

Noah propped his elbows on his knees and plopped his head in his hands. He was finding it hard to concentrate. Somehow nothing seemed as intriguing doing it alone. He missed the companionship of Gavin and Kiryn, and most of all, his sister.

What's the difference? If Aspen never wakes up, this whole thing is just not important.

Now giving in to an overwhelming feeling of sadness, Noah stretched out on the sofa. He put his arm across his forehead and closed his eyes.

<hr>

Drew watched his little brother. In high school, Dylan had been quiet and withdrawn, but since graduation, he had been reckless and obnoxious by most people's standards. He never settled into any one thing. Never could stay in a relationship for more than a month or two, had difficulty holding a job, and trusted no one.

Except Drew.

But now Drew realized Dylan had not even completely trusted

him. His loyalty to their grandpa had overshadowed his life. Practically ruined his life, if the truth be known.

To Drew, he had just been his little brother. Occasionally vulnerability would sneak through, but not very often. Drew never knew why Dylan acted the way he did, but he never asked either. Sometimes, especially when we love someone, we just need to ask.

Drew never did.

It wasn't until the meeting at Rocky's when Drew's son Joseph had given a journal to the Allen kids. A journal which had belonged to Drew and Dylan's Grandpa Dixon. A journal which exposed their grandpa for the man he really was and Dylan had carried that burden his entire adult life—alone.

Their grandpa, Kenneth Lloyd Dixon, had hired the murder of Sumer Munoa and her husband, Juan. Dylan had been in love with Sumer. She was the only girl Dylan had ever loved. Their grandpa had also been instrumental in the murder or disappearance of Rhonda Allen and her boyfriend.

Looking back over the last twenty or so years, and now knowing what had been torturing Dylan all this time, Drew was surprised Dylan hadn't gotten into more serious trouble—gone to prison— or dead.

Drew realized that it was their relationship that had kept Dylan from going completely off the deep end, and he was grateful that at least, he had been some sort of stability for his little brother.

Dylan stood at the counter and fidgeted with his keys. The constant clinking was irritating Drew, but he didn't say anything. He glanced at an older lady who sat near him, but she didn't seem to notice the clinking keys.

Dylan had just finished his first counseling session. The idea was to help Dylan move on. Drew wondered if it was possible. He hoped it was.

Drew had come with him and waited for him. Now they were waiting for the receptionist to schedule Dylan's next appointment. Finally, she handed Dylan a card and told him she would see him next Tuesday.

The brothers walked into the lobby. Dylan gave Drew a nervous smile as he pushed the button for the elevator. They waited. Again.

"So, how was it?"

Dylan shrugged. "Okay, I guess. She just wants me to talk about what comes to my head."

She was the therapist Dylan was seeing. Dr. Majewski. She wasn't the least bit attractive, for which Drew was grateful. Dylan did *not* need any distractions, but she was nice, soft-spoken and possibly had the kindest eyes Drew ever investigated. After the initial meeting with her, to which Dylan insisted Drew accompany him, they had both agreed Dr. Majewski was a good place to start.

"What's with this stupid elevator?" Dylan smashed the down button again.

Drew glanced toward the stairs. A sign plastered to the door read "Please only use in an emergency today. Fresh paint."

"Probably busy because of that," and he motioned to the sign.

Dylan scoffed, "I guess."

Finally, the door opened, and the two stepped inside. Drew reached for the button to take them to the first floor when they heard someone coming down the hall. He pressed the "door open" button to hold the elevator for whomever it was.

It was two men, and they were talking in anxious whispers.

"I don't want any part of it," hissed one of them.

"I told you that kid has to go. She has gotten too close, and it has to be soon."

The first voice sounded familiar, but Drew couldn't place it. He quickly pushed the "close door" button.

"Dammit!" the angry voice echoed through the hall.

The elevator doors closed, and Dylan stared at his brother. "What the—"

Drew shook his head. "I don't know. Did you recognize either of their voices?"

Dylan shook his head. "No. Have no idea."

"Me either." But Drew did. At least he thought he did. Especially the last word—when the person wasn't whispering. But he couldn't believe it. He quickly blew it off. "Well they didn't sound happy that's for sure."

Dylan laughed. "Nope, they didn't at that."

When they got to the first floor, Drew walked over to the gift shop.

"Where are you going?"

"Just going to grab a bottle of water."

"Are you going to die? We are going to lunch."

Drew laughed, "Yeah, we are. I'm just thirsty. All that waiting and all—"

"Whatever. Get me one too." Drew leaned against the open door to the gift shop and picked up a magazine.

Drew placed two bottles of water on the counter and swiped his debit card. He heard the elevator doors open, and he cautiously glanced over his shoulder. Dylan was still leafing through the magazine.

Two men emerged from the elevator. It was obvious they were in a heated discussion. Drew didn't recognize one of the men who had his back to him, but the other one— Drew could hardly believe who he was looking at. He tried not to stare and not to draw Dylan's attention.

"Sir?"

Drew turned around. The cashier was waiting for him to finish his transaction. Drew absently pushed "no" for cash back and "yes" to okay the transaction.

"Thank you."

"Yeah." Drew picked up the water.

Dylan plopped the magazine back in the rack. "Thanks." He took a bottle from Drew.

"C'mon little brother. Let's go eat."

"Sounds good to me. That session made me hungry."

Drew laughed, "I'm sure it did. You'll have to tell me about it."

They walked through the glass door and into the parking lot.

Drew glanced back over his shoulder. The man was nowhere to be seen. A chill ran through him. He just couldn't grasp what he had heard or seen. Maybe he had misunderstood. All this stuff about the past had made him jumpy.

They climbed into Drew's truck, and he started the engine.

"What would you think of going by the hospital to see how that little Allen girl is doing?"

Dylan shrugged. "Okay."

Kiryn covered the space between Gavin's bed and the door in seconds and threw her arms around Rocky's neck. "I'm so glad you came, Dad."

Rocky hugged his daughter and then furrowed his eyebrows. "Why wouldn't I come? Did you plan on walking back to Sommerville?"

"No, I just mean this is perfect timing. We need to talk to you."

They both walked over to Gavin, and Rocky sat on the edge of the bed. "How are ya?"

"Tired of being here for one thing."

Rocky nodded. "Yeah, but how do you feel?"

"I'm still sore, and I still have one more surgery before I can start therapy. This sucks."

"Yeah, that's what your mom told me." Rocky looked at Kiryn. "So, why is this perfect timing?"

Kiryn curled up in the chair on the other side of the bed. "Because Gavin wants us to break him out of here."

"Oh, well, that's a great idea," said Rocky flatly. "That would take care of my never seeing you again until you are eighteen."

Gavin rolled his eyes. "Mom wouldn't do that to you."

"I think she would. She is pretty upset about your scholarship."

"She never asked me what I wanted to do."

Rocky's eyes widened. "What do you want to do?"

"I don't know—"

"Marry Aspen."

Rocky scowled at Kiryn, but then he noticed the look in Gavin's face. "Is that true?"

"That actually has never come up." Gavin glared at his sister. "But it isn't something I haven't thought about. But no, that's not it. I just don't think I want to play ball. I want to do something else. Something important."

"Well, you can do anything you want, Son. A basketball scholarship is a means to an end. It pays for school."

Gavin shrugged. "I know, but it also takes up a lot of time. I don't know. I have just lost interest in basketball."

"Why is that?"

All three of them turned to see Cassie walking into the room.

"Well, Cassie, what are you doing in Memphis?" Rocky stood and smiled at her.

Cassie walked right over to Gavin and handed him a chocolate shake, and without taking her eyes from him, she said, "Oh, my mom has an appointment here today, so I came with her. Hi, Kiryn."

Gavin took the shake, but he didn't smile. "Thanks, Cassie. Since when have you brought me chocolate shakes?"

That question startled Cassie, but Gavin knew he had hit a nerve.

"Well, I just thought—" Cassie abruptly turned to Rocky. "I just figured I could hang out with Gavin."

"Don't you ever call?" asked Kiryn dryly.

"Kiryn!" Rocky glared at his daughter.

But Cassie didn't even miss a beat. "I knew Gavin wouldn't care."

Gavin looked from his dad to his sister. "So, will you guys talk about it? See what you can do?"

Rocky's puzzled expression almost made Gavin laugh.

"Oh! The breaking out thing. Oh, sure." Stammered Rocky.

Kiryn stood and rolled her eyes. "I'll call you later, Gavin."

"You guys don't have to leave just because I came." Cassie cooed.

"Oh, yes we do." Kiryn didn't look at her dad to get his disapproving scowl.

Gavin and Rocky exchanged a quick glance.

"I'll talk to your mom." Rocky patted Gavin's good shoulder. "Love you, Son."

"Love you too, Dad. See you guys later."

Kiryn waved as she disappeared into the hallway, and Rocky followed.

"Geez what got her panties in a wad?"

"Are you kidding me, Cassie?"

She looked surprised. "What?"

Gavin sighed. "Cassie, I appreciate you being nice to me and all, and coming all the way out here to see me, but seriously, other than friends, we are through."

"I don't think you mean that. I think you just got caught up in the thrill of the new girl in school."

"No, I didn't."

"Well, she will be going back to California anyway. They don't fit in around here. Once she's gone, you'll see you still have feelings for me."

"No, I don't, and they are not going anywhere."

"Well, that's what I've heard. I've heard she may never wake up."

"That's enough!"

Cassie jumped at the forcefulness in Gavin's voice.

"But—but that's what I've heard."

"I don't care what you've heard, Cassie. It's not happening. Aspen is going to be fine."

Gavin's arm throbbed, and beads of sweat formed on his forehead.

"Geez, I didn't mean to upset you."

"That's exactly what you meant to do, Cassie. You need to leave and take this with you." Gavin thrust the shake at Cassie, but it slipped from his hand as Cassie jumped out of the way. The shake landed on the floor and splattered all over Cassie's shoes and legs.

"You know what, Gavin Fielden! I am sorry I came here!"

"So am I!"

Cassie spun on her heel and stomped to the door. "You watch, you will come crawling back to me once your little California girl has gone home—or is dead!"

"Get out of here!"

Cassie stormed through the door and into the hallway.

"Cassie? Cassie!"

Gavin heard his mother's voice coming from the hall.

Apparently, Cassie didn't answer, and Sara came through the door. "What was that all about?" Sara stopped when she saw the ice cream all over the floor. "What happened here?"

Gavin didn't answer. He slid down in his bed and turned onto his side. He didn't want his mother to see him cry, but it was no use.

"Gavin?"

"Mom, please go. I don't want to talk right now."

Sara stood still for a few seconds, then she went into the bathroom and returned with some towels. She laid them across the ice cream mess.

"Gavin," she said quietly.

"Mom, please. I don't want to talk."

"Did Cassie—"

"I don't care if I ever see her again, Mom. Don't you get it?" He suddenly sat up and confronted his mother.

"Why haven't you told me about Aspen?" His tears ran freely down his face now, but he didn't care.

"I—I just—"

"Just what, Mom? Do you have any idea how much she means to me? Can't you see that? Or don't you care?"

"Gavin, I—"

"Mom! I do *not* love Cassie. I have been trying to get away from her for months. Even before Aspen came here. I do not love her. I love Aspen, and I thought you knew that."

"I do—"

"I thought you cared enough about me that you could— What?"

"I do, Gavin. I do know that."

Gavin fell back against his pillows and covered his face with his free hand his body shaking with sobs.

Sara walked across the towels and sat on the bed. She leaned over and wrapped her arm around her son's shoulders.

"I do know that, Gavin. I do."

Jackson and Noah ushered Grandma into Aspen's room, and Suzann jumped to her feet.

Emotion welled up in Suzann's chest when she saw her mother, and she hurried across the room and into her open arms.

"Mom!"

Both women cried.

Over Suzann's shoulder, Grandma could see Aspen's still body.

"I can't believe this is happening," she whispered.

Grandma walked slowly toward Aspen, but before she reached the bed, she stopped, covered her face and wept some more.

Jackson stepped up next to her, but Grandma straightened her back and smiled. "I'm okay. Aspen would want us to be okay."

Noah stared at the floor. Grandma was right, of course, but he didn't feel like Aspen should have any input in how they felt. After all, she wasn't here looking at her dead-looking body.

Grandma sat in a chair and reached for Aspen's hand. "Her hands are warm. I guess I expected them to be cold."

"It's like she is in a really deep sleep," said Noah.

"This is her food." Dad pointed to a saline bag above Aspen's head. "They say it has all the nutrients in it."

"Well, it's not like she is getting a lot of activity, I guess," said Noah.

Mom sighed and looked over at Noah. "Really?"

"Well?"

"I suppose you're right."

"So, what do we do? What are they telling you?" asked Grandma.

21

F⚭TSTEPS

Aspen hated that she couldn't move. This dense fog was getting old. The only time she could leave was when Max came to get her. She tried calling to him, but of course nothing. Max only came when he thought she needed to see something—or something like that. She wasn't sure.

She listened.

Dad, Mom, Noah, and Grandma were all here.

I want to talk to you guys. I want you to know I'm fine and I'm coming home.

She thought for a second.

Max never exactly told me that I was going home.

Aspen winced. She didn't like that thought.

"How did it go today?" Mom was saying.

"I'll tell you about it. I'm not sure he is going to be much help," said Dad. "We can talk about it later."

What? Who isn't going to be much help? Ahhh! This is so frustrating!

Her family stayed for a long time, and Aspen loved listening to them talk. Grandma had a lot of questions about her, but she also asked Noah about school, their new friends, and Dad's heart attack. She asked Mom about the big house, and if she would get to see it. Mom assured her that she would.

Aspen suddenly felt very alone. Their new friends, the big house, it all seemed so far away—Gavin seemed so far away. She wondered about his arm and about Cassie. She still hated Cassie, and she was a little surprised at that sudden realization.

Hmmm. Spirits still have feelings. If that's what I am. What am I really?

She began crying.

Am I crying?

She couldn't feel any tears on her cheeks, and her nose didn't stuff up, but yes, she was crying.

Hey, does anyone see that I am crying? Does my body cry when my spirit cries?

She was thinking about Kiryn when she heard Dad say they should get something to eat, and take Grandma to the little house so she could get some sleep. She heard Mom say that it had been a long day, and Grandma's flight was long.

Grandma scoffed at that. Grandma. Always the tough guy. It made Aspen smile.

Familiar now were the soft kisses from her parents. Sometimes Noah and sometimes not, but now a new kiss from Grandma.

As they were leaving, Noah was explaining why they called their house the little house. Aspen had never heard any of them refer to it by that name until now. It had been her own little description.

The room was quiet again, and Aspen lay in the silent darkness. She was no longer crying. She wasn't doing anything.

It would be nice if I could sleep. So, if I am dead, I guess spirits don't sleep. Weird.

Aspen heard someone enter the room. It was so quiet she could hear the person's soft footstep on the tile floor.

Hello?

For some reason, she felt uneasy. She tried to listen harder. Open her eyes. Move her fingers—anything!

Hello?

Something on her face. It was foreign. Not like the soft touch of her mom or dad or Noah. Fear suddenly replaced curiosity.

Help! Hello?

Breathing.

"She's in here."

The door opened, and the familiar voice of the night nurse entered the room. Aspen heard her walk across the floor, but also heard more footsteps. Heavy footsteps.

"Please just stay for a few minutes. Her family just left."

Hey! Hey, there is someone in here!

"Okay."

Aspen was sure she recognized Drew's voice.

"Wow, she looks really pale." That was Joseph.

"She does for sure." Aspen thought that might be Dylan.

"I hope she doesn't die," said Joseph.

"Why don't you put those over there?" asked Drew and Aspen heard more footsteps and she thought someone sat something down.

"She probably doesn't care about flowers."

I like flowers! How nice that they brought me flowers! How nice that they even came.

"Well, not much good we can do here. I just thought we should come by." Drew even sounded sad.

"Yeah," mumbled Joseph.

"C'mon," said Drew.

Wait! Wait!

Aspen heard the three leave the room and she listened carefully. Nothing.

But then—

The door closed. Footsteps. Breathing.

22

TRUST ME

"Aspen?"

Max? Max!

She felt Max take hold of her hand, and he pulled her along with him.

Max! I am so happy to see you!

Max grinned. "I am going to miss you, Aspen."

Why? Where am I going?

Suddenly realization hit Aspen. *Home? Am I going back home?*

Max nodded. "Yes, but I need to show you a couple of things."

They were suddenly back on the balcony again. Aspen knew she would miss this part. It was all so incredibly beautiful. There were people everywhere.

Max didn't say anything. He let her survey everything.

She saw the child again. Her dad. She saw a man walking among some trees. Her Grandpa. She saw a couple sitting on a bench near a stream. Ronda and Thomas. She saw the wide road and the boys on the other side. She was certain she knew who they were, or at least, where they came from.

But then she saw another older man. He seemed to be searching for something. There was a woman who appeared to be with him, or maybe she was following him. Aspen wondered why she didn't hurry and catch up, but she didn't. The man seemed not to notice her at all. He was walking toward a large building. *A hospital?* No.

More like a very fancy hotel, or resort, or something like that. The man seemed very anxious to get to that building.

Aspen studied the man. She turned slightly and looked at Max. *Is that?*

Max grinned. "Yes. It will all make sense at some point down the road, but today, just remember that you saw him."

Aspen watched the man who seemed to be going nowhere. It was her Great-Grandpa Allen.

She turned back to where her Grandpa Allen was among the trees. The two did have similarities, just like her dad. It was easy to see that they were all related.

She turned to Max. *But how will I—*

Max put his finger to his lips.

Aspen's eyes widened. *Are you telling me to shush?*

Max nodded, and to her surprise, she simply obeyed.

Aspen noticed the mist changing, and a cold, creepy feeling seemed to permeate the air around her. The mist was no longer swirls of colors. It was black. A horrible heaviness filled the air.

Max!

She felt him squeeze her hand, but then, he let go!

The darkness became almost unbearable, and Aspen couldn't breathe. She clung to the rail, afraid of falling off the balcony as she gasped for air. She could hear moaning and distant screams—or wailing—she wasn't sure.

She suddenly found herself praying. *Please, God, please.* But the blackness only became more intense.

Max, I can't— I need— Help!

She felt as though she could no longer hang on. It seemed easier to just let go.

There was nothing. Not Max's hand. Not the railing. Nothing.

Aspen blinked several times. The blackness seemed to be receding, and the air felt lighter. She breathed in deeply and slowly, and let it escape just as controlled. The coolness felt good in her lungs.

She had been clinging to the railing the entire time, and now she felt the cool metal in her hands again.

Max! His hand was on hers! Relief swept through Aspen, but she still clung to the railing as Max started to pull her with him.

Gently he pried her fingers away and pulled her along.

Max that is the second time since I met you that I have felt that awful darkness. What is it?

He sighed. She had never heard him do that before. He stopped and looked directly into her eyes. Aspen liked Max, he usually had such a playful nature, but right now he looked rather serious, and Aspen's eyes clouded.

Max let go of her hand but placed both hands on her shoulders. "Aspen, do you remember some of the experiences you had with Kenneth Dixon?'

Aspen shuddered. How could she forget? She nodded, *yes.*

Max twisted his mouth, "Well, you will experience much worse. There are, shall we say, major forces of evil trying to stop you and your friends. What you have found so far is only the beginning."

Who? What do you mean?

"That's all I can tell you at this time."

But—

Max put his finger on her lips. "You will know what to do. I suggest you go to your friend Patrice. She can be of great help to you, and to Gavin."

Aspen's eyes widened. *Gavin?*

Max shrugged. "That's up to him, not you."

Aspen's face drooped, and Max smiled. "Things work out the way they should."

What does that even mean? Never mind, I know I know. I will find out.

Max took her hand again, and they started walking. "I'm taking you back now. Before you go home, something will happen. It will be scary. Just know that I—we—are nearby."

We? Who is we?

"Trust me."

Suddenly Aspen was in the dark silent void again. She couldn't move, but she could hear, and what she heard made her blood curdle.

This was the same sound as before when she had felt something weird on her face.

That person was back.

Aspen tried to scream, *MAX!*

Silence.

That same foreign thing covered her face, and she tried to hold her breath. It smelled like—like medicine. She gasped. There was no way for her to push it away. She jerked her head back and forth, but then she realized the movement was only in her mind.

This time, whatever it was, pressed hard against her mouth and nose, and she couldn't breathe.

She tried to call out, but she couldn't form any words, and she knew her cries would fall on deaf ears anyway. There was no one to help her. She was all alone.

Everything was fading. She couldn't contain one thought. In her mind, she saw Mom, Dad, and Noah, and Krista, and Derrick. She saw Kiryn, Gavin, and Rocky. She saw Grandma and San Clemente. Joseph and Cassie. The ocean and the lake. The Iroc, her bedroom in California, and her bedroom in Sommerville, and she saw Sara, Doug, and Patrice. Each person came and went suddenly as if running toward her, and then pulling away fast.

Her body felt heavy, and she couldn't keep her eyes open. She let them close, and she quit trying to fight for air.

Suddenly, she heard a loud grunt, and at the same time, the thing covering her face, fell away, and she sucked in a huge gulp of air.

There was a lot of commotion in her hospital room, but the only sounds she could hear were grunts and groans from, it seemed, just one person.

It seemed like that person hit the floor, and she heard him moaning. She was positive it was a man.

Her head still spinning from not being able to breathe, she thought she heard the person get up, and then she heard footsteps running away and the door close.

Aspen lay still and listened.

Suddenly, she was in a mist and Max had her hand.

He grinned. "Took care of that guy."

You did?

"No, I have friends in low places." Max laughed.

Who was it?

"That I can't tell you. That's for you to find out. I wasn't supposed to bring you out again. Oh, and I forgot to tell you, you won't remember all of this, but you will *know* all of it. And Aspen, thanks for saying yes, you had to say yes." Max quickly kissed her cheek. "Bye Aspen."

Say yes to what?

Nothing. She was alone again in the silent dark void.

23

MIRACLE

GRANDMA HAD BEEN IN Sommerville for two days, and she had kind of settled into the family's routine.

Mom would get up every morning and go to the hospital to help with Aspen's physical therapy, and then Dad, Noah, and Grandma would pick Mom up for breakfast. Dad would stay, and Mom, Grandma, and Noah would leave for a while, and everyone would come back by lunch. Then it was Noah's turn to stay until dinner time. The entire family ate dinner in Aspen's room every night just to be close to Aspen.

They would all leave in the evening and start the entire routine over again the next day. When he wasn't with Aspen, Noah showed Grandma around Sommerville but avoided Great-Grandpa's big house, and Grandma never brought it up.

It was the morning of the third day, and the routine changed a little. Mom and Grandma drove to the hospital together and were there waiting when Dad and Noah arrived.

"I guess Doctor Harward called Mom when she was on the way in this morning. All he said was to get here fast," said Dad and Noah jumped out of the truck, and ran into the lobby of the hospital. Mom was standing by the elevator with Grandma.

When she saw her husband and son, she burst into tears and threw her arms around both.

"Oh, Jackson! What if— What if—"

Jackson held his wife at arms-length. "Suzann, maybe she moved or something. This isn't necessarily bad news."

He turned her around and walked her through the open elevator doors. Grandma was already inside, and Noah pushed the button for the fourth floor.

"But Dr. Harward said someone was in her room last night. That's all he told me, and that he wanted us to come over."

Noah winced. "Someone was in her room, Mom?"

Right then, the elevator doors parted, and the four hurried out and started toward Aspen's room.

Mom's heart raced when she saw several very young-looking nurses and doctors crowded around Aspen's room. Her worst fear nearly paralyzed her entire body.

One of them looked up.

"Look out you guys. I believe this is her family."

The crowd parted, and Aspen's family walked through the midst of them.

The family stopped short, but then Mom screamed, "Aspen!"

Surrounded by medical personnel, Aspen was sitting upright in the middle of her bed.

"Hey, Mom." Aspen's voice sounded weak.

The family ran to her bedside, and Mom threw her arms around her daughter.

"What happened? How did it happen? When?" The words tumbled out of Mom's mouth through gushing tears.

Dad's head was down, and tears ran onto his shirt. He was holding Grandma's hand, who was also crying.

Noah was not crying. Instead, he stared at his sister in disbelief. "Holy cow, Aspen! This is amazing!"

Aspen smiled at them all. "That's what the doctor said."

Dad sank onto the bed and encircled his arms around his daughter and his wife. "It's a miracle. Thank God! It's a miracle."

"What happened to you? Where did you go?" asked Noah.

Aspen looked up at her doctor, and then she turned back to Noah and shrugged, "I don't know."

Total surprise spread over the faces of Aspen's brother and parents, and they too turned to the doctor.

Doctor Harward shook his head. "She really does not remember anything. That is not to say that she won't, but right now, she doesn't. We don't want to press her for anything either. She has been in a coma for—"

"Six days, fifteen hours, and about thirty-seven minutes—give or take." Noah was looking at his phone, but then he looked up. "I have been keeping track since the day she went into the lake. It would be a week at about five-thirty tonight."

"Precisely," Doctor Harward smiled.

"How…how did this happen? I mean how did you know? Who found her?"

Doctor Howard turned to a woman who appeared to be in her mid-thirties. She was wearing hospital scrubs. The badge hanging at the end of her lanyard read Marie Hunter.

"Marie actually found her. Why don't you tell them, Marie."

Marie Hunter grinned. "Well, I came in this morning—about an hour ago—to check on Aspen as I always do, and she was sitting up. Just like she is now." Marie laughed. "She looked right at me and said, 'Do you know where my cell phone is?'"

That made everyone laugh, but Mom. She was still crying too much to laugh.

"I just can't believe this." Dad looked at Doctor Harward. "Is this normal—for people to wake up like this?"

The doctor nodded, "Yes, and no. Sometimes it's a little slower. We don't know if Aspen was waking up for several minutes or hours because, by the time Marie saw her, she was wide awake."

Another person in scrubs, this time a male said, "But when I checked on her at two and five am she hadn't moved. This happened between five am and seven-thirty this morning."

Mom looked at her daughter, "What do *you* remember, honey?"

Aspen squinted. "Only water. I remember being on the dock, and then water. That's all. Then I woke up in this bed with all this stuff hooked to me."

"How do you feel?" asked Dad.

"Kind of weak, I guess. I haven't tried to stand yet."

"And you won't." Doctor Harward shook his head at Aspen. "Not yet." He turned to Aspen's parents. "After you visit for a while, I have ordered some tests for Aspen. We'll pick her up here in about two hours. She'll be gone for about two hours, and then back in her room around one."

"Can she go home?"

The doctor shook his head. "Not yet, Noah. We're keeping her for a few days just to make sure everything is okay. She must eat and get stronger. A week isn't really long for a coma, but it is long for doing absolutely nothing with your muscles, and normal organ functioning. Don't forget; she spent over twenty-four hours under-water."

The doctor sighed. "She's pretty amazing, that's for sure."

He motioned for the other medical people to exit the room. He explained that some of them, as well as the people in the hall, were interns and some medical students.

Marie gave Aspen a hug, "Welcome back, sweetie. Now we can have a conversation during my morning visits. I usually just talk to you." She turned and walked toward the door, but then she stopped, "Aspen is our Sommerville phenomenon."

Aspen smiled, but inside she was rolling her eyes. She wasn't sure how she felt about Marie's comment.

Freak she means. I already was that.

Aspen laid back on her pillows. She was happy her family was here and surprised to see Grandma, but it was her dad she was concerned about. She owed him an apology.

Doctor Harward asked Dad to follow him into the hallway, leaving Mom still sitting on Aspen's bed, and Grandma and Noah sitting in chairs pulled close to the bed.

Aspen investigated their anxious faces. She knew they wanted her to give them some sort of explanation, but she had nothing to tell. She had lost a week of her life.

Dad walked back into the room.

"Dad, I…I'm sorry, Dad."

He looked puzzled.

"I mean…for the things I said to you…yesterday?" Aspen looked at her mother.

Dad chuckled. "Aspen, don't even think about it."

"And it was last week," said Noah.

Aspen scowled. "Oh, yeah. Well, anyway, Dad, I'm sorry that I said those mean things."

Dad waved his hand back and forth. "Needed to be said. We'll talk about that later. I'm just happy you're with us again." He leaned over and kissed her forehead.

As he pulled away, Aspen saw her dad give Mom a concerned look, but she didn't ask about it. Everything was too overwhelming. She would ask about that and try to remember…tomorrow.

24

A New Witch in Town

It had been a week since Aspen had miraculously awaken. She had been poked and prodded and visited by so many doctors she had lost count. She had been put through a battery of tests none of which found any abnormalities. None of the doctors could explain how she could have been in the water that long and not only still be alive but to have suffered no brain damage.

Aspen was at a major disadvantage. Other than being unusually weak when she first woke up she felt fine so it seemed strange to her to not only be in the hospital but to have a policeman outside her door twenty-four seven.

Apparently further investigation seemed to confirm that there had been an attempt on Aspen's life. Her cheeks were bruised and that nurse Marie had found the room in disarray the morning she discovered Aspen sitting up in her bed. At first she thought Aspen had moved things around. But Aspen had not been out of bed. She had been sitting in the same spot since she woke up.

There was also the small pillow that was left behind. It appeared that someone had tried to suffocate Aspen. But who? There were no fingerprints—and the only other evidence they had found was a pen but that could belong to anybody. No one would elaborate on it for Aspen. To her, it was another unsolved piece to the ever-expanding puzzle of her confusing life since coming to Sommerville.

But before—with the comradeship of her brother and Kiryn

and Gavin she had experienced some pretty scary things but she had started to like Sommerville and she and Noah had begun to settle in to this new life.

Now—Aspen had become a media prodigy. The internet had gone viral with Aspen's story and the family was being contacted by news reporters from all over the nation and some even from other countries. They were bombarded by concerned life-long friends from San Clemente as well as the well-meaning people of Sommerville. It wasn't just about Aspen's ordeal—information had leaked out about the Mansion House, her grandpa, the will and who knew what else.

All of this had caused considerable upset for the FBI agents Byron and Larry as well as several local police including Hank. According to Noah it was becoming more and more difficult to keep investigators at bay regarding the Mansion House and the painting in the storage room.

Noah is the only one who would tell her anything and it was making her angry. She tried to understand her parents concern— after all, they said—she had been as good as dead—and having her back was more than they ever expected.

Noah told her they had worried about her being bedridden the rest of her life, if she ever woke up from her coma.

She had rolled her eyes big time at that, "Just shoot me." Was all she had said and that made Noah sorry he had even mentioned it.

Not having any recollection of the full week made it hard for her. She also felt she needed to be helping her dad. He was try- ing to temper the investigations that seemed to be sprouting up all around them, but everything was racing out of control. There were so many loose pieces and Dad had only become involved just recently. Even though he was a major factor in all of this—possibly *the* major factor—Aspen knew that he needed the help of the four teenagers and Rocky for that matter. She wondered if those rela- tionships would ever be the same.

Dad had flown in his attorney from San Clemente to work with another attorney from Memphis who Hank had recommended.

One thing she did know is that the two of them were working with FBI Investigators Byron and Larry to locate her Great Grandpa's will but they weren't letting up there. Byron and Larry wanted access to the Mansion House, and they wanted to talk with Aspen and Noah and their friends.

When Aspen thought about all of that she was somewhat grateful for the guard outside her door—it meant no one could come in without permission.

It seemed she had made a full recovery and would be released on Friday—two weeks and six days since she had first gone to Mystic Lake alone and fallen—or walked—into the water. That point was still out for deliberation and the one person who knew the answer—could only remember being *in* the water not how she got there.

This entire past week had been strange for Aspen. Her family and the doctors and nurses kept talking about things that had happened and she couldn't relate at all. It frustrated her. She hoped that once she was out in the world again she would relax and things would start to make sense.

And her dreams. Vibrant colors and water—always water. There were people too but no one she recognized and she always seemed to be trying to catch up with them—never seeing their faces clearly. Nothing fit together.

Other than a card and flowers from Rocky and Kiryn—they had remained silent. She didn't understand that either but Noah brushed it aside like it was no big deal—which surprised Aspen, because it was a big deal, at least to her. Aspen felt an urgency to get their little group back together and other than the obvious, she wasn't even sure why. She had checked her phone a dozen times a day but never any texts. Not even from Noah.

All she knew right now is that she was anxious to be out of here and go home—to the little house.

When Aspen was alone she wondered about Kiryn and Gavin—and Rocky. She missed them so much.

Gavin's accident had been horrible and Sara, his mother had

put a stop to his seeing Aspen and Noah. Even Kiryn had become distant. It wasn't that they blamed Aspen—but Sara had threatened to keep Gavin away from Rocky if he allowed any more contact with the Allen kids.

Occasionally Aspen would think of Cassie—she couldn't help but wonder if she and Gavin were together again. Nothing made her heart ache worse than those thoughts. She would try to relive her first kiss with Gavin—to recall the sweetness of it. Usually she could but then today's reality stung even worse and she would end up crying.

She was behind in school and so was Noah. He had not been to school since Aspen disappeared. Her parents had entertained the idea of going back to San Clemente before all of this happened, but now it seemed impossible for them to leave with so many loose ends. Dad was willing to send his kids back but he felt he could not leave.

That was not happening if she had anything to say about it. She was beginning to wonder if she would.

Grandma's stay had been a blessing. She came to the hospital every day and she and Aspen talked about their life in California. "You'll be back home one day—just be patient." Grandma had said that more than once the past week.

She had planned to stay until Aspen came home but decided maybe it would be best if she went back to California and returned to Sommerville for another visit after things calmed down. She had come by the hospital last night to say goodbye to Aspen, and then Mom and Dad had taken her to the airport this morning.

Friday was here and right now Aspen anxiously awaited the arrival of her brother.

She slid off the bed and peeked through the blinds from her hospital room on the 4th floor. The parking lot was swarming with reporters, news vehicles and hundreds of other people. Her gaze drifted to the trees beyond the parking lot and she saw something that made her heart race.

The mist…rising above the trees.

A feeling of urgency engulfed her and she wished her parents would hurry.

Fat chance of me getting near Mystic Lake alone again.

"Hey. Mom and Dad will be up in a minute."

The door opened and Noah joined his sister at the window where they both observed the crowd below. "Pretty crazy, huh?"

Aspen sighed. "Yes, I'm not sure what I'm supposed to do."

"Just come home—we'll figure it out from there."

Aspen turned to her brother. "Noah? I feel like I must be some sort of a freak."

"So what else is…?" Noah sobered when he saw the look on her face. "Sorry, just kidding."

Aspen scowled at him. "I know you were. Don't you think I should probably be dead?"

"Yeah pretty much. I didn't think we would ever find you. And believe me I was praying but geez Aspen. You were under water a long time."

"I guess."

"You were."

"Have you seen…?"

"Kiryn and Gavin? No—Dad has been talking with Rocky though."

"About what?"

"I'm not sure but they have talked quite a bit the past two days."

"How is he—Gavin I mean?"

"Okay I guess."

"You don't know?"

"No, Aspen. We have been pretty occupied around here."

Aspen nodded.

Her parents walked through the door.

"Ready to go?" Dad gave her a hug.

Aspen motioned to the window, "Do we have to talk to them?"

"No." said Mom. They are going to want pictures of you but just walk with us to the car. We already answered a lot of their questions."

"Okay. Let's do this," said Noah and he clapped his hands together.

When Aspen and her family stepped through the hospital doors cameras went off from every direction. Cell phones were taking videos and pictures and some people even cheered. Aspen thought that was a strange since she hadn't done anything heroic. The crowd was a little overwhelming even though several policemen walked in front of the family. Kind comments came from every direction but just as they reached the car Aspen heard one girls voice call out, "Are you the new witch of Sommerville?"

Aspen didn't recognize that voice.

An unsettling silence coursed through the crowd.

Aspen stopped and turned around.

"C'mon Aspen, get in the truck." Her parents were already inside and Noah was holding the door open for her.

"That's what I'm thinkin'—we have a new witch in Sommerville."

Aspen knew that voice and right then Cassie emerged from the crowd—folded her arms across her chest and glared at Aspen.

All eyes were on the two girls.

A thousand thoughts ran through Aspen's mind as she locked eyes with this girl she despised. She remained calm trying to choose her next words carefully. She knew whatever she said would be all over social media within minutes.

She took a deep breath—decided to say nothing and turned to climb in the truck.

"Well?" demanded Cassie.

Aspen turned slowly and she said nonchalantly, "Well—I'm not sure what you mean by that. But I guess if that were the case, you might want to be careful."

With that Aspen climbed in the truck and Noah climbed in after her and closed the door leaving Cassie standing with her mouth hanging open.

Dad pulled away from the crowd and Noah turned to his sister, "What was *that*?!"

Aspen was fuming, "I don't know! I would love to clock that girl!"

Noah was surprised at her response. Laughing, he leaned back in his seat and covered his face with his hands. Oh my gosh, Aspen! I can't believe you did that!"

Dad turned around. "Aspen what were you thinking?"

Noah laughed again. "She wasn't."

Their startled mother stared at all of them. "That was a rude girl. I don't find this so funny."

"That's the understatement." Mumbled Aspen.

Dad stared straight ahead. "It wasn't—but I don't blame her."

"Well what could she possibly mean by such a comment?" Mom was visibly irritated.

"You have no idea." Noah whispered but their parents didn't seem to notice.

"Yeah, Dad, what could I mean?" Aspen glanced sideways at Noah and he returned a 'you better be careful' look.

Dad didn't look back at her. "Nothing really."

Mom was still musing about the rude girl and something about this crazy life they were living.

Aspen flipped her hair over her shoulder and threw Noah a satisfied look.

"Welcome back little sister." Noah held out his fist and Aspen laughed and bumped knuckles with him.

Mom slowly turned around and looked first at Noah and then at Aspen. "Do I want to know what that means?"

Noah and Aspen exchanged a quick glance.

"Naw probably not," said Noah but then he suddenly sat up in his seat. "Hey isn't that...?"

"Kiryn." Aspen had seen her too. She was standing next to Rocky's truck on the side of the road.

"Should I stop?" asked Dad.

"No...no not right now." But she opened the window and lifted her open palm to Kiryn.

Kiryn didn't respond immediately but then she returned the wave and Aspen closed the window.

Aspen turned to Noah and he gave her a brief nod.

Aspen willed back the tears that were stinging her eyes. *I just want to go home.*

25

MESSAGE

GAVIN MANEUVERED THE MOUSE with one hand and scanned through his computer for the zillionth time. He still couldn't move his left arm freely, so he had to put the mouse down to type with one finger. It was tedious, but he was getting used to it.

Aspen headlines were everywhere: *Miracle Girl. Amazing Girl. Wonder Woman. From Another World. Died and Came Back to Life. Witch?*

He had seen the confrontation between Cassie and Aspen online and on the evening news. It had been posted and tweeted so many times it was ridiculous.

He watched it again and couldn't help but chuckle at Aspen's calm demeanor when she responded to Cassie. He would love to have been in the truck afterward, though. He knew Aspen had more to say than that.

Finally, through with surgeries, Gavin was home—at least one of his homes. He was still in Memphis, studying with a tutor to catch up in school. He was still hoping for a scholarship. Aspen had been home from the hospital for over two weeks, and he had been at his mom and Doug's house the entire time.

The last surgery had been minor, and even though he experienced quite a bit of pain, and his arm was in a sling, he worked with a physical therapist three times a day. It would be a long time before he had the full use of his left arm, or maybe he never would, but he seemed to be making progress, and he was able to do a little more each day. At least, until the pain was too much, and he would be forced to let it rest.

Gavin was also being obedient to his mother. He didn't want to, but she loved him, and he loved her. She was making sure he received good care, and he appreciated it. He knew she was just worried about him and didn't want to hurt her.

But now, it was time for him to stand up for what he really wanted. He wasn't sure how his plan would go, but he had to try.

His mom had confiscated his cell phone the day he had texted Noah about Aspen, but she had finally returned it three days ago. He hadn't heard from Cassie, maybe she finally got the hint, but it was obvious she wasn't letting up on Aspen. He felt like he needed to be there to protect Aspen if she would let him.

Gavin stared at his phone. He had carefully typed the text and checked it to make sure he had spelled everything correctly. His heart pounded as he tried to get the courage to push send. Finally, he put his finger on the little icon and pushed.

Nothing.

He waited.

Nothing.

Exasperated, he dropped his phone on the desk, stood and walked across the study to the window.

"Can I get you something, Mr. Gavin?" It was Cynthia, his mom's housekeeper.

Gavin hated that she called him Mr. anything, but she insisted.

He smiled at her. "No thanks, Cynthia. I'm good." He walked past her and down the hall toward the kitchen when she started the vacuum.

Almost immediately, the vacuum shut off.

"Mr. Gavin?" Cynthia stepped into the hall and called him.

Gavin turned around, "Yep?"

"I think you have a message on your phone. I saw it light up, and it made that silly noise you have on there."

Gavin nearly fell racing back down the hall and into the study.

"Thanks, Cynthia!"

She laughed and turned the vacuum back on.

He picked up his phone and pushed the little envelope to read the text.

"Yes."

He leaped into the air and then suddenly stopped. *Now I just need to figure out how to make it happen.*

He quickly typed a response, "Thanks."

He grinned. Everything else was just details.

≈

Drew folded the letter and stuffed it in his back pocket. He decided not to mention it to Dylan. His brother hadn't been himself lately, and Drew was worried about him. He had refused to continue his counseling with Dr. Majewski and had become more easily agitated with everything it seemed.

All Drew hoped for was to get all this stuff with the Allen will settled, and move on with his life. He had even thought of just forgetting about it, but he couldn't bring himself to do that. There was a lot of money at stake for him and Dylan. It could make a huge difference in both of their lives.

He started the riding lawn mower again and absently drove across the massive back lawn of the Allen Mansion. He wondered about the contents of the letter and what it would mean for him and his brother. He also wondered why the sender of the letter had never mentioned anything about this before now.

One thing he did know, and that was whom to contact about it.

≈

This was the fourth time in two weeks that Byron and Larry had met with the Allen's, but this time they had some promising news. They were all sitting in the living room around a raging fire in the fireplace. It was unusually cold outside. With Aspen in the hospital, Halloween had come and gone with not so much as a thought from Aspen or Noah.

Now with Thanksgiving less than a week away, the weather projected an ice storm. Even through the midst of the constant upheaval, Mom and Dad had decided to have a real holiday and invite his sister Dana, and her husband Jerry down. It looked like Grandma may be coming too.

"Well," Dad had observed, "The invites have gone out. We'll see what happens."

Today, however, there was a bit of excitement and anticipation in the air.

Aspen and Noah were both sitting on the hearth. She noticed Noah looking at his phone, but he didn't say anything, and she didn't give it much thought.

Both of their phones had been blowing up with texts from their friends in San Clemente. Even though it took a near tragedy for them to reconnect, Aspen was happy they had. Derrick had even suggested he might come out during the holidays.

Larry placed some folders on the coffee table, but he kept glancing at his watch.

"Are we waiting for someone, Larry?" asked Dad.

Larry nodded. "He should be here any minute."

Aspen and Noah exchanged a quick glance, and then looked at Dad, who seemed unconcerned.

Dad had been different since Aspen had come home. He was more willing to talk and more interested in what was going on with his kids. He still didn't have much to say about his own past. He seemed to guard those feelings, and the family tried to respect that—for now, but Aspen knew at some point that would have to change for any real healing to begin. She just didn't know when or how that would happen.

As for her, she worked with the investigators, she answered questions from the police and her father's attorneys, but she simply could not throw herself into everything that was going on. She noticed the same apprehension in Noah. A huge part of both was missing, and there was a loneliness that would not dispel.

She had not seen, nor heard from Kiryn since that day on the side of the road, but Aspen had seen on social media that Kiryn refused any interviews about her friends, and she protected her brother, it seemed, with her life. If anyone had contacted Gavin, it wasn't obvious, from what Aspen had read.

Drew's landscape company kept the mansion house grounds looking fantastic as usual, but no one had been inside. Dad had seen to that. The Allen family even steered clear, but that was about to change, and there was nothing Dad, or anyone else could do about it.

Just then, the doorbell rang, and Mom went to answer it.

When the door opened both Aspen and Noah gasped.

Rocky.

In his usual casual manner, he made his way into the room, greeting every person without stopping. He walked directly to the fireplace where Noah and Aspen were sitting. He stood in front of them for a few seconds and then, his eyes brimming with tears, he held a hand out to each of them.

Almost simultaneously, both kids grabbed onto one of Rocky's hands, he pulled them to their feet and hugged both of them.

Aspen couldn't hold back tears as the three of them held each other in a long silent hug. She thought of that first day of school when they first met Rocky Fielden. His casual, quirky manner had won Aspen over immediately, and she and Noah both learned to love this kind man.

When Rocky released them, he quickly brushed the tears from his cheeks. "I've missed you kids."

"We've—" Noah choked, "We've missed you too, Rocky." He too brushed the wetness from his cheeks.

Aspen cried freely, and she didn't care. She glanced at Dad. His face wore a look of approval, and relief washed over Aspen. Mom appeared to be struggling with her emotions, but she obviously approved.

Finally, Aspen and Noah sat back down on the hearth, and Rocky sat next to Noah.

Byron seemed to be waiting for a signal from Rocky. When he nodded, Byron began.

He looked around the room, acknowledging each person who was there, Mom and Dad, Aspen and Noah, Rocky, Hank, and Larry.

"Aspen, we're glad you made it." He said it so casually everyone in the room laughed, and then he did too.

"Well, you know, through all of that."

"I knew what you meant."

Byron looked at her for a minute and then nodded, "Good."

Aspen smiled. Of the two agents, Byron was by far the stricter, business type. Larry was more like an old friend, but they seemed to make a good team.

Byron turned to Larry, who handed him one folder from the stack on his lap.

He opened it and laid it on the coffee table, and then carefully opening a yellowed envelope he said, "Larry and I have been working on this case for weeks now. We have found several things that are probably pertinent to this entire case. I think we can all agree that the first thing we are looking for is Jackson Humphrey Allen's will. Hopefully, once that is found, we will at least have some direction with the Allen estate."

Byron waved his hand toward Aspen and Noah, "But, thanks to these kids and their friends, and with the help of Joseph Dixon, we now know that at least two murders were committed, but we also have evidence that points to the possibility that approximately two hundred young men may have been murdered as well. This could be one of the biggest mass murder schemes in history if it plays out the way we think it might. Again, you kids play a vital role."

An image flashed through Aspen's mind. *Boys.*

He continued, "Tomorrow we have ten more FBI agents coming to Sommerville, and we have good reason for this. He turned toward Rocky, "Do you want to tell us what you have?"

Rocky nodded, "Well, I kind of backed off all of this after Gavin's accident. His mother pretty much put the crunch on Gavin spending any more time with these kids, and none of you really know the reason for that, but I do, and so do they." He glanced at Aspen and Noah, and they both nodded.

Aspen noticed the puzzled look on both Mom and Dad's faces.

"Rocky continued, "Most of you would assume it was because Gavin got hurt, but that's only the beginning." Rocky paused and looked directly at Jackson. "Your family coming here, particularly Aspen, has really stirred things up. For one thing, your daughter has a gift—"

"Now wait a minute—" Dad started to stand up.

"Jackson sit down."

Aspen was shocked to hear her mother be so abrupt with their dad, especially in front of other people.

Dad's eyes widened, hesitated, then sank back into his chair. He picked up a bottle of water and took a few swallows.

His response, or lack of, surprised Aspen even more.

Unscathed, Rocky continued, "She does, Jackson, and she has seen a lot of things this past summer. She has been threatened, hurt, experienced anxiety that none of us—except for you—Jackson, could even imagine."

Aspen cringed. She was afraid to look at her dad this time.

"Not only Aspen but with all of this information, we now know that Gavin must have inherited his mother's gift as well. It's different from Aspen's. Nevertheless, it is a gift, and it is valuable. Do you know that he knew Aspen was in the water before anyone told him anything, and he hadn't seen her since his own accident."

Mom interrupted, "So Sara has some sort of—gift?"

Rocky shook his head, "No, not Sara. His birth mother, Sara's sister, Sumer."

"Oh, you were married before Sara?" asked Mom.

"No, I was never married to Sumer."

Now both Mom and Dad really looked confused, and Noah jumped in. "There is way too much to explain all of that, but we will, you should probably hear everything. We've told you a little bit, Mom."

Mom nodded and turned to her husband, "Okay?"

Dad sighed, "Okay."

Aspen couldn't help but assume Dad was feeling a little cornered. She kept waiting for him to either retreat or come out fighting, but so far he just listened.

Rocky picked up the envelope from the coffee table and pulled out a letter, just as yellowed. The letter was on standard notepaper, maybe five inches by nine inches. "Drew Dixon brought this over to me yesterday."

"*Drew?*" Noah expressed what Aspen was thinking.

Rocky nodded, "Yes. Let me read it to you."

To Whom It May Concern:

Assuming one day, someone will find this and read it. I left this out of my journal when we couldn't find the two kids—Ronda and that kid...

"Thomas."

Rocky stopped, and everyone looked at Aspen.

"Thomas?" Noah looked surprised.

Aspen quickly looked around the room.

"How did you know that?"

"I—I don't know. It just popped into my head. It's probably nothing."

Rocky took a deep breath. "Hardly nothing, Aspen, he continued reading the letter:

...when we couldn't find the two kids, Ronda and that kid, Thomas Blackburn, we hired a diving team. It was a team from Memphis, and we told them we had a suspicion that Mystic Lake was deeper than we had originally thought. That lake seemed to take on a life of its own after it was built.

Rocky paused and looked up. "Seriously, Aspen, how did you know that? This letter was the first evidence of his name."

Aspen's brow furrowed, and she twisted her mouth. "I honestly don't know." *How did I know that?*

Rocky looked around at everyone. "See what I mean? It's a gift." He waited for their reaction. When he got nothing but blank stares, he turned back to the letter.

The divers found something we never expected, and that gave us an idea.

Rocky stopped.

Aspen closed her eyes. *Water.*

Noah looked at her curiously. "Are you okay?"

She quickly nodded.

Noah turned back to Rocky. "And?"

"That's it. It may have been two pages, but this is all that was in the envelope. He wrote big and kind of scribbled." Rocky held it up for all to see and pointed to the very bottom of the letter where there was something printed. "The only reason we think Kenneth Dixon may have written it is because his name is printed on the stationery, but it is not signed, and it was never mailed."

Dad leaned over and picked up the envelope.

"Jenson Hamilton Neilson Phillips-Attorneys at Law. Seven Fifteen Dexter Blvd Memphis, Tennessee."

Dad turned to Mom.

"That's the same address we went to, right?"

Mom nodded.

Dad closed his eyes for a second and shook his head. "Interesting."

"Is that the law firm that handled your grandpa's will?" asked Larry.

"I honestly don't know. I have never found anything with any names on it."

"Maybe this will help." Larry produced another folder and handed it to Byron.

Byron retrieved a sheet of paper that had a copy of an envelope on it. He handed the copy to Dad. "We have been in contact with your sister in Oregon, Mr. Allen. She found this right after Aspen was hurt. She said she was going through the boxes again and came across a jacket of your dad's. She could feel something inside and found this envelope. She said it looked like it had slipped through a hole in the inside pocket. She faxed a copy and said she wanted to keep the original."

Jackson read from the copy, "The return address is that same attorney's office. It's addressed to Jackson Humphrey Allen, Sommerville, Tennessee."

"There's no street address?" asked Noah.

"They didn't need them then. Small town. People only needed the name, city, and state."

"No zip codes?" Aspen was surprised.

Larry laughed. "No zip codes. Look at the price of the postage stamps. Three cents."

The first envelope had a stamp on it, but no postmark. The copy, the one addressed to her grandpa, had a stamp with a postmark over the top of the stamp. It obviously had been mailed.

Dad sat back in his seat. He took a long labored breath. "So, we do have the law firm. Are they still in business?"

Byron shook his head. "No. Well, sort of. Corey Baker was right. The law firm did change hands about ten years ago, and Corey Baker and his father purchased the firm, but—"

Larry handed Byron another folder. Inside was one sheet of paper.

"According to this, ten years ago, two kids of the original founders, Marc Jenson, and Tyler Neilson, continued the practice, only in another city, and they changed the name. Looks like they used their wife's maiden names. It is now known as Curtis and Demot, Esq., and they are in Chattanooga."

"Most importantly though, is that an extensive skip trace and internet search of their records found a file for none other than Jackson Humphrey Allen Estate." Larry's eyes brightened.

"The will?" asked Dad.

Larry's expression changed. "No will."

"Yet," said Byron. "We are just getting started on that. We have not actually been to see these boys."

"Yes, this is all good news, but there are a couple of other things that we have to take off the back burner."

"So, this will not be good news?" asked Mom.

"Let's just say it's all a little jumbled," said Rocky.

Noah rolled his eyes. "So, what else is new?"

"Seriously," agreed Aspen.

"What Rocky is trying to say, Mr. and Mrs. Allen is that we are convinced that someone tried to either harm or maybe kill Aspen that last night before she woke up," said Byron.

"Why would anyone want to kill Aspen?" Mom's voice sounded frantic.

"Better question is who? The why isn't so disconcerting. As Rocky has explained, this sleepy little town has been turned upside down since your family came here, and we believe there must be things that these two," Byron waved his hand toward Aspen and Noah, "have not told us."

Rocky agreed. "There are a lot of things we have uncovered. One of them is the painting."

Aspen gasped. She had not wanted to tell her dad about that—not yet.

Rocky looked at Aspen, "I know what you're thinking, but these guys talked to Mr. Weston. He hasn't told them anything, but they do know there is something involving a painting."

"It just makes Great-Grandpa look like a total loser," muttered Noah.

Dad sighed. "Seems as though there may be some truth to that."

"What *painting*? I am so confused," said Mom.

Dad seemed to come back from a distant thought. He looked at his wife and then turned a very puzzled look to first Noah, then

Aspen and then Rocky.

Rocky quickly explained, "There is a painting in the storage room, Jackson, you did not know about that?"

Jackson shook his head, "No. I mean I know there are a lot of paintings and pictures in there. That room always, well it always kind of scared me. I just stayed out of it." He paused and again seemed to trail off into his own thoughts.

Aspen and Noah turned to each other.

"Uh, Dad, maybe you should know about some of the things Aspen has experienced in that room."

Aspen's heart started to pound. She was immediately fearful of what her dad might do or how he would react to that comment. She threw a concerned look at Rocky, but he just slowly nodded and didn't say anything.

They all waited for Dad to say something, but he didn't. He just stared at the fire. His eyes looked vacant, and his face drawn and sad.

Finally, Mom reached over and took his hand. "Jackson?"

Aspen could barely breathe. She was so afraid of her dad getting angry, or worse sick again. Tears started to well up in her eyes. "D...Dad?"

Byron and Larry didn't move. They, too, seemed to wonder what would happen next.

Several minutes passed when without warning, Dad started to cry. It was not a fearful cry or an anguished cry, but a sad, almost lonely cry.

Aspen couldn't stand it, and she quickly rushed to his side. "Dad?" she knelt at his feet, her hands on his knees, looking up into his face, tears streaming down her cheeks.

Dad covered his face with both of his hands and wept freely.

Noah stood and sat on the floor next to his mother, who was not only confused but obviously concerned.

Aspen glanced at her mother. She knew her mother must be thinking of things the family had just gone through—her husband's heart attack and nearly losing her daughter. Aspen sensed the apprehension her mother was feeling right at this moment.

Jackson finally looked up and peered into his daughter's eyes. "It's true, isn't it Aspen?"

She heard her mom whisper to Noah, "What? Oh, the spirit stuff?" and Noah nodded.

"Yes, Dad. I—guess you and I share that same gift?"

Through his tears, Dad scoffed, "Gift? Is that what you think it is?"

"It seems so," said Aspen quietly.

Rocky's next words were slow and deliberate. "What do you think it is, Jackson?"

Dad was quiet. He took some tissues his wife handed him, wiped his eyes, and blew his nose. "I—I suppose it could be a gift. I never thought it was. I was always ridiculed for it. I could never talk to anyone about it. I was punished because of it."

Aspen laid her head in her dad's lap and cried, and Dad stroked her hair. "I'm sorry, Aspen," he whispered.

Aspen lifted her head, "I'm not, and you shouldn't feel that way."

Dad looked around the room and suddenly seemed embarrassed for showing his vulnerability. He turned to Mom, "Do we have anything to eat?"

Mom's eyes opened wide at his random question. "You want something to eat?"

"No." Dad motioned to Byron, Larry, and Rocky. "I was thinking maybe these guys do."

Mom stood, but then immediately sat back down. She laughed, "No, Jackson, there is nothing to eat right now."

Larry jumped in, "We don't need anything, Jackson. I was just thinking, though. Maybe you folks would like to continue this another day."

Noah blurted, "I think that's a great idea."

Dad laughed now, "Oh, you do, do you?"

"Well, yeah. I think… I think we need—"

"Time," Rocky finished the thought for Noah.

"Yeah, time. We need some time."

"I believe that can be arranged." Larry looked at Byron, who quickly agreed.

"A day or two?" asked Byron.

"Why don't you give us the weekend? We could meet on Monday?" asked Mom.

"I have a suggestion," said Rocky. "Would you all be okay with going over to the big house Monday? I think the place to start is for us to backtrack. Tell you where we have been, let Aspen explain what she has experienced, and the things these kids have found. I think it may make this whole transition a little easier on you both," he was talking to Mom and Dad.

"We could—take you on a tour?" asked Noah.

"Of Grandpa's house?" Dad sounded a little indignant.

"Yeah."

"I think I know that house. I lived in it for almost ten years." As though feeling he needed to explain, he added, "Grandpa and Faith moved out of there when I was five or six. They had a home in Memphis since Grandpa was Governor, so we moved in. Grandpa and Faith moved back in the early 90s, and then he died. Dana and Jerry stayed there after that, then we came."

"Where did Faith go?" asked Mom.

Dad shrugged. "I'm not sure. I never asked. She died around 2005, I think."

"You have never told us what happened to your other brothers and sisters, Dad."

Dad's eyes narrowed, but again Aspen noticed no anger, just a very deep pain.

"No. I guess I never did."

Dad's words kind of hung in the air.

Aspen didn't think Dad was ready to volunteer any more information about his siblings, so she steered the conversation back to the house

"Dad, I don't think you know that house, not like we do."

He looked surprised. "Really?"

Noah nodded, "Really, Dad."

"Humph. Well, maybe not." He looked at his daughter and said nonchalantly. "Maybe it's time for me to find out."

Larry and Byron stood, and so did Dad and Mom. The four walked out onto the front porch.

"Rocky, I'm kind of afraid to tell them all of this stuff," said Aspen quietly. "Could you please be there?"

Rocky put his arm around her shoulders. "On Monday for sure, but if your parents want more information before then, tell them. This is the first time I have seen Jackson so receptive."

Noah sighed. "That's true, but I agree with Aspen."

"It will be okay."

Dad and Mom came back in the house, but Byron and Larry were still with them, and Aspen didn't like the look on either of her parent's faces.

"Looks like you had a visitor while we were here." Byron held up a half size sheet of poster paper neatly printed with black letters. He handed it to Rocky.

TIME TO LEAVE SOMMERVILLE, JACKSON FOR THE SAFETY OF YOUR DAUGHTER JUST LEAVE.

Aspen's eyes widened. "Who could that be?"

Larry shook his head, "Don't know, but just wanted to let you know we will have the house staked out through the weekend. He looked directly at Aspen. "Please don't go anywhere alone."

Aspen nodded. "Okay."

"Do you think someone would really try to hurt her?" asked Mom.

Byron said dryly, "Someone already did."

26

TORTURED PAST

MOM DID NOT AGREE with the rest of her family's choice as a place to have a long talk, but clearly, she was outnumbered. They drove up to the big house and parked in the driveway. Noah carried a bunch of wood, and the rest of them carried blankets, food, folding chairs, and roasting sticks.

Mom thought the idea of going back to where Aspen nearly died was ludicrous, but Dad wanted to be away from everyone. He had suggested, or rather insisted, that the cell phones stay home.

Aspen felt nothing one way or the other. She had no negative association with the lake, which Noah still found hard to believe.

It was early when they left, so Mom had made hot chocolate.

Noah expressed relief in seeing that there was still wood from the last fire, and it had even been covered with plastic. It didn't appear anyone had been up here though, so they assumed the police had done that, but for what reason they didn't speculate.

It was cold, but not freezing, so they were quickly warmed by the sun as well as the bonfire Noah started.

Aspen noticed a man leaning against a tree in the yard of the house on the other side of the lake. At first, it made her uneasy, but then she remembered the agents. She pointed him out to her dad, and when Jackson looked in the man's direction, he waved.

Good, he was an agent.

Dad rested his elbows on his knees, balancing a hot cup of chocolate.

"There is a lot we need to talk about, and I know that, but I was wondering if we could start with this lake." He looked at his kids and his wife. "Would that be okay with everyone?"

They all nodded.

"Actually I would kind of like to see where I was…found."

"Fair enough." Dad stood up and started walking toward the water. They all followed him some distance before he stopped.

"Noah, can you tell her where she was?"

"Sure." Noah walked ahead of them and between some rocks to the water's edge. He turned and pointed to an area of trees—the only trees that came this close to the water. "They carried you right to there, but apparently you floated up here."

He turned back to the water. It was shallow, to begin with, but then dropped off suddenly.

"I didn't see you, well, they wouldn't let us see you until you were on the stretcher."

"It was awful. You looked like you were dead," said Mom.

Aspen strode slowly over to the edge of the water and stood next to Noah.

"I can't believe I was in there and I can't remember it."

"You do remember water, right?"

"Yes, but not like scary. Just water. The sound of water, the feeling of water, and the movement. A strange kind of movement."

"Well, you're out. That's what's important." Mom came up behind Aspen and hugged her shoulders.

"Let's go over here. I want to show you all something." Noah continued around the lake.

Aspen kept looking back at the place she had been rescued. *Why would I just suddenly float to the top?*

She hadn't ever been on this side of the lake, not that she could remember. For sure, she had never walked all the way around it.

Noah stopped near a path that led to one of the houses, but the house was shrouded in trees.

"That's Sara and Doug's house." Noah motioned toward the house they couldn't see.

Aspen couldn't stop the knife-like pierce to her heart. She quickly turned and walked ahead of Noah.

"Sorry, Aspen."

She shook her head, shrugging it off. "No worries. Just...just nothing."

Noah touched her arm as he walked past her, and then he stopped. He backed up a few steps. "This is where I landed."

"Landed? What are you talking about?" Aspen eyed him suspiciously. Then slowly she turned toward the water. She saw it—the cement culvert protruding from the lake.

"Is that?"

"Yes. I'm sure it is."

Their parents had stopped for a few minutes and were now just catching up to them.

Noah whispered, "I'll tell you about it later. This would be like starting in the middle of a story."

Aspen nodded.

Noah spoke louder now, "Gavin's mom and his step-dad own that house." He again motioned to one of the houses hidden by trees.

"Hmmm..." Dad mused but didn't volunteer any other thoughts.

They strolled around the lake—Dad telling about more experiences he had as a boy—row boat and swimming races and how at one time the lake was stocked with fish.

"That didn't go over so well though because the kids would leave dead fish or fish guts laying around, which didn't impress any of the uppity folk around here, so they only did that for a couple of years.

He talked more about the picnics at the lake on the Fourth of July and times when his cousins came up for the day. "When I was a kid, the trees weren't so tall here, and we could see the tops of all of the houses surrounding the lake. We used to spend hours out here."

They had reached the dock now, and Aspen and Noah walked out on it. Their parents followed.

Aspen was surprised she didn't feel any apprehension. The tire swing hung limp at the end of the rope. It didn't look at all foreboding.

Dad continued, "One day, though, when I was maybe thirteen or fourteen, I was standing right where we are now."

"Was all of this the same, Dad?" asked Noah.

He nodded. "Yes, except like I said the trees. They are much bigger now."

"What happened, Jackson?" Mom sat down on the dock and curled her legs under her.

Aspen did too, and Dad sat down and leaned against one of the corner posts of the dock.

Noah elected to stand. Aspen thought he looked like he was on guard the way he kept glancing around the water. She decided this was a good time to tell their parents about the swing. She was pretty sure that's what he was thinking about.

"We had been swimming all day, and then we built a big bonfire. Most of the kids left, but it was still light, so some of us decided to get some hot dogs to roast."

He pointed to the house next to Gavin's parent's home. "Dixons lived there." He quickly looked around at his family. "Yes, I did hang out with Drew and Dylan when we were kids, just up here though, we didn't associate at school. They were a lot younger than me. Their parents were dead, and they lived here with their grandpa during the summer, but they had an aunt on the other side of town they lived with during school. Their grandpa ended up moving out of that house kind of quietly. One day they were just gone."

Aspen shuddered.

"Anyway, I volunteered to stay and watch the fire because they were just little kids. I had a friend here, and he went with Drew and Dylan to their house to get the food and stuff." Dad turned his attention to the water.

"There wasn't any sound or anything. I was just poking at the fire with a stick when, for some reason, I turned around and looked at the lake. The strangest thing—a mist was rising off the water. It started in the middle, but then it spread all over the lake. I couldn't believe it, and I just stood there and stared at it, but then I heard Dylan and Drew coming, and as fast as the mist had appeared, it was gone."

"Did you…did you ever figure out what it was?" asked Aspen.

"Naw, and you can bet I didn't tell anyone either, but so many times I would see that mist rising above the trees when I was standing on the balcony of our house, and sometimes from my bedroom window. Strange."

Dad shrugged. "I've even seen it from my hospital room." He looked at Suzann, and his eyes narrowed. "Do you think I'm crazy yet?"

Mom smiled. "No, I'm not really sure what to think. It's like a mystery novel."

Dad chuckled. "Exactly."

"Well, if you're crazy, Dad, so am I." Aspen looked at Noah, and he took a deep breath.

"Remember that day we came up to the lake, and we came back wet?" asked Noah.

Suddenly Aspen remembered that was also the day Dylan had confronted their dad in the front yard. She wondered why he didn't seem to know who it was, but she decided not to bring that up right at this moment.

Aspen didn't wait for Dad to respond to Noah. "I—we told you that Noah pushed me off the dock, but that was only partly true."

Aspen and Noah explained what happened that day; the swing, Aspen falling off, the whirlpool she saw, the lights, and shooting out of the water like someone had pushed her up. They explained how she had nearly drowned, but she didn't want Noah to tell their parents because they already thought she was crazy."

Mom looked shocked. "I can't believe all that I am hearing! This is almost unbelievable. Why didn't you at least tell me?"

"Seriously, Mom?" Noah rolled his eyes.

"I guess you're right. I wasn't in a very good place. It's just that—"

Dad sighed. "Believe it, Suzann. The kids are telling you the truth."

Aspen nodded quickly, "Dad, I saw the mist. Right when we were walking away, I saw the mist. I didn't tell Noah until—well, until just a few weeks ago. It seemed so strange, but like you, I saw it from the hospital too and—"

Suddenly Aspen's eyes lit up. "That day! I saw it again that day I went into the lake. The mist covered the entire lake just like you said, Dad, and then it turned bright, like lights shining from the bottom of the lake. That's what happened that day."

Noah looked confused. "What's what happened that day?"

Aspen pressed her hands to her forehead. "Ahhh…I don't know! I can't remember, but I do remember the lights and the mist! That's got to mean something, right?"

Dad stood and extended a hand to each his daughter and his wife. "I'm exhausted."

They all walked over to the fire, and each sat back down.

"Well, that was some information I wasn't expecting to hear," said Dad.

"I wasn't expecting *any* of this," said Mom. "I think I want a Coke!"

"You don't even drink Coke." Aspen laughed.

Mom reached for the bottle of soda Noah handed her. "I do now." She twisted the cap off and took a long drink, and then she smiled. "Yep, tastes as yucky as I remember. Why don't we have some sandwiches?"

Aspen helped her mother pass out plates, each with turkey sandwiches, pickles, and chips. It was a little warmer then, with the sun directly overhead, but Noah added more wood to the fire anyway.

When they were all seated again, Dad said, "Why don't I give you a little Allen history to begin?"

Everyone waited for him to continue.

"As I told you before, I have five brothers and sisters. Sandra was the oldest, then Jim, Helen, then me. Rob was just two years younger than me, but died when he was eight—he had leukemia. Then Dana, she was born right when we moved to this house. She's five years younger than me."

"How come we have never met any of them?" asked Noah.

"Well, I left when I was eighteen. I did bring your mom back, and she met Dad and Mom and Dana. Do you remember that, Suzann?"

"Of course, I do." Mom said quietly.

Dad sighed. When he started talking again, it seemed more labored. "My older brother and sister were really close; I think maybe fourteen months apart or something like that. They were best friends." He looked at his kids. "Like you two. They did everything together."

"Well, just after my tenth birthday, I overheard Dad talking to Sandra—more like yelling at her. She was fifteen, I think, and they were at the top of the stairs. I was just coming out of my bedroom, so I sneaked back in so they wouldn't know I was there."

Dad was telling her that she was crazy and that she and Jim needed to quit making up stories. Sandra was crying hard, insisting she was not lying and that she and Jim had seen spirits, but Dad freaked out. He became angrier than I have ever seen him. Mom was trying to get him to calm down, but he didn't. He just kept yelling. I didn't know Jim was there too until he suddenly got in Dad's face. He told Dad to quit yelling at Sandra and that she was telling the truth. He asked Dad if he had ever read any of his dad's journals, but still, Dad just told him to shut up, and that was none of his business. Then out of nowhere, Dad hit Jim."

Dad's voice cracked, and he began weeping. "He—he hit him so hard, Jim fell all the way down the stairs. The fall broke his neck and he died. It was—the worst thing."

The pain in Dad's voice was awful. Mom was crying, and so were Aspen and Noah.

To see her dad like this was horrible, and Aspen immediately thought of the day Dad had pushed Noah. They were standing in almost that same spot in the mansion house. Her heart ached for her dad, and when she looked at Noah, she was pretty sure he was remembering that same day.

No one said anything—no one seemed to know what to say.

When Dad was able to talk again, he went on. "My dad was never the same again. To make matters worse, Sandra committed suicide on the morning of Jim's funeral. One of the workers found her out in the yard—I don't know exactly where. They never did tell us."

Dad was sobbing now. Agonizing sobs. He leaned back and covered his face with his hands.

Mom hurried to his side, but he was utterly inconsolable. So, Mom stood behind him with her arms around his chest, her head resting on his shoulder.

Aspen stared at her dad. This was worse than she had ever imagined. It all made sense now. Why he had left Sommerville, and why he had never come back—why he had never told them anything.

Noah, too, was overwhelmed with this news. He was staring at the ground, tears wetting the dirt at his feet.

They were all crying. Aspen couldn't ever remember feeling this sad, not even when Krista died. This was worse because it was her dad who was hurting, and she had no idea how to ease his pain. It was easier to feel your own pain, but awful to see someone you loved hurt like this.

She was sitting near Noah, and she reached over and took his hand.

Noah did not let go. He held tightly to her hand and wept even harder. Aspen's heart ached for her brother, just like the day their dad had pushed him.

She thought she had experienced all the hurt a person could feel these past few months, but she was wrong. This had to be the worst day ever.

Their crying subsided, and the little family sat in silence for a long time.

Finally, Dad said, "And that's why I never tried to talk to Mom or Dad ever again."

Mom asked quietly, "About anything?"

"Oh, about some things, but not about spirits. Never. I was terrified."

Aspen stared at her dad. "So…so you did see…see spirits?"

Dad nodded. "Started when I was maybe five or so. I kept seeing this girl in my room. She didn't scare me. She didn't do anything. I couldn't speak to her. I was too afraid to do that. Her just being there didn't really bother me, but when I tried to tell my mother, she told me to never say it again. It had actually happened to me a few times, but usually just glimpses, nothing too significant."

"So the next time it happened, I told my dad. He lost it. He— he locked me in the storage. I could never get the light to turn on either. I just stayed close to the wall till Mom came and let me out. Sometimes it was for hours."

"*Why didn't your mom get you out of there?*" Mom almost yelled her question.

"Don't blame my mom, Suzann. You have never lived in an abusive home; you don't know the fear. Dad had literally killed one of her children. Not intentionally, but he did. Of course, he never went to jail or anything, Mom told the police it was an accident, which technically it was, but they both knew, and they both lived with that lie. Then when Sandra hung herself, I guess Mom had a nervous breakdown. She was gone for a while. I know that. Grandma Homer came and stayed with us for almost a whole school year, but then Mom came back."

"So…so you had two funerals in one week? Said Noah.

"One day. They got Sandra ready for burial and we had both funerals the next morning." Dad's sigh was heavy, and his eyes swollen. He wiped his face with his hand. "Hard…hard times."

"Did your dad lock you in the storage more than once?" asked Aspen.

Dad nodded. "Yeah, and I did see all those paintings, but I never went near them. I never left the wall. I was too scared. The girl always came, but she never came close to me. She just stayed clear across the room. She helped me feel not as afraid to be in there, but I never dared to talk to her, but there were other people too, and I was afraid of them. They didn't do anything either. Just walked around. It was weird."

He looked at Aspen. "You ever have anything like that?"

Aspen nodded. "Y…yes."

"To say the least," said Noah.

Dad nodded almost like he was relieved. He didn't seem to want to hear about it right now, and he went on.

"Well, that left me, Helen, and Dana. After a year or so, our life seemed kinda normal. We all went through school, played sports, and my sisters danced, and liked to swim."

"What I told you about that first day? We did have parties—fun parties—big parties with our cousins. Sometimes the whole town and our Grandpas and Grandmas would come. Lots of good times. When Dana was in the seventh grade, Helen had graduated, and I was a senior, I thought Dad and Mom had gotten past all of that, but of course, we were forbidden to talk about it. Dana was barely five when it happened, so I don't know how much she remembered."

"I was ten, and Helen was twelve. We remembered every detail. She and I talked about it once, but then we never talked about it again. Not even to each other. It was like Sandra and Jim just disappeared from our lives." Dad's voice trailed off.

Aspen didn't think it seemed right to comment right now, and she sensed Noah and Mom felt the same. This was probably the first time Dad had ever talked about any of this, so his family let him have time to gather his thoughts. He struggled, as the pain was fresh, and it seemed almost like he had been through all of it just yesterday.

He took a deep breath and continued. "It seemed like tragedy followed us around. Mom and Dad could never have peace. Right after Helen graduated, she was on her way to Memphis with some girlfriends and had a head-on collision. All four of them were killed."

At that, Mom gasped, and Noah and Aspen stared at each other.

"*How much pain does one family have to go through?*" asked Mom.

Dad slowly shook his head. "I wondered the same thing."

"So when you left home, Dad, weren't you worried about Dana?" asked Noah.

"Yeah, I was, Noah, but again, Mom fell apart. Our Grandma Homer, Mom's mother, offered to take Dana and keep her with her. She lived in Nashville. Dana was just starting seventh grade, so it seemed a perfect time, and Grandma felt like it would be best for Dana. I don't remember Mom or Dad putting up much resistance, and I don't even know if she saw Mom and Dad much after that."

"This is *so* sad," said Aspen.

"Yeah, your dad comes from the red-letter dysfunctional family."

"But you made it through all of that, right, Dad?" asked Noah.

Dad looked into his son's eyes. "I don't know, Noah, did I?"

Noah looked away briefly, and then back to his dad, "Yeah, Dad. You did."

Dad had a hint of a smile.

"So, how come Dana ended up living in the house?"

"Well, my parents were killed in a plane crash in 1989."

"Geez, Dad!" Aspen wasn't sure she could bear to hear any more tragedy!

"What plane? A big plane?" asked Noah.

"No, it was my dad's plane. Mom left a note, but they did find the plane had engine trouble, so it was never ruled a suicide. I think Dana has the note somewhere. It said they wouldn't be back, but it was written months before the crash.

She said she loved Dana and me, and she knew we wouldn't want for anything because of the estate. Mom said she and Dad had a will, but when we found it, all it said was we were supposed to honor Grandpa Allen's will, who was still alive at the time. I don't think Mom knew that's what it said." He chuckled, "And we have never found that one, as you well know."

"So when did your Grandpa die?" asked Mom.

"He died in 1998 when he was eighty-two. After Dana was married, she and Jerry moved back in the Mansion House, so that they could take care of Grandpa. Faith was in a home somewhere, and she died in 2005."

"Did you go to any of the funerals?"

"My parents, yes. I told you I was on a business trip, Suzann.

The same when Faith died. Sorry. I just came back and went to the cemetery both times. Had no desire to be anywhere around any of the family or to bring you into this mess."

"What about Dana?"

"She knew, Aspen. I saw her both times. I left here when I was eighteen and never looked back. I always sent gifts to Mom and Dad and Dana, and I called Mom on Mother's Day, but that was it."

"How did the plane go down?"

"Mom was a pilot, too, Noah. She was flying that day. They were on their way back from Nashville after visiting Dana. I really don't know, guess in some ways I really didn't care to know."

"Wow." A thousand thoughts were racing through Aspen's mind.

"You mentioned to me one time that your grandma's name was Nina," said Mom.

"Oh, yeah, but I never knew her. My dad's oldest sister ran away with some guy, they didn't find her for months, and Nina had a nervous breakdown. She never recovered and died soon after that. My Grandpa married Faith. I don't know all of the details."

The only sound that anyone could hear for several seconds was the crackling of the fire.

Noah glanced at Aspen, absently stood, and put a log on top and stirred the coals. "Is there any more Coke, Mom?"

"Noah, you are addicted to Coke," said Aspen.

He shrugged. "No, I'm not. It just sounds good."

"Yes, Noah, it's in the cooler."

He pulled a bottle of soda from the cooler. Dad held out his hand, and Noah handed him a Coke. "Anyone else?"

"No, I'm having more hot chocolate," said Mom and Aspen agreed.

Dad guzzled some of his Coke.

Aspen was struggling with what she should say or shouldn't say right now. Although their dad seemed receptive, there was a lot he didn't seem to know about his grandpa. She finally decided to stay on the same subject Dad had introduced himself. She hoped

Noah would do the same.

Aspen asked, "So, Aunt Dana never had any kids?"

Dad shook his head. "And my dad didn't have any cousins either. He had one brother who died when he was just a baby. All the cousins I had were from Mom's side of the family. She had seven sisters if you can believe that."

"Wow, and you never see them either?"

"Nope. I didn't want any connections to this place, Aspen. I did send Grandma and Grandpa Homer Christmas cards, but I asked them not to contact me, and they respected that. Besides they had Dana."

"We weren't very close to my Grandpa Allen's family. My dad had two aunts and an uncle. His aunt Riley died of cancer before I was born and Dad's uncle David, died in a plane crash. He was on a skiing trip in Colorado—it was a small plane too—I think six or seven people—it went down in the Rockies, and his Aunt Jeanne died of cancer when she was only twenty-nine."

Mom sighed. "Good grief."

"So that's it. You kids are the only Allen heirs." Dad moved his arm across his body in one long sweep. "To all of this drama. See why I have never told any of you. Just such a mess."

Aspen studied her dad's face. He almost looked relaxed but tired at the same time. She hesitated, but she had to ask this question. Something was bothering her.

"Hey, Dad? That…that day in the big house, that day that…"

"That I pushed Noah?" Dad didn't look up from the fire.

Aspen hurried on. "Yes, that day. I was wondering if that was the reason that you stopped on the stairs. That you remembered your dad hitting your brother?"

Dad took a long deep breath. "Partly, but what stopped me was what I actually saw— I hadn't seen anything like that since I left Sommerville."

"What did you see Jackson?"

He hesitated and then said softly, "Her."

Mom's face looked puzzled. "Her? Oh, you mean the girl?"

Aspen looked at Noah for reassurance, and he nodded. "He means Ronda."

"Who?" Dad and Mom said in unison.

"Ronda, Dad, you saw Ronda."

27

SECRET PLAN

It took Aspen and Noah most of the afternoon to explain to their parents about Ronda. That she was Riley's sister, the oldest child of Jackson and Nina and that she was the one who was missing so many years ago, not Riley. Also, that the boy she left with, who they now know was Thomas, was never found either.

They told their parents about the journals, both of their Great-Grandpa as well as that of Kenneth Lloyd Dixon, their grandpa's business partner. Aspen explained how she had seen the second girl in a picture and painting in Grandpa's house, and about the girl coming to her, but she couldn't figure out why or what she wanted.

"Remember that first day, Mom, when I asked you to look at that picture upstairs?"

Mom remembered. "This has been going on since then?"

"Yes, and there is a lot more. Krista came to Aspen."

Mom and Dad both looked surprised when Noah explained how that had happened. "This entire summer has been crazy, Dad."

"You are a lot braver than I ever was, Aspen." Dad's troubled eyes made Aspen sad.

"No, Dad, I had Noah, and Gavin, and Kiryn."

"And Rocky," added Noah.

"Yep, and Rocky. We were hoping to find some clue about Ronda and Thomas."

Somehow, Aspen did not feel impressed to fill her parents in about what they had found in the journals.

"You may never find what happened to them," said Mom.

"That's true, but we have to keep looking or at least trying to figure this out."

"What boys were Byron and Larry talking about?"

Aspen turned to her mother, "That is a whole other story. It's about boys that worked for Allen-Dixon, Inc. They have been missing for, well for more than fifty years."

"And they think your Dad's grandpa had something to do with that?"

"Maybe not directly, but yes."

Dad stood then and ran both hands through his hair. "You kids are sure about all of this?"

"We can show you all that we have on Monday, Dad. It's pretty convincing."

"There's more, too, about Gavin's family, but we should let Rocky tell you that. Don't you think, Aspen?"

She nodded, "Besides we have only told you a little."

She described how she had seen Grandpa in a dream and how the spirit of Dixon had tried to interfere with her and stop her from finding the truth. She stopped there.

Dad suddenly seemed more tired than he was only half an hour ago.

"Maybe we should head back home. It's getting dark and colder."

Aspen was a little surprised at his sudden change of heart, but she also knew they had probably overloaded him today.

Mom quickly agreed with her husband, and she started gathering the remnants of lunch.

Dad began folding the chairs, and Noah put out the fire.

Aspen hadn't noticed the cold, but now she did and hurried along with the rest of her family to clean everything up.

They left the lake and walked back to the truck in silence.

Aspen couldn't deny the uneasiness she felt when they crossed the backyard of the mansion house. She and Noah hadn't been in there since the day they had been in the tunnel. She shivered involuntarily.

Noah caught up to her, glancing at their parents who had already reached the truck. He whispered, "Are you sure you want to get back into this stuff?"

She glanced at him and smiled weakly. "We don't have a choice, Noah. It isn't just about me. It's about Dad, too. He needs to put all of this behind him once and for all."

"Do you honestly think that's possible?"

"I don't know. I hope so—for all of us."

Aspen walked into her bedroom and plopped down on her bed, staring at the ceiling. She was awake well before dawn, so she took advantage of the empty bathroom before everyone else woke up.

A thousand things were rushing through her mind. Someone was apparently trying to hurt her. Only this time, it must be a living breathing person, not a spirit. She wasn't sure which she should fear the most.

They were going to Great-Grandpa's house tomorrow, and she was feeling a lot of apprehension about it. Partly because she hadn't been back since being locked in the tunnel, but also because she would be telling her parents a lot of things that only she, Noah, Rocky, Kiryn, and Gavin knew about.

The mere thought of Gavin's name caused pain to well up in Aspen's chest. She rolled over on her side and curled into a ball. She wasn't sleepy at all, so after a while, she decided to get the blow dryer from the bathroom, and dry her hair. She laughed when she got close to the bathroom and heard the water running. She would never get used to one bathroom.

She strolled into the kitchen. Dad was sitting at the table, staring out the window.

"Hey, Dad."

She obviously startled him, and he looked up." Morning, Aspen."

She got a glass from the cupboard and poured some orange juice from the pitcher on the counter. "Want some, Dad."

"No, I'm good."

Aspen sat in a chair across from her father quietly sipping her juice.

"I'm not going to like what I'm about to find out, am I?" Dad asked the question, but he didn't look at her.

"I don't know. Seems like you already have a lot in your past that is unhappy. Maybe some of this will be good. Give you some closure."

Dad didn't say anything, and Aspen continued.

"The thing is, we still have a lot to do. Rocky convinced the FBI people to hold off until you got better. Aunt Dana pretty much told them to jump off a cliff."

Dad laughed. "That doesn't surprise me. She has always spoken her mind."

They were both quiet again, but then Aspen reached across the table and put her hand on top of her dad's. She was a little surprised that she thought she could comfort her dad, but somehow, she knew she could. "It will be okay, Dad. No matter what we go through, it will be okay. We still have each other, and Mom and Noah."

Dad smiled and nodded.

"Did I hear my name?" Noah burst into the kitchen, way too cheery for this early in the morning.

"Well, we didn't call you, if that's what you mean," said Aspen.

"Hmm. That's okay, but Aspen, something came for you this morning."

Aspen's eyes narrowed. "Is it safe?"

"I think so, what do you think, Dad?"

"I think it will be okay."

Aspen eyed them both suspiciously. "What is going on?"

"Nothing." Mom walked in from the hallway. "Except I have some errands to run this morning, and I was thinking you two could help me."

"Okay." Aspen started to stand.

"Not you, those two," said Mom, and she motioned to Dad and Noah.

Aspen sat back down. "What am I going to do?"

Noah took her arm and pulled her up from her chair, "I told you. Something came for you this morning," and he pulled her into the living room.

The blinding sun streaming through the front window made it hard for Aspen to see. Noah planted her right behind the sofa and then disappeared.

Aspen's hands shot to her mouth, and immediately tears welled up in her eyes.

"Aspen?"

Gavin emerged from the sunlight and walked toward her. He stopped within a few feet of her.

Aspen heard the kitchen door close.

She didn't move.

She heard the truck start and drive away.

She still didn't move.

She tried to comprehend Gavin being here, in her house, in front of her, alone. He looked like he had lost a little weight, and his left arm was plastered against his body in a sling, but his broad smile against his dark skin and his chin-length hair looked the same. His green eyes glistened, and she thought he might start to cry, but he didn't. He walked slowly toward her, and when he was close, he encircled her waist with his free arm and pulled her to him.

Aspen's head was spinning, and for a second, she couldn't move, but then she wrapped both arms around his neck and buried her face in his shoulder.

She cried, and he let her.

When she could finally speak, she stuttered, "What—what about your Mom?"

Gavin pulled away from her and placed his finger on her lips. "Shhh."

He leaned toward her again, cupping the back of her head with his hand, he softly pressed his lips against hers.

Aspen's tears ran freely as she pulled him to her, kissing him back with more passion than she ever thought possible.

Gavin buried his face in her wet hair. "I love you, Aspen Allen."

Aspen could not stop weeping. "I love you too. I have missed you so much."

They stood still for a long time, hugging each other.

Aspen did not want to let him go out of fear of losing him again.

Finally, they walked over to the sofa and sat down. Aspen was surprised to see a fire going.

"Noah started that for us."

"But how, when—"

Gavin laughed. "I couldn't stay away any longer Aspen. I'm so sorry I wasn't there to support you—in the hospital—through all of this."

Aspen's eyes widened, and she looked at his arm. "What about you? I wasn't there either."

"But you would have been."

"So would have you."

Gavin squeezed her hand. "No one is going to keep us apart again. I have been miserable."

Aspen nodded quickly. "Me too, but how did you do this—today? Noah acted like he knew."

"I texted him a few days ago and asked him if he would help me with this. I had to let your parents know. I had to see you, Aspen."

"Aren't you still living in Memphis?"

He nodded. "Yes. Kiryn sneaked me out early this morning when Mom and Doug were still sleeping. Rocky met us some ways from Mom's house, and then Kiryn went back to talk to Doug and Mom. Rocky brought me here."

"Poor Kiryn." Aspen honestly felt bad for her.

"She's got this. I talked to Mom a few days ago. She knows how I feel about you. I decided I needed to make the first move."

"I hope they aren't mad at her."

Gavin grinned. "They will be."

Kiryn sat across from Doug and Sara. "I don't know why you are so mad. You know he has a gift too; this isn't all about Aspen."

Doug glared at her, but Sara sank back into her chair.

"I know that Kiryn, but none of this would have happened if they hadn't moved here."

"So, do you think by keeping them apart this will all go away for Gavin? It won't. He knows who he is now, and he can't hide from that. And *you* shouldn't expect him to."

Doug stood up. "Kiryn, watch how you're talking to Sara."

"I'm not trying to be disrespectful, but you both must know how silly it is to assume you can keep Gavin and Aspen apart. They really love each other, Sara, and they are kind of the same—I mean with the spirit stuff, and all that crap."

Sara looked surprised. "Don't you believe any of it?"

"*What?* I believe *all* of it! I've seen it. I just don't want to be *in* it like them. Too scary!"

Doug sat back down. "So, there is some truth to all of this?"

"You were there, Doug when Dylan told us about their grandpa. Why would you wonder if it's true?"

"I don't mean that. I mean these so-called 'gifts' these kids have."

Sara sighed. "They are not so-called 'gifts,' Doug, they are as real as you and I. This has been in my family for centuries."

"How come you never told me?"

"Because I was afraid of your reaction. Good grief, the entire town thought my sister was a witch."

"Well now, thanks to Cassie, they think Aspen is too," mumbled Kiryn.

Doug squirmed but searched Sara's face. "Do—do you have any of that?"

Sara laughed. "No, not me. It was just Sumer, and Gavin is *her* son."

Kiryn felt encouraged, "So we just need to let them be together. With all of us, Rocky, too. We have a lot of stuff to talk to the FBI about. This all needs to be done."

"I suppose you're right, Kiryn, but I, for one, am afraid of what else might be found out in all of this," said Doug.

Kiryn sighed. "Me too, and so are all of us, but it's started now. One thing we need to find is that will, and we found a bunch of other stuff in their grandpa's house before Gavin's accident."

Sara had an odd look on her face.

"What's the matter?"

Sara leaned toward Kiryn but seemed to be trying to decide what to say next. Finally, she said softly, "It wasn't an accident. I do know that."

Kiryn's eyes widened. "Did someone do that to Gavin?"

Sara shook her head. "Not someone," she paused. "I think Gavin needs to talk to Patrice."

"I thought you wanted that stopped—"

"I did, Doug, but I was wrong. They all need Patrice's help. She may be the only one who *can* help them right now."

Doug seemed to relent to Sara, but the look on his face made Kiryn a little uneasy. Why did it seem like he didn't believe Sara?

28

I LOVE YOU TOO

KIRYN CAME OVER AFTER she talked to Doug and Sara, and she and Gavin had dinner with the entire Allen family.

After dinner, they poured over the journals and talked about what they would do tomorrow. They tried to catch up on the time while they had been apart, but they all knew there was too much to cover in one afternoon.

For Aspen, it seemed like old times. It even seemed that her life was complete. They were communicating with Mom and Dad again, and having Kiryn and Gavin, and Rocky too, back in her life was more than she had dared hope for these past few months. She felt whole again.

She had more courage and felt more empowered to move forward, not sure of what she would have to face.

Still, Dad distanced himself a little. He and Mom sat on the front porch for about an hour, and then they came in to get ready for bed. When Mom walked through the living room, she suggested they call it a night because tomorrow was going to be a long day.

Reluctantly, they all agreed.

After Kiryn and Gavin left, Aspen got ready for bed and stopped by Noah's room on the way back from the bathroom. She gently knocked and slowly pushed his door open. His light was off, so she knew he might even be asleep.

He wasn't. "Hey."

"Thanks, Noah."

"No problem. I couldn't stand to watch you mope around much longer."

Aspen smiled, and she knew he was smiling, too, even though she couldn't see his face.

"Well, anyway, I love you, Noah."

"I know."

She turned to walk away.

"Hey, Aspen."

She stopped but didn't turn around.

"I'm—I'm happy they're back."

"Me too." She started to walk down the hall, but she wasn't too far away to hear her brother.

"I love you, too."

$$29$$

TOUR

Aspen was up and dressed early. She was tying her shoes when Noah knocked on her door.

"Hey!" she greeted him when he walked in.

"Hey." He sighed and sat down on her bed.

"What's the matter? You're not getting cold feet, are you?"

"No, but— Aren't you nervous?"

Aspen took a deep breath and let it slowly escape before she answered. "Really nervous. Picking up again with Gavin and Kiryn is like we have never been apart, but telling Mom and Dad all this stuff— I don't know." She sat down next to Noah.

"I'm hoping we can just go through the house and tell them everything that we have experienced, and nothing, you know, *unusual* will happen."

Noah laughed nervously, "Fat chance. Do you realize there are rooms in that house we have never even been in?"

Aspen's expression suddenly sobered. "You know, I hadn't really thought about that, but you're right. At least on the main floor."

Noah shrugged, "Yeah, at least that's what we think."

Aspen scowled, "Let's hope there are no more big surprises." But an uncomfortable uneasiness swept over her. She tried to shrug it off. "C'mon let's see if Mom and Dad are ready."

"Dad's been in the backyard for over an hour."

"Doing what?"

"Just sitting in a chair."

Aspen's eyes narrowed. "That's all?"

"Well, I saw him there when I first got up. I took a shower, ate a doughnut, and he was still there, then I came in here."

"Hmm, let's go check."

Through the window, they saw Dad was sitting in a chair near the garden. His head was down.

"He's sleeping, Noah, duh."

"No. He wasn't sleeping a few minutes ago."

Aspen pushed the kitchen door open, "Dad?"

He didn't look up.

Aspen looked anxiously at her brother.

"Well, let's go see." He gently pushed on her back.

"Dad?" Aspen cautiously approached him.

He lifted his head and turned toward them.

Aspen slowed. She thought she heard him say *amen*. "Were— Were you praying, Dad?"

Dad's eyes were somber, and he nodded.

"We're sorry, Dad, we didn't—"

"Don't be sorry, Noah." Dad stood. He put an arm around each of his children. "I just have a feeling I may need a little help today, that's all."

They walked toward the house.

"Do you do that often, Dad?" Noah seemed honestly surprised.

"I used to, Noah. I haven't much for many years."

"Why did you stop?"

"I didn't actually stop. I just got out of the habit. It's a good habit to have."

"I do sometimes," said Aspen.

"I do too, only I wonder if there is anyone listening," said Noah.

"Don't ever hesitate to pray, Noah. He's always listening."

"So you believe in God, Dad?" asked Aspen.

Dad stopped walking and turned to both. His face we expressionless.

"I always did, but then I just decided I didn't. It seemed like a real God wouldn't put my family through all they've gone through."

"Do you think God did that, you know, to your family?"

Dad shook his head. "No, Noah. I don't know, but I guess I did. I guess I am just not sure where things went so wrong. Somewhere, but I'm not sure where."

Aspen looked at the ground, "Do you think these 'gifts' came from God?"

"I don't know, Aspen, I really don't know, but one thing I do know, all that is good comes from God."

Aspen studied her dad's face. He looked somehow more peaceful this morning. She even thought that he looked younger than he had the past few weeks, but she knew that might be her imagination.

Unexpectedly, he hugged them both, and a wave of happiness swept over her. For a minute, she was a little girl, playing in the sand with Noah when Dad came behind them and hugged them both. She wondered why at that very second, that was the memory that surfaced for her.

She smiled and hugged him back.

It didn't really matter why. She felt warm inside, and she liked that.

～

Aspen and Noah rode up to Grandpa's house in the Iroc. They had plans with Gavin and Kiryn this afternoon, and Mom and Dad drove the truck. Rocky's truck was parked on the street, and Rocky, Kiryn, and Gavin were waiting inside. Dad opened the gate, and the two trucks parked in front of the house. Even before they got out of their vehicles, Larry and Byron pulled in, followed by two black SUV's. Four agents piled out of each one, and immediately dispersed around the grounds.

Aspen glanced at Noah, and they both rolled their eyes. Maybe this was a little bit of an overkill. Nothing unusual had happened since she left the hospital. Well, there was the note.

Gavin walked directly over to Aspen and planted a kiss on her cheek.

"Is this going to be a regular occurrence?" Noah pretended to be annoyed.

Gavin grinned, "Maybe, I have to make up for lost time."

Aspen's heart did somersaults, and when Kiryn linked arms with Noah, and he didn't pull away, Aspen smiled. Maybe things really were back to normal.

Rocky and Dad shook hands when he and Mom joined him, Larry and Byron on the porch. The five spoke briefly, and then they turned to the four teenagers.

"We are going to follow you kids through the house. Just explain what happened and where," said Rocky.

Dad unlocked the door, and Noah started to walk in, but then stopped. "Wait, we need to go to the side of the house."

When they reached the side door, Dad had a curious look on his face. "This is where I saw you kids with Drew."

"Exactly, but this is what we were doing. Noah grabbed the handle of the door and pulled it open, revealing the brick wall.

"Why were you going through a side door?"

"That would be sneaking in," Rocky clarified for Dad.

"Ohhh…"

Noah hurried on, "What door opens to a brick wall?"

"I honestly don't ever remember that door being there when I lived here," said Dad. "I had so much on my mind the day I saw you kids here. I didn't give it any thought."

"Well, Drew made sure he was standing in front of the door, so that could be the reason," said Noah.

"Maybe." Dad put his hand on the brick, closed the door, and examined it for a few minutes. He slowly shook his head. "This door was never here." He backed up and looked at the bushes on either side of the door. "Or maybe it was, but it was covered with that vine. It was not visible. I know that. I wonder where it opens to."

"We think we found out," said Gavin. "We'll show you."

The group started to follow Noah back to the front of the house, but Dad did not immediately join them. He walked around the corner of the house and pulled at some vines. "Dana let this stuff almost cover the steps to the balcony."

Noah glanced at Aspen. "One place we have never been."

She nodded.

The steps were almost entirely hidden by the thick vine that crawled up the side of the wall and crept around the balcony railing.

"Did your family use the balcony, Jackson?" asked Mom.

"All the time, but I remember as a kid thinking it was strange that we couldn't get to the balcony from the inside of the house. We had to come outside."

The four teenagers all exchanged a quick look.

Rocky laughed. "We all wondered the same thing."

They went back to the front of the house and walked into the entry. The two massive paintings towered above them, and Aspen asked, "So Aspencia was your mom, right?"

Dad nodded.

Aspen pointed to the other painting. "But Faith was not your grandma?"

"Well, sort of. She married Grandpa. My grandmother, who died was Nina."

Rocky asked, "Did you know her?"

Jackson shook his head. "No. She died before I was born. I have never even seen a picture of her."

Suddenly Kiryn walked directly over to the painting of Jackson Humphrey Allen and Faith Allen. With her fingernail, she scratched Faith's dress. Tiny fragments of paint dropped to the floor. She slowly turned her eyes wide. "Holy cow."

"What?" Mom's puzzled expression made Aspen laugh.

"Nothing. We'll explain in a few minutes."

"I am totally confused."

"You won't be, Mom. Well, maybe you will be. Just come on."

Aspen was surprised her dad did not have anything to say about

Kiryn scratching the painting, considering his protectiveness of the house when they first arrived in Sommerville.

Noah led the group up the wide staircase.

Aspen stopped at the painting of the three children. "This is where I saw the girl the first time. She was just a shadow, but I noticed she had a chipped tooth and that her necklace was opposite of the necklace in the same smaller picture in the bedroom. She took them into the bedroom and pointed out the picture. "Remember Mom?"

Mom nodded. "I have to admit, I had a strange feeling that day when we walked past that painting, but I just thought it was, well, this house."

"This is the same room that Noah felt someone touch him, and once I was inside the painting."

All the adults in the room except for Rocky were gaping at Aspen as though she were crazy. "Okay, maybe too much information right now."

Without elaborating, she skirted past all of them into the hallway. She pointed to the end of the hall, just past the staircase. "That's where I saw Ronda—"

"And I saw Krista," said Gavin.

Kiryn pointed to the storage. "And that's where Gavin's mother was."

"Gavin's mother?" Mom's eyes widened.

Rocky jumped in. "Yes, Suzann. Gavin's mother died when he was born. Sara and I adopted Gavin. We were married at the time."

"So—so you kids have seen all of these spirits?" Mom looked a little unconvinced, not to mention the looks on Byron and Larry's faces.

"Don't judge," said Rocky. "You have to hear everything."

Aspen noticed that Byron was taking notes so fast, she wondered if he would run out of paper in his notebook. Larry, on the other hand, looked somewhat amused, and she tried not to be irritated by that.

"If I may clarify, I have seen no spirits," said Kiryn with a look of satisfaction.

"Well, neither have I." added Noah.

"Yeah, but you felt them." Kiryn's eyes suddenly widened. "Wait a minute! I saw the doorknob—"

"And my arm went through the door."

"*What*? When did your arm go through a door, Aspen?"

"It was downstairs."

"Downstairs?" Dad's eyes were as wide as Mom's now.

"Oh, wow, this is going to take a while." Rocky paused. He started for the end of the hall. "Come down here."

"This is where we, well the kids, broke through the wall."

"We didn't mean to, Aspen fell through it," said Kiryn quickly.

"We were just trying to move that plant because it looked like there had been a door here once, and when we leaned against the wall to push it away, the wall gave way, and Aspen fell through it."

"Where does it go?" Dad was running his hand over the wall. "I had it fixed. I didn't even come up here to look at it."

"It goes to a shaft, like an air conditioning shaft, it goes down, and then it drops off. There is a ladder and another room, and there are two staircases leading from that room—one up and one down and—"

"Kiryn!"

Gavin startled Kiryn, and she clamped her mouth shut.

"*Geez*! You are so psychotic! Slow down!"

Kiryn blushed, and Aspen and Gavin laughed at both.

Rocky casually walked past all of them. "C'mon Kiryn, since you can't wait to tell all, let's take them there."

They went into the master bedroom, but when they passed the storage room, the four teenagers all exchanged anxious looks. None of them said anything. Aspen knew what they were thinking—the painting. She wondered how her dad would react to that disclosure.

Larry whistled through his teeth when he saw the gun collection in the master bedroom. "Now that's worth some bucks."

"I'm sure it is. I had no idea these guns were here, but now that I think about it, they could have been. We were never allowed in Mom and Dad's room," said Dad.

"*Never?*" Kiryn looked stunned.

"Never," confirmed Jackson. "I don't even think I ever came this far down the hall. We weren't allowed, and we obeyed," he eyed Aspen and Noah, "Unlike some kids I know."

Neither of them responded, and Dad didn't elaborate. He just chuckled and shook his head at Mom.

Aspen shot a look of relief at her brother.

"This is a bit tricky, but it's easier than going down the shaft," said Rocky.

With Noah and Gavin's help, he moved the clothes in the closet, removed the fake wall, opened the backpack he carried, and retrieved two high-powered flashlights.

Aspen recognized those lights. They were the same ones used to go into the tunnel that day. A shiver trickled down her spine.

Rocky crawled through the hole, and the rest of them followed while Rocky explained.

"When we get to the bottom, you will see why we looked for this entrance." He led them down the short hall, and to the long, narrow staircase.

"This is creepy," said Mom.

Kiryn quickly agreed, "No kidding."

At the bottom of the stairs, they turned and went down the second even more narrow, winding staircase.

"Where does that go?" Larry was referring to the small part of the stairs that went up.

"In a second," said Gavin. "We need to show you this part first."

When they reached the small room at the bottom, Noah pointed to the wall of brick. "See Dad. That's the brick wall that the door opens to."

Dad observed from where he was standing.

Aspen motioned to a second door. "A doorknob was on this door, but it was fake." She picked it up and showed it to everyone. "It was glued on."

"See if your arm will go through that door now."

Aspen glared at Kiryn, but she pressed her hand against the wall, and nothing happened.

Kiryn shrugged. "Well, it *did* happen."

"Your arm—"

Aspen touched her mother's shoulder. "Be patient, Mom. I promise I will tell you."

Mom shrugged, but eyed first Aspen, and then Noah.

"Where does that go?" Larry was looking at the third door.

Noah shrugged. "We don't know. We were just going to check it out when we heard the commotion upstairs and left."

The words had barely left Noah's lips when a cold wind whistled through the room. The sound became deafening, and Aspen could only assume this might be what a tornado sounded like. In seconds, she was being pulled toward the third door, and to her horror, she was swept off the floor and sucked through it up to her waist. She had been standing closest to Gavin, and he grabbed both of her hands, but he was being pulled toward the door with her.

The suction on Aspen's legs was so strong; she felt as though they might be snatched from her body.

Mom screamed, "*What is happening?*"

"We don't know!" yelled Rocky. "Everyone help!" He wrapped both arms around Gavin's waist and held onto him. Each person, in turn, did the same, forming a chain.

Aspen was screaming, "Don't let go of me! Gavin, please!"

The sound was deafening.

Dad, who was at the back of the chain, suddenly let go and leaped toward Aspen.

Immediately, he was sucked through the door. Aspen was propelled back into the room, crashing into Gavin.

The wind stopped, leaving them all in a heap on the floor.

"Jackson!" Mom screamed and scrambled to her feet.

Rocky grabbed her arm, "Wait! Don't go over there!"

"Where is he? Aspen where did he go!?"

Aspen was as shocked as everyone else. Suddenly filled with fierceness, she jumped to her feet and slammed both hands against the door.

Nothing.

"Aspen, don't!" The terrified look in Gavin's eyes made her stop, but he was looking at her mother. "She can't lose you again."

"Dad!" wailed Aspen. "We have to get him out of there!"

~~

The blackness was so thick Jackson could barely breathe.

Daring not to move, he stood perfectly still, waiting.

In seconds, a tree materialized, surrounded by a dim glow. Thick branches protruded from the massive trunk and twisted every which way. Large red leaves clung to every inch of each gnarly branch.

Jackson knew this place.

"Did you think you could run forever?"

Fear gripped Jackson as he turned in the direction of the voice.

Three teenage boys. He had gone to school with them.

"Well?" It was the same voice, but Jackson noticed his lips didn't move.

Jackson stared at the three familiar faces. He hated these three boys. Well, at least two of them. They never really were his friends, but they found out about Jackson's gift, or at least they thought they did.

What do you want? Jackson thought he was talking, but he realized he couldn't hear his voice.

Nevertheless, they seemed to hear him.

"What we always wanted and never got. Where is it, Jackson?" Spat the second boy.

"Yeah," the third boy's face had no expression, and he quickly looked down when Jackson turned in his direction.

The images faded, and Jackson was left alone with the tree. He searched the ground until he found what he was looking for. A feeling of dread engulfed his entire body, and he hung his head.

I can't— I can't—

~~

To the shock of everyone, Jackson was suddenly sucked through the door but now, just as suddenly, he lay in a heap at their feet.

"Mr. Allen?"

Jackson was on his back, looking up at Byron and Rocky.

"Dad!"

"Jackson!"

He heard Aspen and Suzann.

He tried to sit up, but someone gently pushed him back down.

"Dad, just stay there for a second." Noah's worried look alarmed Jackson.

"I'm fine. I really am fine."

"Well, *I'm* not! Don't you *ever* do that again!" Suzann knelt beside him and hugged his shoulders.

"I didn't—" Jackson stopped.

They were all waiting for him to continue.

He didn't, so Aspen spoke up, "Dad, you went through the door."

Dad pushed them away, and with Noah's help, got to his feet.

"I don't know what you're talking about. I must have fallen. Where did that wind come from?"

Everyone was looking at Jackson.

"Are you sure you're okay, Dad?" Aspen knew these experiences left her feeling strange, but not like she couldn't function. She knew her dad had gone somewhere, but for some reason, he was unwilling to disclose what had happened to him. The best thing to do was to move past it. *For now.*

Jackson nodded. "I'm fine. What were we going to do now?"

They all looked at each other, but no one seemed to know what to say right at this moment.

"Well, why don't we show you the coolest thing ever—"

Aspen grabbed her dad's hand and pulled him up the staircase. Everyone followed in silence.

They passed the staircase leading to the master bedroom and walked through the thick wooden door. They emerged into another room. In one corner was a ladder. Just below the ladder was a hole.

A metal box with no lid lay next to the hole, and the dirt from the hole was collected strangely into a neat little pile.

"What is this place?" asked Byron, but he asked it in such a reverent tone, it surprised Aspen.

Aspen looked at Rocky, Kiryn, Noah, then finally at Gavin. They all nodded to her, so she knelt next to the hole, and explained how she had dreamed about Great-Grandpa Allen and the box.

She had left the wooden box next to the hole, and lifted it so they could all see it.

She explained how when they first came down, Gavin jumped from the ladder, and the floor gave way.

"Lots of things happened that made us decide to come here again, and we found this box. There was a note that your grandpa had written, Dad, and a small gold statue of a girl."

Dad looked as if he wasn't sure he followed what Aspen was trying to say.

"Dad, the note was to Ronda, Grandpa's oldest daughter. In one of the journals, Kenneth Dixon confessed to killing Ronda and her boyfriend, Thomas—"

Sudden irritation pulled at Dad's mouth, and he interrupted Noah, "But why? Why would he do that? Where's this statue and note?"

Rocky quickly stepped in, "Apparently those two kids overheard Dixon planning what to do with some boys that worked for them. He said he was drunk, and he told a guy that worked for your Grandpa and Dixon to get rid of them—the boys."

Noah continued, "Ronda must have sneaked out of the house, and she and Thomas were hiding in a rowboat at Mystic Lake. That's where this all took place. Dixon pulled them out of the boat and even though they begged him not to, he drowned them both."

Dad sank to the floor and buried his face in his hands. He wept silently but didn't say anything.

"I have the statue and note at home, Dad," said Aspen quietly.

Slowly the rest of the group sat on the floor as well. Mom sat close to Dad on one side, and Aspen did the same on the other.

Aspen couldn't think of a single thing to say to console her dad. There was really nothing to say. She knew he just needed time. Rocky and the four kids had already absorbed all of this, but for Larry, Byron, Mom, and especially Dad, this was horrific information.

Dad's voice cracked when he whispered, "So my grandpa kept this secret his entire life?"

"Oh, no, Dad. Grandpa thought Ronda ran away. He didn't find out the truth till just before Dixon died."

"Are you sugar-coating this, Aspen?"

"No, you can read the journals yourself."

Dad looked at his two kids. "There is more, isn't there?"

Noah looked away, and Aspen twisted her mouth.

Rocky finally answered his question, "There is, Jackson. If you've had enough for today though—"

Jackson pulled himself to his feet and brushed the wetness from his cheeks. "No, let's continue." He took a couple of steps, stopped, and turned around, "Where to?"

"Uh—back upstairs." Gavin stepped out in front of the group, took one of the flashlights from Rocky, went down the few steps to the other staircase, and led the way back up.

Everyone followed.

Mom was in front of Dad, Noah, and Aspen.

Aspen pulled on her dad's hand and said softly, "Dad, did you— Did you see something on the other side of that door?"

He glanced at his wife who turned around when she heard Aspen ask that question. He shook his head, "No, Aspen. Nothing." And he followed the rest up the staircase.

Aspen stared at his back. *But he didn't say that he did NOT go on the other side of the door.*

Rocky took up the rear, and Aspen turned to him and Noah.

"He's lying," she mouthed.

Rocky and Noah both raised their eyebrows and nodded.

"What are you waiting for? Let's go." Noah nudged his sister.

Aspen took the flashlight from Rocky and pointed the beam

toward the door. She wrinkled her face as she handed the light back to Rocky and then started to ascend the stairs.

"What?" Noah eyed her suspiciously. "Do you know something?"

She shook her head, "No, just thinking."

Why do I hear water and see images of boys? And I don't even think I know a kid with red hair and freckles.

30

FUNNEL

THEY EMERGED FROM THE closet in the master bedroom.

Jackson stood in front of the wall of gun cabinets. He studied the display for a few minutes, then turned to face the group.

"I haven't been through all of the stuff in Grandpa's office. Maybe the keys to the gun cabinets are in there somewhere."

Noah shrugged. "Maybe. They have to be somewhere."

"One more missing piece," mused Rocky.

"What?"

Rocky sighed before he answered Suzann.

"I meant there are so many missing pieces to all of this."

Mom turned to her husband. "Will you let us help you go through the office, Jackson?" she seemed a little apprehensive.

Now it was Jackson who sighed, and then he chuckled as he looked at his kids. "Yes. I don't think there is much reason for secrecy at this point."

Aspen linked arms with her dad. "Well there *are* a few things—" She glanced at Noah, who rolled his eyes. She knew what he was thinking; there were *a lot more* than a "few" things.

"Where to?" asked Noah.

Kiryn all but skipped ahead of all of them, and said lightly, "I'm thinking the storage." She stopped and turned to face the group. "In there is the most amaz—" Kiryn suddenly stopped talking. "Mr. All—"

The group was just passing the long staircase. Kiryn made Aspen laugh, but when she saw the look on her face, she sobered. At that moment, she felt her dad's grip on her arm suddenly weaken.

When Aspen looked up at her dad, his face was turned away from her. Sweat poured from the back of his neck, and he was visibly shaking.

"Dad?" Aspen touched his shoulder.

Noah was immediately at his side. "Dad, what's wrong?"

"Could we just— Could we—" Jackson stammered and leaned against the wall.

Aspen turned to where her dad was looking. He seemed to be staring at thin air.

"What in the heck—" Noah too looked at the place his father seemed to be staring.

"Could we what, Jackson?" Mom slipped her arm around her husband's waist. "Do you want to leave?"

Jackson nodded weakly. "I—I think so." He mused.

Aspen turned to Noah. "There is something here. Remember the day he had his heart attack?"

Noah nodded. He glanced back at Rocky, who also nodded.

Gavin was standing behind Rocky.

Noah tugged on Aspen's arm. "What's up with Gavin?"

Aspen turned to look at Gavin, but as she did, she noticed the look on Kiryn's face. She too was looking at Gavin, but with wide, fearful eyes.

Aspen could see why. Gavin seemed to have fallen into a trance of some sort. He stood completely still. His arms hung limply to his sides, and his face turned upward. His wide-open eyes stared past them, toward the storage door, but more towards the ceiling.

Aspen quickly glanced at Byron and Larry, who stood silently staring at all of them. Byron wasn't even taking notes.

A sound like rushing wind came up the stairs and blew past all of them. Everyone's hair and clothes moved as though they were standing outside in a light breeze.

To Aspen, everything seemed to be moving in slow motion. She clasped Noah's hand and pulled him with her toward Gavin, but Noah resisted, electing to stay next to their dad.

Aspen looked at Kiryn as she walked past her. Her face still wore the same fearful expression.

Aspen touched Gavin's hand. When she did, he suddenly shook his head and looked directly at her.

"Are you okay?" Aspen's voice sounded hollow and distant.

Gavin slowly nodded, but then his eyes widened. "I saw them, Aspen?"

"Who? You saw who?"

"Boys—a huge group of boys."

"*You saw the dead boys?*" Kiryn shrieked, but even she sounded hollow; like she was talking from inside a can.

Gavin shook his head. "The boys I saw are not dead. At least they didn't seem to be."

The sound of rushing wind, louder this time, again came from the stairs.

Aspen whirled, frozen in place by what she saw.

There in the air, on the staircase was an opening—it was swirling—like when water swirls down a drain. The silver funnel appeared to be about two feet in diameter.

Suddenly Dad yelled, "*See there! Do you see it?*"

"See what, Jackson?" Mom was on the verge of tears.

"What is wrong with everybody?" Kiryn was starting to panic.

Rocky moved next to Gavin, his arm around his son's shoulders, and Gavin leaned against him.

Aspen looked at her dad. "Is it swirling, Dad?"

He didn't answer her but continued to stare at the same spot.

The sound of wind was getting louder, and Aspen yelled to be heard above it. "*Dad! Is it swirling?*"

Suddenly Jackson looked at his daughter with tear-filled eyes. He nodded vigorously, "*Yes! It wants me to come! I don't want to go!*"

Jackson started to back away from the stairs, nearly knocking his wife to the floor.

Suzann scrambled to keep her footing, assisted by Byron, who quickly jumped to her side.

"*Dad!*" Noah ran to his dad's side, wrapping both arms around him. "*Dad it's okay! It's okay!*"

Larry helped Noah subdue his father while mom, weeping, clung to Byron's arm.

Kiryn clung tightly to Rocky's free arm.

Aspen turned to the opening. "*NO!*" she screamed. "*Not now!*"

Noah turned to her. "Not now? What's wrong with you? Not ever!"

Aspen quickly scanned the faces of her family and friends. "We need to find out what this is!"

Everyone stared at her in disbelief. Everyone but Gavin. He suddenly bolted toward her and grabbed her hand.

Clarity suddenly hit Aspen, and pulling Gavin with her, she latched onto her dad's hand, and then she turned back to the opening. The wind was louder now, and she screamed. "*NOT NOW!*"

Immediately the wind stopped, the opening closed and Aspen, Gavin, and Dad all collapsed onto the floor.

No one said anything for several seconds.

From the back of the group, Larry breathed, "What. Was. That?"

No one responded to Larry, and now everyone but Kiryn sank onto the floor.

"Shouldn't we just get out of here?" she demanded.

They all looked up at her but said nothing.

Noah extended his hand, and she reluctantly took it. He pulled her down next to him. It was then that she started to cry, and mumbled, "We are all crazy. I think we should burn this house down."

Aspen sighed. "But that was not scary. I mean it was scary, don't get me wrong, but it was not *evil*. Something, or someone, wants us to do something. I think."

"Exactly! Maybe they just want our bodies!"

Gavin looked at his sister. "Kiryn really? They don't want our bodies."

"He's right, Kiryn." Rocky patted his daughter's arm. "Whoever, or whatever, it is has had many opportunities to take any one of us if that's what they wanted to do."

Dad studied Rocky's face. Sweat still poured down his face, and his voice trembled. "What is that supposed to mean?"

"I mean, Jackson, that with all the spirits Aspen and Gavin have encountered, if someone wanted to possess their bodies, it probably would have happened by now."

"Did any of you see what Dad and I could see?" asked Aspen of the group.

Everyone shook their heads.

She turned to Gavin, "Not even you?"

"I'm not sure what you saw. I only saw a light."

Aspen shuddered, "It was silver, but it was swirling like into a hole or something."

Gavin shook his head. "I didn't see that."

"I did, and it's not the first time," said Dad softly.

Aspen squeezed his hand and released it. She turned to Noah, then Rocky. Sniffles only remained of Kiryn's outburst. Larry and Byron both leaned against the wall. Byron was now taking notes. Mom leaned her head on Dad's shoulder but said nothing.

Dad looked at his daughter. She gave him a weak smile, but then turned to Gavin and said quietly, "Patrice?"

Gavin squeezed her hand.

"Dad?" began Aspen. "Would you be willing to talk to Patrice with us?"

Immediately Dad's expression became puzzled.

Rocky spoke quickly. "The Native American lady, Jackson. She is Sara's aunt. She is the one the kids talked to when you were in the hospital. She may be able to help you understand what is happening."

Jackson's sigh was long and labored. He touched his wife's hand. "What do you think, Suzann?"

"I guess. I can't see any harm in it. I just—it's just that I feel like we are—or this is all—"

"Crazy, right?!" Kiryn blurted.

Rocky took her arm. "Calm down."

Kiryn glared at her dad, but then with a deep sigh, she shrugged.

Mom looked directly at Jackson and said, "Strange."

Jackson nodded. "It is strange, and yes, I suppose it's time to face whatever this is."

Aspen squinted and twisted her mouth to one side. "Dad, do you— Do you want to tell us about the…the door?"

When his head jerked up, she knew immediately this was not the right time.

Jackson hesitated. "Blackness. Only blackness."

Aspen and Noah exchanged a quick glance.

"Let it be for now," Gavin whispered softly practically into Aspen's hair, but Dad heard him.

"For now," agreed Dad, and a weak smile crossed his face. "I'm so tired."

Everyone must have felt like Jackson did because no one made any attempt to move.

Aspen looked again at the place on the stairs and then turned toward the storage. Something beckoned her to turn back to the stairs.

Briefly—almost a flicker—an image of a boy with red hair.

Puzzled herself, she turned to Gavin, whose electrifying green eyes engulfed her. He squeezed her hand again, and she could not look away, but there was something else in his eyes—something she had not seen before—a flash of red, and then it was gone.

She leaned her head against his chest and closed her eyes. The steady beat of his heart and the quiet breathing of those in the room was all that she could hear.

31

HAUNTED PAST

ROCKY SAT UP QUICKLY. Sleep had left him, and he was sweating profusely. His t-shirt was cold and damp. The dream had invaded his entire night. Waking up periodically, he would simply fall back into the same fitful nightmare.

It wasn't just a dream, though—it was real. For some reason, he was reliving a dark time in his past. He trudged downstairs to the kitchen, opened the fridge, guzzled the rest of a quart of orange juice, and then he grabbed a cold bottle of water.

As he walked to Kiryn's door, he screwed the cap off and took a huge gulp. He peeked into her room—she was sleeping soundly.

Rocky dragged himself back up to his room, only to come face to face with Gavin, who was standing at the top of the staircase.

"Dad? Are you okay?"

Rocky sighed. "Just a bad dream, that's all."

"Want to talk about it?

"No, that's okay." Rocky changed the subject. "How's that arm?"

"Hurts—I was going to get something for it."

Rocky put his hand on Gavin's shoulder. "C'mon, I have something in my room, then maybe you can sleep. We don't want your mom to be sorry she let you stay the weekend."

Gavin laughed and followed Dad into his bedroom.

The blind was open, and Gavin walked over to the window. Without turning to his father, he asked, "Dad, do you think I'm weird?"

Rocky chuckled, "You mean because you can see spirits and—"

"No—" Gavin smiled. "No, I know that part of me is weird."

"Unique." Rocky handed his son three small white tablets and the opened bottle of water.

Gavin popped them into his mouth and flushed them down with the water. "Oh, okay—unique. You're my dad, you have to say that, but I mean about basketball?"

"No Gavin. I did wonder though. You hadn't even mentioned basketball since you met Aspen and Noah."

Gavin sank into the chair by Rocky's desk, and Rocky sat on his bed.

"I don't know, Dad, it's just that. When I met Aspen, even when I first saw her, something switched inside my head. She is the only thing that seemed important. I even tried to hang out with Cassie a couple of times, but I didn't feel anything. It's like Aspen is, I don't know, part of me. I feel more— Complete. That sounds lame, but that's kind of how I feel when she is with me."

Rocky took a deep breath and let it slowly escape as if giving himself some time to think before he said anything. "Does she feel the same about you?"

"Yes, I think she does. She said she loves me."

"You kids are pretty young, Gav, I just—"

"I love her."

Rocky raised his eyebrows, and his head jerked in a brief nod. "Well, okay, I can see that."

Gavin eyed his dad. "You can?"

"Yes, I can, but you are young. You're still in high school."

Now Gavin sighed. "I know, it totally bites."

Rocky started to laugh. "No, it doesn't. Just look at it as a good time to sort things out. To make sure of what you're feeling for her and what she feels for you."

"There's something else—"

Rocky sobered. "What?"

"I don't know. It's like we are connected or something. Like I have known her, or knew her or— Ahhh! I don't know how to explain what I mean because I don't *know* what I mean!"

Rocky smiled, and his eyes suddenly looked faraway. "You are in a lot better place than I was at your age."

"You mean with Mom?"

"No, not your mom. I was in college when I met your mom. I mean in high school." Rocky sighed. "The dream— That was the dream I was having."

Gavin cocked his head to one side. "I'm totally lost."

Rocky rubbed his face with his hands, and leaning both elbows on his knees, he looked at the floor. When he started to talk, it was slow—he chose his words carefully.

"When I was sixteen, I drank—a lot. I lived in Memphis, and one night a bunch of us went out to Lake Matthews for a party. There were some kids at the lake from Sommerville—two guys in particular—"

"Was—did you know Jackson—you guys are about the same age?"

Rocky shook his head and half-smiled. "He is six years older than me and, no, I didn't know him at all. Didn't even know the Allens existed back then. I didn't care much about politics and that sort of stuff."

"Oh."

"No these were two—I guess you could say, lowlifes. They were just hanging around bugging the girls we brought with us. I was with a girl named Miranda. She and I had been dating a while. She was hanging all over those two—she had been drinking too—it made me so mad I just left her there and went home."

Gavin's eyebrows shot up. "Wow."

"Yeah." Rocky's voice cracked.

"What happened?"

"I didn't know until weeks later. She came to me and told me she had slept with those guys that night. I was dumbfounded. She and I had never done anything like that—ever. I guess she found out she was going to have a baby, and she wanted me to let her tell her parents it was mine. Well, there was no way I was doing that.

I didn't even like her that much." Rocky chuckled. "But that was beside the point."

Gavin waited for him to continue.

"I thought I was pretty tough back then. I was pretty good with a rifle. My dad and I hunted a lot. So, I decided to threaten those two guys. I drove to Sommerville and looked them up. I had my loaded gun on my seat. I was just going to scare them, but lucky for me, I was pulled over for speeding. Officer took my gun. I went to court and spent a night in juvenile detention. The next several weeks, I was doing community service. Now that totally bites. I washed police cars every weekend for thirty-six weeks. Not fun."

Gavin couldn't help but laugh. "At least you didn't shoot them. What happened with the girl?"

"Well, she was mad, to say the least, and probably scared. I tried to ignore her, but it didn't work. One night after a football game—we had all been drinking, of course—she asked me for a ride home. I told her no. She was really drunk, and I had been drinking too much to drive my car. I was going to stay at a friend's house that I could walk to. I suggested she do the same—go to her friend's house and go home in the morning."

"But she found my jacket and took my keys. The next thing I knew, I heard my car start. I chased her. The car was barely rolling, so I opened the door and jumped in, pushing her to the other seat. She begged me to take her to her sister's house because her sister wouldn't tell on her. So, I agreed. It was only two blocks away, and besides, after what had happened the last time, I left her—" Rocky sighed and then mumbled. "Dumbest thing I have ever done though."

Rocky looked up at his son with tear-filled eyes. "I told her to put her seat belt on, but she didn't. She cried and told me what a loser I was because I wouldn't be her baby's dad. I couldn't believe it. I wanted to just dump her out on the sidewalk. I should have."

He stopped talking for a few seconds, but Gavin sat quietly waiting for him to start again.

"All of a sudden, she grabbed the wheel and turned the car right in front of a truck. I was able to turn it farther, hoping to get out of its path because I didn't have time to correct it and bring it back into my lane. Well, the truck nailed us right in the passenger door. She was thrown into me and then smashed into the windshield. It killed her."

Gavin gasped. "Holy cow, Dad! I'm sorry! What happened to you?"

"I spent the next three weeks in the hospital and the next year in jail. When I turned eighteen, I went to prison for two more years."

"For a DUI?"

"And murder, but my attorney was able to get it to involuntary manslaughter. I was supposed to serve a total of nine years, but because of my clean record and the testimony of the kids at school who knew the situation, and even her own parent's testimony, I was finally let out after three years. I was on parole for another four years. It was a mess."

The room was silent.

Then Rocky said, "Haven't had a drink since that night."

Gavin stood and then sat next to his dad. He put his arm across his shoulders, "I'm sorry, Dad. I had no idea."

"I didn't want you to have any idea. I can't believe you haven't found out before now, though. You may have had I stayed in Memphis, but I met your mom in college, and when I graduated, we moved here. Your mom had spent some time here with her family, and she really liked the small town, so we came here, and I got a job teaching at the high school. The rest, as we say, is history."

"You both went to the University of Memphis, right?"

Rocky nodded. "Yep, we did. Those days seem so far away."

"So, that was your past you were talking about that day at the Allen Manor?"

"Yes. Now you know."

"Doesn't change who you are now, Dad."

"I know it doesn't, but it took a long time to get over Miranda's death. I did feel responsible. I should have just told her no. I guess I am just trying to tell you—"

"Not to drink? You and mom have made that quite clear."

Rocky laughed. "I guess we have, but that's only part of it. Be careful with Aspen, Gavin. I do believe the two of you love each other. Just be careful. Don't let things get out of hand. You have your whole lives ahead of you."

"It would be a short life if I ever took advantage of Aspen, Dad. Mr. Allen would kill me."

"Ah, he isn't so tough. He would have to get through me first."

"Then you would kill me."

"Exactly."

32

INSIGHT

When Dad pulled the truck into Patrice's driveway, Aspen's heart jumped, and she realized what she had been feeling this morning was excitement, for herself and Gavin, and especially for Dad. She desperately hoped meeting with Patrice would be a breakthrough for Dad.

She climbed out of the back seat, just as Rocky drove up with Gavin and Kiryn.

Patrice was sitting in the same chair on her front porch. Larry and Byron were already there, and while walking up the path, Aspen spotted four FBI agents. She was holding Gavin's free hand, and she whispered, "This is nuts with all of these guys hanging around."

Gavin shrugged. "I don't think so. Someone must be pretty anxious to harm you."

Aspen couldn't deny that. When they had arrived back at the little house on Monday afternoon, another note was plastered across the front door. It read simply:

ALLEN'S GET OUT!!!!

That note was the reason Byron and Larry stayed the night with the Allen's. When they left the big house, the two agents went to the little Sommerville Motel, took a nap, showered, changed, and were back at 8 pm to relieve two other agents from their posts outside in the yard. That's where they stayed until morning.

As the two families approached the house, Byron stood and walked up to Jackson and Suzann. "We think we may have found the will. We're not positive, but two of our agents have been working around the clock on this. We are meeting with them right after we leave here."

Jackson shook Byron's hand. "Thank you."

"Don't thank us yet," Byron grinned. "Let's make sure."

This time, Patrice already had a spread of muffins and juice on a low round table that was surrounded by chairs.

"It's early, I thought you might be hungry," she called.

"I'm always hungry," said Gavin.

"You got that right," said Rocky, as he took Patrice's hand in his. "That was very thoughtful, thank you!" He turned immediately to Jackson and Suzann.

"Patrice, these are Noah and Aspen's parents, Jackson and Suzann Allen."

She extended both of her hands, and they each grasped one.

A small smile spread across Patrice's lips. "Finally, I meet the famous Allens."

Jackson shrugged. "I don't know about famous. Topic of conversation and gossip, but I don't know if that is the same thing."

Patrice laughed heartily. "Same thing Mr. Allen! Here, please sit down." She motioned to two chairs and turned to the four teenagers. "And how are you, kids?"

Each armed with a muffin and juice, they had found a place to sit.

"We are all good," said Noah, and the rest of them nodded. "Well, if you don't count Gavin nearly being killed, and Aspen's near-death experience, constant threats on her life; I suppose all is well," said Kiryn, and then she stuffed a muffin in her mouth.

Patrice laughed again. "I am so happy the funny girl is with us today."

Rocky, Noah, Gavin, and Aspen burst out laughing while Byron,

Larry, Mom and Dad looked puzzled.

A car pulling into the driveway caught their attention, and they all turned around.

"It's your mom," said Kiryn to Gavin.

Gavin stood and walked to the steps. "Mom?"

Sara hurried toward him, and up the steps, quickly hugging her son. "Hi, Gavin." She turned to Patrice. "Thank you for calling me. You too, Rocky."

Rocky chuckled, and he winked at Patrice, "Great minds."

Gavin said to his mother, "Where is Doug?"

Sara brushed his question aside, "He is in Memphis."

Jackson pulled a chair into the circle for Sara, and she quickly took a seat.

"So, we all know each other, right?" asked Patrice.

Sara looked over at Byron and Larry, and Rocky quickly jumped in with introductions. "Sara these are the two FBI agents assigned to the Allen case."

"Nice to meet you, Mrs. Fielden," said Larry.

Sara looked surprised, "Oh, no, Mrs. Mendel. Rocky and I are no longer— We're not—"

"They are divorced," said Gavin.

Aspen smiled at his comment, but her thoughts drifted elsewhere.

First, we are a legend, and now we are a case. I need to write a book.

Larry was apologizing to Sara, who was blushing, which surprised Aspen. She didn't seem like the blushing type. Right then, Aspen also noticed Sara was wearing a light sweatshirt and jeans. Usually dressed to the hilt, this was not normal for Sara either, and Aspen couldn't help but be curious.

It had been raining all day, and it was cold out. The four porch heaters Patrice had going full blast, provided just enough warmth to keep everyone comfortable. Still, Aspen wondered why they didn't just meet inside.

Patrice turned to Jackson. "There is something on your mind,

Mr. Allen." It was a statement, not a question.

Jackson was startled, but he nodded.

"What would that be?"

Jackson sighed. "Your last name, Munoa. It sounds, familiar."

Patrice's eyes twinkled. "My family has lived in this area for many years. You may have heard that name before."

Jackson nodded, but Aspen couldn't help but notice he didn't seem satisfied.

Patrice was unscathed by Jackson's apparent uncertainty.

She sat back in her chair. "Are we ready to begin?"

Aspen immediately turned her attention to the sweet lady who, hopefully, could provide wisdom and answers for this confused group.

Before Patrice said anything more, she studied each of their faces. She started with Kiryn and went all around the group, still saying nothing. She skipped past Gavin, Aspen, and Dad.

After looking at Larry so long he started to squirm. She turned to Gavin. "May I start with you, dear?"

Gavin stood and took the chair in front of Patrice. Just like before, she leaned forward and took both of his hands in hers. Gavin scooted forward in his chair so that she could reach his hand in the sling.

Patrice closed her eyes and slightly bowed her head. After several minutes, she released Gavin's hands and sat back in her chair again. Gavin sat back as well.

"Gavin, your gift is developing, isn't it?"

Gavin nodded.

"Can you tell me a little about it? What has happened?"

Gavin took a deep breath. "Well, one thing was when I saw Aspen in the water. I hadn't seen or talked to her for a few weeks, but then one day, just sitting in my room I saw her—in my mind—I saw her in water."

Aspen noticed Patrice's eyes narrow when Gavin said he hadn't seen Aspen in weeks.

"Was she?"

"Yes! She was—in the lake—Mystic Lake, but no one had told me."

"What was she doing?" Patrice glanced over at Aspen and then turned back to Gavin.

"She was just—floating—but it was strange because she was under the water. She was completely covered with water, but I didn't get the feeling she was drowning or had drowned."

"And this we know now to be true, correct?" she was addressing Suzann.

"Yes, yes that's true. She was not dead, but then when she was found, she was in a coma."

Patrice nodded and turned back to Gavin. "Go on."

"Well, that's about it until this past Monday. I saw a bunch of boys. A whole crowd of them."

Patrice raised her eyebrows. "What were they doing? Were they also in water?"

Gavin slowly shook his head. "No, but they seemed, I don't know. Restricted or trapped or something. They seemed anxious, but I couldn't tell where they were."

Patrice nodded slightly. "And your arm. What happened to it?"

Aspen noticed Sara stiffen.

"A tree branch fell on me—in the Allen's backyard."

Patrice looked around. "Were any of you with him?"

Noah spoke up. "Oh, yeah, we all were. I mean me, Kiryn, and Aspen."

"How did this happen?"

"I had just come out of the shed—" Gavin stopped. As though something had just occurred to him, he glanced toward Noah. "We—the four of us—went into the backyard because Noah and Aspen had seen a light or something the night before."

Noah quickly interjected. "Actually, Aspen saw it first. I came into the kitchen, and she pointed it out to me." He looked at Aspen as if waiting for her to continue the story.

Aspen hesitated, as she scanned everyone's faces, but then she stopped and looked directly at Dad. She suddenly realized she and

Noah had never told anyone about the light in the backyard. Well, except for Kiryn and Gavin.

"Aspen?" Patrice was waiting for her to say something.

Aspen swallowed. "Well, I went into the kitchen in the middle of the night to get a drink of water, and while I was in there, I saw a bright light outside the window. When Noah came in, we both saw it, and it was so bright, it was hard to look at. Then it seemed to move to the back of the yard, maybe toward the shed."

She turned to Noah.

He quickly nodded. "It was pretty strange. We just went back to bed—"

"We didn't really. We couldn't sleep," said Aspen.

"True. We texted Gavin and Kiryn to see if they wanted to come over early and go to breakfast. Before we left, Aspen and I took them into the backyard to show them where we had seen the light, and to hopefully find the source."

Gavin continued, "I was in the shed. I was telling Noah that there was no light in the socket, so that the light couldn't have come from the shed. Nothing seemed unusual, so I followed Noah out, but then I heard a loud cracking sound—"

"We all did," said Kiryn.

Gavin nodded. "They got out of the way, but I didn't make it, and that's when the branch hit me."

Dad gasped involuntarily, and all eyes turned to him.

Patrice simply said, "Mr. Allen?"

Beads of sweat formed on Dad's forehead and his face suddenly looked drawn.

"I— That—that happened to me and my dad, in the same place."

"Did the tree hit you?" Kiryn's voice shot up a full octave.

Dad shook his head, "No, but it was what my dad said."

Everyone waited.

Dad looked down as he spoke, "My dad, he said— He said it was my fault, that I was a menace to the family."

Now Mom gasped and closed her eyes. She shook her head in

disgust. "Your father was a horrible man!"

Dad didn't even comment, and Aspen noticed a tear splatter on the wood plank next to her dad's shoe.

"Do you think your father was afraid of something, Jackson?" Patrice's tone was slow and even. That was the first time she had called him by his first name.

When Dad spoke, his voice caught, and he quickly cleared his throat and brushed the wetness from his eyes. "I don't know. I just don't know." His voice trailed off.

Aspen was staring at her father when Gavin said, "What?"

She looked up, but he was not talking to her. Gavin was looking at his mom, and then at Patrice.

The two women seemed to understand something the rest of the group was not privy to. Finally, when Patrice gave her a quick nod, Sara explained.

"For many years, there has been a sort of presence if you will, in this valley."

Rocky was nodding as if he understood.

"Dad?"

Rocky held his open hand toward Gavin. "Wait."

The tension was unbearable as Aspen waited for someone to continue with an explanation.

Rocky was looking at Sara, who said nothing. Instead, she turned her attention to Patrice.

"For a very long time, there has been what some folks called a curse. I personally do not think of it as such. It began after Mystic Lake was constructed and the homes built around it, but soon after the Allen girl disappeared, it became more intense, more present I guess. Most people would not have noticed, but my family did. The gifts that have been passed down through the generations of my family are all a little different, but they also have one common thread—a sense of the unknown—of another world."

"The spirit world?"

The question came from Larry which surprised not only Aspen, but seemingly everyone else as well.

Patrice smiled. "I knew I sensed something in you." She continued to eye him for several seconds, obviously making Larry uncomfortable. He shifted in his seat but did not take his eyes from Patrice.

Finally, Patrice continued, "Yes, another world, or dimension. No one has ever been able to explain why the presence became so strong after the death of the young girl, but it did. What Sara is talking about—the tree falling—has always been assumed was caused by someone from another dimension—or world."

Patrice paused briefly, but then continued, "Like an attempt to stop something from happening in this world."

Gavin's eyebrows furrowed, and he asked flatly, "Like what?"

"Well, we know that several attempts have been made to stop Aspen from uncovering the information about the Allen girl. At least, we assume that is what was going on, and obviously, that did not work. Whatever is trying to stop her, maybe elected to turn the attention on you, Gavin, as you are someone Aspen cares for very much."

"But Aspen wasn't even heard of when my dad and I had that experience," said Jackson.

Patrice raised her eyebrows and threaded her fingers together. "Obviously it—they—whatever, was not able to get through to you."

"So, you're saying that now because I didn't respond the way I was expected to, this—thing—is coming after my daughter?"

"What was who, or what, trying to stop?" Mom sounded exasperated.

"This must be very confusing to you, Mrs. Allen."

"Please. Call me Suzann."

Patrice paused, "Of course, Suzann." She began again only more deliberate this time. "Your daughter and your husband have a gift of the spirit—or of connections—I am not sure how to best explain it, but they act as conduits for people from other worlds—or dimensions, as I like to call them. They are subject to portals which allow communications."

"From dead people?" It was as though this reality still had not occurred to Suzann.

"Welcome to my world," mused Kiryn, and after a few seconds of silence, everyone laughed.

Aspen and Gavin exchanged a quick glance, and he reached for her hand. When he took her hand, a feeling of comfort swept over her, but then looking at Mom, she noticed a sort of fear in her eyes.

Mom jumped to her feet, "If this force, or *presence* as you call it, can actually cause physical danger to people, maybe Jackson did the right thing by leaving this valley!"

What started as anger now sounded like pure anxiety, "Maybe we should do the same, tonight!"

"Suzann—"

"Jackson, no! I hate this. We nearly lost you, and then Aspen. Let's just go home."

Mom stood by her chair, fists clenched at her sides.

Dad stood slowly, hugged her, and then putting his hands on her shoulders; he gently pushed Mom back onto her chair. He sat down too, but he held onto her hand.

Aspen felt complete empathy for her mother, but she was also glad that the realization of all that was going on finally seemed to sink it. It was not as though she had not acknowledged what they had all been going through, but now she was internalizing it, and that seemed to make all the difference in her reactions now.

Patrice simply waited and said nothing.

Finally, Byron spoke up. "I hate to be the bearer of bad news, Mrs. Allen, but your daughter can't really leave just yet."

Mom spun on him, "What? What are you talking about?"

Larry and Byron exchanged a quick glance, and then Byron continued. "She is the main lead we have to what could be one of the biggest serial murders in the history of this state."

"The nation," added Larry.

"That too. We have to get to the bottom of all of this if we can. We have allowed the investigation to kind of map its own course, but we are getting a lot of pressure to step up the pace."

Mom rubbed her forehead and ran her fingers through her hair. She took an exasperated breath and sighed. "Okay, so let's move it along."

"It isn't that easy, Suzann." Rocky gave her a sympathetic look. "There are so many little pieces of information, and every time we turn a corner, something else rears its ugly head."

Mom started to cry and buried her face in her husband's shoulder.

Jackson stroked her hair, and Aspen's heart ached at the vulnerability both of her parent's seemed to possess.

Noah stood, walked up behind his parents, and put an arm around each of their shoulders. "We can do this. We *are* doing this." He looked at everyone in the room. "We have a lot of support here, and think of what this could mean to get all of this out in the open."

"If we survive." Mom sat up quickly and patted her son's hand. "Okay, okay. I'm sorry. I just lost it for a second."

Rocky laughed, "Well, it won't be the last time, believe me."

Patrice raised two open hands to the group. "Let's take a break for a few minutes. There are more muffins in the kitchen and plenty of juice and milk."

Aspen asked for directions to the bathroom and then stepped into the tiny living room. Immediately, she could see why Patrice did not have them come inside. Two overstuffed chairs and a matching sofa were the only places to sit, but the startling thing to Aspen was the amount of clutter on the end tables, bookshelves, extra chairs, and the coffee table.

When Aspen emerged from the bathroom, she took a closer look. The clutter wasn't just junk like she thought it was. Instead, there were several trinkets, tiny picture frames, little glass vases, plastic flowers, ceramics, and dozens of small wood carvings.

"Quite a collection, huh?"

Aspen jumped and whirled around to face Patrice, who was leaning on her cane and holding a plate of muffins.

Embarrassed, Aspen hurried to relieve Patrice of the muffins.

"I'm— I'm sorry, I was just—"

"Curious?" Patrice laughed. "I know. It seems like junk."

Aspen winced, "Well, I wouldn't say junk."

"Yes, you would! It looks like junk." Patrice smiled. "But it is not. Everything here has meaning. Many things were gifts from people who felt they had been helped by my family."

"Family?"

"Oh, yes! All these things weren't given to me, but I am the last surviving child of my parents, so all of it fell into my possession."

"Ahh, that makes sense."

Patrice chuckled. "Probably not, but you are kind to agree."

She picked up a tiny plastic bear. "For example, this was from a friend of my mother's. Her husband was attacked by a bear in the mountains of Utah. His remains could not be found, so it was assumed the bear had eaten him."

Aspen's eyes widened, "Seriously?"

Patrice nodded, "Seriously. She was in agony, but my mother was able to direct her to find his remains, what was left to be found."

She opened her hand, and the tiny bear lay in her palm. "Each has a meaning."

Patrice placed the bear back in its place, and saying nothing more; she stepped out onto the porch.

Aspen followed.

She placed the fresh plate of muffins on the table and again took her seat. Aspen was the last one to sit down, which drew curious looks from everyone.

Patrice settled into her chair and turned to Sara. "Aspen found my collections."

Sara smiled. "She has a lot."

Aspen's eyes widened. "I'll say." She glanced around. "You should all take a look."

They were all still staring at her, and she especially noticed a kind of disapproving look from her mom and found it satisfying in a funny sort of way that her mom was being—Mom.

"We were just trying to figure out where to go from here,"

Rocky explained. "Byron and Larry are pretty anxious to get into the office at the mansion."

Aspen nodded.

Patrice seemed to brush all of that aside when she turned to Gavin.

"You have the same gift as your mother, Gavin, and it is a wonderful gift. You could see Aspen when she was in trouble, and now you can see some boys."

"Not *some* boys. A *ton* of boys. I just have no idea where they are," said Gavin. "I knew Aspen was in water, but these guys— I have no clue." He suddenly looked thoughtful.

"What?"

"I don't know, Noah, I keep seeing a red flash. Or orange. Yeah, maybe orange."

Aspen's head jerked up.

"Is that something you see as well?" asked Patrice.

Aspen nodded. "Yes, only it seems to be a person. With freckles."

"Have you seen a person, Gavin?"

He shook his head. "No. It's just a flash. I've only seen the boys once, but the flash of orange is random. I've actually seen that quite often since I've seen those boys."

"What about the—the bones?" Kiryn asked cautiously.

"What bones?" Byron stood up.

Gavin's eyes narrowed, and he glared at his sister.

"Sorry," she mouthed, but then she turned to Noah. "Did you bring your cell phone?"

Noah rolled his eyes and nodded. He pulled it out of his pocket, scrolled down the screen, tapped on the picture icon, and scanned through the pictures. He clicked on one to make it bigger and held it up for Byron and Larry, who were both now standing on either side of Noah.

"*Holy cow!* Where is this?" Byron took the phone from Noah.

"In a tunnel," said Rocky flatly. "Under the Allen Manor."

"You've seen this?"

"No, I haven't seen them. The kids have."

Byron handed the phone back to Noah, who passed it to his Dad's outstretched hand.

Byron motioned to Larry, and they both took their seats.

When Bryon was settled in his chair, he spoke directly to the four teenagers, "After this meeting—"

They all nodded reluctantly.

Now, Dad's eyes narrowed when he handed the phone back to his son. "What else don't we know?"

"Oh, the list goes on and—" Kiryn's mouth clamped shut when she saw the glares she was getting from Gavin, Aspen, and Noah.

33

JIMMY

Patrice interjected quickly, "Possibly, we should continue with what you came for, and then it seems there is much to attend to."

"Sorry." Kiryn ducked her head.

"There is absolutely no reason to be sorry, Kiryn. So much is going on for all of you folks, and I am aware of that. I think maybe understanding how Gavin, Aspen, and I believe, Jackson's, gifts can help provide a little better understanding of what has been happening could prove beneficial."

"I hope so," said Rocky.

"So do I," said Jackson.

Appearing satisfied, Patrice turned to Gavin. "Is there anything else for you, Gavin? Anything we haven't covered?"

Gavin shook his head. "No, that's all."

She turned to Aspen. "Could you come over here, Aspen?"

Aspen stood, and she and Gavin changed places.

Patrice took Aspen's hands and held them for several seconds and then, as with Gavin, she released them and sat back in her chair.

"Aspen, you have been through a harrowing experience."

Aspen's eyes widened, but then she nodded. "Oh, yes, the lake and the coma."

Patrice smiled slightly. "I mean, where you have been."

Now Aspen was puzzled. "The water?"

Patrice nodded. "Where did you go while in the water?"

Aspen shrugged. "I have no idea."

"Yes, you do. Think."

Aspen looked from Gavin to Noah, to Kiryn and then at each of her parents.

"I don't know. I just remember standing on the dock, and then water, and then waking up in the hospital."

"You mentioned a person—"

Aspen's eyes widened. "A—a boy. With red hair—"

"And freckles?" asked Noah.

"I think so, but I don't know anyone like that."

"Could you have met this person while in the coma?" asked Patrice.

"You mean in a dream?"

"You tell us."

Aspen winced and squeezed her eyes shut. When she opened them, she shook her head as if to clear her thoughts. "It seems like there is this memory of something, and I am like right on the brink of remembering, and then it is gone."

Patrice sighed and patted Aspen's hand. "It will come. Something will spark your memory, and it will come to you."

Aspen nodded slowly, but then she looked past Patrice. There it was again. An almost remembering. She closed her eyes and then suddenly opened them. "Boys! A road or a divide or something and boys! I can see boys, too, Gavin."

"Does one of them have red hair?" Kiryn leaned toward Aspen.

"No. I can't see individual boys. Just a group of them… I think."

Kiryn plopped back in her seat, "Oh."

"Aspen, can you remember anything else while you were in the coma?"

Aspen sat quietly for several seconds and then finally answered, "No. I honestly can't."

"Okay. Let's leave that alone for now." Patrice turned to Jackson. "Could you take this chair?"

Aspen stood now and sat by her mother while her dad took the chair in front of Patrice.

Patrice grinned as she held her hands toward Jackson. He hesitated and then allowed her to take both of his hands in hers.

Patrice closed her eyes, but she did not open them soon as she had with Gavin and Aspen.

A bird chirped in a nearby tree and Patrice's cat meandered across the porch, but there were no other sounds or movement. Everyone was perfectly quiet.

Finally, after at least five minutes, Patrice opened her eyes. She still held Dad's hands as she looked deep into his eyes, but then she released them and sat back in her chair.

But Dad did not sit back. He stayed erect, his hands on his knees.

When Patrice didn't speak immediately, he blurted, "What?"

Patrice closed her eyes briefly, and then she began, "Jackson, there are so many things that I can see when I hold your hands. You have experienced a lot of sadness and grief in your past. I believe that your grandfather was a tortured man, and subsequently, he passed that onto your father."

This was not news to Aspen, after Dad's description of his relationship with his father.

Rocky said quietly, "We believe Jackson's grandfather knew his daughter had been murder before he died and also that he had information about something going on with the disappearance of several boys that worked for the company Allen owned with Kenneth Dixon."

Patrice listened intently, but then suddenly she turned to Jackson, looked directly at him and completely changed the subject.

"What about the three teenagers from school?"

The look on Dad's face was unmistakable agony.

"They were— They— I didn't participate, but they threatened to—"

Jackson covered his face with his hands.

"To what? Who were they, Jackson?"

Three boys were news to both Aspen and Noah, and they exchanged a puzzled look. By the look on Mom's face, Aspen could see this was news to her as well.

Dad did not offer an explanation, but instead, it was Rocky who started to explain.

"I— I think I know what Jackson may be talking about."

All eyes turned toward Rocky, but he was looking at Jackson, and he hesitated.

Jackson slowly raised his head, but he didn't say anything.

Rocky said slowly, "Landon. That was you?"

"If you're talking about the deaths that wasn't me—"

"I know. I mean that was you the boys were talking about before they died."

Jackson nodded.

Rocky coughed nervously, and Aspen looked around at the bewildered expressions on everyone's faces, and she knew hers would be included.

Jackson still addressed Rocky. "How did you know?"

"I'm a history buff and a teacher. I have read a lot about the history of Sommerville, and, well, just history."

Jackson sighed. "Jimmy Landon was my best friend in middle school. His family wasn't wealthy or anything like that. We just hit it off and hung out together all the time. He had twin brothers who were three years older than us, Russ and Mike. They were always in trouble. It was hard to believe they were even related to Jimmy.

"I had confided in Jimmy, you know, about some of the problems I had with my dad, and stuff." Jackson looked at his wife, and she nodded.

"Anyway, I guess Jimmy told his brothers about my—my gift…" he looked at Aspen and rolled his eyes. "They took it completely out of context. They thought I could find stuff—hidden stuff— that kind of thing, and they wouldn't let up."

"What did they want you to find?"

Jackson's sigh was labored as he contemplated Noah's question.

"Maybe I can explain—" said Rocky, and he waited.

Jackson nodded.

"According to the newspaper articles, someone had buried a lot of money. The reports suggested it was money that had been either earned or stolen from the old Allen-Dixon company. Supposedly it was a lot—over a million dollars, and it was apparently in cash."

"Russ and Mike wanted me to find it for them," said Jackson. "Well, of course, I had no idea how to do that. One afternoon, they invited Jimmy and me to go with them to see a movie in Memphis. I didn't want to go, but Jimmy begged me. He was always trying to get his brothers to like him. He was kind of a nerd. Smart kid, you know, and his brothers were dumber than stumps."

"We never did go to Memphis. They had never planned on that. Instead, we drove all over Sommerville. They were told the money was buried under a tree." Jackson shook his head. "A tree! Like there are so few in this state!"

A low chuckle, almost a grunt, came from all of them at his reference to the obvious.

Jackson continued, "We went to every old tree in the city, and then some. Every time they would make me get out of the car and stand under the tree. Every time nothing happened. I had no idea how to find anything!"

"We were only thirteen. His brothers were big, tough high school guys, and soon they started slapping Jimmy around because I couldn't find the stupid money. I tried to get them to stop. I have to admit they scared me."

"Did they hit you, Dad?"

"No, Aspen, I think they knew better. They were afraid of my dad, well at least of his money and influence. Finally, they told me since they knew my family had money that I had better figure out a way to get them some cash or they would hurt my sister. I believed them. They were notorious for beating people up. They were always in juvenile detention."

Jackson stopped talking as if he didn't want to tell them what happened next.

After a few seconds, Rocky said, "There was an accident. According to the reports, they had a gun with them, right, Jackson?"

He nodded, and then said quietly, "Yes, they did, and they were messing around with it. I wasn't afraid they would shoot us. They weren't that crazy, but then the gun went off. Mike was holding it, and he shot Jimmy—dead. I mean the bullet went right into his chest. I knew it was an accident, but Mike freaked out and started screaming and waving the gun around. Russ grabbed him and shoved him in the car, and they took off."

Jackson looked at Rocky who explained further, "No one is sure what happened after that except that there was an accident. The boys were both killed. Russ was driving and had a gunshot wound in the head and must have wrecked the car. Mike was thrown out of the car, and it rolled on top of him."

Suzann began weeping. "I honestly don't think I can take any more of this depressing information."

This had all been hard on their mother. Her life in California was never tainted by abuse or murder or any other such things. She came from a normal family—as normal as a family can be. Now she was learning about things her husband had experienced that she would only imagine as something to be read in a book or seen in a movie—a horror movie.

Jackson turned in his chair to face his wife. "I'm sorry, Suzann."

Sobbing, Mom all but jumped out of her chair and flung her arms around Jackson. "I'm just so sorry that you had to go through all of this, Jackson!"

Dad hugged her but didn't say anything.

Rocky quietly summed things up for the group. "Jackson was never blamed for anything, but the stories that circulated had to be hard to listen to. I never put it together, Jackson. Your dad was pretty good at keeping your name out of the papers. I had no idea."

"Money talks," mumbled Jackson then he said, "More validation for my dad to think I was a freak." Jackson chuckled, and the gift? Well, guess who I started seeing?"

Aspen gasped. "Those boys?"

Jackson nodded and looked at Patrice, "All three of them. Jimmy is always in the background with his head down. Mike and Russ are always mad and demanding to know where the money is. They are always by some stupid tree."

"Was it ever found?" asked Gavin.

"Not that I know of." Jackson looked at Rocky, who shook his head.

"Me either."

Patrice had been silent—listening. Now she said quietly, "The same tree?"

Jackson's eyes widened, and then his brow furrowed. He looked at Rocky, and then at Noah and Aspen. He slowly nodded. "Yes, I think so."

Patrice took a deep breath. She slowly let it escape before she said, "Jackson, stop running from this gift. Embrace it as Aspen has done. You too, Gavin."

Gavin sat up as if to say, "*Me?*"

Patrice smiled. "All of you. And don't be afraid. There are many mysteries to be solved with these types of gifts, but most people ignore them or push them aside, either because they don't think they are real or fear stops them. Many times, it is fear—not only of the gift itself but of ridicule from friends, family, teachers, or clergy."

Sara suddenly reached for Gavin's hand, and he stood and walked over to her. "I have been afraid for you, Gavin. I'm sorry. I just saw what my sister experienced in this town, and I—" she glanced at Rocky, "We, didn't want that for you."

"It's okay, Mom. I get it." Gavin hugged his mother and then turned to Jackson, and his eyes twinkled. "Maybe you should concentrate a little more on that tree."

Everyone laughed, including Jackson, and even Mom.

34

DECEIT

"Well, everything looks good, young lady. I still can't believe you came through that ordeal unscathed."

"We can't either." Tears welled up in Mom's eyes, and she quickly glanced at Aspen. "Sorry."

"She promised not to do this anymore." Aspen laughed and hugged her mom's shoulders.

"You are a miracle, that's for sure." Doctor Harward patted Aspen's knee. "Makes me emotional too!"

Dad had been sitting quietly in the corner of the exam room, but now he spoke up, "So, we have nothing to worry about?"

Doctor Harward gave Dad a sympathetic look. "I know you're concerned, Mr. Allen, and believe me, if I thought there were any dangers that she could face because of the water, the coma, anything, I would tell you. There isn't. She checks out perfectly normal."

Dad sighed and stood. He put an arm around the shoulders of his daughter and his wife. "So, there is no way I can slow her down?"

Doctor Harward laughed, "I'm afraid not, at least not from a medical standpoint."

Finally, Dad smiled, "Okay." He looked at Aspen and kissed her forehead. "I guess you get free rein again."

"Thanks!" Aspen grinned at the doctor, spun around, and exited the exam room. She practically ran into the waiting room where

Noah, Gavin, and Kiryn were holding vigil until she returned.

"I'm free!"

"Yay!" Kiryn jumped to her feet and hugged her friend. "Now we can drive to Memphis to see Gavin's doctor."

"Oh, yay." Gavin was much less enthusiastic, but he pulled Aspen to him with his free arm and kissed her cheek.

"Oh, please. You can do better than that." Kiryn teased.

Gavin raised his eyebrows. "Yeah, I can." He pressed his lips firmly against Aspen's, and she kissed him back.

"*Really?*"

Both Aspen and Gavin jumped, and Kiryn and Noah laughed.

"Busted!" Noah chuckled when he turned to see his parents standing in the door of the waiting room.

Mom smiled, and Dad shook his head. "I guess freedom deserves a kiss."

"Uh, yeah. Sorry, Mr. Allen." Gavin's dark complexion had turned a flaming shade of crimson.

Mom brushed the whole thing aside and walked directly to Gavin. "So, you are going to the doctor today as well?"

Gavin nodded as he quickly stepped away from Aspen. "Yes. I was supposed to go tomorrow, but Mom moved the appointment so that I can be here when we go to the big house."

"I hope all is well. How is your arm anyway?"

Gavin sighed. "I still have pain, but the good thing is, I am supposed to go without the brace for a few hours a day."

"That's good. How about physical therapy? Is that helping?"

"I guess it is. It hurts if that counts."

Mom laughed. "I'm sure that has to mean something."

"What are you guys doing today, Dad? Are you meeting with the attorney?"

"Not yet, Noah. Byron and Larry found the firm, but the owners are tight-lipped about any knowledge of the will, so they must subpoena them. Mom and I are going over to the house, and start going through things in the office."

Aspen quickly jumped in, "But not the storage, right?"

Dad smiled, "No, Aspen, not the storage. We'll do that tomorrow with you kids and Rocky."

Aspen sighed. "Good. I—we—want to be there when you—Never mind! See you tonight!"

She hurried out of the doctor's office, followed by Kiryn, Noah, and Gavin. She passed the two agents and sighed. "Well, I'm kind of free."

Sara told Kiryn the appointment with Gavin's doctor could take up to two hours, so she Noah and Aspen decided to get lunch.

Rocky was waiting for them when they dropped Gavin off at the clinic, and Sara arrived shortly after. Gavin was surprised Doug wasn't there because he usually was there for his appointments, but Sara said he had some things to take care of and would meet them in an hour.

Noah pulled the Iroc into a parking spot at the mall and the three piled out.

"Do those guys follow you everywhere?" Kiryn was looking at a black SUV parked three spots down.

Aspen sighed, "Yes. Sorry."

"Oh, I was just asking. I think they're cute."

Noah scowled. "They're a little old."

Kiryn laughed and punched his shoulder. "Oh, cool. You're jealous."

"I'm not jealous."

"Yes, you are." Kiryn chided. "They are old. Well, older than us, but they are still cute."

"Whatever."

Aspen laughed at Noah's sudden coolness.

Sometimes he is such a dork. Why doesn't he just admit that he likes her?

They found a table at a Chinese restaurant and started pouring over the menus.

"Well, that's interesting."

Aspen and Kiryn both looked up and turned to see what Noah was looking at.

Immediately, Aspen felt a stab in the pit of her stomach. Cassie was standing in the center of the mall with her back to them.

In Memphis? Is there no escaping her?

Aspen hadn't heard much about the witch rumors in a couple of weeks, but just the sight of Cassie caused immediate anxiety.

"What the—" Noah was still staring at Cassie, but now Aspen noticed the unusual group of people in the mall.

Cassie, Brandon Tuttle from school, and Dylan Dixon.

"So, are they dating?"

Aspen shrugged, "Who? Cassie and Brandon or Cassie and Dylan?"

Kiryn did not hold back her sarcasm, "Well, *Brandon,* of course, but I wouldn't put it past Cassie to be dating Dylan!"

"You're not serious?" Aspen didn't like Cassie, but she didn't know her well either. Brandon did not seem her type, but maybe he was.

"No, I'm not, but even Cassie and Brandon seems weird. He is a really nice guy."

"Yeah, he seems nice."

The girls turned back to their menus.

"C'mon, Noah, lets order," said Aspen.

Noah still didn't turn around. "Well, what do you make of that?"

Again, both girls looked up, but this time, they gasped in unison.

Dylan, Cassie, and Brandon seemed to be in a deep conversation, which seemed odd enough, only Aspen really didn't know what kind of connections they had. It was the next person that joined them that startled Aspen, and visibly Noah, and Kiryn.

Doug Mendel.

Gavin's step-dad, approached the group in the mall, and they chatted for a few seconds, Doug handed something to Dylan, which he immediately stuffed in his jeans pocket. Then Doug turned and abruptly walked away.

Noah, Aspen, and Kiryn were staring in silence.

Suddenly Kiryn stood, "I think I will just go find out."

Noah grabbed her hand and pulled her back to her chair. "No, didn't Sara say Doug was meeting them at the clinic?"

"Yes." Kiryn sat back down.

"We are going back there, let's see what Doug says—if anything—I don't think we should let him know that we saw him with those guys."

"Why? What do you think is going on?" Aspen drank some water, and then looked up when the server approached their table.

Noah shook his head. "I don't know, but something does not feel right.

Aspen's eyes narrowed. "Do you think it has anything to do with us—me?"

"Absolutely," said Kiryn flatly.

Aspen stared at her friend, and Kiryn added, "Everything right now has to do with you, Aspen, face it. There must be something up with them."

Aspen looked back out into the mall staring at nothing. "But what?"

Gavin and his mother were walking out the front door of the clinic when Noah, Aspen, and Kiryn arrived.

Doug was visibly missing.

Gavin grinned and waved at the sight of his friends and sister.

"So, what's the verdict?" Aspen linked arms with Gavin.

"Well, I'm afraid his prognosis isn't quite as good as yours, Aspen," said Sara. "But it isn't bad either."

"When I had the surgeries, they had to reattach muscles, stuff like that. Doc said if I ever want my arm to completely straighten out again, I will have to go through some pretty painful physical therapy."

"Why haven't they started that before now?" asked Kiryn.

"Couldn't. Had to wait for the bone to heal and the muscles, I mean I have been doing therapy, but now it's going to intensify—" Gavin dragged the last word and squeezed his eyes shut. "Hurts already."

"Hey! Sorry I'm late!"

They all turned to see Doug jogging up the steps.

"No worries. Took you longer than you thought, huh?" Sara kissed her husband on the cheek.

"Yeah, just drove here from Sommerville. Lots of traffic out on the main road."

"A meeting in Sommerville?" snapped Kiryn, and Aspen subtly elbowed her.

Doug gave Kiryn an annoyed look but turned to Gavin. "I'm sorry, buddy, I really meant to be here."

Gavin shrugged, "It's no big deal, Doug. Mom and Dad were here." He looked around, "Where is Dad anyway?"

Sara glanced at the door, "He was filling out some paperwork for your physical therapy. He wants you to be able to have it at home in Sommerville."

"Someone is going to come to my house to torture me?"

Sara laughed, "Or you can make the trip here three times a week."

"Uh, no thanks."

Rocky pushed the glass door open, "All done. Ready to go? Hey, there you are, Doug."

"Rocky." Doug reached for Rocky's hand.

"Has everyone eaten?" Doug looked around the group.

"Yeah, we did, we were at the—"

Aspen elbowed Kiryn again.

"Dairy Stop."

"That's where you went for lunch? You had plenty of time to go to a restaurant."

Kiryn nodded, "Yeah, it was yummy."

Sara shrugged, "Okay. Are you hungry Gavin?"

He shook his head, "No, I'll get something later."

Noah's phone buzzed, and he looked down at it, "It's Joseph Dixon."

"Wow, haven't heard from him in a while," said Gavin.

"What did it say?"

Noah looked at Kiryn. "Call me."

"Humph, well, okay, call him."

Noah scrolled the front of his phone. "Later."

Aspen looked curiously at her brother, but he wasn't paying any attention to her.

"Rocky, would you like to join Doug and me for lunch?"

"No thanks, Sara, I have a couple of things I need to do before tomorrow." Rocky quickly explained, "I am meeting with Mr. Weston."

"Who's that?"

"He's the guy who worked on the paintings in the storage," said Rocky.

"Ahh." Sara changed the subject. "Well, then we are going to get some Christmas shopping done."

"Oh, wow, Thanksgiving is next week." Aspen's eyes widened. "I can't believe it."

"Me either. That's why I am going to take advantage of this time."

"Did my parents mention to you about Thanksgiving?" asked Aspen.

"They did, Aspen, and it was sweet of them to invite us, but we actually have plans with Doug's family this year."

Aspen quickly looked at Gavin.

"I— We'll come over after dinner."

"What's this *we* stuff, Gavin? Rocky and I are going," said Kiryn.

"Oh." Gavin's face fell. "Okay, well, I will come over after dinner."

Aspen gave him a sympathetic look, but Sara did not waver.

"From what I hear, you are having quite a reunion over there. Gavin doesn't need to be there the whole day."

"Yeah, I guess Aunt Dana and Grandma are coming." Noah's eyes lit up. "I can't wait to meet Aunt Dana."

"She sounds like a character," said Rocky.

"I think she gets here day after tomorrow?" asked Noah. "Dad and Mom want her to go through Grandpa's office with them. That's where they are today."

Suddenly Doug seemed anxious to leave. He put his hand on Sara's back, "Well, we better get going. Good to see all of you. See you later, Gavin." And he gave his step-son a quick hug.

"Yeah, later," said Gavin.

Aspen noticed the puzzled look on Rocky's face when Doug abruptly ended the conversation, but then he shrugged and turned to the kids. "Okay, I will see you guys later. Are you coming to our house?"

They all nodded.

"Well then, guess I had better get some grub going."

35

WARNING

THE FOUR TEENAGERS CLIMBED in the Iroc and Noah started the engine, but didn't put the car in gear. Instead, he punched some numbers on his phone and waited.

"Hey, Joseph, it's Noah, what's up?" Then Noah punched the speaker icon.

"Thanks for calling me back." As usual, Joseph sounded nervous. "I overheard my Uncle Dylan talking on the phone, but I don't know who he was talking to."

"Okay—and?" asked Noah.

"Well, I just think maybe he is thinking of doing something stupid, it wouldn't be the first time. He gets these really radical ideas, and then he follows through with them."

"Like what? Did he say anything specific?"

"No. Well, sort of. I didn't hear all of it, but he said 'Maybe that will make them leave.' I think he might be talking about you guys."

Noah immediately turned toward Aspen, but she shrugged.

"Okay, Joseph. Hey, thanks for the information. Don't worry though. Aspen has FBI agents all over the place. I'm sure we'll be fine, but I will tell them this information."

"Yep. Okay, Noah. Uh—happy Thanksgiving."

Noah smiled, "You too, Joseph. See you at school." He touched the red phone icon, scrolled the front of his phone, and then put the car in gear, and backed out of the parking space.

"What was that all about?" asked Aspen.

"He sounded pretty worried."

Gavin nodded in Kiryn's direction. "He really did. What should we do?"

Noah hadn't said anything, but now he told Aspen, "Text Byron and Larry. Tell them so that they know in case anything comes of it."

Aspen nodded and immediately began sending a message to Byron. Seconds later, her phone rang. "Hi, Byron."

Pause.

"He didn't have any specifics, and he didn't know who Dylan was talking to."

Kiryn reached over Aspen's shoulder and touched the speaker icon on her phone.

Aspen laughed. "Byron you are on speaker."

"Oh, great, and whom might I be talking to?"

"Just us. Me, Kiryn, Noah, and Gavin."

Noah stopped the car in the parking lot before pulling onto the street, so that they could hear Byron through the speaker.

They all laughed, "Hi, Byron!"

"Uh, hi. So did Joseph have any kind of a time frame?"

"No," said Noah.

"And no other people involved."

"He didn't say," Noah repeated.

"He just said Dylan was talking about something, but he wasn't sure about what?"

"No, I mean, yes," began Noah, "But he also said he heard Dylan say, 'Maybe that will make them leave.'"

Byron was quiet.

"Are you still there?"

"Yes, I'm still here, Gavin. Just thinking. Where are your parents?"

"*My* parents?" asked Gavin.

"No, sorry, Jackson and Suzann."

"Oh, our parents are at the big house. They wanted to go

through some of the stuff in the office," said Aspen.

"And you have agents with you, right?"

Aspen looked around and immediately located the black SUV parked close by. She nodded, "Yes."

Again, Byron was quiet for a few seconds, and then he said, "Where are you kids? Still in Memphis?"

"Yes!"

The other three looked at Kiryn.

"Well, I wanted to talk too," she said quietly.

Even Byron laughed at Kiryn's outburst. "Okay look, don't worry about anything. I am going to send a couple of my guys over to your house just to be safe. Please let me know when you are back in Sommerville."

"Where are you and Larry?" asked Noah.

"Almost back to Sommerville. We spent the morning at the attorney's office."

"Any luck?"

"We'll see."

Noah shrugged, "Okay. See you tomorrow."

"Okay, you kids be careful."

The phone went dead.

Noah put the car in gear and pulled onto the street. "Do you guys think we have anything to be concerned about? I mean with Dylan and whoever?"

"You don't suppose—"

Aspen scowled, "No way, Kiryn. Cassie and Brandon wouldn't be involved in anything so stupid."

"What about Cassie and Brandon?"

Aspen suddenly realized Gavin didn't know what they were talking about. By the hesitant looks on Noah and Kiryn's faces, she wasn't sure how much they should tell Gavin.

Suddenly Kiryn said, "We saw them at the mall talking to Dylan."

"Oh, that's all." Gavin sank back into his seat.

"What do you mean is that all? Don't you find it a little odd?"

Gavin shook his head. "No, Dylan is Cassie's uncle."

"*What?* I didn't know that!" Kiryn sat straight up.

"It isn't well known because Cassie is an illegitimate kid of Dylan's sister, who was adopted by a cousin of Dylan. Cassie's adoptive parents stayed in the area, so Dylan's sister could see Cassie grow up. She was only fifteen when Cassie was born." Gavin said all of that so casually it irritated Kiryn.

"How come you never told me?"

"Because Cassie asked me not to tell anybody."

"Well, that makes sense. She may not want people to know," said Aspen and she was annoyed at herself at the sudden rush of jealousy of Gavin discussing Cassie—especially a secret the two of them held.

Gavin reached up and squeezed Aspen's shoulder. "First of all, why aren't you riding in the back seat with me, and second, it wasn't about Cassie at all. It was about protecting Cassie's birth mom. They wanted her to finish school and have a normal life, but Cassie's adoptive parents wanted her birth mother—"

"Is it Andrea?" asked Kiryn.

"No, the youngest sister, Melissa."

"Oh, wow, you would never know that!" Kiryn explained further for Noah and Kiryn, "She's a model, and she is beautiful."

"That's cool, Cassie isn't exactly ugly," said Aspen.

"Anyway..." Gavin continued, "They wanted Cassie's birth mother to know her. Cassie was fourteen before they told her who Melissa was."

"Okay, so maybe it isn't so odd that they were talking to them," said Noah.

An uncomfortable silence followed for Kiryn, Noah, and Aspen, but Gavin was oblivious to the deliberate omission of Doug's name.

36

YOU'RE USING ME

"I'M NOT SURE HOW I feel about this, Cassie. I don't want anyone to get hurt."

"Don't be silly, Brandon, no one is going to get hurt. Dylan just wants us to scare them."

"Why are you so bent on helping them?"

Cassie immediately turned and planted a passionate kiss on Brandon's unsuspecting lips.

"Money, silly—for you and me—lots of it!"

"I didn't think Joseph's family had much money."

"Well, they don't, yet, but, according to Dylan, they will."

"Have you even talked to Joseph about all of this?"

Cassie looked indignant, "No, of course not. Joseph and I don't associate at school. He's kind of, well, kind of a loser."

"He's actually a pretty nice kid if you get to know him."

"Humph, maybe. I don't care, whatever, Brandon. Don't go getting all soft on me."

"One more thing. What does Gavin's step-dad have to do with all of this?"

Cassie flipped her head to one side, whipping her long hair in Brandon's face, "I have no idea. I don't ask questions. He's a nice man, and he likes me. More I think, than that Aspen Allen witch girl."

"Cassie, she's not a witch."

Cassie spun around to face Brandon, who was looking down at his hands. "You don't know that. You haven't lived here your entire life like I have. There are stories—"

"Exactly. Stories—" Suddenly Brandon looked up. "You want her gone so that you can have Gavin back, don't you? You don't really care for me at all, do you?"

"Don't be silly," cooed Cassie. "I don't want Gavin back. He is annoying. Dylan just wants the Allens gone." She leaned into Brandon's shoulder. "C'mon, let's finish what we started, and get out of here."

Everything was in place now. They had followed Dylan's instructions to the tee. They jumped back in Brandon's truck and drove away. As they did, Brandon noticed Dylan some ways off, camouflaged by trees. His heart began pounding, and he suddenly felt sick to his stomach.

Out on the main road now, Brandon slammed on the brakes jerking the truck to a stop. He grabbed his cell phone off the dash and punched in only three numbers.

"Yes, I'd like to report a fire."

Cassie grabbed the cell phone and pushed the end icon. "What are you doing?! You are such an idiot!"

Brandon glared at her, and leaned across her and opened the passenger door, "You're right, I *am* an idiot for ever getting involved with you and this mess. Get out of my truck."

Cassie laughed nervously, "C'mon Brandon. You're just scared. No one will ever know we were involved."

"Yes, they will because I'm going to tell them. This is insane. *You're* insane! *GET OUT!*"

Cassie scooted across the seat and jumped out of the truck. She screamed as she slammed the door. "You'll regret this, Brandon Tuttle! I promise you will!"

Brandon floored the gas pedal. He was shocked at what he had just done. In his rearview mirror, he saw Cassie standing on the side of the road and from his side mirror, smoke started to billow above the trees.

Sirens screamed in the distance. Relieved, he slowed down, steered his truck off the road, and slammed it into park. Leaning his forehead on the steering wheel, he cried.

37

FIRE!

SUZANN WAS EXHAUSTED. THE search through the office had not revealed much. Mostly a lot of books. She and Jackson had decided to call it a day as they had found nothing significant.

She looked up to see Jackson standing in the doorway of the office, looking out into the hall.

"What's wrong, Jackson?"

"I was just thinking that I wish I had the courage to go back up the stairs and try to figure out what—"

Suzann was immediately to his side and put her hand on his shoulder. "It's okay, Jackson. Maybe that will not be necessary. Maybe that was just something from the past."

Jackson shrugged. "I hope you're right."

"The bookcase."

"What did you say?"

"Huh? I didn't say anything."

Jackson turned around and looked back toward the massive wall of bookcases. "You didn't just say 'The bookcase?'"

Suzann chuckled. "No, Jackson, you really are tired."

Jackson gently pushed her hand away and walked deliberately to the bookcase. He felt a strong presence, and this time—for the first time—rather than turn away, he stood quietly, listening.

Suzann still stood in the doorway, "Jackson, you're scaring me."

Jackson pumped the air with one hand. "Shhh. Don't be afraid."

"The bookcase."

Jackson heard it again and then noticed movement at the bottom of the bookcase, where the bottom panel met with the floor. The corner was moving as though someone was pulling on it.

"Suzann come here! Help me!"

Anxious now, and with Suzann's help, he pulled on the edge of the panel. It appeared to be simply an oak panel that typically would be used for cosmetic appearance to hide unusable space and unfinished wood.

After several attempts, the panel finally gave way, revealing small finish nails that held it in place. They pulled the end loose and then, like a domino effect, the entire panel fell away and onto the floor. It wasn't nailed at all, but simply lodged into place and fit so perfectly, it did not move.

Jackson and Suzann stared in disbelief at the row of wood file drawers. There were at least fifteen and each with the same small square label on the front.

Jackson bent down and rubbed his hand across the first label and read aloud, "Allen-Dixon Inc. Worker Files." He turned and looked at his wife, and for a second, he froze.

Quickly he turned and pulled the handle on the first drawer. It did not give easily, but with a little force, he was able to pull it out a few inches. He reached in and removed the first file.

Jackson stood and read the name on the file to Suzann.

ROBBIE ACKERMAN — 17

"Jackson, do you think?"

"What else could it be?"

"This is amazing. We have to call Larry and Byron."

At that second, Jackson's phone rang. He punched the green phone icon and said to Suzann, "It's Hank."

The expression on Jackson's face changed from elation to horror. "Where are the kids?!"

Immediately, panic gripped Suzann. *"Jackson?"*

"Okay, we are on our way." He grabbed Suzann's hand and pulled her down the hall toward the front door of the Mansion House.

"*Jackson, what is it?*"

"A fire, but the kids are okay." He pushed her in front of him, and as they exited the door, he reached back to pull it shut.

Shocked at what he saw at the end of the hall, he hesitated only briefly, closed the door, and ran with Suzann to the truck. Already he could see smoke billowing above the trees.

Jackson started the truck and screeched out of the driveway, not bothering to lock the gate. His mind a jumble of confusion at the phone call he had just received, and the image he had seen in the hallway.

Krista?

"Looks like a fire somewhere." Kiryn directed everyone's attention to the smoke snaking into the sky.

"That's a pretty big fire," said Gavin.

Noah kept driving, but asked for a direction, "Where are we going? To your house?"

"Well, I want to eat. We drove all the way from Memphis, and I am still starving."

"Of course you are!' Kiryn smacked her brother on the shoulder.

"Want to go to Bill and Nada's? We haven't been there in a while."

"Sure."

They pulled up in front to see men rushing from the popular café and jumping into vehicles.

Noah turned off the engine just as Bill exited the café. He immediately saw the kids and rushed up to the car. "Gavin, there is a fire."

"Yeah, we saw that. What is it?"

Bill looked directly at Noah. "From what I understand, it's your house?"

Noah started the engine and threw the Iroc into reverse, but Bill grabbed Noah's arm. "Leave it. Rocky is on his way."

"Here?" Gavin jumped out of the car this time, not caring if Noah minded that he did not open the door.

"Yes, he had just finished lunch and left when he got the call, but then I saw you kids pulling in."

Rocky's truck screeched to a halt behind the Iroc, and the four kids climbed in.

"Dad, what's happening?"

"I'm not sure, Kiryn. I just got a call from Hank. All I know is that there is a fire at the Allen's."

Aspen's heart felt as though it would burst. She didn't think her parents were there, but she really wasn't positive. What about the journal, the statue, her book about Krista, her beloved stuffed giraffe, Sprinkle. She was a little surprised at the things that suddenly seemed most important.

She looked over to see Noah staring at her.

Could this be what Joseph was talking about? It seemed improbable.

She felt Gavin's hand on her shoulder, and he attempted to pull her back toward him.

She turned, smiled, and instead took his hand. She simply could not relax. He squeezed her hand. She looked over at Kiryn, whose silent tears were streaking her face.

Is there something wrong with me? Why aren't I crying?

There was no way to get to the little house as the main road was lined with cars and trucks, so Rocky found a place to park and the five jumped out, immediately running toward the driveway.

Two police officers Aspen didn't recognize stopped them. She fully expected Kiryn to call them by name, but surprisingly she didn't.

Aspen glanced at the patrol car parked nearby—Tennessee Highway Patrol—these were not local cops.

"This is their house," Rocky explained, referring to Noah and Kiryn.

"Sorry. We can't let them go down there."

"Are their parents in there?"

The first policeman shook his head. "I have no idea, sir."

The second policeman added, "We do know this though, someone called it in. It would have been a lot worse. From what we understand, it's pretty much confined to the garage."

"If it helps at all, we have not heard there was anyone inside," said the first policeman.

"I wonder who would have seen it? It's pretty isolated down there," said Gavin.

"Maybe someone from the street."

"Rocky!"

They all turned to see Drew and Dylan running across the street toward them.

"What happened? We came as fast as we could," said Drew.

"No clue," said Rocky. "I guess the garage caught fire."

"Was anyone hurt?" asked Drew.

"We're not sure, but we don't think so."

"Neither Dad or Mom are answering their phones!" Noah sounded anxious. "I wish—"

Aspen's phone rang, and she punched the phone button, "Hello?"

Pause.

"*MOM!* Where are you? We have been trying to call you and Dad!"

Pause.

"Yes, we're okay, we're at the end of the driveway."

Pause.

Noah reached over and punched speaker on Aspen's phone.

"I'm sorry, Aspen, I left my phone at the big house and Dad dropped his somewhere between the truck and here. I borrowed this phone, but for a while, I couldn't remember any phone numbers."

Aspen looked down the driveway. Dad's truck was parked haphazardly off to the side. She hadn't noticed it before.

"We're coming out right—"

Screaming sirens made it impossible for them to hear Mom, and the policemen ushered them out of the way to allow another firetruck to get through.

"I didn't even see the smoke. I'm parked on the road on the other side of the lake."

Noah looked at Dylan. "Why were you parked there?"

"My truck broke down. I called Drew, and he came and got me. Didn't know there was a fire till the trucks passed me."

Drew said, "I was clear on the other side of town when Dylan called, and while I was on my way, Bill called to let me know about this. Once I was headed this way, I could see the smoke."

"Aspen! Noah!"

They both turned to see their parents running toward them.

The minute Aspen saw them, she burst into tears. "What happened?"

Dad hugged his wife and two kids. "We're not sure. The garage is pretty much gone."

"Along with my car," said Mom.

"Oh, Mom, I'm sorry!" said Noah.

"Sorry? Don't be silly. It's a car! We are all okay; that's what matters." She hugged her kids tighter.

One of the police officers said, "Folks, could we get you to move across the street, please?"

They all immediately obeyed.

Aspen wiped the tears from her cheeks, relieved that her mom and dad were okay.

While they were walking, Dylan lit up a cigarette.

"Don't do that here, Dylan. These folks don't smoke."

Dylan glared at his brother, but dropped it to the ground and crushed it with the toe of his boot.

Aspen couldn't help but notice how nervous he seemed. She locked eyes with Kiryn who was biting her lip. Aspen knew she was dying to say something sarcastic to Dylan but, impressively, she said nothing, and just glared at him. Although Dylan wasn't looking in Kiryn's direction, so he didn't see the death stare. Despite everything, it made Aspen chuckle. Kiryn's glare intensified as though staring harder might make Dylan look at her.

"So much for Thanksgiving—" Mom said.

"That's right! And Aunt Dana and Grandma! What are we going to do?" wailed Aspen.

"We could stay at the big house—" Dad ventured slowly.

"Not on your life!" said Mom.

"No!" said Noah at the same time.

"I was only kidding. I don't want to stay there either."

"What about the little house, Dad?" asked Aspen.

"There is plenty of insurance on this place, Aspen. It will be repaired in no time."

Aspen shrugged.

Mom walked away from the group and sat down on the ground. She leaned against a tree. "I'm really tired."

Mom wasn't crying, but she suddenly looked drawn. "What are we going to do with Grandma and Dana, Jackson?"

"Well, Thanksgiving is no problem, and we can make room for all of you to stay with us," said Rocky.

"Oh no—"

"It will be fun, Mrs. Allen!" said Kiryn. "Noah and Aspen stay all the time."

Mom laughed. "It's okay Rocky, we can stay at the hotel, but we will take you up on your kitchen for Thanksgiving."

Rocky nodded, "Done."

"Mr. Allen?"

Dad and Rocky turned as the policeman approached, and Dylan and Drew joined them.

Suddenly Mom started to cry.

Noah walked over and plopped down next to her. "It's okay, Mom. As you said, we are all okay."

Aspen, Gavin, and Kiryn joined Mom, and they all sat in the dirt.

"I know," said Mom quietly. "I guess I was just hoping for some semblance of normal for the holidays."

"I can't see that happening any time soon," said Kiryn.

"Thanks for that, Kiryn," said Gavin.

"Well, it's the truth."

"No, she's right. What was I thinking?" Mom chuckled softly, but tears still ran freely down her cheeks.

Aspen looked across the street. The black SUV that had been following them had parked just down from Rocky's truck, and now two more FBI agents walked from the driveway and joined the first two.

"Are they coming to dinner, too?" mumbled Aspen.

They all looked in the direction of the four agents, who suddenly looked more official than ever in their black suits and ties.

Mom sighed. "Probably. Kiryn's right. I guess normal won't happen for a while."

38

COMPANY

ASPEN LOOKED OVER AT Kiryn who was still sleeping. She quickly dressed, pulled on her sweats and running shoes, and stepped out onto the front porch of Rocky's house. She stopped short at what she saw.

Snow.

Aspen had never seen snow falling from the sky. Tiny snowflakes fluttered through the air, immediately melting upon contact with the ground.

She whirled around and ran back inside. She jogged up the stairs and knocked on Gavin's door.

"You guys, it's snowing!"

Several seconds passed before the door cracked open.

"What?" Gavin was still rubbing the sleep from his eyes.

"It's snowing!"

Gavin perked up, "Seriously?"

"Yes! Noah, come on, it's snowing."

The door flew open and Noah, still in boxers, and a t-shirt, burst past Gavin.

Aspen followed him down the stairs, and Kiryn met them at the bottom. Gavin stumbled down the stairs behind them.

"This is amazing!" Aspen squealed.

"I take it you've never seen snow before," laughed Kiryn.

"No, not ever like this!" said Aspen. She stepped out onto the sidewalk and held her hands out in front of her allowing the snow-flakes to fall onto her open palms and disappear.

"Well, once at Big Bear, but it wasn't snowing. I think a lot of it was made with snow machines that year."

Kiryn and Gavin exchanged a puzzled look.

Noah explained, "When it doesn't snow in the mountains in Southern California, they have these big machines that make snow, but it's usually only on one ski run."

Noah followed Aspen and let tiny snowflakes melt into his hand.

Kiryn and Gavin snapped pictures of them with their cell phones.

"This is kind of a miracle," said Gavin.

"Yeah, it is, we don't get much snow around here, and this is usually what it does too—melts. Mostly it just rains." Kiryn continued to take pictures.

"This is a great day!" laughed Aspen. She looked at Noah and then ran to him and threw her arms around his neck. "Isn't this a great day?"

Noah laughed at his sister but hugged her back. "Yeah, it is."

Grandma and Aunt Dana's planes were landing at 7:30 am and 8:00 am, so Mom and Dad assured their kids, and Rocky they would be back to the big house by 10:30. When they pulled into the driveway, Aspen and Noah were waiting for them. The snow had stopped, but both kids couldn't wait to tell their parents about it.

Rocky decided the Allens needed some time, so he told Jackson that he, Gavin, and Kiryn were going to join them after Gavin's physical therapy.

Noah rushed to the truck and opened his mom's door, "Did you see the snow, Mom?"

"Yes! I wished we had all been together. I don't think you kids have actually seen it snowing, right?"

"First time, and it was awesome!" Aspen opened the back door and took Grandma's arm when she jumped out.

"Be careful, Mom!"

"I'm fine. Do you think I'm old?"

Suzann laughed and rolled her eyes, "Okay, Mom."

Grandma pulled her grandkids into a tight hug, and they hugged her back. "So good to see you kids, and you're standing!" she said to Aspen.

She released them and laughed, "But is it safe? I mean, the last time I was here, Aspen, you were in the hospital, and now your house had a fire?"

"Seriously!" Aspen laughed too. "We're sorry. Mom wanted this to be a normal Thanksgiving."

"*Normal?* With this family? I doubt that. Since your mom met your dad, they have been traveling—spending way too much time in the ocean where I am sure sharks were awaiting their arrival—and then they took you two little kids to the same probable fate! You survived that, but now more trouble." Grandma laughed heartily.

Noah looked puzzled. "Grandma, you live on the beach."

"Yes, but I do not go *in* unless I am in a boat. I *look* at and *listen* to the ocean." She laughed again and then she lowered her voice. "But, shhh, don't tell your parents. That's why I love to spend time with this family. Always so much happening; crazy as it is at times!"

"I heard that, Mom."

"Well, it's the truth." Grandma lifted her chin toward Suzann but winked at Noah and Aspen.

Aunt Dana and Dad walked around the truck and joined them.

"Aspen, Noah, this is my sister, Aunt Dana."

As tall as Aspen, Aunt Dana had long dark hair and a smile that spread across her entire face. The only person Aspen knew with that broad of a smile was Kiryn.

The resemblance to their dad was unmistakable. Aunt Dana was as pretty as Dad was handsome and dressed in jeans, a t-shirt, and tennis shoes. Aspen liked her already.

Noah held out his hand, but Aunt Dana pushed it aside and

pulled him into a tight squeeze. "I've waited a lot of years to meet my brother's kids, and I don't intend on just shaking your hands!"

She released Noah and pulled Aspen into the same tight hug, stood back, and looked them both up and down. "So these are the trouble causers, Jackson?"

Dad laughed, "These are they."

Aunt Dana continued, "I've heard all about you from your Grandma and your mom. Your dad hasn't said much except to agree. I can't wait to get to know you both." And without warning, she removed her sunglasses and wiped tears from her cheeks.

"Dana?" Dad sounded surprised.

"Oh, be quiet, Jackson. I am just so happy to finally meet your family." She smiled at Mom and then hugged Dad. "I love my big brother."

Aspen suddenly choked up, and so did Mom.

Dad squeezed Aunt Dana. "It's been a lot of years." He too, choked on his words. "But here we are."

"What should we do first?" Aunt Dana rubbed her hands together, and Noah and Aspen quickly exchanged smiles.

She's cool.

"Well, we have hotel rooms for both of you, since our house is uninhabitable right now," said Dad.

"Can't we stay right here?"

"*NO!*" Mom, Dad, Aspen, and Noah all responded in unison, making everyone laugh.

Aunt Dana raised her eyebrows and pursed her lips, "Alrighty then." She turned to Grandma. "Hopefully, we will know why sooner or later."

"Oh, it will be soon."

"Noah!" Mom glowered.

"Sorry—"

Aunt Dana's eyes became narrow slits. "Well, I can see I will need to collaborate with the kids to get any information."

"We'll tell you. There's just a lot to tell," said Dad.

"Well let's get going! We're burnin' daylight here! That's from an old—" Aunt Dana must have caught the look on Aspen's face.

Aspen could not believe her ears. She was shocked to hear her aunt, whom she had never met, use the same phrase Krista had used about wasting daylight instead of surfing.

"Did I say something wrong?"

"No," Dad put his arm around his sister. "That's an expression that a close friend of Aspen's used to say when they surfed."

"I would like to meet this friend. Great minds you know!"

"Uh, she's— She's not here. I mean she's dead."

"Oh, I am so sorry, Aspen! I will try not to say that anymore."

"No, it's okay. I mean, it's kind of nice to hear it again."

Aunt Dana linked arms with Aspen. "We need a drink, Jackson."

Now Jackson's eyebrows shot up. "You drink now?"

"Oh, good grief, I was talking about a Coke!"

Noah grinned. "You're going to fit right in, Aunt Dana. C'mon, let's go to Bill and Nada's."

The same welcoming hospitality was shown to the group when they arrived at the café, except even more so today in the aftermath of the fire.

The servers pushed some tables together when Noah told them there would be three more people joining them and quickly texted Kiryn to tell them to come to the café instead of the big house.

"How bad was the damage, Jackson?" Bill asked as he approached their table. Then he turned to Dana. "Wow, good to see you around here again!" and he gave her a quick hug.

Jackson shook his head. "I have no idea. They haven't let us in yet, but from what I understand, we can go over today." He turned to Suzann. "Maybe we should do that after we leave here."

"Yes, please, Dad," said Aspen.

"Well, I would have gone over first thing this morning, but when I called the fire department, they told me they still had people there checking for hot spots."

Noah looked puzzled, "Why? I thought it was a fire in the garage."

"Didn't the snow help?" asked Aspen.

"There wasn't that much snow, Aspen, but apparently that little bit of snow helped in other ways."

"What does that mean?" asked Mom.

"I'm not sure. We'll find out when we go down there." Dad turned to Noah, "Is Rocky meeting us here?"

"Yeah, Kiryn just texted me."

"Let's order then."

The next hour was spent eating a late breakfast and filling Aunt Dana and Grandma in on all the details. Those Dad thought they needed to know. He had cautioned Aspen and Noah earlier that some of this stuff needed to be told gently and in pieces, and not to bombard them—especially Grandma—with all of the unusual details.

They were constantly interrupted by people stopping to say hi to Aunt Dana. Once again confirming for Aspen that Sommerville was a small town.

After hearing all that they *did* tell them, Grandma seemed unaffected. "What I want to hear about is these friends, Kiryn and Gavin. Aren't these the new love interests of you kids?"

Noah's face immediately flushed, and Aspen laughed, "You'll have to ask Noah about that, but yes, they are the best friends ever."

That familiar twinge hit Aspen's heart, and she immediately thought of Krista.

Grandma's eyes twinkled, "C'mon, Noah, give."

Noah scowled at Aspen, "Yes, I like, Kiryn. Of course, I like Kiryn!"

"Well, gee, that's good news."

Noah spun around in his seat coming face-to-face with Kiryn, who cocked her head to one side.

Noah jumped to his feet, "Hi! Grandma, this is Kiryn—"

Grandma grinned at Kiryn, and Gavin quickly reached for her hand. "And I'm Gavin. This is our dad, Rocky."

Grandma laughed out loud. "So nice to finally meet all of you."

Dad introduced Aunt Dana and Rocky, who were already casually acquainted, and Kiryn and Gavin took the empty chairs on either side of Aspen and Noah. Rocky sat next to Aunt Dana.

Kiryn leaned across Noah to whisper to Aspen, "So, he likes me?"

Aspen whispered back, "Well, he is kind of a dork."

"Excuse me, don't talk about me like I'm not here." Noah glowered at them both.

"Well—" Kiryn demanded.

"Well, yes, I do like you, duh." He turned to his sister, "I'm not a dork." Then Noah said to Gavin. "Are you going to eat?"

Gavin looked surprised, "No."

Noah pushed his chair back from the table. "Good, you can ride with me." And he stood up.

Gavin glanced at Aspen and followed Noah out of the café.

"I guess we're riding with Rocky," laughed Aspen.

Kiryn's eyes widened, "Guess so!" And then both girls laughed along with everyone else at their tables.

"You're Grandma is a riot," said Gavin as Noah sped down the street away from the café.

"Yeah, she's pretty cool, but why would she say that?"

"Someone had to have told her something."

"Aspen most likely."

"Well, is that so bad? You do like my sister, right?"

Noah scowled and did not answer immediately.

"Well?"

"Well, it just seems kind of weird, you and Aspen, me and Kiryn. Brothers and sisters, you know."

"Dude, I'm not even related to Kiryn! Don't forget that, and besides, it's not abnormal. It happens."

"I know. Guess I'm just cautious."

"There is no hurry, to quote Rocky, 'You are still in high school.'"

"What? You talked to Rocky about Kiryn and me?"

Gavin laughed, "No, I talked to Rocky about Aspen and me."

"Oh, well, you two are obvious."

"That's a bad thing?"

"No, I didn't mean that. It's just that you two seem to know what you want, and I don't."

"You want to go back to California, don't you?"

"Eventually, but I wonder if that life still exists for me, or any of us."

"Of course, it does. You just left for a while."

Noah nodded.

"Do you think you can remember how to surf?"

"See! That's what I'm talkin' about! I don't know!"

"You don't lose skills like that, Noah, it will all come back to you, and, you will go back—" Gavin paused.

Noah looked over at him. "But?"

"But nothing, except Kiryn and I will go with you." Gavin leaned back against the seat, obviously satisfied with his statement.

Noah raised his eyebrows.

I hadn't thought of that.

39

ARSON

Hank was waiting at the driveway of the little house. Yellow tape stretched across the entire opening.

"What's going on?" Noah parked the car, and the two boys climbed out. The smell of smoke was unmistakable.

"How are you kids?" but Hank didn't wait for an answer. "Looks like we have a crime scene."

"*What?*"

"Yes, Noah, this fire was set intentionally. We told your parents we were all lucky someone called it in, or the house probably would have been leveled."

"Who was it? I mean, who called it in?"

"I can't tell you that, Gavin, everything is still under investigation, but we do have some leads."

They all looked up the road to the sounds of trucks approaching.

Jackson and Rocky both parked their trucks. Mom, Dad, Grandma, and Aunt Dana piled out of Jackson's and Rocky, Kiryn, and Aspen from Rocky's.

More introductions, and then Hank lead them all down the driveway.

"Do you know what's going on, Hank?"

"I do, Jackson, but I will let you talk to Kendall. He's heading up this investigation from the Fire Department. He actually asked for the assignment."

When they rounded the turn in the driveway, and the little house came into view, the gasps from the entire group was a vivid indication that they were not at all prepared for what they saw.

Even though Mom had seen the house earlier, she immediately started to cry, and so did Aspen. Dad put an arm around each of them. They all walked in silence until they reached another expanse of yellow caution tape.

Aunt Dana caught up with her brother, and he stepped back when she did.

They linked arms, "This is so sad, Jackson." Her voice caught.

He didn't have time to answer. A tall African-American emerged from the house, and walked deliberately toward them, extending his hand to Jackson.

Noah immediately spoke up, "Hey, aren't you one of the divers who were at the lake?"

The man smiled, "Kendall Washington, and yes." He immediately looked at Aspen. "You sure are looking better than the last time I saw you!"

Aspen only smiled. She had no idea who this man was.

Dad shook Kendall's hand. "Hank said you asked to be assigned here. Do you work for the fire department?"

Kendall nodded. "Arson investigations."

"Arson?" Mom's eyes widened.

Kendall nodded, "Yes, ma'am."

"Well, thank you for taking the job," said Dad.

Kendall smiled and looked directly at Aspen, "I kind of want to see the whole thing through, and besides I have kind of a personal interest."

"How so?"

Kendall answered Dad's question, "I'm not sure, sir."

Except for a portion of the roof that was still attached to the breezeway, the garage was completely gone. The burned skeleton of Mom's BMW was still sitting on the cement slab. Everything that was not burned to a crisp, or at least beyond recognition, was black or covered with pink fire retardant. Or wet. Very wet.

The outside kitchen wall which was connected to the breezeway was charred, and in some places burned entirely through.

When they went in the through the front door, the entire house smelled of smoke, and the walls had a thin layer of black dust, as did the furniture, floors—everything.

Kendall gave them the go-ahead to walk through the rest of the house, but more yellow tape across the kitchen entrance stopped them from going in there.

"Just until we make sure the roof is stable," Kendall explained.

Gavin, Kiryn, and Grandma stayed on the front porch, and Dana talked with Hank and Rocky.

Mom, Dad, Aspen, and Noah walked into each room together. Except for the smell and the black dust, everything looked the same.

Aspen quickly checked her bottom drawer for the journal and statue, and her closet for the huge scrapbook of her and Krista. Satisfied that all was in place, she asked her parents, "Can we take our stuff?"

Kendall heard her and responded, "Can you give us today? Then tomorrow you folks are welcome to come and get whatever you need." Then he asked Dad, "Have you contacted your insurance adjusters?"

Dad nodded, "Dana has. She has handled all of that for years."

"Okay. Well, no one else will be allowed into the house except for your family, and of course, officials. You will need to let us know when you will be coming, please."

Dad nodded.

"We found some more fire starting spots all the way around your house. Whoever did this, planned for the entire place to go up in smoke."

Dad's eyebrows furrowed, and he looked at Mom.

"Don't worry. We've got this." Kendall looked out the front window. "I assume those guys are with you."

Dad turned in the direction Kendall was looking and saw four agents standing in the front yard. He nodded, "Yes, they have to be with us. This mess makes it even more apparent."

"Understood." Kendall nodded to all of them. "We'll be in touch."

Dad shook his hand. "Thanks."

"Jackson, Hank was telling me about the snow. I guess it stuck in some imprints around the back of the house," said Rocky.

"Imprints? What kind of imprints."

"Footprints. The snow made them more noticeable because it stayed in them a little longer. They think they have some pretty good leads."

"I hope so. I didn't think anyone would go this far, did you?"

"No," said Rocky flatly. "I sure wish I knew who was behind it."

"I'm sure we'll know soon enough." Dad looked at his watch, "It's only 1:30. Why don't we go up to the house." His expression changed, and his eyes suddenly twinkled as though he had just remembered something, and he said, mostly for Rocky, "You will not believe what Suzann and I found."

"Okay, let's go," said Rocky, and they all started down the driveway.

Suddenly, Aunt Dana stopped, "Jackson, I'm going up the steps." She grinned at the four teenagers.

"Have fun." Jackson waved his hand. "See you up there." And he laughed.

"Anyone coming?" Aunt Dana's eyes twinkled.

All four teenagers jumped at the chance, but Mom, Grandma, and Rocky went with Dad.

Aspen glanced back to see Rocky looking right at her. He winked. She didn't know exactly why, but she assumed it was because they were getting a chance to talk to Aunt Dana.

Halfway up, Aunt Dana plopped down on a step. "Okay, so I forgot how steep they are!"

The rest of them sat down with her.

Suddenly, Aspen looked up at her newfound aunt, "We are so glad you're here."

Aunt Dana smiled, "Me too, Aspen. This—whatever it is with

your dad—has gone on way too long. I am so happy to see him here in this place. It just makes me sad that it never happened while Mom and Dad were still alive."

Noah was obviously using caution when he spoke, "Aunt Dana, do you know much about Dad and Grandpa's relationship?"

Aunt Dana sighed. "I don't think so, Noah. I know that it wasn't very good."

"It was really pretty horrible, or it seems like it was."

Aunt Dana removed her sunglasses, and the look in her eyes seemed far away. "I guess I want to remember only the good. That's about all I do remember. I wasn't that old when Mom and Dad were killed, and I went to live with my grandparents. I was probably twelve, I was just starting seventh grade, but I think a lot of things were kept from me. Our family had a lot of tragedy. A lot of death."

"Yeah, you did. Dad told us about it," said Aspen. We didn't know anything about any of you until we came to Sommerville. Even then, we didn't know details. Dad kept it all to himself."

Aunt Dana stood up now, and the rest followed. Gavin and Kiryn took up the rear, and even Aspen was surprised at Kiryn's silence. It wasn't like her.

When they reached the top of the steps, they all sat down on the benches, and Gavin sat on the steps. The expansive backyard and the massive Mansion House stretched before them.

"I am surprised every time I look at all of this. When I really take time *to* look," said Aspen.

"Surprised, why?" asked Dana.

"That it's so huge?" asked Kiryn, making Aspen smile.

"Exactly," said Aspen. "This place is so big!"

Aunt Dana sighed. "It's home to me, but in two different worlds. I do have fond memories of living here as a little girl, but mostly as an adult when Jerry and I lived here and took care of Grandpa," she said quietly, and Aspen could not help but notice the softness in her eyes.

"What was Grandpa like?" asked Noah.

Aunt Dana thought for several seconds. "Sad. I think that would best describe Grandpa, at least when we took care of him. He was very sad. He spent most of his time in his room or his office. We could never get him into any real deep conversations. He always got emotional, or he would just stare and say nothing."

"So, he was married to Faith, but what about our Grandma, Nina?"

"He loved Faith, he never said anything bad about her, but his entire countenance would change when he talked about Nina. He seemed lighter—or free—or something. It's hard to explain. The only problem is that he would only talk about Nina up until the time she had her nervous breakdown, and then it was as though she did not exist, and we all knew she wasn't dead."

"So when did she die?" asked Aspen.

"I'm honestly not sure. She lived in a home somewhere."

"But it seems like she died soon after she got sick," said Aspen.

Dana looked surprised. "No, I don't think so." She shrugged. "I'm not sure. I don't want to give you kids wrong information because I honestly do not know all the facts."

"Noah! Aspen!" Dad was standing on the back patio of the big house.

"Comin' Dad!" yelled Noah.

"Guess we better get moving." Aunt Dana stood, and everyone, but Gavin followed.

When she realized Gavin wasn't with them, Aspen turned around. "Hey!"

Gavin looked up, "Oh, sorry."

Aspen walked back to him. "What's up?"

He stood, took her hand, and they both walked toward the big house.

"Your aunt seems so in the dark about your Grandpa. Do you think it's possible that she could have lived with him—right in the same house—and not know more about him?"

"Well, I have lived with my dad my entire life, and I had no clue about him. The reality is that if they don't talk, how can we know anything?"

"I guess. It's just so different than my family. I mean, I know everything—" Gavin stopped.

"What?"

"Actually, you're right. I learned some stuff about my dad that I never knew just the other night."

"Is that bad?"

"No, not at all. Just that I didn't know he used to drink heavily, stuff like that."

"Oh, wow. What about your mom?"

"She's pretty much an open book. Doug, too, I don't think there is much to hide in their relationship."

Aspen nodded. She knew she needed to say something quickly to avoid an awkward silence. "That's good, that's the way relationships should be." She thought of Doug at the mall with Dylan, Cassie, and Brandon, and then of his total avoidance in telling Sara about it.

Gavin dropped her hand, put his arm around her, and pulled her close to him, but he winced when he did.

"How was the physical therapy this morning?"

He grimaced. "Brutal."

They went into the Mansion house through the kitchen door where everyone else was waiting.

Aspen couldn't dismiss the uneasy feeling about Gavin's stepdad.

I don't think Doug is all that honest.

40

DEAD FRIEND

Dad was leaning against the counter. He almost looked excited. In the wake of the fire the previous day, and considering how easily he became despondent, Aspen found it a little odd.

Mom, Grandma, and Rocky were sitting at the table when Aunt Dana, Noah, Kiryn, Gavin, and Aspen joined them.

"Okay, Jackson, we are all here. What's going on?" Aunt Dana seemed a little skeptical.

"I want to show all of you what Suzann and I found yesterday." Dad walked out of the kitchen, across the foyer, and into the hall leading to the office. The rest of them followed.

Once inside, he walked purposefully toward the wall of books, but then abruptly stopped and turned around.

"Jackson?" Mom came up behind him, but then she gasped. What the—"

"Mom, what?" asked Noah.

Dad turned and stared at Rocky. "There—yesterday—we found or at least we saw—"

Dad fell to his knees and began prying on the edge of a wood panel near the floor.

"Do you need some help, Jackson?" Rocky knelt next to him.

"It won't budge." Dad looked up at Mom. "How could this be?"

"*What* be? What are we talking about?" asked Noah, and he too knelt on the floor.

"Yesterday, this entire panel pulled away from the wall, and fell on the floor," said Dad.

Noah got closer to the floor to inspect the panel. "Dad, I'm not sure how that could be possible." He ran his hand under the lip of the wood overhang. "This is a solid piece of wood."

Dad laid on his back and looked up at the wood panel where it was joined to the front piece. It was solid. There was no way a piece could have separated without pulling the entire bottom row of books with it.

"What was different yesterday?" asked Rocky.

Dad sat up and leaned against the bookcase.

"The entire panel pulled away, and there were a bunch of file drawers behind it."

Instinctively, everyone turned to Mom.

"It's true. We even took a file out of one of them, and it had a name on it. The file drawers had Allen-Dixon on the front." Mom looked bewildered.

"That's how we left it when we got the call about the fire."

Gavin looked at Jackson, and then he dropped to the floor.

Noah joined him, and the two of them scoured the entire bookcase, running their hands under the edge and attempting to pull it away. Nothing.

"Just out of curiosity, what made you think to pull the panel off in the first place." Rocky stood and brushed his hands together. He was asking Jackson, who looked confused, and then he turned to Suzann.

Mom was looking at Dad as well, but when he didn't say anything, she became flustered and, still looking at Dad, she tried to explain, "I don't know. Everything happened so fast. First Jackson asked me if I said 'The bookcase,' then he started pulling the panel, and then there they were. The file drawers, I mean. Then the phone rang, and it was Hank and the fire———" She looked at everyone, and then seeming even more confused than before, she asked Dad, "Why did you ask me if I said 'The bookcase'? What did that mean?"

Dad was seemingly staring at nothing, and Aspen was afraid he was going to slip into his emotional despondency, but to her relief, he didn't. He looked up at all of them and pointed to the door.

"I was standing right there, we were leaving, and then I distinctly heard a voice—a girl's voice—say 'The bookcase.' I heard it twice. So, I went to the bookcase, and then I saw the edge of the panel moving like someone was pulling on it. Then Suzann and I pulled it off. What she is telling you is the truth. There were file drawers behind the panel, but it was flimsy not like this." And he knocked on the wood panel with his knuckles.

"Did you hear the voice, Mom?" asked Noah.

"No."

"Maybe it was Ronda," said Gavin.

"It wasn't," said Dad.

"*What?* Then who do you think it was, Jackson?" asked Rocky.

"Who's Ronda?"

Dad looked up at his sister. "Ronda was Grandpa's sister. The one who ran away."

Dana shook her head, "No, that was Riley. That much I do know. There was no Ronda."

No one said anything for several seconds, but then Kiryn spoke up.

"Well, actually, there was, *and* a Riley."

Aunt Dana's eyebrows shot up. "Where? How?"

"See, I told you there was a lot to tell you," said Dad.

"I'll say!"

"But wait, if you are sure it wasn't Ronda, Dad, who was it?" asked Noah.

Dad took a deep breath, and then let it slowly escape before he said anything.

"I'm pretty sure it was—Krista."

"What?!"

"I think so, Aspen, I haven't heard Krista's voice for a long time, but I heard it twice."

"You seem pretty sure though, Jackson," said Rocky.

Again, Dad sighed. "When Suzann and I were leaving for the fire, I saw her. She was standing in the archway of the hall. Right out there." He again pointed toward the door.

"Who's Krista?'

Aspen looked at Aunt Dana. "My friend."

Kiryn added, "Her dead friend."

41

THANKSGIVING

"I think that's the last piece of stemware." Kiryn placed the delicate glass back in the box and threw her dishtowel at Aspen. "Sara was kind to lend your mom all of these fancy dishes for us to wash. What is the point of china and crystal if you can't put them in the dishwasher?"

Aspen laughed. "I hear ya." She tossed the towel onto the counter and glanced around Rocky's kitchen. "But actually, it was perfect. Don't you think?"

Kiryn plopped onto the bench in the nook. She sighed deeply. "Yes, perfect."

Rocky and Noah came through the kitchen door.

"Tables are folded and put away."

"Where did you put them?" Kiryn eyed Rocky.

He chuckled. "In the garage. We'll return them to the school on Monday."

"I can't believe you lugged those over here, Rocky. We could have made it work without the long tables."

Rocky smiled. "We could have, but it was nice for Suzann, don't you think?"

The three teens nodded in agreement.

There was no mistaking the excitement in Mom's eyes when everyone took their places for Thanksgiving dinner. Aspen couldn't help but notice the pleased look on Dad's face too, and for a minute, she felt like everything would be okay.

Two long tables decked with white linens, china place settings, and crystal stemware. Turkey, dressing, cranberries, whipped potatoes, and gravy, corn, yams. Not to mention pumpkin and apple pies from Bill and Nada's and every other thing imaginable that Mom could think of to make this Thanksgiving dinner one that none of them would forget.

Suzann had planned to drive to Memphis to pick up some fancy paper plates and napkins and Dad offered to get silverware from the Mansion House, but Mom resisted, so he dropped the idea. When Sara heard the plan, she immediately intervened, and a beautiful Thanksgiving table was born.

Gavin and his mom had shown up Wednesday morning carrying boxes containing some of Sara's best dishes and table linens. She had more than enough for Mom, Dad, Aspen, and Noah. Rocky and Kiryn, Grandma and Aunt Dana, and two unfamiliar FBI agents.

The new agents had arrived that morning, relieving Byron Coulsen and Larry Brimhall, so that they could go home for the holiday weekend.

Aspen's phone rang, and she pulled it from her back pocket. "It's Gavin," she said absently.

"Hey!" she waited quietly and then said, "Oh, okay."

Kiryn, Noah, and Rocky immediately detected the disappointment in her voice.

"So can I do anything? Is everything okay?" Again, Aspen was silent. She listened and then she perked up. "Okay, that will be cool. Just a second." She turned to Noah and Kiryn. "Do you guys want to drive out to Lake Matthews in the morning?"

Noah squinted. "We are going there—why?"

Aspen shrugged. "I don't know. Gavin just asked if we wanted to."

"So, he's not coming over tonight?"

Aspen held up one hand to Noah, but she talked into the phone. "Okay, what time? Okay, we'll see you then. Hope everything is okay. Okay, bye."

Kiryn looked annoyed. "What was that all about? I thought he was coming over so we could all hang out tonight."

Aspen placed her phone on the counter. "He was— I guess Doug asked him to stay home with them."

Kiryn rolled her eyes. "Asked or demanded."

Aspen looked at her friend. "I'm not sure. Gavin didn't seem upset. Just said he agreed to hang out with them tonight." She paused and then as though trying to convince herself she said, "It is Thanksgiving. That's where he should be—I guess."

"I guess." Kiryn stood. "Let's have some pie."

Rocky and Kiryn went to bed about ten, and Aspen and Noah crashed on the floor in front of Rocky's fireplace listening to the adults talk about old times.

Aspen noticed the almost deliberate omission of any discussion of Dad's childhood as Dad, Mom, and Grandma told Aunt Dana about San Clemente, the beach, and a life that seemed forever away right now.

It was nearly midnight when Mom, Dad, Aunt Dana, and Grandma finally decided to go back to the motel.

"What are you doing?"

Aspen whirled around.

Krista was holding two surfboards. She gently pushed one in Aspen's direction, and Aspen caught the edge as it teetered toward her.

Krista looked toward the water. "Surf's up—let's go!" and she turned and ran across the sand carrying her board over her head with both hands.

Aspen heaved the board above her head and followed her friend.

Krista glanced over her shoulder. "We're—"

I know! Burnin' daylight!"

"Aspen?"

Aspen forced her eyes open and lifted her head off the carpet.

"Aspen, we are leaving, and everyone is in bed. You need to go too."

Aspen took a deep breath and tried to focus on her mom's face. She didn't say anything but allowed Mom to help her up and walk her across the den to Rocky's sofa bed.

Mom pulled back the bedding, and Aspen plopped onto the cool sheets. She had barely opened her eyes, but she felt her mom's soft kiss on her forehead and heard her walking away.

"M—Mom?"

Mom stopped and turned around.

"Happy Thanksgiving, Mom."

"Happy Thanksgiving, Aspen."

Noah sat up but then plopped back onto his pillow and pulled the sheet up to his chin. He squeezed his eyes shut and then opened them again, and turned to look at the clock on Gavin's dresser.

He heard the doorbell ring again.

Doesn't he have a key? It's only seven o'clock. I'll kill Gavin. He is supposed to be here at ten. Man, I wanted to sleep!

He could hear mixed men's voices—more than two. It couldn't just be Rocky and Gavin.

Still, he grabbed the blankets and covered his head and made an aggressive effort to go back to sleep.

His door opened. "Noah, are you asleep?"

Noah grunted. "Well, I was. Why aren't you?" He didn't uncover his head.

Aspen hurried into the room and sat on his bed. "Are you grumpy?"

Noah growled, "No. Sleeping."

"You aren't either. Wake up."

"See, even you can see I am sleeping, or you would have said 'get up' not 'wake up.'"

"Oh, please." Aspen pulled the covers from his face.

Noah peered through the narrow slits in his eyes, observing Aspen's disheveled hair. "Well, obviously, you were sleeping. Did the doorbell wake you up too?"

Aspen rubbed her face with her hands and combed through her hair with her fingers. "Yes. It's Hank Cox, and Byron and Larry."

"This early? I thought they all went home for the weekend."

"Well, they're back."

Noah threw the covers back and sat up.

"I'll hurry in the bathroom." Aspen skirted out of the room, but called over her shoulder, "Mom and Dad are here too."

Now it was Noah's turn to rub his face with both hands. "Guess I'm up." He grumbled.

⌇

Noah and Aspen found Rocky and Kiryn still in their robes, in the kitchen with Hank, Larry, Byron, Dad, Mom, and Aunt Dana.

No Gavin.

Aunt Dana laughed, "Morning, sleepyheads."

Noah took a deep breath and let it ruffle through his lips. "Morning, Aunt Dana."

"Hi!" Aspen went directly to the pan of hot chocolate on the stove. "Want some, Noah?"

He nodded and pulled a chair up to the table next to Hank. "What's up? Thought you went home."

Hank chuckled. "I did, but got a call early this morning."

"*Earlier than now?*" Noah's voice went up an octave, and everyone laughed.

"Like this is early for you two," said Mom. "I was actually surprised you were still sleeping."

"Yeah, well it's a holiday. Kids are supposed to sleep in on holidays."

Dad rolled his eyes. "Hasn't ever applied in our house and you two have been kids for some time."

Aspen suddenly noticed the solemn looks on everyone's faces. She took a sip of her hot chocolate, peering over the edge of the mug. Her eyes drifted to Noah and stopped.

He locked eyes with her, his brow furrowed and his head cocked to one side, and she knew that he sensed something as well.

She slowly lowered her mug, handed Noah his hot chocolate, and walked toward an empty chair next to Aunt Dana.

"So, what's going on?"

No one spoke immediately, and that irritated Aspen.

"What?" she demanded.

Always the business one of the group, Byron spoke up. "The police made an arrest last night."

Aspen's eyebrows shot up, and she turned to Noah who looked as surprised as she felt.

"Who? What for? The murders? The—"

"Breathe, Aspen." Aunt Dana touched her arm, and at that same second, the doorbell rang.

"That must be Gavin." Hank jumped up and disappeared into the living room, leaving all kinds of questions hanging in the air.

"Good morning."

To Aspen, Hank sounded like he was trying not to sound anxious.

A wave of relief swept over her when Gavin followed Hank into the kitchen.

"You're early."

Gavin scoffed at Noah's remark. "Yeah, well it wasn't my idea."

"What the heck is going on anyway?!"

Aspen chuckled at Kiryn's usual impatience.

Everyone scooted chairs to make room for the new arrivals and Gavin grabbed the stool in the corner. He plopped it next to Aspen, sat down and squeezed her arm.

He looked at Hank. "Okay, now what?"

Hank motioned to Larry who said, "As I was saying, we made

an arrest last night." He turned to Aspen, "In regards to the fire."

"Really?" It was Mom which surprised Aspen because she assumed her parents already knew what was going on.

"How did you find them so fast?" asked Dad.

Byron grinned. "It helps when one uses his cell phone to report the fire. The agents had him pegged yesterday, with the help of Kendall Washington. Officers went to his house last night, and he gave a full confession, at least of his role in it."

"I'm confused. Who?"

"Someone we never suspected, Noah." Hank looked a little dejected, "Brandon Tuttle."

Aspen nearly choked on her hot chocolate. "*WHAT?*"

She looked from Kiryn to Noah, and then at Rocky. They all had the same expression—total disbelief.

"But we saw— I wonder if— I can't believe this!" The words that tumbled out of Kiryn and Noah's mouths were the same thoughts racing through Aspen's head.

Hank raised one hand to silence Kiryn and Noah.

They obeyed, but then Dad said quietly, "Who is Brandon Tuttle."

"Oh, sorry, Dad, he's—"

"He's a student at the school. Same age as—"

"He's a nice guy—"

"We saw him with—"

Now Hank stood. "Okay, let's back up. One at a time." He motioned to Noah, Rocky, Aspen, and Kiryn.

"They are all right, Jackson, Brandon is the same age as these kids and," he looked at Aspen, "he is a nice guy. How he got caught up in this mess is a mystery, except that I don't think he thought it would ever escalate as it did."

"Is he in jail?" Mom sounded sad. "I mean, he didn't do this all on his own, right? He's just a kid."

"No, he didn't, at least we don't think so, but he won't give us the names of anyone else."

Gavin hadn't said anything yet, but now he asked, "So, you

really don't know who else might be involved?"

Hank shook his head. "Not yet, but we will soon enough." He turned to Suzann. "He is in juvenile detention. He has an arraignment Monday morning."

Aspen caught the disparaging look in Hank's eyes, and she quickly looked at Noah who immediately averted his eyes from hers.

She then turned to Kiryn. She was looking at the floor.

She looked at Gavin, who simply looked confused.

Byron, who had been rapidly taking notes, suddenly stopped, placed his pen on his tablet, and rested his folded arms on top of it. He glanced at Larry, who quickly nodded, and then he turned to Hank, who also nodded.

Byron took a deep breath. "Okay, is there anything any of you want to tell us?"

Mom, Dad, Aunt Dana, and Rocky scanned the faces of the four teenagers.

"Like what?" Gavin's eyes widened. "Do you think we had something to do with this?"

Byron shook his head. "No, but one of you—or all of you—made a call to Hank, am I right?"

Noah sighed. "Yes, we did. After Joseph called me, but all he said was that he thought Dylan was up to something."

"Yeah, but before that—" Kiryn's voice caught, and she glanced at Gavin.

Gavin's brow furrowed. "What?"

"Oh, geez, Gavin. It's just that, well, we saw Brandon and Cassie talking to Dylan at the mall."

"So, we talked about this. Dylan is Cassie's uncle, and Brandon and Cass—"

"Are dating. So to speak." Noah finished Gavin's sentence.

Gavin's eyes widened. "You think Cassie is involved?"

Aspen squirmed at Kiryn's omission of Doug, Gavin's step-dad.

"We don't think anything, Gavin, but we were hoping that maybe Joseph said more than you kids told Hank."

Noah shook his head. "No, he only said that he overheard Dylan talking to someone, but he didn't know who, or even whom he was talking about."

"Did he tell you what Dylan said?" asked Byron.

Noah nodded, "He said, 'Maybe that will make them leave.' He just assumed Dylan was talking about us—our family."

Hank sat down now and ran his fingers through his hair. "I'm inclined to agree with Joseph."

"There isn't much we can do this weekend. I feel bad that Brandon has to spend the weekend in detention, but he committed a serious crime. He may be spending a long time there if he is convicted," said Byron.

"But you said he called the fire department. Doesn't that say something?"

Hank nodded, "It does, Gavin, but it's kind of like remorse, fear, we don't know for sure."

"Regret," mumbled Dad.

"Jackson?"

"Fear, Hank, the kid got scared, and he was already past the point of no return, so he did the only thing he could think of doing."

"Yeah, he was a mess last night. His parents said he didn't even come down for dinner and all his cousins were there. His mother said he had been pretty despondent for several days, but they couldn't get him to talk." Hank sighed. "I have to admit; I felt pretty bad for him. He looked like a scared little kid."

"He is," Mom's voice cracked.

Everyone was silent.

Aspen was trying to make sense of the disconnected pieces of information. Brandon—Cassie—Dylan and then there was—

Hank's phone interrupted the silence. He quickly scrolled the screen and put it to his ear.

"This is Hank."

Pause.

"He did? How much was it?"

Pause.

Now Hank's eyebrows raised. "I guess I didn't think his parents had that kind of cash. Did they get a bond?"

Pause.

"Oh, wow. Well, that was nice of him."

Pause.

"Okay, well, thanks for the information. It will make Mrs. Jackson feel a little better." He winked at Suzann. "I'll explain later. Thanks for the call."

Hank scrolled his phone and stuffed into his shirt pocket. "Brandon was able to post his bail, so they released him to his parents until Monday morning."

"Who posted it?" asked Byron.

Hank turned to Gavin. "Your step-dad, Doug Mendel."

42

TANGLED WEBS

"Okay, I will. Just give me a day or so. They have had a lot with the fire and all, and their classmate is being arraigned this morning."

"Oh, yes, I heard about that. How completely devastating for his family." Mr. Weston stood and reached for Rocky's hand. "Thanks, Mr. Fielden. I'm sure you can understand my frustration at this point."

Rocky shook Mr. Weston's hand and nodded. "Of course, I can. I will talk to the kids later today."

Mr. Weston had started for the door but whirled around. "The kids?"

"Yes, they have not told their parents about the painting yet, Mr. Weston. There is— There is a lot involved here."

"Humph, well I guess. Seems funny to me that they have not at least told their father about a painting of that, well, historical significance."

"I know, it seems strange, but trust me it isn't."

Mr. Weston eyed him suspiciously.

"Please, just trust me."

Mr. Weston sighed. "Okay, I will wait to hear from you."

"Oh, Mr. Weston, I just thought of this. Have you— Do you need to be paid for the work you did on the painting?"

Mr. Weston chuckled. "No, it's not about the money. I know the family is good for it. I guess I am just anxious to get to the history, or should we say, mystery, behind all of this."

Hank sighed laboriously. "You and me both."

He watched as Mr. Weston pulled out of the driveway, and then turned to see Kiryn standing in the hallway.

"He wants to know what's going on with the painting, right?"

"Right." Rocky laughed as he walked toward her. "Oh, Kiryn, the tangled webs we weave in life."

Kiryn laughed. "Uh, okay, Dad."

He grabbed her and pulled her into a tight squeeze. "I love you, Kiryn. I'm happy my sister trusted me with you to raise."

Kiryn hugged him back. "Me too."

"Do I get in on this tender moment?" Gavin loped down the stairs.

"No," chided Rocky. "You're my kid. I didn't have a choice with you."

"Gee, thanks." Gavin covered the distance between him and his dad in three steps and slugged him with his good hand.

"Watch it. You're handicapped right now."

"True," laughed Gavin and followed Kiryn and Rocky into the kitchen.

"I have pancakes and bacon." Rocky opened the microwave, and the smell of freshly cooked bacon wafted through the kitchen. "It will just take a second to heat up the grill and cook the cakes."

"I'm game." Gavin pulled a chair away from the table.

Kiryn slid onto the bench across from Gavin. "Are we going to the arraignment, Dad?"

"It's closed. Only his parents and attorneys will be there, and the arresting officers of course."

"Hank mentioned Kendall Washington. What does he have to do with all of this?"

"Well, he's with arson for the Fire Department, so that would make sense."

"I thought he had diving teams," said Gavin.

"He does, but he is a firefighter as well. "So it still makes sense, right?"

"Yeah, I guess." Gavin made designs on the table with his finger.

"Are you thinking about Cassie?"

Without looking up at Kiryn, Gavin nodded. "She can be, well, she can be pretty ruthless in getting what she wants, but I can't imagine her being involved in anything like this."

"But you do think she is?"

Gavin looked at Kiryn. "For some reason, yeah, I do, and it makes me sick to think of it."

Rocky placed a stack of pancakes and a plate of bacon in front of the kids. He walked back to get the syrup and milk and then joined them.

"Let's not jump to any conclusions. We will learn what's going on soon enough."

Gavin chewed the end from a piece of bacon. "I guess."

43

AUNT DANA

AUNT DANA TURNED THE key and opened the kitchen door. She stepped inside and closed the door behind her. She stood silently taking in every inch of the huge kitchen in the Mansion House.

She had never really cooked much in that kitchen; she, her husband, and dad usually ate in the adjoining dining room, but she had fond memories of this place.

The long counter had rows of cabinets above and below except for above the two double sinks. White-framed windows that cranked open allowed the cooks to see into the massive backyard and patio while they worked.

She let her mind wander, and the sights and smells of the kitchen skipped lightly through her memory.

Back then, the pantry was always stocked with every ingredient to bake whatever one wanted, and the top shelves slanted to make it easier to retrieve an assortment of canned foods.

Two side-by-side refrigerators overflowed with fresh vegetables and fruits, and the freezers were routinely stacked to capacity with an assortment of meat.

A bowl of fresh fruit sat on the end of the counter and fresh cookies, or some other baked pastry was readily available for consumption at will.

Dana allowed her mind to wander to days she couldn't remember well—before she moved in with her grandparents. The memories were still fond, except the day Jackson left. That was a sad day to her.

The days and months taking care of her grandfather were a different story. He had plenty of people to care for him and more than enough money to pay for it, but he wanted Dana and her husband Jerry there, so he didn't feel so lonely.

Dana allowed her thoughts to dwell there for a few minutes, and then she wandered through the kitchen and into the entryway.

She stared at the huge paintings of her parents and grandparents and the long winding staircase that led to the second floor where the bedrooms and storage are located.

After a few minutes, she decided she had better do what she came to do. She promised Jackson and Suzann she would be back within the hour.

Dana walked deliberately to the office, stopping in the doorway. This room had always been off-limits to her and Jerry. The only people her grandfather had allowed in were the cleaning staff.

She almost felt like she was breaking a cardinal rule, and she paused, waiting for a confirmation that it was okay to go in.

None came, and she finally stepped farther into the room. She hesitated again and then quickly walked to the wall-to-wall bookcase. The one where Jackson and Suzann said they had seen the files.

Dana stood in front of it for a few seconds, scanning every shelf. Nothing seemed to jump out at her, but what was she looking for really? She wasn't even sure herself. It was just a feeling. Something she overheard the cleaning ladies talking about many years ago.

She ran her fingers along the bottom edge of the bookcase. Noah was right. It was a solid piece of wood. There was no way it could have opened as Jackson had described without pulling the entire bottom shelf with it.

Dana turned and studied her grandfather's desk. It, like everything else in or around the Mansion House, was massive. The eagle bookends, the brass lamp, the high-backed leather chair, all rested silently in place just like she remembered them. Everything was eerily quiet, and for a second, she almost chose to run.

But she didn't. She felt compelled to help Jackson. She just wasn't sure how she was going to do it.

Cautiously, she walked around the desk and pulled the chair from its place. She sat in it, and the leather felt cool, even through her warm winter sweatpants. She rolled the chair up to the desk and placed her hands on top of the glistening oak surface.

Where would it be?

She ran her fingers under the edges of the desk and tried to open the center drawer. Locked. Subsequently, she tried each drawer, which were all locked as well.

Dana sighed and slumped back in the chair.

Did you see that? The whole bottom just opened right up.

She reflected over the words she had heard one of the cleaning ladies say.

The whole bottom…

Dana glanced at her watch and immediately stood. She rolled the chair back into place, and as quickly as she had entered the Mansion House, she was gone. She had found nothing.

She ran across the back lawn toward the steps leading down to what she remembered as the servants' quarters but was now where her brother and his family lived.

Suddenly, she stopped and looked back at the house, and felt sure someone was watching her.

A chill ran down her spine, and as quickly as she could without falling, she ascended the long cement stairs, knowing full well the chill was not from the cold winter air.

44

NEW ANXIETY

"That was nice of you to post that boy's bail, Doug, but why would you do that?" Sara Mendel zipped into her jeans and pulled a sweatshirt over her head.

Her husband didn't turn from the mirror. He placed his toothbrush back in its holder and casually answered. "He's a friend of Gavin's. I know his parents don't have that kind of money. They would have to mortgage their home."

"Why do you think he did it? It seems so out of character for Brandon."

Doug shrugged. "Who knows what gets into the minds of kids? Look at the stuff Gavin and Kiryn, and the Allen kids have gotten involved in."

"But that is different. Their involvement wasn't willful, at least, not at first."

"So you admit that it is now?"

Sara scowled. "What is that supposed to mean?"

Doug turned to face his wife. "I simply mean that maybe they should back off. Hasn't enough damage been done? People are upset enough that they tried to burn their house down?"

"People?"

"Brandon!" snapped Doug. "I mean Brandon, and whoever else was involved in all of this."

Sara stared at her husband, but he did not make eye contact with her.

He picked up his jacket and walked towards her. Cupping the back of her head in his hand, he kissed her forehead. "I have a meeting in Memphis at noon. Are you staying out here tonight?"

Sara nodded. She wanted to stay in Sommerville until she found out what happened at Brandon's hearing. "Gavin has an appointment at Rocky's today with the physical therapist. I would kind of like to see how he is doing firsthand, not just by talking to the therapist on the phone."

Doug nodded curtly. "Suit yourself."

"Are you coming back here tonight?" she was referring to their home in Somerville on Mystic Lake.

"Possibly. I'll call you. What are your plans for the week? You wanted to get the Christmas decorations up, right?"

Sara nodded. "Yes, I will start on that today. I'd like to get them up in this house and the Memphis house by the end of the week."

"I can have Sydnee and Alice start them."

Doug was referring to their cleaning staff in Memphis, but Sara shook her head. "No, I like to do it."

Doug chuckled. "Okay. I will call you later." He started down the stairs. "Hey, let me know what you find out about Brandon, and with Gavin's appointment."

"I will."

Sara sat on her bed. The familiar anxiety she had been dealing with for over two weeks started to creep into her stomach, and she felt the muscles in her neck and shoulders tighten.

Why am I feeling this way? Has this whole thing with the Allen's and Sumer and Patrice got me all worked up too?

She flopped back on her bed. No, it wasn't just that. It was her son. Gavin was heavily involved, and she was not sure where this would lead. She and Rocky had tried his entire life to keep him away from the history of his ancestors. Her sister Sumer, his birth mother, Patrice. All of it.

We were so stupid. How could we ever think he could escape his— destiny?

Her phone rang from downstairs. She sat up. It quit ringing, and she knew it had gone to voicemail.

Sara dragged herself downstairs to the kitchen. She reached for her phone, but first picked up a handwritten note. It was from Doug.

I love you, Sara. See you tonight.

She smiled, and a little of her anxiety seemed to subside. She picked up her phone.

Missed call from Gavin. Sara punched the little bubble icon and listened.

"Hey Mom, my appointment with the therapist is at eleven today. Just wanted to let you know. See you at Dad's."

Sara quickly clicked on Gavin's name in her phone and sent him a text.

"Missed your call but got your message. I will see you at your dad's at eleven. Love you."

She pushed send and almost immediately she got a text back.

"Okay see you then. Love you too."

45

CONDUIT

Jackson steered his truck out of the airport parking lot and headed towards the freeway. He looked over at his wife and noticed a tear trickling down her cheek.

"You okay?"

Suzann nodded quickly. "Yes. I just—"

"Miss your mom," Jackson finished her sentence.

Suzann nodded again. "Having her here these past few days have been, well, comforting." She turned to her husband and smiled. "Yes. I miss my mom."

She felt a light pat on her shoulder, and she turned to Jackson's sister who, up until now had been silent in the back seat.

"I don't blame you for missing her. She is an easy person to be around, and your kids adore her," said Dana.

"We all do," said Jackson, and Suzann squeezed his hand.

They rode in silence for a few seconds, and then Jackson looked at his sister through the rearview mirror. "So, did you find what you were looking for at Grandpa's house? Or were you just reminiscing?"

"A little of both, I guess." Dana turned to look out the window. "We need to come to Memphis to see the Christmas lights and bring the kids. They really do a nice job of decorating."

Jackson glanced over his shoulder. "Okay, we can do that. Are you changing the subject?"

Dana laughed. "No, I just think we should."

"We will. That would be nice," said Suzann.

Jackson eyed his sister again.

She caught him looking at her. "Okay! Yes, I was looking for something."

Suzann turned around in her seat. "For what?"

Dana squirmed. "I just—*Ahhh!* I don't know."

"Yes, you do. Is there something you're not telling us?"

"No, Jackson. Nothing like that. I keep remembering a conversation I overheard when Grandpa's cleaning staff didn't know I was in the study. They had just come out of Grandpa's office and were talking about the whole bottom of something opening up."

Suzann and Jackson's faces both expressed the same confusion, so Dana went on.

"When you took us to the office the other day and were trying to explain how the bottom of the bookcase just 'fell away,' as you described it, I thought of that conversation. Well, I didn't think of it right then, but later. The point is, they could have easily been talking about the bookcase. Maybe they did something, and it opened."

Suzann's eyes twinkled. "Like a hidden wall, you know, as you see in the movies when the entire wall turns and then there is another wall?"

Dana's face lit up. "Exactly! It would make sense, wouldn't it?"

Jackson was trying to maneuver the truck into freeway traffic, and he didn't say anything for a few minutes. When he did, it was a casual comment. "Don't you think that's a little farfetched?"

"What?" Dana and Suzann spoke at the same time, which made Jackson laugh.

"Well—"

"Jackson! What about this entire scenario is *not* farfetched?" Suzann was turned sideways in her seat, looking directly at her husband.

He pursed his lips and then sighed. "You're right."

Dana continued, "I was trying to find a button or something

that maybe I could push, and it would open.”

“Nothing?”

Dana looked at Suzann. “Nothing.”

Jackson’s phone rang. He glanced down the screen. “It’s Hank. Will you answer that?”

Suzann picked up the phone. “Hi, Hank. It’s Suzann, Jackson is driving. I’ll put you on speaker.”

“Good morning!” the sound of Hank’s voice filled the cab of the truck.

“Morning, Hank. What’s up? Is the arraignment over?”

“Yep and that kid is not cracking,” said Hank.

“What do you mean?”

“I mean, that he is claiming he did it all on his own. His parents are beside themselves. We don’t know whom he is protecting, or why.”

“What did the judge do?” asked Suzann.

“Slapped him right back in juvenile. He’s in jail.”

Tears welled up in Suzann’s eyes. “I can’t believe this. I don’t know Brandon, but I try to picture Noah doing something like that. It’s just so hard to believe.”

“Not so much that he is capable of it, I mean, he is practically an adult. I think the bigger question here is *why*. His parents said he has expressed no personal animosity toward any of your family—ever. They are in total shock,” said Hank through the speaker.

“This is Dana, Hank. What are you going to do?”

“Well, Brandon has a great attorney. He’s a guy from Nashville. Apparently, Doug Mendel hooked them up.”

“Doug seems to be coming through big time in this whole thing. Does that surprise anyone? I don’t even know the guy,” said Jackson.

“Not really. I guess this isn’t the first time Doug has stepped in to help people. His family is worth millions, and on his own Doug is not suffering—at all. He can afford it without blinking an eye,” said Hank. “I’ve known him for years, not personally, but he’s always making huge contributions to all kinds of charities, stuff like that, and he and Sara paid cash for that house on Mystic Lake. That cost them a pretty penny. Didn't seem to even phase Doug."

"Well, it's nice he can help Brandon then."

Hank went on, "Yeah, it is. Well, I will let you go, but Jackson, I had a thought. Think I could meet with your kids a little later today?"

"Sure. I think we are going to the Mansion House this afternoon. Aspen is dying to show us something." Jackson squirmed and glanced at Suzann.

"Okay, I will call you in an hour or so. Talk to you then."

"Thanks, Hank." Jackson glanced at Suzann again.

"Wondering what will happen this time. At the house, I mean?" asked Suzann.

Jackson sighed and nodded. "I can't help it. Makes me nervous."

"Well, I can't imagine why! Ghosts! That house is full of ghosts! Even I can see that now. I don't know why I never noticed it all the years I lived there."

Suzann spoke quietly, but what she said both Jackson and Dana knew to be true. "Because you are not a conduit. Aspen and Jackson are."

A chill seemed to pass through the cab of the truck.

46

KENDALL WASHINGTON

KENDALL WASHINGTON FINALLY FOUND the box he had been looking for. He riffled through the photos, tossing them haphazardly
on the bed. Exasperated, he dropped the nearly empty box on the
floor and stared into space.

His mother had been no help at all when he called her last week.
"You are wrong, Son. Let it lie."

But Kendall couldn't help the feeling that engulfed him every
time he met the Allen family. It started that first day at Mystic Lake
when his diving team began their search for Aspen Allen.

Kendall shrugged, picked up a handful of pictures, and tossed
them back into the box. As he did, a small photo fluttered out
of his hand and landed upside down on the carpet. He finished
clearing the bed of the pictures and then picked up that last one,
dropping it on top of the pile. It landed upright, and Kendall froze.

For several seconds he stared at it, but then he retrieved it from
the box and studied it closer.

This can't be a coincidence.

He walked to his desk, opened the drawer, and took out a small
book. He tucked the picture between the pages, grabbed his coat
and the book and headed out the door.

Today was his day off, and he had planned to do some shopping
and visit his grandfather, but instead, he turned his truck toward
Memphis and the nearly four-hour drive to Nashville.

47

REMEMBER

Aspen finished dressing and started brushing her hair.

"Aspen."

As she turned around, she said, "Why are you whispering?"

She fully expected to see Noah standing at her bedroom door, but he wasn't there. No one was there.

Her parents and Aunt Dana were on their way back from taking Grandma to the airport, so the only person it could be was Noah.

When she stepped into the hallway, she heard the shower running.

Aspen stood still for a few seconds, listening.

Nothing.

She ran her brush through her hair again as she walked back into her room.

"Aspen."

She stopped abruptly and listened again.

"Who? What—who is this?" her voice quivered.

Silence.

"Remember."

Even though the voice startled Aspen, she was not afraid.

"Remember? Remember what?"

But there was only more silence.

Aspen looked around her room. Everything was in place. She wondered who was trying to contact her and why.

The voice came again; only this time, it sounded farther away.

"Remember."

"That voice sounds strangely familiar," she said out loud.

"Who are you talking to?"

For the second time in less than ten minutes, Aspen spun around to see who was standing behind her. Even though this time, she knew it was Noah.

"You scared me!"

"Obviously. I must have interrupted an important—conversation?" Noah chuckled. He held his open hand toward her. "Believe me, Aspen, I am not questioning you. I know better than that, but who was that?"

Aspen shrugged. "Heck, if I know, but—" she twisted her mouth.

Noah raised his eyebrows and leaned forward with both hands open toward her like he was waiting for her to hand him something.

"It was a boy." She scrunched her nose.

Noah rolled his eyes. "So, did he smell, or something?"

Now Aspen rolled her eyes. "Oh, brother. No, but his voice sounded, I don't know, familiar."

"There haven't been any boy spirits come to you, right? Well, except for Dixon, and that one time in the storage, whoever that was."

Aspen shuddered at the thought of Kenneth Lloyd Dixon, the person, well, the spirit of that person, who had tormented her the first few months after her family moved to Somerville. She hadn't heard from him since locating the statue her grandfather had hidden in the Mansion House, the one he dedicated to his daughter, Ronda.

Dixon had been responsible for the murder of Ronda, and her boyfriend, Thomas.

Aspen, Noah, Gavin, and Kiryn were convinced that Dixon was involved in the mysterious disappearance of approximately two hundred boys around that same time frame, but there was no concrete proof—yet.

Aspen answered her brother, "Yeah, just that one, but no one else."

"Then I wonder why he—whoever it is—sounds familiar."

Aspen shook her head, "I don't know."

"What did he say?"

"First, he said my name. I thought it was you, but then he said *'remember,'* twice."

Noah studied his sister. She almost looked sad.

"I'm sorry, Aspen. That must be the worst. I don't even know how to relate."

"Thanks, Noah." She paused.

"What?"

"You are going to think I have lost my mind."

"Well, it won't be the first time!" laughed Noah.

Aspen scowled. "Thanks."

"I couldn't resist, but seriously, what?"

"I wonder if maybe I saw him, or met him when I was in the coma."

"Do you think that's possible?"

Aspen shook her head. "I don't know, but Patrice did mention something like that. I had never considered it. I can't remember anything, except—"

"Except?"

"Water. I remember water and red hair and freckles. I think."

"You think red hair or freckles?"

"I think freckles. I do remember red hair." Exasperated, she threw her arms up. "I don't know!"

"I can't even imagine being inside your head."

Aspen glared at him. "My head is like everyone else's head!"

"*Right.*" He started to laugh, and before he risked making her mad, he turned and walked briskly out the bedroom, but called over his shoulder, "Mom and Dad should be home soon. I'll text Gavin to see if they are on their way."

Aspen sighed. She knew Noah was just teasing her, but it frustrated her to have so many thoughts and voices in her head that she couldn't connect. "I guess my head is not like everyone else's."

"That's a given."

Aspen looked up to the sound of Kiryn's voice.

"Okay, not you too. When did you get here?"

"Just now. Noah said you were back here talking to some guy. You should have seen Gavin's face," she chuckled. "Priceless."

Aspen rolled her eyes and grabbed Kiryn's arm. "C'mon. I'll tell you about it later."

"Okay." Kiryn changed the subject. "I am so excited about today, aren't you?"

Aspen's heart leaped, and she grinned at Kiryn. "Excited and nervous. I'm always afraid for my dad."

"I get that, but don't you think he has really, you know, come a long way?"

Aspen nodded, but her mind wandered. She could understand why Kiryn would think that. Her dad had been doing well since his heart attack, and he was way more receptive to all that was going on around them now, but Kiryn had not been at the lake several weeks ago when Dad told their mom and her and Noah about his childhood and his relationship, or lack of, with his father. To see her dad hurt like that, was one of the saddest days Aspen could ever remember.

Kiryn and Gavin knew some of it, but Aspen hadn't felt at liberty to share the details. They were too sad too. In a way, humiliating to Dad, and in some sort of protection kind of thing, Aspen was still trying to shelter him. Others might find it silly, but Aspen didn't.

She and Noah had sincere concerns about their dad's mental and physical state, and every time some new facts came up about the Allen Family history, an underlying fear accompanied the excitement. Or maybe dread.

"Are you listening to me?"

Kiryn jolted Aspen back to the present.

"How can she not listen? You never stop talking." Gavin stepped between Kiryn and Aspen. He put an arm around Aspen and slipped his injured arm through Kiryn's. "My two favorite girls," he chided.

"Seriously? That was corny." Noah shook his head and rolled his eyes at the same time.

Aspen's eyes narrowed, and she looked directly at Noah. "I like corny."

"That was even worse." Gavin released them both and stepped away from them. "I'm going to have to go with Noah on this one."

"Whatever." Aspen flipped her hand toward them both and walked toward Rocky, who was just now getting out of his truck. He was still on the phone but briefly waved at Aspen.

Everyone turned to the sound of Dad's truck coming down the driveway, and Aspen took a deep breath.

Showtime.

48

UNDER THE LAYERS

"Okay now, before we go in, I need to explain something." Aspen stood with her back to the storage door.

Aspen, Rocky, Kiryn, Noah, and Gavin knew precisely what they would find in the storage, but the rest of them, Dad, Mom, Aunt Dana, Hank, Byron, and Larry had no clue.

Just as Aspen started to speak again, the front doorbell rang.

Rocky immediately headed for the stairs. "I'll get it."

No one said anything, and Aspen's heart started to pound.

Within a few minutes, Rocky was back, accompanied by Mr. Weston.

"I thought he needed to be here." Rocky's voice hinted of an apology, but Mr. Weston did not give anyone a second to respond.

"Hello, everyone." Mr. Weston grinned, and Aspen detected an excitement about him. He stood back for a second, but then went around the room, shaking hands with everyone. When he reached the four teenagers, he said, "This is an exciting day!"

Aspen's heart really pounded now. She caught her dad's puzzled expression.

"See, this is what I wanted to explain."

"Wait, Aspen, let me." Rocky motioned to Mr. Weston.

"Mr. Weston, I would like you to meet Jackson and Suzann Allen, Jackson's sister, Dana, Hank, and I believe you know—"

"Oh, I know Hank, and I also know, or at least know of, Miss

Dana." He laughed and nodded in Aunt Dana's direction.

"Oh, yeah, of course, you do. Byron Coulsen and Larry Brimhall. These are the FBI agents working on this case." Rocky sighed. "Well, several different cases, involving the same case, sort of."

Mr. Weston looked puzzled.

Rocky shook his head, "Never mind. Go ahead, Aspen."

"Okay, so really quick. We went in the storage," she winced, "against your wishes, Dad."

"I think that ship has sailed, Aspen. You kids broke every rule in the book."

Aspen took a deep breath and slowly let it out. She nodded curtly. "True. We did."

She scanned the faces of her brother and two friends, and they all quickly nodded in agreement. She couldn't help but notice the looks of apprehension on Gavin and Noah's faces. Kiryn looked, well, eager.

Dad exchanged a quick glance with Mom. He narrowed his eyes and turned back to his daughter, "Go on."

"Well, Kiryn and I, we were looking at all the paintings."

"Actually, I was terrified to go in there," said Kiryn.

Rocky looked at his daughter, "But you did."

Kiryn nodded, "Well, yeah."

"Anyway, we were looking at these paintings. You must have seen them, Dad, when you were in the storage?'

Dad shook his head. "There were paintings, but I always stayed by the door, and besides, the paintings were all facing the wall." He caught the curious looks on the other men's faces. "Long story."

"Okay, well anyway, we were looking at this one huge painting, and Kiryn noticed that the paint on some parts was thicker than on other parts. So she, well, she scrapped it with her fingernail, and the paint chipped off, but only in certain places. Not on the whole painting."

"One thing led to another, and we called, well Kiryn called—"

"I actually called Miss Greenland, and she told me to call Mr. Weston," said Kiryn.

"Wait." Dad held one hand up. "Who is Mrs. Greenland?"

Kiryn eyebrows shot up. "Oh! She is my art teacher at school."

Dad nodded and Aspen continued.

"Mr. Weston came over to look at it. Right?" She looked at Mr. Weston, who nodded, and then stepped forward.

It was like he could not contain himself any longer. He pointed to the door. "May we go in?"

Aspen reached behind her and turned the doorknob, but she did not immediately open the door.

"I thought that door was locked," said Dad.

"Well, it was, but we got it open."

"I see." Dad now looked directly at Noah.

Noah turned to Gavin. "Actually he got us in."

"Well, not me, actually, my mother—" he stopped.

"Never mind!" Kiryn almost yelled, and she stepped past Aspen and pushed the door open.

Simultaneously, both Kiryn and Aspen gasped. Noah and Gavin crowded around the open doorway.

"What the—" said Noah.

"What's wrong?" Mr. Weston pushed past them, and the rest of the adults followed.

"Oh, my, my," said Mr. Weston. "Well, this is something."

Aspen was speechless, and it seemed as though Kiryn, Gavin, Noah, and even Rocky were as shocked as she was.

Except for one very large painting standing on an easel, and one much smaller painting leaning against one of the legs of the easel, the room was completely empty.

The paintings were both turned away from the doorway.

"This is impossible," Aspen barely whispered.

"What? That the room is empty?" asked Dad.

"Yeah, Dad. There were boxes everywhere and lots of paintings, and clothes, and shoes, and stuff!" said Noah.

Dad nodded, "It was never this empty when I was in here."

"It wasn't empty two months ago!" said Kiryn.

Mom, Aunt Dana, Hank, Byron, and Larry still stood in the

hallway looking through the door.

Rocky and Mr. Weston had already walked over to the paintings, but they stood behind them.

Mr. Weston was carrying a thin briefcase, and now he opened it, placed it on the floor, and retrieved a white envelope and motioned for everyone to join him.

He pulled a picture from the envelope that appeared to be about eleven by fourteen. He held it up and asked Aspen to identify the people in the picture.

Aspen turned to her dad, "You know who they are, right, Dad?"

Jackson nodded and proceeded to point them out. "This is Grandpa, and this is Grandma Faith. He pointed to the girl to the right of his Grandpa, "This is Aunt Jeanne, this boy is Uncle David, and the girl behind Grandma Faith, is Aunt Riley."

"Precisely." Mr. Weston clapped his hands together. He held the photo up. "This is a photo of that larger painting before I worked on it. "Now, if you could all just come around to the front here."

Mr. Weston all but skipped around the large easel, and the rest followed him.

Jackson stared at the painting. He said nothing.

"See, Dad, this is what we found." Aspen took her dad's arm.

"Jackson, is that—" The words were barely audible when they slipped from Suzann's lips.

Aspen lightly touched the face of the woman in the painting. "This is Nina, Great-Grandpa's first wife. Your grandma, Dad."

Dad still didn't say anything.

"And this, "Aspen pointed to the girl sitting on the floor in front of Riley. "This is Ronda, Dad."

Jackson's expressionless face did not even twitch.

Aspen wondered what he was thinking, what he would do, how this would affect him.

Suzann put her arm around her husband's waist but she too, said nothing.

After a long silence, Mr. Weston spoke up again, but this time, he spoke with reverence, and with what Aspen thought, dignity.

"Mr. Allen. Someone, someone with incredible skills, painted over the original painting. This flowerpot covered the girl and the woman, Faith, I believe the kids said, was meticulously painted over this woman, your grandmother, it would seem."

His eyes still fixed on the face of Faith, Jackson asked, "Why?"

"I think I can answer that, Jackson," said Rocky.

Gradually, the teenagers sank to the floor. The adults followed, leaving Rocky and Mr. Weston standing.

Rocky continued, "In everything I have been able to find, and it is backed by bits and pieces of your grandfather's journal, he, your grandpa, did everything in his power to erase Nina and Ronda from his life—his history." He motioned to the smaller painting. "This one was altered as well. We have not been able to locate any paintings that have Ronda in them or Nina for that matter. It's like he simply—"

"Painted them away," said Kiryn.

"Pretty much," said Rocky.

"How does a person just pretend his child, or wife, never existed? That's crazy!" Hank looked bewildered.

"Unless the pain of remembering was greater than the pain of forgetting," said Aunt Dana quietly.

Dad took a labored breath. "This is— This is unbelievable."

"Believe it, Dad. It really happened," said Noah.

"I don't know if I want to believe it," said Dad.

"I don't think anyone does, Dad," said Aspen. "I know this is just adding to your sadness from the past."

Dad ran his fingers through his hair. He turned to his wife and tried to smile.

Suzann touched the silent tears that wetted his cheeks. "I'm sorry, Jackson."

He dropped his head and shook it quickly, and then when he looked up, he turned toward Rocky, "Now what?

Rocky joined them on the floor. "We are not exactly sure, Jackson. We are trying to get some information as to where Nina went, when she died, that sort of thing, but so far we are coming up empty."

"We are hoping the will might help solve some of the pieces," said Larry.

"Any luck on that yet?" asked Dad.

"We have a hearing with them tomorrow in Memphis. They are not giving up easily," said Byron.

"Can't they just pretend it never existed, even if they do have it?" asked Suzann.

Byron nodded. "They can, but we will just seize their computers, property, whatever we need to do. Right now they have the chance to come forward."

"So, you do know they have it?" Jackson's eyes seemed to brighten.

Larry and Bryon exchanged a quick glance.

"Ninety percent sure," said Larry.

That seemed to satisfy Jackson, and he turned to Mr. Weston. "May I keep that?" Jackson pointed to the photo of the original painting.

"Actually, I gave one to your kids."

"He did, Dad. It's in a box in my closet," said Noah.

"But the fire?"

I checked it, Kiryn. It's fine. Not even touched. The closet was closed, and so was the box. Not so much of a fleck of soot.

Kiryn looked relieved.

"We owe Mr. Weston some money, Dad," said Noah.

Dad pulled himself to his feet and then helped Suzann up. "No doubt. What are the damages, Mr. Weston?"

Mr. Weston protested with both open hands. "We will take care of the details later." He then turned to Aspen and Noah. "Didn't I suggest you kids keep this door locked?"

"We did," said Noah. "We even changed the lock."

Rocky nodded. "That we did. We didn't want anyone in here."

"Including me," said Dad.

Noah nodded and ducked his head. "Yes, Dad. Including you."

"Well, the best-laid plans. If there were other things in here like you said, someone got past your lock," said Byron.

"Yeah," said Aspen absently, but her attention was drawn to the far wall. Seven women were standing kind of in the wall. Their pleasant faces looked back at Aspen. She glanced around. The only person paying any attention to her was Gavin. His head slightly turned in her direction, and he looked at her from the corner of his eye.

Aspen's faint smile confirmed what he already knew. She was seeing some of the people she had seen in here before, and he assumed they must have something to do with the disappearance of the contents of the storage.

But now both were left to wonder, where did they take it?

Dad was so intrigued by the painting that he didn't want to leave the storage room.

"I would sure like to know what my grandpa's thought process was to completely wipe out two members of his family."

"Could have been as simple as saving face," said Rocky.

Irritation pulled at Jackson's mouth. "From what?"

"Society, Jackson. You should read through the journals. It might help you understand. It's not something you will agree with, and neither do I, but it was the time they lived in. Your grandparents were high society—*political* high society—and since the beginning of time, politicians have lived by a different standard than the rest of us. I mean, look at the Bible, it was going on even then."

"You mean dishonesty, lying, cheating? That kind of standard?" Aspen had rejoined the conversation.

Rocky nodded. "Unfortunately, yes. It would seem so. I think the disappearance of Ronda, and adding to the humiliation was the fact that she was rumored to be with one of the hired help, who was also, I might add, strictly forbidden to associate with any of the Mystic Lake residences. Least of all, the Dixons and the Allens. It was just too much for Allen. In order to move forward with his life, his political life, he needed to first, get a new wife and second, cover up that fact, that even his money could not protect his daughter and worse yet, find her. He spent nearly half a million dollars searching for her before he finally gave up."

"But didn't people wonder about that? I mean when she never came back? Didn't they question him?" asked Suzann.

"I'm sure they did, but money talks. I'm sure Allen had to silence a few people, but then, those around him, especially those who depended on him for survival, for lack of a better term, just shut up." Rocky's sympathetic eyes turned to Jackson.

"I'm sorry, Jackson. This has got to be hard for you."

Jackson nodded, but he stared past all of them. "It has been hard. Excruciating actually, but now, I just want to get to the bottom of all of this." The sadness in his eyes was obvious when he looked first at Noah and then Aspen.

Blowing out his breath in frustration, he turned to Suzann. "I will tell you this; I knew the day I got Dana's letter that I would be coming back to a nightmare, but never in my wildest dreams did I expect the magnitude of all of this."

"How could you know?" Suzann touched his hand.

Jackson looked at Aspen. "I knew you had the same thing I had, Aspen, that you could see people, but every time your mom brought it up, I dismissed it. I thought if I ignored it, the whole thing would go away. I did not want that—this—for you." He suddenly stopped speaking, and his face became expressionless.

Finally, he said, "I guess I am no different than my grandpa. I just tried to paint away the past."

Aspen looked around the room. All eyes were on Jackson. Even Larry and Byron looked sad.

"Well, I'm glad you came!" blurted Kiryn. "I know it's been, you know, heart attacks, comas, murder, and a fire and some really horrible stuff, but I think it has been worth it!"

Stunned by Kiryn's sudden outburst, everyone simply looked at her.

Rocky's eyebrows furrowed, and he glared at his daughter, but Jackson broke the tension when he started to laugh. "Well, that pretty much sums it up!"

Aunt Dana, who had not said anything, walked over to Jackson. She took both of his hands in hers and looked directly into his eyes. "Well, I agree with Kiryn. It has been worth it. I have my big brother back and I, for one, am ready to dig up all the crap and find out just how much of a rotten scoundrel our grandfather really was!"

She dropped his hands and pulled him into a tight hug, and Jackson hugged her back.

"It's time, Jackson. It's time," she whispered in his ear.

Noah locked the front door of the Mansion House, and ran and jumped in the driver's seat of the Iroc. "It's freezing out here!"

"I think this is the coldest day so far this winter," said Gavin. "Did they decide on Bill and Nada's?"

Kiryn laughed. "Where else?"

"What do you guys think Hank wants to talk to us about that he couldn't talk to us about here?" asked Aspen.

Noah shrugged and followed his Dad's truck out of the driveway. Everyone else had already left ahead of them. "Don't know, but we'll soon find out."

49

WHAT A MESS

"You promised me there wouldn't be any trouble!" Cassie screamed. She pushed the door open and jumped out of Dylan's truck.

Dylan leaped out of the driver door and ran around the front of the truck, intercepting Cassie when she tried to run for the road. He grabbed her arm and shoved her against the grill.

"If your stupid boyfriend wouldn't have gotten all soft on us! I told you he wouldn't be able to carry this through. Big tough football player who is a total wimp!"

"Shut up!" Cassie tried to pull away from Dylan, but he slammed her back against the grill, this time hard enough that she felt the metal dig into her skin through her shirt.

She started to cry. "Let me go, Dylan!"

The loud blast of a horn caused Dylan to step away from Cassie, and she immediately bolted toward the SUV that rolled toward them.

The SUV stopped, and Cassie stopped too, collapsing into a sobbing heap on the frost-covered ground.

Doug Mendel took her arm and pulled her to her feet. "It's okay now."

He kept hold of her arm and walked her toward Dylan, who was leaning against his truck, smoking a cigarette.

"What do you think you're doing manhandling this girl?" Doug shoved Dylan, but he just glared at him.

Dylan dropped his cigarette and crushed it with the toe of his boot. He pulled his coat closed and fumbled with the zipper. "Her idiot boyfriend blew it."

"Yeah, he did, but she didn't, and Brandon is not going to be a problem." Doug still held Cassie's arm, and now he pulled her toward his SUV, and Dylan followed.

Doug had left the engine running, and Cassie welcomed the warmth when she climbed into the back seat.

"Okay, look, the main thing is that we don't get crazy. I got Brandon a good attorney and I—"

"He's back in jail, though."

Doug looked back at Cassie. "Only until tomorrow. The judge was more concerned about him being a flight risk, and he is on suicide watch."

Cassie's eyes widened. "*What?*"

"It's standard procedure, Cassie. One of his parents must be with him all the time. That's the only way they will release him."

"Did you have to pay more money?" asked Cassie.

"No, not yet, but I'm sure that's coming."

She started to cry again. "You know he only did this to get the money to help his sister. His parents are pretty strapped with all of her medical bills."

Doug shook his head. "I didn't know that. What sister?"

"She has bone cancer. She's been in and out of the hospital for months. You probably don't know it because she lives in Memphis. She's married and has two little kids. Her medical bills have eaten up all of their insurance. Brandon thought he could help." She buried her face in her hands. "I can't believe I got him involved in all of this."

"He made his choice," snapped Dylan.

Cassie lunged at Dylan, but Doug threw his arm across her chest and pushed her back into the seat. "That's enough."

Cassie threw herself on the seat and sobbed again.

Doug and Dylan were quiet until Cassie's sobs turned to low

whimpers.

She sat up, and Doug handed her a wad of tissues.

Doug squeezed his temples with his thumb and forefinger and rubbed his forehead with his hand.

"Look, you two have to lay low and stay out of the limelight. I'll take care of Brandon and his sister." Doug looked back at Cassie. "Have your parents asked you any questions?"

Cassie nodded. "My dad has interrogated me. They know that Brandon and I have been dating, but my mom has pretty much convinced him that I am upset because of Brandon. I don't know how much longer he will believe that, though."

"You have to make him believe it."

Cassie nodded. "Yeah."

"What about you? Have you spilled your guts to Drew?"

Dylan's head shot up. "You know I haven't! Drew would have been in your face. Besides, this stuff isn't Drew's style. He's got a kid and all."

Doug stared through the foggy windshield. "Yeah, well, I have two of them. Three, if I count Gavin."

"You hate Gavin."

Doug turned slowly and glared at Dylan. "I do not *hate* Gavin. I just need him and his friends to stop already. They are getting too close."

"To what?"

"Never mind, Cassie. It's nothing you need to worry about."

"She is worried because she's head over heels for that kid." Dylan chuckled.

Cassie glared at Dylan. "How would you know who I like and don't like?"

"I got eyes, don't I? You played poor Brandon right to the last second."

"What would you know about loving someone? Your girlfriend was killed!" Cassie knew she had struck a chord, and she immediately wished she could take the words back.

Dylan's face wrenched and he slumped into the seat saying

nothing.

Cassie's reference to Sumer Munoa who was murdered by Dylan's own grandfather, Kenneth Dixon, was too much. It had haunted Dylan his entire life, and from the look on his face, the pain was still as fresh as it was over seventeen years ago.

"Okay, okay. Both of you stop. For us to get all crazy is not going to help anything." Doug reached across the seat and opened the glove box. He pulled out two envelopes and handed one to each of them. "Here is a little something. Consider it a down payment."

Neither of them opened the envelopes.

Cassie shoved hers in her coat pocket. "I need to get home."

"I'll drive you," said Doug.

Cassie shook her head. "No, I told my parents I was going with Dylan because my mom—my real mom—was going to be at Drew's today. I need to go back with him."

Doug looked at Dylan. "Can you do that without killing her?"

Dylan scoffed. "I'll try." He opened the door and stepped out of the truck. Before he closed the door, he turned back to Doug.

"Look, I'm sorry that it all went haywire. It seemed like a simple thing when we started."

Doug nodded. "Yeah, just lay low. I'll take care of everything, including Brandon." He glanced at Cassie. "And his sister. I need to you find what hospital she is going to for treatments, or the doctor's name."

"Okay." Cassie climbed out of the truck. She shoved her hands in her pockets and followed Dylan, not looking back at Doug.

≈

Doug watched them drive past him. He lifted his hand, and Dylan nodded, but Cassie just stared through the windshield.

Doug sighed. *What a mess.*

He picked up his cell phone but then hesitated. After several seconds, he pushed one of the speed dial numbers and waited.

When a voice came on at the other end, Doug simply said, "It's all good. I will contact you after the weekend. I'm staying out here tonight. Need to calm my wife's nerves. Look into something for me. Brandon Tuttle has a sister in Memphis who is going through cancer treatments. See what you can find out about her."

Doug pushed end and dropped his cell phone onto the seat. After several minutes, he picked it up again and punched in some numbers.

When the call was answered, Doug said, "I need you to go see Brandon, before they release him. Tell him his sister will be taken care of. Tell him not to say anything to his parents."

"Done." Came the response at the other end.

Doug clicked end and again dropped the phone on the seat. He grabbed a half-full bottle of water and chugged the entire thing, tossing the empty bottle on the floor.

Steering his truck back down the deserted dirt road, he headed to the store in Somerville to pick up the new boxes of Christmas lights he promised to get for Sara a week ago.

50

DIFFICULT VISIT

"Why do you want us to talk to Brandon?" Aspen wrapped both hands around her mug of hot chocolate to warm her hands.

Bill and Nada's was quiet this afternoon, so the server pushed four tables together to accommodate the large group.

Hank studied all their faces without saying anything. He looked down at his fingers, which he had been tapping on the table, but his eyes seemed far away.

Aspen caught Kiryn staring at Hank's fingers like she wanted to crush them, and Aspen chuckled.

Kiryn heard her and glared at Aspen.

Aspen quickly took a sip of chocolate, covering her eyes with her mug.

Finally, Hank looked up. "I think maybe you kids could get to him."

"All of us at once? That might be a little much." Kiryn sat back in her chair now that Hank was no longer tapping the table.

"No, not at once. Who is the closest to Brandon? Or are any of you?"

"I played basketball with him last year, and little league football with him too, but that's about it. He made varsity football last year and decided not to play basketball," said Gavin.

"I don't know him at all," said Noah. "Except that last summer, he gave Aspen a ride from the lake, leaving me stranded. He glared at his sister.

Aspen chuckled. "Oh, yeah, I forgot about that."

Noah sneered at her and turned to Kiryn. "What about you?"

"I've known him forever. We both grew up here, but it's not like we've ever hung out together. A few parties maybe, but just because we were both there."

Hank pursed his lips and then sighed. "Okay, well, let's start with you, Gavin."

Gavin's head jerked up. "Do you think he will talk to me?"

Hank stood, and both Larry and Byron followed. "I have no idea, but I do know that they are releasing him to his parents later tonight. We need to go now." He turned to Rocky. "You okay with this."

Rocky shrugged. "Sure. We need to try all options."

"Okay then, will you still be here, or do I need to bring him home?"

"How long will you be?" asked Rocky.

"Maybe an hour tops. We won't get much time with him. His attorney is meeting us there."

Rocky smiled. "What if I would have said no?"

Hank grinned and grabbed his coat as the server delivered a large platter of hot bread and chili to the table.

"Decided I would take a chance. I had to ask either you or Jackson, and I figured one of you would say yes." He glanced at the food. "I'll bring him here. Doesn't look like you folks are going too far very soon."

〰

Gavin fidgeted with his zipper on his coat. The jail visiting area felt cold and foreboding. It was empty, except for the party waiting to see Brandon.

Byron, Hank, and Larry all stood behind him, but Lance Anderson, Brandon's attorney, sat in the chair next to him.

Hank addressed the attorney as Lance, but the two FBI agents called him Mr. Anderson. He asked them to call him Lance and nodded in Gavin's direction, "You too."

Gavin looked over at Lance, who was entering some notes in his tablet. Gavin was surprised at how young he was. Clean cut blonde hair and wearing what appeared to be an expensive suit. Gavin recognized quality in men's suits. His step-dad, Doug, wore nothing but the best, and the light gray tailored suit this attorney wore was nothing short of the best.

Suddenly, Lance looked up. "Are you okay?"

Gavin blushed. "Yeah, I guess. What am I supposed to do?"

"Just talk to him. Ask him what got him involved in it. Just follow your gut. I want to help him, too. His parents are not dealing with this very well."

Lance motioned to the glass partition in front of them, and Gavin turned to face it. He gasped when he saw Brandon.

Hands and feet in shackles, and wearing an orange jumpsuit, Brandon's face was drawn and pale. His weary eyes averted Gavin's as he sat down in the only chair.

Lance picked up the phone, and Brandon did the same.

"Brandon, you know Gavin, don't you?"

Brandon nodded, but he still didn't look up.

"Okay, I am going to leave you two to talk for a few minutes."

Lance handed the phone to Gavin.

"Hey, Brandon."

Brandon nodded.

Gavin didn't know what else to say, so he just sat there.

Finally, Brandon looked up. "Why did they bring you here?"

Gavin shrugged. "I guess since we are, you know, kind of friends, that maybe you would talk to me."

Brandon shook his head. "Nothing to say."

That frustrated Gavin, and he leaned closer to the glass. "Brandon, you didn't plan this all on your own. Geez, you called the fire department. Who put you up to this?'

Brandon looked directly at Gavin. "Can't say."

Gavin looked into Brandon's clouded eyes. "Dude."

Brandon abruptly stood. "I gotta go now. Thanks for coming."

He hung up the phone, nodded briefly at Lance, and then turned and said something to the guard who was with him.

Gavin couldn't hear what he said, but in seconds, both Brandon and the guard disappeared.

Gavin stared at his reflection in the glass. Finally, he hung up the phone and turned to face the four men. He shrugged. "Sorry."

Hank put a hand on Gavin's shoulder. "It's okay. It was a long shot."

Lance hung behind, but Byron and Larry followed Hank and Gavin into the hall.

When they stepped out into the cool afternoon air, Gavin tried to suppress the tears that pricked the corners of his eyes.

51

BALCONY

ASPEN STROLLED ALONG THE *cobblestone path. At least it looked like cobblestone, except it was the color of gold. She stopped, bent down and, rubbed her hand across the surface. She got closer. It is gold, I think.*

She stood and turned slowly in a circle. Flowers everywhere. Trees and bushes the most incredible color of green she had ever seen, and she could not remember ever seeing such brilliant colors of flowers. Some of the colors she didn't even know existed.

The only sounds she could hear was running water somewhere in the distance and the beautiful singing of birds.

"They are singing, not chirping."

This time she whirled around quickly.

"Where am I?"

She thought she heard something above her and she looked up. Before her, seemingly in a cloud, or a mist, was a tall white building. It appeared to be about three stories and had several windows side by side on each level.

A balcony encircled the entire second level for as far as she could see. The building appeared to be made of stone, or marble. She wasn't sure.

A girl appeared at the edge of the balcony. She looked down at Aspen and waved.

"Krista?"

The girl turned slightly, and another girl stood next to her. Immediately a boy appeared. The girl and the boy were strangely familiar to Aspen. He grinned, but the girl did not, and then all of them were gone.

Aspen opened her eyes and stared at the ceiling. She could hear rain pelting the window of Rocky's living room where she was sleeping.

She looked at the clock on the desk.

Five am.

Suddenly, she jumped up. She grabbed her cell phone and without thinking, punched Rocky's name in her contacts.

It rang several times and then finally she heard Rocky.

"Hello?" he croaked.

"Rocky! Can you get us in the school?"

"Aspen, what time is it?"

"It's five am. Don't kill me. Can you get us in the school—today?"

"Uh, yeah, I guess I can. Sure. What for? What is this all about?"

"I'm not exactly sure, well, at least I think I'm sure, but not totally."

Rocky sighed. "Okay, okay. I'll get up. You know you could have just knocked on my door."

"True. Didn't think of that. I need to wake up Noah, and Kiryn, and Gavin but—"

"No, it's okay. I'll wake the boys. You get Kiryn."

"Thanks, Rocky! Really, thanks!"

"Yeah, yeah. No worries."

Since the fire, she and Noah had been staying with Rocky.

Noah was sleeping in the other twin bed in Gavin's room and Aspen on the pull-out sofa in the living room. Their parents and Aunt Dana were still at the Sommerville Motel.

Mom was hoping they could have the little house back by Christmas, which was just three weeks away.

Aspen fidgeted with her hands while Rocky unlocked one of the side doors to the school. When the five of them entered, they were met by a custodian. The school smelled of fresh-cut pine from the huge Christmas tree in the front foyer by the offices.

"Hey, Mr. Fielden? Making these kids come to school on the weekend?"

Rocky laughed. "No, but it couldn't hurt, Bill. I need to get into one of the storage rooms upstairs. Could you help me with that?"

"Sure thing." Bill pulled on a round silver key ring that held, as much as Aspen could tell, at least thirty keys.

They all followed him up the stairs. Bill and Rocky chatted as they walked ahead of the kids.

Kiryn yawned. "So you have been pretty quiet about this adventure. What gives?"

Aspen took a deep breath, but then let it out before she said anything. Her silence caused her brother and two friends to stop and turn their attention to her.

"Remember that first day in the classroom when that desk hit me?'

"Yes! That was crazy!" said Kiryn.

"Totally weird," said Gavin.

Noah rolled his eyes. "Well, it seemed weird then, but now it's all in a day's work."

Aspen smacked his shoulder.

"What? It's the truth."

Aspen twisted her mouth and then rolled her own eyes. "True."

"Anyway," Kiryn drawled.

"Well, last night I had a dream, and I think—wait let me back up—that day after the desk hit me, I saw a kid, sitting at a desk. Only for a second, but I did."

"A kid?" Gavin's eyes narrowed. "What kid?"

"Do you think it may have been Thomas, Ronda's boyfriend?"

Aspen shook her head in response to Noah's question, but she did not look at any of them. She was looking down, trying to make sense of what she was about to say.

"No. But, okay, so now the dream. I was in a place that seemed familiar. Like I had been there before, but I haven't because there is no place on earth, at least I don't think there is, that has colors like that. But—"

She looked up, suddenly aware of the complete silence. All three of their faces displayed serious questionable looks.

"Are you kids coming or not?" Rocky and Bill had disappeared into the open storage room, but Rocky stepped into the hall and called to them.

"Coming!" called Noah, and the four slowly walked down the hall.

Aspen continued, "So, in the dream, I saw Krista, some other girl, and some guy, who I swear I know, or have known or something! *Ahhh*! I am not sure!"

"So, do you think the kid at the desk was the same guy?" asked Gavin.

"Kind of. I have nothing to base it on except a feeling."

Noah chuckled, "So that's normal, go on."

Aspen scowled at him. "I hate that my not normal is so normal!"

They all laughed.

They reached the storage room, and Aspen stopped at the doorway, turned and said to her friends, I hope I can see him again. If I can't, this is a wasted exercise."

When the four walked into the room, Rocky said to Bill, "Do you think I could have a few minutes alone with the kids?"

"Sure, no problem. I am heading back downstairs." He walked out into the hall and pointing to the door and said, "Just turn that latch before you close the door, and it will lock. I will deadbolt it later."

Rocky was a little taken back by that comment. "Why does it have to be deadbolted? It's just storage."

Bill shrugged. "Don't know. Got my orders. Something about history. Nice to visit with you, Mr. Fielden."

"Likewise, Bill. See you on Monday."

Bill waved and his footsteps became quieter as he walked away from them.

Rocky turned to Aspen. "So what is the mystery?" He pulled a chair away from a round table and motioned for them all to sit.

Aspen remained standing. "I just need to go over by the window."

Rocky, Noah, Gavin, and Kiryn stayed seated at the table. No one said anything. They just watched her.

Aspen walked to the window, stopped and peered out. That first day's experiences ran like a movie through her mind. Meeting bubbly Kiryn, mesmerized by gorgeous Gavin, Noah standing aloof away from all of them, finding names on the desks, the strange feeling she had when she passed one of the desks and, the boy sitting at the desk.

She turned toward the few desks crowded together. There weren't as many as the first day. The project that day was to clean them for the historical society, or something like that, to purchase them.

She stared silently, nothing.

She turned back to the window, remembering the desk that sailed across the floor and smacked her side, knocking her to the floor. It all seemed so strange and distant now, and yet she couldn't dismiss the fact that it was somehow important that she come here this morning.

"Anything?" Kiryn whispered.

Aspen shook her head. "Rocky, do you know who bought the desks?"

"No, but I can find out. Why? Is the desk you were thinking of missing?"

"I'm not sure. The only significant thing about it was that I got kind of an eerie feeling when I walked by it, and then I saw a boy sitting there, just for a second."

Rocky's eyebrows shot up. "Really? Could it have been Thomas?"

"We already crossed that bridge," said Kiryn.

"We thought that because that is the only boy spirit, right, Aspen?"

"Right." Aspen nodded. She still stared at the desk. She felt absolutely nothing.

Finally, she walked directly across the floor toward the door. "I'm sorry you guys. This is a total waste of time."

They all stood.

"There is no hurry," said Rocky. "Nothing is really a waste of time because we can just cross it off the list."

"You mean the one we don't have written down?" asked Noah.

"Yeah, that one. That keeps growing and growing," said Gavin.

Aspen rubbed her face with both hands. "I guess I was wrong. Let's go. We all have Christmas shopping to do right?"

"I haven't even thought about Christmas shopping," said Noah.

"I'm not buying anybody anything," chided Rocky and followed the kids to the door.

"Well, gee, that's great," said Kiryn, and she glared at her dad.

"Well, how good have you been this year? And let's be honest," laughed Rocky.

"I have been perfect!"

"Oh, wow, that must be some other daughter."

"Seriously, none of us know that perfect girl," said Gavin.

"What's happening with Brandon? Do we know yet, Rocky?" Noah suddenly changed the subject.

"I'm not sure. I did get a text from your dad while we have been sitting here. He wants us to go to the big house today."

"Did he say why?"

"He said it has to do with the office."

Everyone was in the hallway except Aspen, and the other's voices sounded strangely distant to her. She stopped and turned one more time toward the desks.

Are you here? She silently pleaded.

Nothing. She sighed and turned again to walk out of the room.

"Aspen."

She whirled, and for one brief second, she saw him. The kid at the desk. He grinned, just like he had that first day, but then as quickly as he had appeared, he was gone.

Aspen gasped. "Oh, my gosh!"

But no sooner had the words escaped her lips when another

figure appeared. He was near or maybe in the window. She couldn't tell. Her mind raced. The kid at the desk had red hair.

She moved toward the window. The morning sunlight peering through made it hard to see the figure clearly.

Directly in front of the window now, Aspen stared with disbelief.

The figure was a boy with red hair and freckles.

Aspen could barely breathe. She put the palm of her hand on the window, but she only felt the cold glass.

The boy grinned. It was the same boy.

Wide-eyed and stunned, Aspen stared at the familiar face of this boy, but then he was gone. She pressed her nose against the glass as if she could maybe see him outside the window, but there was nothing but the treeless brown winter grass of the school courtyard.

Back at Rocky's, they gathered in the kitchen for BLTs for breakfast. They all helped put the meal together. All but Aspen.

She sat at the nook, staring out the window.

Where had she seen that kid before? She had no idea. *No recollection of ever meeting a red-haired boy.* Trying to figure it out was giving her a headache.

She turned around in her seat when Kiryn plopped a BLT and glass of apple juice in front of her.

"I have egg nog if you would rather." Kiryn was saying.

"No, this is perfect. Thank you."

Noah took a bite of his sandwich and munched it slowly while studying his sister.

"What?" Aspen demanded.

"Well, we were thinking." Noah swallowed before he continued. "You said the place you saw was something you had never seen before, right?"

Aspen nodded.

"But it was familiar to you?" asked Gavin.

"Yes."

Kiryn looked quickly at Rocky, Noah, and then Gavin. "Aspen, do you think maybe you like died or something? That maybe you went to heaven?"

Aspen looked at Rocky. "Did they say I died?"

"I don't think so, but you were in a coma. Maybe then?"

"Maybe you didn't die, Aspen. Maybe you met this guy then, in the coma," said Gavin.

Noah looked around at all of them. "Is that even possible?"

Rocky sighed. "I wouldn't discount anything at this point."

They all nodded and continued to eat in silence.

Aspen leaned back and rubbed the back of her neck with her hand. "Ugh. This is so complicated! Why, if I am supposed to know this guy or he is supposed to help me or us or whoever, why doesn't he just come up to me and say, 'Hi Aspen. I'm Max. I knew you in the coma.'"

Aspen froze, and everyone stared at her.

"*Max!* His name is *Max!*"

"Who do you know named, Max? We don't know a Max." Noah blurted.

"That kid! The red kid. I mean, the red-haired kid! His name is Max! I am sure of it!"

They continued to stare at her.

Aspen slammed her fists on the table. "I am telling you that kid is Max! I don't know where from or how I know him, but he is Max!"

"Okay, calm down." Gavin covered her fists with both of his hands.

Kiryn leaned toward her friend. "We believe you, Aspen. You said, just now, that you knew him in the coma."

Aspen's eyes widened, "I did?"

Noah nodded. "And we believe you, Aspen. We just need to figure out who—"

"Or *what*—"

Noah and Gavin glared at Kiryn, but she shrugged.

"I'm just sayin'. She met him in a *coma?*"

Tears welled up in Aspen's eyes.

Kiryn threw her arms around her friend, "Oh, good grief! The only thing I meant was how are we going to meet him? I, for one, am not willing to go into a coma to meet this Max guy."

Aspen forced back the tears. "I just thought for a minute you all thought I was crazy—again."

Kiryn pulled away from her and cocked her head to one side. "Well—"

"What she means is, I think we are all accustomed to that, right Kiryn?" Rocky chuckled. "And you should not be offended by it."

Aspen wiped her face. "I'm not. I'm really not."

The doorbell rang, and Rocky glanced at the clock on the microwave as he left the kitchen to answer it.

"Does everyone have to start so early on Saturday? It's not even eight yet," he mumbled as he opened the door.

"Hey! Good morning! Come in and join the party. We have been up for hours!"

"You answered my text, so I figured you must be up."

Aspen heard her dad's voice.

"Hey, Dad!" called Noah. "We have just confirmed Aspen has been two-timing Gavin with some guy named Max."

Aspen glared at him. "Thanks."

Noah shrugged. "Well, it could be."

Jackson said hi to everyone and then turned to Aspen, "Who's Max?"

52

UNDER THE DESK

ASPEN RODE WITH HER dad on the way to the big house. She told him all that had happened; the dream, going to the school, the red-haired kid at the desk, and at the window. She said his name just suddenly popped into her head while she was eating her BLT. She said there was probably no connection, but that was what she was doing.

That made Dad laugh.

Mom and Aunt Dana were already in the office of the big house when Dad arrived with Aspen. Rocky, Gavin, Noah, and Kiryn came right behind them.

"Good morning!" Aunt Dana seemed even more cheerful than usual if that was possible. Aspen could not believe how upbeat she was all the time.

"She hasn't told us anything. She read her emails this morning and was pounding on our door at six AM," said Dad.

Rocky rolled his eyes. "No one sleeps anymore."

Noah turned to Aunt Dana. "What?"

Aunt Dana's eyes twinkled. She reached in her jeans pocket and pulled out a folded piece of paper. When she opened it, Aspen could see it was a printed email message.

"Listen to this," Dana unfolded it and read:

Dana, I found this last night. I have been going through every single paper we have of your dad's, hoping maybe we missed something. We did, and it is something big. It was not your dad's however; I believe this belonged to your grandpa. —Jerry

Dana spread the first page out on the desk and then opened the second page. "This was an attachment to the email Jerry sent."

It was easy to see the attachment was a copy of a very old type-written note.

```
Dixon - You have to move the desk. There
is a small door under the rug. Open it,
and there will be a latch. Just turn it.
It's kind of hard to move. The cables run
under the floor to the bookcase. Everything
is there. You need to destroy all of that
before Allen gets back. If that ever gets
uncovered, we are all ruined.

- Demot
```

"What is that?" Jackson took the paper from Dana's outstretched hand.

"Who is Demot?" asked Gavin.

"Great a new name, and we were just getting to know everyone." Aunt Dana put her hands on her cheeks and shook her head. "This is *crazy!*"

"E-er. craz*ier*," said Noah.

Dad was studying the note. "Do you recognize that name?"

Dana shook her head, No, but remember I told you about the conversation between the two-cleaning staff that I overheard? I told Jerry about it, and it reminded him of a paper that he had seen. He had put it aside because it did not have Grandpa or Dad's name on it, but then, just in case it might mean something, he emailed it to me last night."

Everyone turned to the massive oak desk.

"Well, let's move it!" Noah grabbed the eagle bookends, and quickly, everyone moved something off the desk while Dana pushed the leather chair out of the way.

"This thing must weigh five-hundred pounds!" said Dad.

Mom grabbed his arm. "Don't you help Jackson. You just had a heart attack!"

Reluctantly, Jackson backed away and watched while the others inched the heavy desk off the large circular rug and onto the wood floor.

As soon as it was clear, he got down on the floor, and with Noah, Gavin, and Rocky's help, rolled the thick rug until it was in a long thick tube shape, and out of the way.

Sure enough, under the rug was a door. It was about two feet square and had a recessed handle.

Jackson reached for it, but then suddenly, sat back on his heels. He looked up at Dana. "Is there a date on that note?"

Dana quickly scanned the document. "Yes. December 10, 1982." She looked up at Jackson and said quietly, "Dad and Mom were killed on December 11th that year." She winced. "Do you think Dad knew about this?"

Jackson shrugged, "Maybe." He looked at Suzann, shook his head, and again reached for the handle.

The small door creaked when it opened.

Dad brushed the cobwebs aside and reached for the handle and attempted to turn it, but it did not budge. He tried again. Still nothing. He grabbed it with both hands and tried one more time. This time it moved, just a tiny bit.

No one noticed that Gavin had left the room, but now he jogged back in. He was holding a can. "It was behind the seat of your truck, Dad."

"I know," said Rocky. "Good thinking."

Gavin knelt and sprayed the crank with the chemical.

Dad waited a few seconds and then tried the handle again. This time it moved easier, slowly, but it did move.

Loud creaking and groaning coming from the bookcase made all of them all turn around. It reminded Aspen of something from a scary movie.

To the astonishment of everyone in the room, the entire bookcase separated in the middle and each section pivoted from the center. The huge shelves turned ever so slowly, completely reversing and falling awkwardly into place, revealing an entirely different set of bookcases.

"Holy smokes!" said Kiryn.

Mouths gaping, they all stared at the dusty bookcases.

There were a few random books on some of the shelves, but what caught Jackson and Suzann's attention was the panel that ran the full-length across the bottom.

Jackson stood and walked directly to the corner with Suzann right on his heels.

He knelt and grasped the end of the bookcase just like he had done the day of the fire.

He jerked on it, and the entire panel fell away, revealing a row of file drawers that extended from one end of the bookcase to the other.

Mom squealed, and immediately knelt and pulled open the first drawer. Pulling out the first file right from where she had put it back nearly three weeks earlier. She held it up and waved it back and forth. "Look! Robbie Ackerman—Seventeen!" She squealed. She turned to her husband and threw her arms around his neck. "Oh, Jackson! They really were here!"

Jackson stood and pulled her to her feet, hugging her back as the file folder dropped to the floor.

Rocky picked it up. He leafed through it, and then pulled open a second drawer. The kids followed suit, each opening another file. "These files have the kid's names, birthdates, phone numbers, addresses! You hit the jackpot, Jackson!"

Every drawer was crammed with dusty manila file folders, each revealing the name of a different boy. They read a few random folders, and not one was over the age of nineteen.

"What does this mean?" Kiryn's wide eyes described what all of them were thinking.

"It means the boys did exist. That's what it means," said Rocky.

"But that information is over fifty years old, how good can it be now?" asked Suzann.

"I was wondering the same thing," Jackson turned to this sister, "Dana I don't think Dad ever saw that note."

"I don't either."

Gavin suddenly blurted, "Aspen, did you see that?"

Aspen was looking in the same direction as Gavin, and she nodded vigorously. "Yes! Boys! I can see boys!"

Kiryn looked in the same direction, "Where are they?"

But it was Dad who pointed toward the picture window behind where the desk had stood. "Right there," he said quietly.

53

STRANGER

AFTER GAVIN, KIRYN, AND Aspen rolled the shelves away from the wall, and Noah removed the poster board. With flashlights, the four made their way down the narrow staircase, and to the small room at the bottom.

They knew this would be the last time they would see it this way.

Dad had given the okay to reopen the wall where Aspen first fell into the shaft, as well as to the staircase. So, they knew it would all change, and they just had to go back one more time.

Aspen plopped down on the floor next to the open hole where the box had been safely tucked away for over fifteen years, maybe longer. One thing for sure, the secret her Great-Grandfather Allen had kept in his heart, tormented him a lot longer than that.

His daughter, Ronda, disappeared around 1939, and depending on when he found out that she had been murdered, he could have harbored that secret for over fifty years.

"We've come a long way since this room," said Gavin.

"No kidding. Remember when you jumped off the ladder and landed on this spot? Who knew that you were standing right on top of one of the Allen secrets?"

Gavin shrugged at Noah's comment. "That was just an accident."

"I don't believe that. Nothing is really an accident," said Aspen. "Things happen for a reason, and one thing leads to another until—"

"Until we find statues of dead—" Kiryn noticed the scrutinizing looks she was getting from her brother and friends. "Okay…statues *representing* dead people, and then…" she flipped her hand in the air, "the actual *bones* of dead people." She shuddered. "Still gives me the creeps."

Aspen picked up a handful of the dirt they had taken out of the hole. She let it fall through her fingers. "Noah, do you remember that soap opera Grandma used to watch?"

Noah rolled his eyes. "You mean the one *we* watched with her? So, lame."

Aspen laughed. "Yes, that one." She explained to Gavin and Kiryn.

"Sometimes, when we went to stay with Grandma, at about one in the afternoon, she would get us a snack, and we would all sit down and watch this half -hour soap opera."

"She means every time, not sometimes," said Noah.

"Soap opera?" Kiryn was obviously puzzled.

"Yes, it's a half-hour show that goes on day after day and tells a story. It's all so crazy, and the drama is unbelievable, so I guess that's why they named them 'soap' operas because they were basically ongoing dramas," said Aspen.

"And Grandma would talk about the characters like they were real. It's pretty funny, now that I look back at it."

"So, we are living our own soap opera!" Kiryn laughed. "Maybe we should sell the rights to our story."

"It would take so long to write the story," said Gavin. "Makes me tired just thinking about it."

"Well, we would hire writers." Kiryn seemed satisfied that this was a good idea.

Gavin gave his sister a disparaging look. "Calm down. I think we should just forget the soap opera." He turned to Aspen. "Why did you bring that up anyway?"

"Huh?" Aspen was repeatedly picking up the dirt and letting it sift through her fingers. She looked up. "Oh! Well, I was thinking of the beginning of the one we watched with Grandma. There was an hourglass on the screen."

She changed her voice to a lower octave. "Like sands through the hourglass, so are the Days of our Lives."

Noah laughed. "That was perfect! *Days of our Lives*. Yep, that's what we watched over peanut butter sandwiches, chips, and soda."

"Sounds like lunch, not snack," said Kiryn.

"To Grandma, that was a snack," said Noah.

Aspen suddenly stood up. "Well, thank heavens, this is not our life." She brushed her hands together, and tiny particles of dirt fell from them.

They all stared at the small pile of dust and dirt. The falling particles fell right back into the pile.

Now Kiryn stood, "Yep, still creepy."

They all laughed, picked up their flashlights, and started for the narrow staircase, but Aspen went a different direction.

"We have to go down to the room one more time."

Saying nothing, they all followed.

The small room at the bottom of the winding staircase looked the same. The brick wall, the thick door they had just come through now stood open. The door Aspen's hand had gone through. The same one that pulled her and Dad into it—Dad right through it— still stood, mysteriously untouched.

The fake doorknob still lay where it had dropped.

"This is one place I am anxious for them to investigate. I really wonder what is beyond that door," said Noah.

They all nodded. "Me, too. I hope they will show us," said Aspen.

"They *have* to show us. It's your dad's house," said Kiryn emphatically.

"Them, not us," said Gavin.

Aspen put her arm through Gavin's. "We are only us. There is no *them*. The four of us are *us*."

Gavin turned to her, and his eyes narrowed.

"Was that corny?"

Noah answered for Gavin. "Pretty much."

Aspen raised her eyebrows. "Fine." She let go of Gavin's arm, and he followed Noah to the staircase.

Aspen turned to Kiryn, but before she said anything, Kiryn said, "Yeah, I'm going to have to go along with the guys on this one." And she followed the boys.

Aspen picked up her flashlight. "Whatever."

Just before she ascended the stairs, she turned back.

It was only a flash, but they were there. The entire room was filled with boys, and then they were gone.

Aspen turned, and again started up the stairs, but she glanced back one more time.

Nothing.

Bye, little room.

Discovery of the file folders once again brought the Allen Family mystery to the front headlines of the news, and Sommerville was swarming with more FBI agents and news media. The files revealed two hundred and eleven names. All of them were male, between the ages of sixteen and nineteen. Most were white or African American, but there were also a few Mexican and Asian names.

Investigators set up a command post at the city office building, where they were pouring over the files. The team hoped to contact the person whose name was in the file, the family of that person, or at least relatives of all two hundred and eleven boys.

The same team was also researching archived articles from the 1930s through the 1980s which included the time frame that Allen-Dixon, Inc. became a company, until both of their deaths. Dixon in 1995 and Great-Grandpa Allen in 1998.

Another investigation born from the latest finding was the instigation of a forensic team. Dad and Aunt Dana gave the FBI access to the tunnel under the Mansion House after Noah showed them the pictures he had taken of the pile of bones. They also had access to the shaft and the staircase leading from the master bedroom.

The fact that Aspen, Gavin, and now Dad had *seen* some boys, was hardly evidence that would hold up in any sane court in the country, so that part of the mystery was not disclosed to the media or the investigators.

However, it only fueled the fire for Aspen to get to the bottom of why this was happening. *What did they want from her?*

Having Gavin and Dad now able to see them as well, gave her confidence that maybe there truly was a meaningful message in all of this. Could it really be possible that all of them were dead? It made her shudder to think about it.

It was two weeks until Christmas, and the renovation of the little house was nearly complete. The family would be moving back in on Sunday, which was in two days.

News media were everywhere, and because of the latest findings, they were pouncing on every opportunity to take pictures or get an interview with any member of the family.

For some strange reason, possibly because Aspen had recovered, the news media didn't pay much attention to Mystic Lake. So, that Friday afternoon, the four friends took refuge there. They wanted to get away from everyone just for a little while.

But there were some people they could not escape. The FBI agents. Same black suits, same neat haircuts, same black SUV, just different faces. Aspen didn't even know any of their names.

Hank called Dad and Rocky just before the kids started their trek to Mystic Lake. He told them he would like to stop by later tonight for a few minutes. He said he had an update on Brandon, but he wouldn't give them any more information than that.

It had not rained in several days, but it was cold. They built a big fire, and huddled on a blanket, drinking individual thermoses of hot chocolate and reminisced about the time since they had first met at the school.

So much had happened. Dixon—Dylan and Drew, Krista's death, the mysteries in the Mansion House, Dad's heart attack, Mom's mysterious secret about Drew when they first arrived in Sommerville, Rocky getting beat up, Joseph, the paintings, the mist in the lake, the lake itself, the bones, the statue, Great-Grandpa Allen, the tunnel under the house, the rooms under the other side of the house, secret passages, Patrice, Gavin's accident, Aspen's coma, Cassie, Brandon, Aunt Dana, the journals and notes, the fire. They hashed through it all, and it was exhausting.

At one point, they sat quietly staring at the lake. It wasn't cold enough for the water to freeze, so it lapped lazily onto the muddy shores.

Mystic Lake held so many unsolved mysteries for them.

The lights that appeared to Aspen, and the mist that lifted from the top, then there was the cave the divers told them about, and the culvert that loomed about twenty feet off the shore, forbidding anyone to go near it.

Probably the most incredible fact, at least to Aspen, was that she had spent more than twenty-four hours under the water.

"And now this Max guy," said Noah. "Who *is* he?"

No one responded because no one had anything to say about Max. If he was even real. The only person who had seen him was Aspen, and she wasn't even sure if he was an imaginary being or someone she knew.

Two things for certain, his name suddenly came to her, *and* she had seen him at the desk in the storage room at Sommerville High, months ago. Other than that, she was not sure of anything concerning this so-called Max person.

Well, was she even sure of that? The kid at the desk had red hair and freckles, and she kept thinking of a boy with those same characteristics, but were they the *same* person? Who knew?

"Do you guys even know any of these people that live in the other houses on Mystic Lake?" asked Kiryn. "I mean, you all live here. Do you ever see anyone else?"

Gavin shrugged. "I haven't seen anyone when I've been here. The properties are secluded from each other. Mom said a lot of the people don't even live here year-round. The people who built these homes are either dead or really old."

Aspen looked at Noah, and they both agreed with Gavin.

"We haven't seen anyone either, except for Drew and the other gardeners," said Noah.

Kiryn quickly scanned the trees around the lake. "Seems weird. The trees could be hiding just about anything."

"That's unsettling," said Noah.

"But true," said Aspen.

With evening coming, it was starting to get dark and significantly colder. They decided to go back to Rocky's and started to put out the fire.

"Hey."

Startled, they all turned to see a man walking toward them. He was coming from the path that most likely led to the house next to Gavin's mom and step-dad's house.

The shadows of the trees made it hard to see him, but when he came into view, they all stared in disbelief.

About the same height as Gavin but older and more muscular. He appeared to be in his mid-twenties.

Before he reached them, two FBI agents were on either side of him.

The stranger stopped immediately and held up both hands. In a strong Australian accent, he said, "Sorry, I just wanted to talk to them." He motioned to the four teenagers.

"About what?" one of the agents stood squarely in front of him, the other next to him, his hand on his gun.

"Just about— It's hard to explain."

"I'll bet it is," said the first agent. "You need to come with us."

The second agent motioned to the kids, "You guys get the fire out now and head back. We'll be right behind you with our new friend."

Without saying anything, they all obeyed. They quickly doused the fire and started toward the path leading to the Mansion house.

Aspen glanced back. The man with the shocking red hair and freckles was looking right at her.

54

SUSPECTS

Hank, Rocky, Jackson, and Suzann gathered around the small desk in the Allen's room at the Sommerville Motel.

Mystified, Rocky read the information that Hank had provided one more time. He looked up at Hank, "Do you have any idea who paid for this?"

"Well, we didn't, but now we have an idea, at least a possible lead."

Jackson eyed Hank. "But you're not going to tell us, are you?"

Hank grinned. "No, but I will tell you that a couple of other things have surfaced over the past week."

Rocky plopped his elbow on the desk, chin in hand. "Do tell. I am still trying to figure out who has that kind of money to pay a half-million dollars to a hospital."

"And why?" asked Suzann.

"The *why* we know," said Hank.

They all looked at him in surprise.

"But—"

"You are not going to tell us," said Jackson.

Hank avoided the question. "I will tell you that Drew called me last week. He said Dylan suddenly came into some money. Not a lot of money, but more than he usually has. Guess he was spending more than normal and Drew asked him about it. The other curious part about Dylan; remember his truck broke down out near Mystic

Lake the day of the fire?"

Rocky nodded, but Suzann and Jackson didn't seem to know about that.

Hank went on, "Well, supposedly it did. That's why Drew was out there the day of the fire. To help Dylan, but when Drew called me, he also told me that after things settled down that day, he and Dylan went to get the truck, and the only thing wrong was the battery was dead."

"Why would that be unusual?"

"It wouldn't be, except that Dylan didn't say that to Drew when he called him. He didn't say, bring jumper cables, he said that he broke down. I guess Drew found that odd, where Dylan is concerned."

"He probably knew Drew always had cables in his truck. He's a gardener. I'm sure he has tools," said Jackson.

"Maybe," said Hank. "I don't know Dylan that well, but he is Drew's brother, and he found that odd I guess."

Rocky shrugged. "Okay, and as far as the money, maybe Dylan was doing some extra work for someone."

Hank nodded and again said, "Maybe." But he didn't volunteer anything else.

"There's more?"

Hank smiled at Jackson. "Yes, Brandon finally broke down and talked to his parents."

Suzann's eyes widened. "Why? What made him do that?"

"That's the curious part. I guess Brandon's older sister lives in Memphis. She has two little kids and has been in and out of the hospital with cancer. The bills are killing them, and they have exhausted all of her husband's insurance."

"The money was for her? Who would do that?"

"That's what we are not sure of yet, Suzann. But Kirk Tuttle, that's Brandon's dad, called me yesterday. He said Brandon told them who put him up to all of this, and why." Hank quickly clarified, "Why Brandon did it, not why they wanted your house set on fire. He has no idea."

"So wait, whoever wanted our house burned, paid the hospital a half-million dollars for Brandon's sister's care?"

Hank nodded in response to Jackson's question. "Apparently."

"Well, no wonder he did it! It isn't rocket science. He's a kid and saw a chance to help his sister. I wouldn't think he intended to hurt anyone," said Suzann.

"Pretty much, but arson is a serious crime, Suzann."

"I know." Suzann sighed. "I know. It's just that—"

Jackson patted her hand. "He's just a kid."

She nodded but said nothing.

"I'm sure all of this will be taken into consideration at his trial."

"When will that be?" asked Rocky.

"I believe it is scheduled for February or March."

"So who put him up to it?"

"Well, Rocky, that is the curious part. He said it was Cassie."

This news shocked everyone in the room.

"Cassie? Why would she— Better yet, where did she get that kind of money?"

"Both good questions that I don't know the answer to."

"Isn't she the one who called Aspen a witch?" asked Suzann.

"Yes, but you wouldn't think she would go to his extent to hurt Aspen."

"I don't know, Jackson, teenagers can be pretty ruthless. Maybe she just wanted you guys to leave."

Rocky nodded. "Yeah, she and Gavin have been off and on for a couple of years or more. Although, I didn't weigh too much into it. They were only sophomores when they started dating."

"But is that reason to burn someone's house down, because someone stole your boyfriend?" asked Jackson. "That's ludicrous."

"I agree, and we don't know. There may be more to it than that. We are bringing her in for questioning Monday morning."

"Why not tomorrow or Sunday, or doesn't the FBI question people on weekends?"

Hank laughed, "Yes, Jackson, they work every day. But Cassie is in New York. She dances, and I guess she is at a national competition or something. She gets home late Saturday night or early Sunday morning; I'm not exactly sure."

"Can't her parents bring her back early?" asked Jackson, and it was not hard to hear the irritation in his voice.

"She isn't with her parents. She went with her dance studio and a lot of other students. We are just trying to let her come home, trying not to alarm her so that she doesn't try to contact whomever her hookup is—if there is a hookup."

"So, you don't think it was her idea?" asked Suzann.

Hank shook his head. "No."

Suddenly there were no more questions. Everyone was quiet for several minutes, and then Hank broke the silence. "I know it's a lot to take in."

Suzann shook her head slowly. "There is so much going on. The fire, the files, the bones under the house— "She looked at Jackson, "And then there is that painting? That is so curious."

She turned to Hank, "Do you think we will ever figure all of this out?"

"I don't know," said Hank. "Your kids—all four of them—have really made some progress. Maybe had we been involved early on, we could be farther along by now."

"That's our fault." Jackson quickly stepped in. "Well, my fault. I was just hoping to get into Sommerville, sell the house, and go back to California. I haven't even worked since we got out here."

"That's not a worry, Jackson. Your clients understand. Besides Clint is taking care of everything, right? And your attorneys are there." Suzann clarified for Rocky and Hank, "Clint is Jackson's partner, sort of partner, the business is Jackson's."

"Well, it was." Laughed Jackson. "Guess we'll see about that."

55

SHOCKING NEWS

TWO MORE FBI AGENTS were waiting when the kids approached the back patio of the Mansion House. One of them spoke into a cell phone. "We have the four kids. Suspect heading your way with Simpson and Fry."

Neither of them spoke to the teenagers, they just motioned them to the front of the house and then to the Iroc parked in the driveway.

The second agent spoke directly to Gavin. "We will follow you to your dad's."

Gavin nodded, and the four piled into the Iroc.

"Was he ordering us to go home?" asked Gavin after he closed the door.

"I would say so," said Noah. He started the engine and pulled slowly out of the driveway. He looked in the rearview mirror. The black SUV was right behind them.

"Who was that guy? Do you know him, Aspen?"

"Why would I know him, Noah?"

"He has red hair—"

"He does, but he is way older than the kid I saw. And bigger. *Way* bigger."

"He has a cool accent," said Kiryn.

"Do you think he lives in that house? The one he was walking away from?"

Gavin shrugged. "Have no idea. I have never seen him before in my life."

"Weird that we were just talking about never seeing any other people around Mystic Lake and then he appears," said Aspen.

"Well, I liked his accent," said Kiryn.

Gavin rolled his eyes. "Okay, we got that."

Kiryn lifted her chin and turned to Aspen. "Didn't you?"

Aspen laughed. "Yes, he did have a cool accent, but I was looking at his hair and freckles. And his eyes. They were green."

Gavin looked back at Aspen from the front seat. "You noticed his eyes?"

"Not at first, but when I turned back around, I did. His eyes were an intense green, and I remembered seeing those eyes before."

"Where? In your dream, at the school, in the coma?"

Aspen smiled. "Maybe, but also, right there." She leaned forward and pointed directly at Gavin. "He has the same eyes as you."

Gavin glared at her. "So, now I am the same as creepy Australian guy?"

Aspen leaned back. "Who said he was creepy? I didn't think he was creepy. Did you think he was creepy, Kiryn?"

Kiryn grinned, "No, not creepy at all."

Gavin turned around in his seat. "Okay, whatever."

Aspen caught Noah looking at her through the rearview mirror, and his eyes narrowed, but he was smiling.

Aspen smiled back, and then she took a deep breath. "Well," she sighed. "One more piece of the puzzle."

Gavin didn't look at her but said, "He may be nothing." He was quiet for a few seconds, then added, "But he did want to talk to us."

"Yeah, he is something," said Kiryn. "I mean something to do with— With everything—not that he is something—you know, even though he totally is, but I mean something with all of the, you know, stuff."

"The guy is in his twenties, Kiryn, don't get your hopes up."

"I'm not, Gavin, about him anyway. I just mean that he is

probably something to do, you know, with the Allen Legend." She grinned at Aspen her eyes twinkling.

Aspen chuckled at Kiryn's giddiness.

They were at Rocky's now, and they all piled out of the car. The black SUV pulled in right behind them, but the agents didn't get out.

As they walked to the house, Aspen said, "I haven't heard that for a long time, Kiryn."

"What?"

"Allen Legend."

Rocky put the two large pizzas on the seat of his truck and pulled away from Bill and Nada's.

This weekend, Noah and Kiryn would be going back to the little house with their parents and Aunt Dana. The house was finally ready for them to move into after the fire destroyed the garage, Suzann's BMW, and blackened the inside of the house, and furnishings.

Rocky had just left the Allens at the Sommerville Motel where Jackson received a call that the rest of the new furniture would be moved in tomorrow morning, and the house was ready to go.

Noah and Aspen had not heard the news. They were expecting to move on Sunday.

He knew this would be bittersweet for the kids. Even though Aspen and Noah would be glad to be back home, the four had enjoyed the past two weeks, staying together at his place.

Rocky chuckled as he walked toward the front door.

When the kids first came, just before Thanksgiving, Suzann had expressed concern, mainly about Aspen and Gavin since they were dating, and seemed to honestly love each other. She wasn't sure them being in the same house together day and night was a good idea.

Rocky had assured her that they had all stayed there several times and not to worry. Besides, Gavin was aware of imminent death—so to speak—enforced first by Jackson, and then by Rocky himself if anything went on between the two.

He juggled the pizzas and reached for the doorknob.

Now to tell them about Cassie.

56

I HATE TUNNELS

HANK FOLLOWED AN AGENT down a steep ladder and onto a dirt floor. He tried to see into the darkness, but his eyes wouldn't adjust. The agent clicked on a high beam flashlight, and Hank followed him through the musty tunnel.

After nearly ten minutes of walking, he saw some yellow caution tape up ahead and to the right of the tunnel, and he assumed that was the spot where the kids had located the bones.

The agent stopped so Hank could take some pictures. He counted eighteen tags which appeared to be attached to eighteen skulls. He shuddered and motioned for the agent to move on.

The agent continued through the tunnel. "Never get used to it, do you?"

"No. No, you never do."

Ahead of them, the tunnel was partially lighted. As they got closer, he could see large battery-operated floodlights illuminating what looked like a cinder block room. He remembered the kids telling him about this, but it was hard to imagine. Now he did not have to wonder any longer.

The small room was crowded with the eight agents, and now Hank. There was an open door opposite the side they had entered from.

A tall, skinny agent stepped forward and offered his hand. "Agent Skoresby."

Hank shook his hand briefly. "Detective Cox. What is it you wanted to show me?" He motioned to the door. "Where does that go?"

"I'll show you in a second, but first take a look at this."

Another agent turned one of the lights on the wall to Hank's left, and Agent Skoresby ran his gloved finger along a groove about a foot above his head. He stopped and continued to follow another groove all the way to the floor. He pointed out a matching groove directly opposite of the first one.

"This section looks like it has been walled up at some point. If you notice, the entire room is of cinder blocks, except for the door, but right here, there must have been another door or opening."

Hank stepped toward it and looked more closely. It was a section of cinderblocks, but each had been cut to fit into space contained inside the mortared grooves.

He looked at agent Skoresby.

"What do you want to do?"

"Cut it out. I have some people up top who are waiting for you to give the go-ahead."

"Do it."

Agent Skoresby nodded to the agent next to him who spoke into a two-way radio. "Bring them down."

Hank started for the open doorway. "Does this go to the ladder?"

The Agent looked surprised.

"The kids who found it told me about it. Well, their dad did."

The agent followed Hank, and the two of them walked to the end of the shaft."

Hank shielded his eyes from the morning sun, which shone directly down the cement pipe. "That's a bit of a climb."

Agent Skoresby pointed to the grate on top. We haven't moved that. Right now, we don't have to worry about anyone coming down here. That thing has eight locks on it."

Hank nodded and turned back toward the small room.

"Call me the minute you get through there. How long do you think it will take?

"Two or three hours, at least. We have to take it slow. We have no idea if we have dirt or cement on the other side, so we don't know how stable it is."

Hank nodded. "Okay, thanks."

Agent Skoresby nodded and motioned for the same agent that had brought Hank down, to take him back up.

Once outside, Hank climbed into his truck and grabbed an open bottle of water. He guzzled it and tossed the empty bottle onto the seat.

I hate tunnels.

He leaned on the steering wheel and stared at the massive Mansion House.

What else are you hiding?

At one time during this investigation, he had obtained a copy of a map of Mystic Lake properties. He pulled it out of the glove box and stretched it out across the seat.

He located approximately where the closet was in the Mansion House that had the tunnel entrance. With his finger, he traced an imaginary line from there to the lake in the vicinity of the culvert opening.

Then he turned his finger and traced it in a straight line to the trees between two other properties.

Bingo.

57

DOES GAVIN KNOW?

"ROCKY?" ASPEN WHISPERED SO Gavin and Noah would not hear her from Gavin's room. Noah had promised to keep Gavin busy.

Rocky cracked open his bedroom door.

"Aspen, why are you whispering?"

Aspen put her finger to her lips and motioned for Rocky to follow her.

Rocky had just taken off his socks and shoes, so he followed her in bare feet, hoping she was not taking him outside. She took him to the kitchen where Kiryn was sitting in the dark.

"What in the world—"

"Dad, shush!" Kiryn's piercing whisper was almost as loud as Rocky's normal voice.

"Okay, okay. What is going on?"

Aspen and Rocky joined Kiryn at the nook.

"Dad, we have something to tell you."

Rocky eyed them both. "What?"

"Remember when you and Sara went to that doctor appointment with Gavin, and the three of us went to lunch, and we saw Cassie and Brandon at the mall?"

Rocky nodded. "And?"

"They weren't alone," said Aspen. "They were with Dylan."

"What were they doing?"

"Just standing there talking."

Kiryn continued again, "We told Gavin about it, and he said it was no big deal because Dylan is Cassie's uncle. She is adopted, and her biological mom is Dylan and Drew's sister and—"

"Okay, I knew that."

"You did? Well, how come I never knew that?"

"You didn't need to know. Everyone protected Cassie for years. Once she was old enough and was told the truth, it was old news. Nobody cared anymore."

"Well, that's only a part of it," said Aspen.

Rocky raised his eyebrows. "How so?"

"When they were standing there, Doug Mendel walked up to them. Only for a few seconds. He handed something to Dylan and then walked away."

"Yeah, he wasn't in Sommerville as he said," added Kiryn.

Rocky thought for a minute. "My guess is that they borrowed money from him."

"For what?"

"I'm not sure, but that wouldn't be too surprising if Cassie planned something. Maybe she asked Doug for money to pay Brandon."

"Wouldn't Doug wonder what for?" asked Aspen.

Rocky squinted. "Most likely, but I still don't think it's a concern."

"Maybe. We just never told Gavin about Doug being there, and now we're worried that we should have," said Kiryn.

Rocky stood. "I don't think it's an issue, but I do appreciate your telling me. I think we should tell Gavin in the morning."

Rocky opened the fridge and retrieved a bottle of water. He saluted the two girls with the bottle. "Goodnight, ladies. I'm going to bed." He winked and disappeared from the kitchen.

Aspen and Kiryn stared at each other.

"Well, that didn't go as I thought it would," said Kiryn.

"No kidding. Let's go to bed."

Aspen pulled both blankets up to her chin and closed her eyes, but her brain didn't shut down. *There is something going on with*

Gavin's step-dad. I know there is, and so does Rocky.

⁓

Rocky quietly closed his bedroom door, went directly to his dresser, and picked up his phone. He waited anxiously for an answer.

"Hank?"

⁓

"Doug is loaded, you guys. He loans, and gives money to everyone. I wouldn't put it past Cassie to borrow from him." Gavin popped the last bite of his pancake into his mouth and chased it down with milk.

"Is she poor?" asked Aspen.

Gavin laughed. "No, but they aren't rich either. Her parents keep a pretty tight rope on her. She spends every dime she gets, and she wants to attend a ridiculously expensive dance school in New York."

"Yeah, pretty tight. she has been to New York twice since we moved here."

Gavin turned slightly and eyed Aspen. "I don't see you guys suffering much." He grinned and turned back to his sausage.

Aspen thought for a minute. "Guess you're right. Maybe if I had someone to borrow from."

"You wouldn't," said Rocky.

"How do you know I wouldn't?"

"You and Noah both had jobs in San Clemente, right?"

"Gavin did, and I would have, but we moved."

"I rest my case. Cassie has never worked. She dances, that's it. She is spoiled. Her adoptive parents have really overcompensated for the fact that they are not her biological parents, and they have tried to give her a better life than she may have had with her biological mom's family. They overextend themselves to do it too."

"How do you know they do?"

"Because they are both teachers, Noah. She teaches elementary, and he is at the middle school." Rocky rolled his eyes, "And we all know what teachers make."

Kiryn rolled her eyes as well, "That we do, Dad."

And they both laughed.

"But, Drew doesn't seem to be a bad guy, not really," said Aspen.

"He isn't now that he's older, and has a kid. He used to be a real hellion."

"Guess everyone has a past," said Gavin casually.

"That they do," said Rocky, and he winked at his son.

Kiryn and Aspen finished the last of the dishes, except for Gavin's plate.

"You can load that one yourself," said Kiryn.

He glared at his sister, "Like I don't know how?"

Noah stood, "Well, anyway, we had better get going, Aspen. Mom wants us to help put up the Christmas tree," said Noah.

"Now, this morning?" asked Gavin.

Aspen laughed, "You don't know our mom and Christmas, and now she has to make up for lost time."

"We are doing the same thing this morning." Kiryn grinned and linked arms with Rocky.

Gavin winced. "We are?"

"You like getting Christmas trees, and you know it." Rocky lightly slapped the top of Gavin's head.

"Yeah, I do, but we are kind of late this year. Everything will be gone."

"Dad picked one up at a place called—"

"Morey Has More Trees," said Gavin and Kiryn in unison.

Noah nodded. "Yeah, that place!"

They all laughed at the reference to the little man with the oldest Christmas tree lot in Sommerville.

Rocky added, "No chance of there being none left. Morey over-buys every year."

Gavin walked over to Aspen and gave her a quick hug. "See you guys in the morning then, at Patrice's?"

"Will do," said Noah. He started toward the door, but then

spun around, walked directly to Kiryn, threw his arms around her, and pulled her into a tight hug.

He looked at Gavin, raised his eyebrows, and walked past Aspen and out the front door.

Surprised, Kiryn still stood in the same place.

"How can I deal with this?" sighed Rocky.

Noah and Aspen hashed over the Doug Mendel mystery all the way to the little house. When they pulled into the driveway, Aspen said, "I don't know, Noah. I have a really bad feeling about this."

Noah shut the engine off but stared straight ahead. "Me, too. This is going to end badly; I just know it."

58

NEW LITTLE HOUSE

THE LITTLE HOUSE WAS like new, but somehow bigger. Aspen and Noah peered through the windshield of the Iroc. They had been given strict orders to stay away until the construction was done so this was the first time they had been here since they had retrieved what they needed to stay at Rocky's.

The garage looked like it had never burned, the new roof on the breezeway only showed signs of being brand new because the shingles were a tiny bit lighter than the rest of the house, but, there was an extension that hadn't been there before.

"Are you coming in or not?" Mom threw the door open and stepped out onto the porch.

Aspen and Noah both jumped out of the car and hurried into the house, only to be met with Dad and Aunt Dana, who stopped them in their tracks.

"Everything smells so new!" said Aspen.

"That's because it is," said Mom. She could hardly contain herself. "Go look at your new rooms." And she gently pushed on each of their backs.

Aspen and Noah started toward their rooms, but the hallway looked different. They walked right past their bedrooms and through a new door at the end of the hall.

"This is awesome!" squealed Aspen, when she saw the newly added bathroom.

"We thought you might like that." Dad grinned.

"It's mine, right?" Noah pushed past his sister.

"Nice try funny man." Aspen then ducked around him and stepped into the shower. She closed the door and grinned at them through the glass.

"What are you doing?" asked Mom.

"Staking my claim!" she pushed the door open and stepped out. "Seriously this is fantastic! Thank you so much!"

"Yeah, it really is! Thank you both."

Aunt Dana hardly waited for Noah to finish his sentence before she scurried past her niece and nephew, turned down a short new hall, and threw open the door at the end.

"My room!" she exclaimed.

"Wow, Aunt Dana! This is awesome!" Aspen hurried to share in her aunt's excitement.

"It was your Dad's idea," said Aunt Dana. She pointed out the window that looked past the garage to the trees at the edge of the grass. She explained that Suzann had her choose the different shades of orange décor since that was her favorite color, and they chose a queen size bed in case Jerry came down at some time.

"This really is great." Aspen hugged her aunt.

"Better than staying at the motel or sleeping on the couch," said Noah.

"Oh, that wasn't going to happen. We were going to give her your room," said Mom.

Noah winced. "Oh."

"Well, we thought of that when she first came, but then we figured since we had to rebuild that side of the house anyway, we might as well expand a little and give you kids your own bathroom and add a room for Dana," Dad explained.

"Great idea." Noah eyed his dad as they all followed Mom to the kitchen.

"And, we added this window." Mom was saying.

From the new window, you could see across the breezeway to the garage.

"It gives the kitchen more natural light," explained Mom.

Dad put an arm around each of his kids.

"Just thought we would make it a little more like our home, that's all."

"It's the best, Dad, it really is," said Aspen.

"Yeah, thanks you guys." Noah hugged his Mom and then pulled Aunt Dana into the same hug.

"I love my new family." Aunt Dana quickly whisked away the tears at the corners of her eyes and then hugged Jackson. "So happy to have my brother back."

Aspen curled her legs under her and snuggled with her favorite soft Christmas blanket.

Now the little house really did look like a Christmas card. Five stockings hung on the mantle above the crackling fire. Fresh pine permeated the air and other than the fire, the soft glow of the Christmas tree was the only light in the house. Aspen loved this.

After dinner, they all played a board game until Noah wiped them all out twice. Now they were listening to Christmas music. Aspen could not believe they had this entire day to themselves with no interruptions from anyone.

She had always marveled at her mom's ability to put together the most amazing Christmas experiences for their family, but this time, she had out-done herself. Aspen was relishing in this moment.

Unbeknownst to the rest of the family, Mom had asked Grandma to go to their house in San Clemente and locate the Christmas decorations. She boxed them up and shipped them to Sommerville, which is why Aspen was enjoying her Christmas blanket with the huge Santa Claus on it.

Mom had ordered new Christmas stockings so that Aunt Dana would have one to match the rest of the family, but everything else was familiar. All the traditional Christmas decorations that were near and dear to their family.

Aspen especially loved the nativity scene that her great-grand-mother had given Mom over fifteen years ago. Pearl white ceramic trimmed in gold, Great-Grandma had made it herself and given it to Mom for Christmas when she and Noah were just little.

Mom carefully packed it away every year, and it was still as beautiful as ever.

When Noah was little, he used to take the baby Jesus, manger and all, to his room. He did it so many times that Mom finally bought each of them their own little manger scenes.

But even then, Noah was still partial to the white ceramic one.

The tree was adorned with ornaments, representing each year since Mom and Dad had been married, and every ornament had a story about something significant for that year.

Aspen silently surveyed some of them. The baby ornaments the years she and Noah were born, the airplane for their first plane ride, and she especially loved their little surfboards. Those were added when each of them turned two. The first year they were taken into the ocean on a surfboard.

A twinge tugged at Aspen's heart. Surfing, San Clemente, the beach, her friends. It all seemed almost a distant memory, and yet, it was just over six months ago.

Dad was asleep on the sofa, and Mom's head rested on his lap. She was staring at the Christmas tree, and Aspen wondered if she was loving this night as much as Aspen was.

Aunt Dana was texting Uncle Jerry, whom Aspen had never met. He wanted Aunt Dana to come home to Oregon for Christmas to be with him and his father, so she promised that she would leave on the 23rd and stay until the 26th. Jerry indicated on a phone call earlier this morning that he did not think his dad would be with them much longer.

Aspen hoped that their Uncle Jerry could come back with Aunt Dana, so they could get to know him, but she knew that wouldn't happen unless Jerry's father passed away, so she quickly dismissed that idea. Feeling guilty for ever having thought it in the first place.

Noah was laying on the floor, right in front of the fireplace. He was on his stomach, his head resting on top of his crossed arms. He looked comfortable. Maybe he was sleeping, she couldn't tell.

Aspen took a deep breath, and once again surveyed her family and the perfect little room. She basked in the quiet Christmas memories their family had made this totally uneventful day in the little house, in Sommerville, Tennessee.

"So dinghead, you going to bed or are you going to sleep in that chair all night?"

Aspen tried to open her eyes, but they just wanted to stay closed.

"Hello—"

Noah was starting to irritate her.

Aspen forced herself to wake up and rubbed her face with her hands.

She looked up, just in time to see Noah turn off the Christmas tree. Glowing embers were all that was left of the fire, and her parents and Aunt Dana were nowhere in sight.

She stood and dragged herself down the hall behind her brother.

When he turned into his room, she said, "Isn't this perfect, Noah? Life is just perfect."

Noah leaned back out into the hall and watched his half-asleep sister stumble into her bedroom.

He pulled his t-shirt and pajama bottoms off, opting only for his boxers. He climbed between the new sheets and closed his eyes.

Yep, everything is perfect. We have FBI agents sleeping in the driveway, we are going to see Patrice tomorrow to see if she can figure out why Dad, Gavin, and my nutty sister can see ghosts, a kid our age is in jail, Gavin's old girlfriend tried to kill our family, and that is just the beginning.

He yawned and pulled the sheets up around his chin.

Things couldn't be more perfect.

59

TRAIN TRACKS

"Hank? It's Agent Skoresby. We didn't get through that wall until 3:00 am. We are back over here now."

Hank glanced at his watch. It was 9:00 am, and he had two meetings later today; one at 2:00 pm at the Tuttle residence, and one at 4:00 pm with the attorneys regarding the Allen will.

"I'm on my way."

Hank picked up Agents Larry and Byron and headed for the Mansion House. Just like the first time, an agent met him in the bedroom closet and took the three of them into the tunnel, and subsequently to the cinderblock room.

Hank had warned Larry and Byron about the bones, but it still startled them a little. Most agents were used to seeing one or two dead bodies, but rarely a pile of bones like this. It was a little unsettling for everyone.

The cutting team was gone, and there were only two other agents with Agent Skoresby. The wall was gone, and a huge dark hole loomed in its place.

Hank briefly introduced Larry and Byron and then asked, "So what do you have?"

Agent Skoresby leaned over and flipped a switch on a floodlight, illuminating the hole. He then turned to Hank. "That's what we have. What do you make of this?"

Hank knelt on one knee and blew a low whistle through his

teeth. "What the—

"Yep, that was pretty much our reaction," said one of the other agents.

The hole opened to another tunnel—this one considerably narrower, only wide enough for one adult to walk through.

Hank took one of the high beam flashlights and pointed it down the tunnel. It went straight for quite some ways, but then appeared to turn to the right.

He shined the light directly on the floor of the tunnel to see more clearly what he thought he was looking at.

"Those are tracks."

Agent Skoresby nodded. "They are. Reminds me of an old mining tunnel. Looks like they could be for one of those small mining cars."

"Have you been down there?"

"Nope."

"Well, let's find out where it goes." Hank turned to Larry and Byron, and the other two agents. "Wait here. We may not come back," he joked.

But no one seemed too humored by it.

Hank and Agent Skoresby walked slowly through the narrow tunnel. There were places where they had to duck, some places that were wider, and some so narrow they had to turn sideways. They came to the bend in the tunnel, and Hank stopped.

"Something wrong?"

Hank shook his head. "No just thinking. I was looking at the map yesterday of the estates around this lake. I think this is headed right for the Mendel's place."

Suddenly Hank remembered the call from Rocky. He tried not to put too much credence in the kids seeing Doug Mendel with Dylan, Cassie Garrett, and Brandon Tuttle. After all, Dylan was biologically Cassie's uncle.

But Doug?

Agent Skoresby shrugged. "And that means?'

"I'm not sure. Except that when these places were first built, the Mendel's place was owned by a guy named Tygert. He was in business with some of the principal partners in this whole case.

They turned the corner. The tunnel seemed to go on forever.

"Ev-ry-hng o-y do-n t-er-?" The radio in Hank's hand crackled.

"We're good," Hank yelled into the radio, but he wasn't sure if Larry heard him.

"You understood that?"

Hank chuckled, "No, but I'm pretty sure that's what he was asking."

The two kept walking. The tunnel turned again, but then stopped. They were met with another wall. Just a cinderblock wall, not a room.

"These tracks run right into, or under that wall," said Hank.

"I'm betting under it, and then even farther."

The two men turned, and Hank briskly led the way back out of the tunnel.

Once out, Agent Skoresby punched a number on his cell phone. "Hey, see if you can get those guys back to cut another wall, but tell them it's all dirt around it. They need to bring something for reinforcement, so the thing doesn't cave in."

He scrolled the screen of his phone and stuffed it into his shirt pocket.

Hank shook his hand. "Let me know."

<hr>

When they got in the truck, Hank noticed a missed call from Rocky. He punched the call back icon on his phone.

"Hey Hank, thanks for calling me back. I had an unusual request from Patrice just now. Do you know where I can find Larry and Byron?"

"They are here with me, what do you need?" asked Hank.

"We are on our way to meet with her, and she asked if I could bring them.'"

"What time? Did she say why?"

"We're on our way right now. We are all meeting her at 11:30, and

no, she didn't say why. Would that be a problem?"

Hank glanced at his watch. "No, they— Well we, will just have to starve a little longer."

"I'll spring for lunch."

"We might take you up on that. We're on our way."

Hank ended the call and turned to the two agents. "You didn't have any pressing plans, did you?"

"Would it matter?" asked Larry.

Hank laughed, "Not really."

60

CONFERENCE

Aspen was surprised to see that Gavin's step-dad, Doug was there, but Sara explained that Patrice had called her and asked that he come.

Rocky told them that Patrice also requested that Larry and Byron come as well.

Hank joked that he hadn't been invited and that he could get something to eat, but Patrice stopped that in a hurry and asked him to take a seat.

Patrice was in an odd mood today, at least from the other times they had met with her, and she was doing things a little differently this time.

When everyone arrived, she had all the chairs in a circle on her porch. It was crowded, so they were squished together.

There were two small sofas and Aspen, and Gavin took one, but Patrice asked them to move. She explained that she wanted them in a certain order.

When everyone was seated, and Patrice seemed satisfied, she had Larry on her left, then Aunt Dana, Rocky, Sara, Noah, Byron, Gavin, Hank, Kiryn, Dad, Doug, Mom, and Aspen on her right.

"Welcome." Patrice took her chair, placed her hands in her lap, and smiled at the group.

"Thank you for entertaining my little plan today. I have had very little sleep these past two nights preparing for you to come."

"Are you okay, Aunt Patrice?" asked Sara.

"Yes, dear, I'm fine. It's just that there are a few things that have been bothering me. I need to figure something out, and I hope, with all of your help, I can do it today." She sighed and sat back in her chair. "There are actually a few things I want to do today, so I hope you have a little time."

Hank and Rocky exchanged a quick glance, but Patrice did not seem to notice. They looked a little stressed, in a funny sort of way, and it made Aspen laugh, but not out loud. She didn't dare.

Patrice reached for Larry and Aspen's hands. Aspen took hold of her hand, but Larry hesitated. He seemed uncomfortable.

"I won't bite you." Patrice smiled.

Larry shrugged, glanced around the group and then took her hand.

"Now, will all of you please join hands?"

Everyone obeyed.

"Please just sit quietly." Patrice closed her eyes. After several seconds, she opened them again and asked Larry and Aspen to let go, and she then took hold of Mom and Aunt Dana's hands, the rest remained intact.

She closed her eyes again, and after a few seconds, she asked Aspen and Larry to rejoin them and Mom and Aunt Dana to let go.

Patrice continued the same process until she had everyone in the group let go and then rejoin them.

"Okay, we can all let go of hands now." She sat back in her chair and folded her hands across her chest. "I would like to talk to you for a minute."

"I wonder if all of you realize that we live in a world where there are several dimensions. In fact, there are other worlds, or realms, or spheres, right here with us, separated only by time.

"For reasons unknown to me, some of us can see beyond this life, into another. It may be the next life. it may be a life that existed before we came here. It may be what we consider heaven, or maybe hell. The fact simply remains that there are other dimensions, and sometimes we slip through the portals for a time. Sometimes it is only a glimpse. It can happen in a dream, or while you are wide awake."

"More people than you realize have this gift, but it can, in many ways, be suppressed by an individual, but not indefinitely. The person with the gift may ignore it, they may fight it, but they will always have it, and it will rear its head in the most unexpected and surprising ways."

Leaning forward, Patrice scrutinized her audience and then smiled. "Some of you simply do not believe it exists, and I understand that, but I am here to tell you that it does."

She made a circular motion with her hand. "All of us are helped, and sometimes hindered, from forces beyond this world. Most are out of our control. There are those who choose not to believe in anything of the sort, and I am sad for them. They are missing an important, mysterious, miraculous part of life."

She sat back again and was quiet for several seconds, but no one said anything. They were all waiting for her next comment.

Finally, she told them, "That being said; sometimes, the gift allows a person to read, if you will, something in another individual, a living, breathing person. When that happens, it is because there is a sort of energy that emulates from the one that is being read."

"You have all done it. When you are attracted to a person, and you can tell they are also attracted to you. Or, when you sense negative energy from someone and your instincts tell you to steer clear of that person. These are all part of our intuition, our inborn senses. A sixth sense if you will."

"So what are you trying to tell us? That we all have that gift?" Doug sounded a little impatient.

Not to be rushed, Patrice slowly shook her head. "Not at all. Exactly the opposite."

Doug sighed. "Well then, *what?*"

Not phased at all by Doug's impatience, she simply said, "You, Mr. Mendel, may step out of the group."

Doug couldn't hide the startled look on his face. Obviously, that was not what he was expecting. Awkwardly, he pushed his chair back and stood, and walked to the corner of the porch and leaned against the house. He glared at Sara, but she ignored him.

Looking directly at each individual, Patrice then said, "Suzann, Noah, Kiryn, Hank, Byron. Could all of you join Doug in time-out?"

She laughed at her own joke, and so did everyone else. Well, except Doug.

She asked the remaining members of the circle to slide the chairs in closer and again take hands.

After a few seconds, she asked Byron to trade places with Larry, who gladly obliged, making Byron chuckle.

Larry did not join the rest of them. He stopped and leaned against the support post.

Again, the group held hands. The people who had been removed, simply stood by, saying nothing.

Then Patrice said, "Dana and Sara. You both have a gift. You just need to develop it."

"That's okay!" Aunt Dana practically jumped out of her chair. "I had a tiny taste of it, I think, and I am not interested. Nope! Not in the least!"

Everyone was laughing as Dana made her quick exit. "I'll be happy to go to time out!"

Patrice laughed with everyone else at Dana's reaction but then turned to her niece. "Sara?"

"I don't have a gift, Aunt Patrice. That was Sumer, and it's Gavin."

"You do not have *their* gift, Sara, I didn't say that. I am simply telling you that there is— There is something."

Sara stood. "Let's just have one of us." She touched Gavin's shoulder as she walked past him. She kissed her aunt on top of her head. "But thank you."

Patrice smiled at her niece but then turned to Byron. "You, my dear man, do not have the gift I am looking for."

Byron stood. "But, I am one heck of an FBI agent." He laughed and left the circle.

"Can't say I'm disappointed," he said when he walked past Rocky.

Patrice turned back to those remaining. Gavin, Aspen, and Dad. "No surprises here."

"So what was the point of all of this?" asked Dad.

Patrice took a deep breath. "The only reason this is working for me, and not the three of you right now is because I have spent years developing my gift." She turned to Jackson. "You have spent years suppressing yours, and you two, well this is still very new, and your gifts are very different."

"What is working?" asked Aspen. She felt the hair standing up on the back of her neck.

"That I can see them," said Patrice.

"See who?" Gavin turned and looked behind them.

"The boys, Gavin. There are many boys here right now, young boys, about your age."

"I can't see them," said Gavin.

"Me either," said Aspen, "but I can feel—something."

"I have only seen them once, and it did not last long," said Dad.

Patrice chuckled, "They have about given up on you, Jackson. You have been running from them for years."

Dad shook his head, "No, from a girl."

"Yes, but she couldn't reach you, so they didn't try. They have always been there."

Dad suddenly looked sad, and Patrice quickly added, "It's okay, Jackson. It's actually quite normal."

Dad rolled his eyes. "I guess."

Patrice nodded. "Trust me."

"So back to these boys. What are they doing?" asked Aspen.

"Nothing. That is the problem; they can't do anything. Or they won't do anything. I'm not sure. I have only been seeing them for maybe a week, but they are hanging around all the time now."

Aspen slowly turned toward the group in the corner. She squinted to focus a little better.

"Patrice?"

Patrice was looking in the same direction.

"Is there? No, there *is* a boy over there," she whispered.

"Yes, there is." Patrice turned to Jackson and Gavin. "Do either of you see him?"

They both shook their heads.

Aspen furrowed her brow. "Why is he walking over to Larry?"

Cassie grabbed her duffle from the bag claim carousel and threw the strap over her shoulder. Hers was one of the last bags to come down, and when her teacher left with her husband and kids, Cassie assured her she would be fine.

The hour was late, and the plane was too. Her teacher's young kids were tired and cranky, and her husband wanted to get them home.

Cassie's parents had already texted her to let her know they were in passenger pickup.

She hurried through the crowd towards the exit doors.

Cassie was tired. It had been a grueling five days of competition, but she had won the solo division in jazz, and their team placed a high gold in ballet. She had made sure of that. She knew this game she was playing was a dangerous one, and if her parents ever found out, they would kill her.

But it was all about the scholarship for her, and each win was another plus for her application. She needed to get a full ride in order to go to the college she wanted to attend. It was very expensive, and her parents told her without the scholarship, she may need to settle for a different school at least for the first two years.

Cassie was not going to let that happen, no matter what she had to do. So, she had taken things into her own hands over a year ago. She had not lost one competition since and was rated the top solo dancer at every competition since that time. They were always so impressed with her effortless dancing. It was becoming her trademark. Her picture was all over the dance world, and Cassie relished in the spotlight.

Just a few more months and once I have it in the bag I won't need to see that doctor anymore. Besides, it's costing a fortune.

She pushed the glass door open. she could see her parent's car across the road in line with several others.

Suddenly, a man ran through the open door directly at her. He slammed into her, nearly knocking her to the floor. Struggling to stay on her feet, Cassie glared at him, but she couldn't see his face behind his sunglasses and ball cap pulled over his eyes.

"Geez, you moron! Watch where you're going! Take off your stupid sunglasses. It's almost midnight!"

The man did not even so much as glance back at her.

A sharp pain stabbed in her hip, and she stood still for a minute.

"Are you okay, Miss?"

Cassie nodded to the older couple who had stopped to help her.

"Yes, I'm fine. Just threw me off balance for a minute. Thank you."

She continued through the door and onto the sidewalk.

"I hate people."

≈

"The kid won't talk. Don't worry about him."

"Don't be too sure. He is just a kid."

"I made sure of it. I bought insurance on him."

"Okay, well if you say so. I'm getting a lot of pressure on this end."

"I said the kid is under control, and the girl too. I've figured out how to keep her quiet."

"That girl is a loose cannon. We'll take care of her."

"What is that supposed to mean?"

"Don't you worry about that. You just need to figure out how to stop the Allens."

"Don't you listen to the news? That's taken on a life of its own."

"We've noticed."

The phone was silent for several seconds.

"Just leave the kids alone. I got this. I just need a little more time."

"Too late, it's done."

"Wait? What? What's done?!"

The phone went dead.

Sweat poured off his face, and his hands shook as he stared at the black screen on his cell phone.

For the first time in his life, Doug Mendel was engulfed in sheer panic.

Still baffled by what Patrice was trying to accomplish this morning, Hank had sent Larry and Byron onto Memphis to meet with the attorneys regarding the will of Jackson Humphrey Allen, grandfather to Jackson Allen and Great-Grandfather to Aspen Allen.

Reluctantly, they all had taken a rain check on Rocky's offer to buy them lunch.

Hank pulled up in front of the Tuttle residence. He wasn't sure if there was any other information Brandon Tuttle could—or would—give him, but he had to try.

Normally, he wouldn't press so hard on a Sunday afternoon, but all bets were off now. Things were coming rapidly to a head, and he had to force the issue from every angle.

Up until now, the FBI had given him a lot of control, but now they were moving in quickly. They were still consulting him and keeping him informed since he had been on the Allen case since its inception, but who knew how much longer that would last.

He took a deep breath, grabbed his worn notebook and pen, and then stepped out of the truck. Before he even reached the sidewalk, the front door opened.

It was Brandon's mother.

"Mrs. Tuttle?"

"Hi, Mr. Cox."

"Hank."

She nodded, and Hank immediately noticed she was upset.

"Is everything okay?"

"Not really. We—Brandon—just got some bad news. Some very bad news." She started to cry.

Now on the porch, Hank asked, "May I come in?"

"I'm not sure if that's a good idea."

Hank stopped. "Okay, well—"

The door opened slowly, and Hank looked up.

Brandon stood in the doorway. Wearing shorts, a long-sleeved t-shirt, and bare feet. He looked like maybe he had started getting ready to meet with Hank, but his swollen red eyes told a different story.

"Hey, Brandon. What's going on?"

Brandon started to cry, and his dad walked up behind him. He pulled his son into a hug and motioned to Hank and his wife. "Why don't we all come inside?"

Hank's phone buzzed, but he reached in his pocket and put it on silent. This was no time to be answering phone calls.

Brandon was crying so hard he could hardly talk, but when Hank closed the front door and followed the Tuttle family into a small living room off the hallway, Brandon suddenly turned and blurted, "She's dead, Hank. Cassie is dead."

Reeling from that news, Hank stopped short and stared at the teenager.

"*What?* Did you say? How do you—"

"Cassie's aunt called us about an hour ago." Mr. Tuttle rubbed the back of his neck with his hand, and then his forehead and face. He was pale. Hank hadn't noticed that at first.

"But how, what? When? I thought she was in New York, or coming back from New York."

"All we know is that her parents picked her up at the airport, and about fifteen minutes later, she fell unconscious in the back seat, and they took her to the hospital."

Hank's mind was racing with a million different thoughts. His cell phone had not stopped buzzing.

"Uh, I'm sorry, do you mind? My phone has been buzzing non-stop. May I take just a second?"

Mr. Tuttle nodded, and Hank walked back out into the entry-way. He pulled his cell from his pocket. Five missed calls and three missed texts.

He scrolled the screen. They were all from his boss, Sean Thornton, the police commissioner in Tennessee.

"Need to talk to you now."

"Call me—now."

"Cox what are you doing?"

He punched speed dial on his phone as he walked out of the house onto the front porch. He didn't bother to listen to the messages. He was pretty sure what they were about.

When the commissioner answered, Hank said, "I just heard. I'm at Brandon Tuttle's place."

The commissioner wasn't very good with small talk.

"Did you feel at any point she needed to have police protection?"

"No, sir. We just learned that she was involved on Friday. Maybe Thursday. She has been in New York at a dance competition. We don't even know how involved."

"Well, she won't be dancing anymore."

"No sir."

"Any reason why you didn't pick her up and bring her home? Scratch that—for what? She hadn't been charged with anything.'

"Exactly, sir."

"A kid dead. Was she sick?"

"I don't know sir. I don't know the family that well. I knew of Cassie, but not much about her."

"She's the one that accused the Allen girl, right?"

"Of being a witch, yes sir, that was her."

"Thought so. Stupid kids."

"Yes, sir." Hank's voice cracked.

"You okay, Cox? You can't let this be personal."

Hank nodded as if it would convince the commissioner, or maybe himself.

"I know, sir, it's just—just so unexpected." But it was becoming personal to Hank. Maybe he had gotten too close.

The commissioner was quiet for a few seconds.

"Yes, it is. Listen Cox, you and your men have done a good job with this so far. I get the reports in from Chief Wilson out there every day. You're going to have to dig. I have a bad feeling that this little girl was murdered. We need to get to the big fish."

"Yes sir, we have some pretty good leads, I think, we are just not exactly sure what we are looking for, but you've seen the report about the files found in the Allen house, right?"

"I have. If this pans out the way it looks like it will, this could be one of the biggest schemes and murder cases in history."

"I think it may all stem back to that. Why Cassie and Brandon were involved, I'm not sure yet. At least we think Cassie was involved, we only have Brandon's word on that, and this kid is a basket case right now."

"Hasn't been a good month for that family, either."

Hank nodded again. "No, sir, it hasn't. This is sad on so many different levels."

"That it is. Okay, Cox, I just wanted to personally talk to you. If you need anything—anything at all, let Chief Wilson know or call me directly. Let's get to the bottom of this mess."

"Okay, sir. Thank you."

"Oh, and Cox, one more thing. Any reason to believe the Allen's are persons of interest in this case?"

Hank sighed. "I believe that there are people in their past that were involved, but these folks. No, sir, I believe they are the victims in all of this."

"Okay then. Thanks for the information. Chief Wilson will visit with Cassie Garrett's parent's tomorrow."

Hank clicked end and stood still. He couldn't focus on any one thing. This was the last thing he expected—the death of one of these kids, and what if the commissioner was right? What if Cassie was murdered? Is that even possible? It can't be. There had to be something wrong with her. He knew they would do an autopsy simply for the mysterious way she died.

Hank's heart was filled with dread. He had to call Jackson and Rocky. He doubted Byron and Larry knew. He had sent them into Memphis to meet with Jackson's attorney who was trying to get his hands on the infamous Allen will.

This was going to have a huge impact on the four kids who had opened this can of worms.

He shuddered. Where to start right now?

He took a deep breath and stared absently at the Tuttle's front door.

After a few seconds, he reluctantly opened the door and walked back inside.

61

PROTECTIVE CUSTODY

"WELL, THAT WAS AN interesting meeting with Patrice." Jackson scanned the menu then handed it to his wife."

"I don't even know why you look at the menu. You always order the same thing."

"Well, I was considering stepping outside of the box."

Noah pulled a chair out next to his dad and plopped down. "Doubt it, Dad. You're a grilled chicken sandwich kind of guy."

"No, I'm not. I prefer deep-fried." He twisted his mouth and handed the menu to Noah. "But those days are gone."

"Well, it's better for you, anyway." Dana looked over her menu. "They have the best salads here, but I think I'll have the crispy chicken." She waited for a response from her brother, but Jackson just glared at her.

"Just kidding! I'll have soup and salad."

"Everyone ready to order?" the server had been chatting with Kiryn and Aspen, but now she pulled out her order pad.

"What's wrong with Hank?" Gavin was looking toward the door where Hank had just entered the café.

They all turned, but Rocky stood immediately. "Hank?"

Hank motioned to Jackson. "Rocky, we need to talk."

"You and Jackson?"

"No, I mean the three of us."

Jackson stood and followed Hank and Rocky out of the café.

"What do you suppose that's all about?" asked Kiryn.

"Who knows, but he didn't look very good," said Gavin.

"Maybe something is up with Brandon. He said he was going over there today." Noah turned toward the door.

The three men had not come back in.

Suzann got a text. "It's your dad? Why doesn't he—" She read the text and then turned to Gavin.

"Gavin, text your mom and ask her to meet us at Rocky's as soon as she can. She hasn't left Sommerville, has she?"

"I don't think so." Gavin typed in a text and sent it. "What do I tell her?"

"Just to meet us."

Gavin threw a questioning look in Noah's direction and shrugged.

Mom called to the server. "We need to cancel that order. Do you have some pizza we could take with us?"

Visibly surprised, the server nodded. "I'm sure we do. Right now?'

Suzann looked back down at her phone. "Apparently." She turned to the kids and Dana. "So, Dad and Rocky left with Hank. They want us to meet them at Rocky's."

"Mom, what's going on?" Aspen took her mom's debit card and handed it to the server.

"I honestly do not know. We'll find out soon enough."

"Noah, will you and Gavin grab those pizzas? Gavin, did you get a hold of your mom?"

"Yes, she said she couldn't find Doug. He is not answering his phone. Did they want him to come?"

Suzann sighed and shook her head. "He didn't say."

They all exited the restaurant and the kids piled in the Iroc.

"This is weird," said Kiryn.

"Something feels wrong," said Gavin. He turned and looked out the window. "Really wrong."

Aspen turned to Kiryn. "This is scaring me."

"Me too."

When Noah turned the car into Rocky's driveway, Hank, Rocky and Jackson were standing on the porch talking to Larry, and Byron.

Before he even shut the engine off, Sara pulled in behind him, followed by a police car and the black SUV which had followed them from Bill and Nada's.

"What the heck is going on?" Gavin opened the door and stepped out of the car.

His mom rushed up to him. "Gavin, what happened?"

"I don't know, Mom. We were just starting lunch when Hank came and got all of us."

Two policemen walked briskly past them, but the two FBI agents hung back.

Rocky opened the door to his house, turned and motioned for all of them to come in.

Once inside, Rocky asked everyone to sit down.

The somber looks on all the men's faces gave Aspen major anxiety.

Suddenly an image flashed through her mind. It was so startling, she gasped.

"Aspen?" Mom took her arm. "Are you okay?"

"Yes, I just— It's nothing." She looked over at Gavin. His expressionless face stared at Hank.

"Jackson, could you please tell us what is going on here?" Suzann sounded exasperated.

Hank stood. "I will."

"I got some very bad news when I was over at the Tuttle's. You will all find out soon enough, so I wanted to tell you all together." Hank choked and paused so long it seemed like he would never speak again.

"*What?*" blurted Kiryn.

"There has been an accident—or something—we are not sure." Hank paused and quickly looked around the room, and then he said quietly, "Cassie is dead."

The policemen and the FBI agents stood silently, but there was a collective gasp from everyone else in the room.

Reeling from that information, questions flew at Hank.

"How did—

"When?"

"Was she in a car accident?'

"Was she with her parents?"

"Was she mugged in New York?"

Aspen couldn't speak.

She stood the same time as Kiryn did, and they threw their arms around each other.

Crying, Sara immediately pulled Gavin to her and held him tight.

For the next several minutes, the room was total chaos as they all tried to make sense of it.

It was especially difficult for Gavin, Kiryn, Sara, and of course, Rocky. They had all known Cassie the longest. The kids had gone to school with Cassie for several years, she had been in Rocky's classes more than once, and she and Sara had developed a friendship while Cassie and Gavin were dating.

Aspen looked over Kiryn's shoulder at Gavin. He was visibly distraught, and Aspen had no idea how to comfort him. She was an outsider when it came to Cassie. The two girls had been at odds since the first day they met, and now Aspen was struggling with her own feelings, and she was confused and upset. She didn't feel sadness, and that bothered her. She simply felt empty—nothing, and as fast as those feelings came and went, she was engulfed with guilt.

She became aware that Hank was talking to them all again, "We will know in the next day or so exactly what happened to Cassie. In the meantime," and the sigh that escaped from him was heavy and labored. "In the meantime, we are putting you four kids, and Brandon, in protective custody."

"What does that mean?" Noah looked at his dad and then at Hank.

"It means we need you all to stay in one spot, and the three of us," he motioned to Jackson and Rocky, "we determined the best place is here."

Hank turned to Suzann. "Sorry."

Mom stared back at him. Finally, she said, "Jackson?"

Dad nodded. "They have four more agents coming, Suzann. They need the kids in one spot."

"Brandon?"

"We are taking him into police custody, Gavin."

"What is this all about? Why?"

"We're not sure, Aspen, but we have reason to believe all of you could be in more danger than we originally thought. This was the commissioner's idea, not mine."

Jackson could see Suzann was going to cry, and he walked quickly around the chairs to reach to her and pulled her to him. Then she did start to cry.

Sara was holding on to Gavin's arm, and Aunt Dana put an arm each around Kiryn and Noah.

Rocky was talking to the two policemen, for a second, he stopped, read a text, and then sent a text. He then turned back to the conversation.

Aspen sank into a chair. She covered her face with her hands and rested her elbows on her knees. No tears.

Again, the image—it flashed through her mind like a lightning bolt—she forced it away.

What is going on?

Aspen felt two hands close around her wrists, and she looked up.

Gavin pulled her to her feet and wrapped his arms around her. Weeping, he buried his face in her shoulder.

Aspen felt nothing.

〰

"Did you tell him?"

Hank shook his head. "No, this is not the time. I really am happy about it, though. One more thing to hopefully help us get into the nitty-gritty of this case and maybe keep commissioner

Thornton off my back."

"Don't you mean cases?" asked Byron.

Hank laughed nervously. "Yeah, I guess I do."

"That girl's death sure put a damper on things."

"That's for sure. Merry Christmas."

Byron sighed. "Yeah."

Hank pulled the truck into the Allen Mansion House driveway. The gate was always open now that the FBI had been given access. It seemed there were people there 24/7.

When Dad and Dana turned the Mansion house over to the police and the FBI, they had two specific requests. No one was to go into the storage or the master bedroom.

Hank had resisted at first, but Jackson and Dana asked for a couple of weeks and promised that if they found anything they thought would be pertinent to the cases, they would tell Hank. He reluctantly agreed but had quickly followed up that he could not promise anything.

The team they hired to cut through the cinderblock walls would be back early Monday morning to cut through the brick wall on the outside that led to the rooms at the bottom of the shaft.

The old hand-drawn map Gavin found several weeks ago depicted a cellar there. Now they needed to find out if it existed.

Hank opened the truck door and started to climb out but paused,

"You're awfully quiet, Larry. What's on your mind?"

Larry's head jerked up. "Nothing."

Hank eyed the agent. "Okay, well c'mon."

Larry sighed, "Why are we here again?"

"Agent Skoresby said we wouldn't believe what they found through the second wall."

"Geez, these people were a bunch of freaks back in the day," said Byron.

"Seems like it."

They walked into the entry hall, up the stairs, and to the bedroom.

As they followed the agent down the ladder, Hank said, "All I know is that I hate tunnels, and I have been spending way too much time in them."

"Don't know if will end any time soon," said Byron.

Larry grunted, and Hank curiously turned around to look at him, but Larry was looking at the ground.

Agent Skoresby was waiting for them. He handed each of them a flashlight and told them to follow him.

The team that had been working had placed half-inch thick U-shaped, steel reinforcement plates every few yards from the cinderblock room to the newly discovered wall, and Hank observed, beyond.

Referring to the steel plates, Byron asked, "How did they get those in here?"

"We used the cement pipe at the other end of the tunnel. It's five feet in diameter, and these are four feet wide, so it was tight but easier than trying to get them down that ladder. Let alone dragging them through that tunnel. They are not exactly light."

When they reached the new hole, two workers were waiting.

Agent Skoresby said to one of them, "Jim, could you explain what you guys found?"

Jim nodded, "Sure. Come with me."

He led the group through the hole and into a continuation of the tunnel. The tracks were still there—Hank had been right—the tracks went under the wall.

After about fifty feet, Jim stopped. He pointed the beam of his light straight ahead, but then moved it to the left and slowly to the right.

Hank was flabbergasted.

They were looking into a room, not a small room either. It was huge or reinforced with railroad ties that stood on end.

The ceiling was wood, but the walls were cement, like the foundation for a house, only deeper, like maybe for a basement. The dirt floor was damp, and along two sides, the bottom of the concrete was darker than the rest of the wall. It appeared there had been water in here at some time.

Other than the railroad ties, there was nothing else in the room. Or so he thought.

"Look at this." Jim walked farther into the room.

Hank nervously blew air through his lips "Is it hot down here? It's hot down here."

Jim chuckled. "Not really." He walked in about ten feet and pointed his light at the floor.

"My guess—vaults."

Hank stared at the rectangular cement slab at his feet.

Jim waved the flashlight around.

Hank stared in disbelief at another, and another. There were at least ten of them from what he could see."

Hank looked up at the ceiling and thought of the map he had in the truck, but Byron spoke up before Hank could ask the question he was thinking.

"What is above this?" asked Byron.

Larry hadn't said much and stood back some ways from the other men.

"Doug Mendel's house," he said casually.

The untouched boxes of cold pizza still sat on Rocky's table. It was 7:00 pm and no one had eaten anything all day.

Hank, Larry, and Byron left hours ago, as the policemen stayed and interviewed all of them. Seemingly satisfied with what they had, they finally left.

Now four FBI agents were posting watch.

A heaviness hung in the air. It was dark outside and even darker inside.

Aunt Dana stood, walked over and flipped on the Christmas tree lights.

Aspen stared at the multi-colored lights and the decorative Christmas tree skirt.

Life is not perfect. What was I thinking?

Suddenly Mom stood. "So, are we having cold pizza or Rocky do you have something we can fix?"

"I took care of it." Dana smiled. "We all need to eat."

Curiously, they all turned to Aunt Dana, and she laughed. "I ordered chicken."

"From where?" the thought of food resonated with Gavin.

"Well finger-lickin'-good, of course."

"What? Where in Sommerville?" Noah was surprised.

"Way on the other side of town. You must drive there deliberately. It used to be on a main road, but when the state highway was built, they were bypassed." She added, "And Bill and Nada's right in the center of town hasn't helped much."

"Humm, I didn't know," said Noah.

"I forgot about it," said Kiryn.

"I knew it was there. I, like everyone else, just never drive over there," said Rocky.

There was a knock at the door, and Aunt Dana answered it. She summoned help from the kids to take the food to the kitchen while she paid the driver.

The familiar smell of the famous recipe wafted through the entire house, and they all clamored to the two buckets and boxes for fried chicken, coleslaw, mashed potatoes, and biscuits.

Aspen hadn't felt hungry at all, but now her stomach growled, and when she bit into a chicken leg, it tasted even better than she remembered.

Things were already confusing, but now the saga had taken a shocking twist. Cassie was dead. It was so hard to believe.

Aspen had never liked Cassie, and the feeling was mutual, but she would never want her dead. It sickened Aspen to think about it.

The last time she had any communication with Cassie was in the hospital when she went to see Gavin. It had not been pleasant at all, and Aspen, at least that day, did feel as though she hated Cassie.

But what is hate? In this case, it was jealousy, and it had nearly eaten her alive for a while. But Aspen had never in her life been so angry with someone, even Cassie, that she would want them to die—not ever.

A promising dancer, it seemed as though Cassie had just dropped dead.

The whole thing was just so unbelievable.

It was ten o'clock, and the food had been devoured, along with the uneaten cold pizza, and all containers deposited in the trash outside.

When Noah opened the can, he chuckled. There was already an empty chicken bucket in the trash.

Gavin looked past Noah and motioned to the black SUV.

"I heard Dana tell your mom she had ordered some for the agents."

Noah shook his head. "Of course she did."

The two walked back to the house.

"Well, they are practically family," said Gavin.

"Sure seems so, strange, but yeah they seem like family, sort of."

They both laughed.

Under the circumstances, Mom didn't want to leave her kids at Rocky's. It was one thing to let them stay but entirely another to be forced to have them stay. She wanted to remain with them, but Dad and Dana convinced her she needed to come home with them, and she finally relented, comforted in the fact that it was only for forty-eight hours.

Rocky closed and locked the door behind them.

We hope it's only for forty-eight hours.

The house was quiet. Aspen had asked Rocky to leave the Christmas tree on when she made up the sofa bed, but now that she was alone, she got up and turned it off.

Somehow, it seemed the right thing to do. Even though the lights gave Aspen comfort, the sadness prevailed, and she didn't want the two to mix. It probably wouldn't make sense if she tried to explain that to anyone, and in a few weeks or months from now, it may seem silly to her as well. At this moment, it felt right.

Aspen crawled into bed, rolled to her side, and stared at the clear night sky through the French doors.

There must be a million stars out tonight.

She tried not to think of anything, but it was impossible.

You live, and then you're dead. There must be more. There just has to be.

Silent tears trickled down her cheeks and onto her arm, which was supporting her head. She closed her eyes.

Heavenly Father, if you're there, could you please help us find the answers we need?

She opened her eyes briefly and then closed them again.

And, Heavenly Father, please, no more deaths.

62

TOBY

Jackson, Suzanne, and Dana finished packing the last of the office at the Mansion House. Most of what was left were just remnants that would be found in any office: pens, notebooks, a stapler, blank receipt books, and other miscellaneous items.

Even the few books on the shelves were a meaningless assortment of random novels and finance aids.

Dana explained that she and Jerry had packed all their father's papers and personal items and had taken them to Oregon when they moved.

The master bedroom, however, was a different story.

The first thing Jackson did was call and arrange for an appraisal of the gun collection. With only one week until Christmas, and Dana leaving on the twenty-third, he scheduled it for the twenty-seventh so that Dana would be back from Oregon.

It took the three of them nearly two hours to box the clothes in the closet so that they could be picked up by Goodwill.

"They are so out of date, no one will even want them," said Suzann.

"You never know," mused Dana. She pulled a picture out the pocket of a dress she was folding. "Look at this."

She held the photo so Suzann and Jackson could see it.

"That's Nina, I'm sure of it," said Jackson.

"With all four of her children," said Dana.

They all studied the smiling faces of those in the picture.

Nina, Jackson's grandmother, and his aunts, and uncles. Ronda was the oldest and maybe twelve in this picture. That would make Jeanne, who was the youngest, about five. Riley and David in between the two.

They looked happy then. The girls and Nina were in swimming suits and shorts and David just a swimsuit. Maybe they had been at Mystic Lake that day.

It must have been a good day. A day-long before the ominous tragedy took over their lives.

Jackson focused on Nina's face. She had a pretty smile, and she looked so content with her four children. He suddenly felt very sad for her, knowing the fate that awaited just six years in the future.

Suzann plopped down on a box full of clothes. "I'm exhausted. Can the storage wait until tomorrow?"

"Fine with me," said Dana.

"Do you think we need to take these boxes down to the entry-way for them to be picked up? The Goodwill drivers don't usually come into the houses."

Dana surveyed the more than fifty boxes and then scowled. "Is there a way to request a special pickup? One where they *will* come in the house to pick up?"

Suzann sighed. "I'm with her. Let's check on that tomorrow."

Jackson sighed. "You're right, Okay. Suzann, did you hear from the kids?"

"Yes, just got a message from Aspen. They spent the day going over your grandpa's journal before they turn it over to the FBI."

"Did they find anything new?" asked Dana.

"She didn't say, but I'm sure she would have if they— Well, no probably not. She would have called though."

"Does Rocky need us to do anything?"

Jackson pulled a face. "No, Suzann, the kids are practically adults. It's not like he is babysitting them."

Suzann rolled her eyes, that's true. I guess nothing much can happen at Rocky's."

"And with four FBI agents guarding the place," said Dana.

"Yes, they will be fine. Don't worry about them," said Jackson.

Suzann and Jackson walked into the hallway, and Jackson locked the door to the master bedroom. He stood back and surveyed the entry lock and deadbolt on the door. "Can you believe this?"

"I can! Jerry and I were never allowed in that room," said Dana. "We never tried either, even when Dad wasn't home. I think the lock served its purpose."

"Why do you suppose that was?' Suzann had already started down the stairs.

Dana shrugged, "Maybe the guns, maybe the hidden passageway in the closet—"

"Or," said Jackson, "maybe there were other reasons that are no longer there."

When they passed through the entry hall, he stopped and surveyed the paintings of his dad, mom, and grandparents.

"I'm having these moved up to the storage tomorrow."

"That's probably a good idea. Maybe we should have all of the pictures and paintings moved up there."

"That's a better idea. Let's take care of that today."

Jackson started the truck and pulled out of the driveway.

"Do you think they will have Cassie's funeral before Christmas?" asked Dana.

"They haven't even released the autopsy yet, so I doubt it."

"How do you know that, Jackson?"

Jackson turned to his wife. "I called Rocky this morning."

"About the autopsy?"

"No, I was wondering if there was anything we could do for Cassie's parents."

Suzann touched her husband's shoulder. "That was sweet of you."

"I just feel so helpless. Remember when we thought we would

lose Aspen. I can't imagine how horrible they must feel having had their daughter actually die."

"I hope there are no repercussions, you know since she was adopted," said Dana.

"They have had a pretty good relationship with her birth mother, right?" asked Suzann.

"I don't know. Talk about adding insult to injury."

Jackson just stared straight ahead. "I hadn't thought of that."

〜〜

"Who is this guy? Where did he come from, and why does he want to talk to these kids?"

Surprised, Hank looked at his phone and then put it back to his ear. Rocky seemed irritated, and it wasn't his usual demeanor, so Hank spoke slowly and cautiously.

"He came from Australia, and his name is Toby. He mainly wants to talk with Aspen, but has no problem talking to all of you."

Rocky didn't say anything.

"Look, Rocky. He has been in police custody, and he underwent a full interrogation by the FBI. They claim he is clean—no risk."

"Yeah, well what do they know?"

"Rocky, are you okay?"

Again, Rocky was silent.

"Do you want me to ask them to wait a day or so?"

"It's December twenty-first!"

"Yeah, I'm aware of that."

Rocky sighed, and Hank felt the heaviness of it through the phone.

"Sorry, Hank. What time did you want to bring him over? Or is he just coming alone?'

"No, I'll come with him. We had to bring the tunnel investigation to a halt until after Christmas. We need a search warrant, and we all decided not to stir that pot until after the holidays."

"A search warrant? Why? Jackson gave you full access, didn't he?"

"He did—it's complicated. I will fill you in later."

Another labored sigh. *"Okay, when are you coming?"*

"Will 11:00 be okay?"

"It's not like they have any place to go."

"Okay, see you then."

"Yeah."

Hank ended the call and leaned back against the seat of his truck.

I hope the commissioner will be okay with us waiting on the search warrant.

Hank had a meeting with Commissioner Thornton and Chief Wilson at 2:00. He hadn't been able to get ahold of Larry all day. He had called Byron and told him he was not feeling well, but he wasn't answering his phone.

He decided to go down to the station. Maybe they had some information on Cassie's autopsy. He cringed. He knew he should call her by her last name since she was part of a police investigation, but he couldn't bring himself to do it. It seemed so—impersonal. But, he knew, it was supposed to be impersonal.

When he walked into the station, he was greeted by Christmas decorations, chocolate candy, and homemade treats everywhere he looked, and he felt a sudden sadness.

Hank Cox had been a policeman for nearly ten years, had been in Sommerville just over a year, and was promoted to detective six weeks ago. He had seen some pretty bad things when he was in Memphis, but this? This case was turning Sommerville upside down.

He grabbed a small candy cane from a dish on the receptionist's desk, tore the wrapper off, and popped it into his mouth.

"Merry Christmas, Hank." The receptionist looked up from her computer.

Hank smiled, "Merry Christmas, Penny."

He walked into his office. There was a stack of mail on his desk, and he sat down in his chair. He whirled around and looked through the window at the gloomy sky.

I wonder what's got Rocky wound so tight.

Aspen was speechless.

The same red-haired man who had walked out of the shadows at the lake was standing at Rocky's front door.

Rocky shook Hank's hand and at the same time, pulled him into the house.

"Sorry about earlier."

Hank brushed it aside with the wave of his hand. He grinned. "I figure you'll tell me about it when you're ready."

Gavin watched his dad. He had taken a phone call out in the yard earlier in the day and had seemed a little on edge ever since.

"So, you must be, Toby?"

The tall redhead extended his hand toward Rocky. "That's me. I appreciate the opportunity to visit with—" he motioned to the four teenagers, "With all of you today."

Aspen was still staring at him when Kiryn took her arm and pulled her down on the sofa.

Hank made quick introductions and then sat down in an empty chair. He noticed that all four teenagers were sitting on the edge of their seats, studying this new stranger.

"What brings you here, Toby? I understand you just arrived in the U.S. this week?"

Toby nodded. Yes, last Thursday.

"Do you know, Max?" Aspen blurted.

Toby looked surprised. "Do you?"

Aspen blushed, "Sort of, I think, anyway."

Now it was Toby who was puzzled. He studied Aspen for a minute. "Max Smith. Must be a different Max. The only Max I know died years ago."

Aspen gasped. She looked at Noah, then Kiryn, and then Gavin.

"I guess I don't understand. Is there another Max that I should know about?" asked Toby.

Rocky reached over and put his hand on Aspen's knee. "Why don't you tell us why you are here? Then we can go into that."

Toby shrugged. "Okay. The reason I'm here is because of a story my grandmother told me when I was— I don't know, maybe ten. I used to live here, at Mystic Lake."

"You lived here? When? I've never seen you before," said Gavin.

"My mother took me to Australia when I was five. That's where she was from. She divorced my dad, and we left America, and haven't been back until now."

"Which house did you live in?" asked Kiryn.

"The one I was coming from when I saw you all at the lake. No one has lived in it for years. Well, off and on, but not regularly since my dad died."

"I'm sorry about your father. When did he die?" asked Rocky.

"Well let's see, I'm twenty-five. Probably about fifteen years ago. That was why my grandmother told me the story. We got word that my father had been killed, and— It's okay, I barely remember my father."

Hank had been looking at the floor but now looked directly at Toby. "How? How was he killed?"

"Car accident. A rollover, I think. The details were pretty sketchy, and my mom didn't care to find out more. She remarried when I was seven, but she never got over my dad. At least that's what I believe."

"Where did your red hair—"

Aspen jumped in the middle of Kiryn's question, "And freckles come from?"

Toby laughed. "That would be my mom's side." He looked around. No one seemed to want to say anything, so he continued.

"My great-grandfather and his partner opened a cabinet shop in Memphis. My grandfather and his two brothers, and then later, my dad and my uncle worked for them for about ten years before my dad and mother met. That's how they met."

"How?" asked Hank.

"The cabinet shop did a lot of work on a house for a guy who owned a home on Mystic Lake. He was the one who convinced my great-grandfather to build out here as well.

Apparently, my great-grandfather had a falling out with his brothers when he moved out to Sommerville. That's when my mother and my dad's great-grandfather became partners in the cabinet business.

He and his wife were divorced, so my grandmother had not seen her grandfather for years. She brought her two granddaughters, my mom, and her sister to the U.S. for a visit, and they came out to Mystic Lake. Mom met my dad, and they were married six months later."

"We lived in Memphis, but after my great-grandfather died, my parents moved out here. I was just two. That's the house I mentioned."

"Do you know whom your great-grandfather worked for?" asked Rocky.

"I don't. I could ask my grandmother though, maybe she knows."

"So your mother's mother is whom you lived with? She is still living."

"Oh, yes. Of course, in Australia."

Rocky looked at Aspen and then Noah. "Interesting."

Noah nodded, but Aspen said nothing. She had not taken her eyes off Toby.

Toby continued, "This story about the girl who survived an apparent drowning in Mystic Lake, was all over the internet." He turned to Aspen. "Is it all true? I mean, obviously it is. Here you are in front of me."

"It's all true," said Rocky flatly.

Toby shifted in his seat, he nodded and went on.

"Well, of course, I recognized the name Mystic Lake. My mother talked about the lake and the beautiful house all the time. She died of cancer when I was nineteen."

"When this story of Mystic Lake came into the news, my grandmother and I were looking at pictures of the lake on the internet, and my grandmother asked me if I remembered the story she had told me when I was younger."

"I did, but I hadn't thought about it for a long time. I thought it was just a story."

Toby stopped talking. He suddenly realized that everyone was now listening intently, and he looked nervous.

"Go on," said Rocky.

"Any chance I could get a drink of water? You guys are making me nervous."

Rocky stood. "No one is trying to make you nervous. You just—you just have no idea what you walked into, that's all." He disappeared into the kitchen.

"Should I leave?"

"No!" Aspen leaned forward, "I need to know about Max."

"As I said, the only Max—" Toby's eyes widened, but then he seemed to change his mind about whatever he was thinking.

Rocky came back with several bottles of water. He handed one to Toby and put the rest on the coffee table. No one touched them, but Toby opened his and drank half the bottle.

He looked at all of them. "Okay, so the story was that this guy needed to hide a bunch of papers or something, so a cabinet maker built him a revolving shelf. Or shelves. They turned, you know like you might see in one of those old movies."

"The shelves turned so that in the room, it looked like a regular bookcase, but when they turned, the shelves revealed the concealed papers. When I was ten, my grandmother told it like a mystery story. She was somewhat fascinated by it."

Rocky's eyes widened. "Did you read about this too? Because it has been all over the news."

Toby nodded and guzzled some more water. I did read about that, but that's only part of what brought me here. It was the name on the note. Demot.

Hank looked at Rocky and then back to Toby.

"This would be?"

"Considering the time when this probably all happened, it is most likely my great-grandfather. Actually, I'm positive it was."

"Why?"

Toby reached in his pocket and pulled an envelope. He handed it to Hank.

"It's a letter to my mother, open it. The contents are not really significant, but the signature is what caught my attention."

Hank opened the letter and read the signature,

Harold Demot

"Does that ring a bell with anyone?"

Everyone shrugged.

Toby then asked Rocky, "Do you have the note that was found? The one that was in an email that they talked about in the news report?"

"Oh! The one to our Aunt Dana about the door under the rug in the office?" asked Noah.

Toby pointed his finger at Noah, "Yes, that one."

"I think the police took it?" asked Noah.

Rocky and Hank exchanged a quick glance.

Hank nodded, "Probably."

"Then if you have a laptop, let's pull up the picture. It's there."

Gavin stood, jogged upstairs and immediately returned with his laptop. He turned it on and handed it to Toby.

"Funny," said Noah. "We have never even looked at this stuff online."

"Why would we? We live it!" blurted Kiryn.

Noah gave her a nonchalant look. "True."

"Here it is." Toby placed the computer on the table. "Now look at the signature."

"It's the same," said Rocky. "The way he printed his D's, with that little squirrely thing at the bottom is a dead giveaway."

Satisfied, Toby sat back in his seat. "I don't know if it helps much, but I am quite sure my great-grandfather built that revolving shelf in your grandfather's office." He was looking at Noah.

"It was originally my great-grandfather's office," said Noah.

"May we keep this letter?" asked Hank.

"You will have to give it to the FBI. They allowed me to bring it to show you, but then you are supposed to return it to them. I assured them I would leave it in your safekeeping."

Hank nodded.

Aspen hadn't said anything in regards to the letter. Now she looked directly at Toby.

"Who is Max?"

"Oh, Max. He was my distant cousin. He lived at the house on Mystic Lake until he died sometime in the late 40s I think."

Aspen furrowed her brow. "Well, then you don't actually know him, right? I mean it seemed like you did from the way you were talking."

Toby laughed. "No, I don't actually know him, but I have seen pictures of him. He and I could practically be twins. Only he was a lot younger than I am when he died."

"How—how old was he?" asked Aspen with trepidation.

"Umm. From what I understand, he was sixteen or seventeen."

"What happened to him? How did he die?"

Toby took another drink of his water and then said nonchalantly, "No one knows for sure, he just up and disappeared. But that was in the late 50s. He would be in his 70s if he were alive." He set the empty bottle on the table. "So obviously, not the same Max."

63

ARREST

Jackson and Suzann had just arrived at Rocky's when a police car pulled in behind them. The young officer got out of his car, nodded to them both as he passed and walked right up to Hank and Rocky who were on the porch.

He handed Hank a paper, who appeared to sign it, and returned it to the officer. He turned and walked directly back to his patrol car. In less than five minutes, he was gone.

"I'm glad this quarantine has ended," said Mom when she reached the porch. "Where are the kids? It's cold out here, why are you two standing outside?"

Hank and Rocky glanced at each other, and they both looked at Jackson who shrugged.

"Do you want them to answer those questions one at a time, Suzann?" asked Jackson.

"No need." Suzann didn't look back at the three men when she opened the front door. "*Kids?*"

Jackson followed her with his eyes for a few seconds and then turned back to Hank and Rocky.

They both laughed.

Jackson changed the subject, "What was that all about?" He motioned toward the driveway.

Hank sighed. "He needed me to sign a warrant."

Jackson looked surprised. "For whom?"

"Doug Mendel."

Jackson's eyebrows shot up. "What?"

"Don't misunderstand, we don't think Doug is involved in what we are looking for, but we found a room under his house. That tunnel under your place took us right to his house. There are some slabs under there, and we needed a warrant to dig them up."

"Why didn't you just ask him?"

"Right? That's what I asked," said Rocky.

"Well, I would have, but the Commissioner wouldn't hear of it. He wants everything done by the book, and documented."

"He's going to be surprised by this," said Jackson.

"I called him. He knows the officer is coming over. I thought the FBI would wait until after Christmas, but they are over there right now. The warrant is just a formality."

Hank sighed. "Things are coming together rapidly, at least regarding those boys whose names are in the files. The FBI put out an internet search. Of course, there are always a ton of people who answer those things with he said-she said. Blah blah blah, but they have actually confirmed relatives of four of the boys."

"That is amazing. They did that pretty fast."

Hank nodded.

"So, what does the FBI think they are going to find?'

Hank shrugged. "I'm not sure. They are also going down in the cellar under your house—the Mansion house. The Commissioner is convinced those boys are buried around here somewhere and he wants answers for the families."

"Interestingly enough," said Rocky. "Every one of the families that have been able to prove relationship to one of the four had genealogy records that linked them right to the boy's parents and subsequently to our four victims."

"Do we know their names?" asked Jackson.

"I don't," said Hank.

The door opened, and Suzann stepped out onto the porch. "Hank, the kids are wondering if Brandon was released from protective custody."

Hank shook his head. "No, they will let him come home

Christmas eve, but not before, at least, that is the last I heard."

Suzann looked down at her feet. "Oh." Suddenly she looked up again, "Jackson and Rocky, I am going to see if Dana wants to drive into Memphis with me and take the kids to see the Christmas lights. Are you two okay with that?" she looked at Hank, "Are you?"

"You'll have to take them." Hank nodded toward the four agents in the black SUV.

Suzann smiled, "Okay." Saying nothing more, she turned and went back inside.

"Doesn't feel much like Christmas anymore," said Rocky.

"Sure doesn't." Jackson sighed. Suddenly he asked, "Hank, what about you? You need to go home for Christmas."

Hank chuckled, "Not this year. You guys have fixed that for me."

Jackson's eyes widened. "I'm sorry, Hank. Why can't you just go?"

"I'm just kidding. It's all good. Worked out fine. Remember, my mother-in-law passed? My wife flew up to New York with the kids the day before yesterday. My father-in-law needs the company. I'll go up once this has settled down."

"I feel terrible. I didn't even think about that," said Jackson.

"Don't feel too bad for him," laughed Rocky. "His check will be worth it."

Hank smiled. "Yeah this has been grueling, and I never expected to be this heavily involved, but it won't hurt my career, that's for sure. Already got the promotion."

"Really? That's great, Hank!" Rocky slapped his shoulder.

Hank grinned, "Detective Hank to you, buddy."

64

UNDER THE SLABS

"TEN! THE REMAINS OF ten persons were under the first slab!" Commissioner Thornton shook his head and plopped back into his chair.

He continued, "And what is even crazier, the slab you were standing on was the top of the vault. A cement coffin for ten people—boys, no doubt—just four inches under your feet!"

Hank felt sick. "They just left them there for anyone to stumble over?"

"Not exactly, look what it took to find them. I wouldn't say they were stumbled on," said Chief Wilson.

"Well, I know, but I mean, you would think they would have covered up the cement slabs."

"I think they did," said Commissioner Thornton. "You said it looked like water had been under there, maybe over time, it just washed away."

Hank shuddered, "Maybe. What in the world would drive someone to do this?"

Chief Wilson lifted his hand and rubbed his fingers against his thumb. "The same thing that has driven men to corruption since the beginning of time, money."

Hank sank into a chair. "Did they find anything in the cellar under the Allen's house?"

"Not yet. They just got through the brick wall. They are trying not to destroy everything. I told them to call me as soon as they know."

Hank nodded. "Okay, so far, we have four families that have positively been linked to some of the victims. We have ten corpses and a pile of disconnected bones."

"Skeletons," said Chief Wilson. "And they were not carefully put in those vaults. They were just thrown on top of each other."

"Like the ones in the tunnel?"

Chief Wilson nodded, "It's a slow process. They all have to be removed, and then I guess they will try dental records to identify who they are."

"Do you honestly think they are going to find dental records for those kids?"

They were all silent.

Finally, Commissioner Thornton sighed. "No. No, I don't think we will be able to identify any of them."

"What about DNA?"

The commissioner turned to Chief Wilson, "Yes, that's a possibility. Expensive though. That could take months, too, maybe years."

"These kids had families, sir."

The commissioner had been looking at his hands. He now looked at Hank. "Yes, I know. I know."

Doug Mendel opened the front door to his house on Mystic Lake.

"Thanks for seeing us, Doug."

Hank was immediately taken back by the sheer majesty of the entryway he was standing in. Not quite as tall as the Allen's entry, but the décor looked like a mini version of the Las Vegas casino, Caesar's Palace.

"This is a huge house!"

Doug laughed, "Too big for us. I think I am going to sell it. Especially now."

Hank nodded. "I'm really sorry about all of this, Doug."

Doug shrugged. "Don't be sorry, except that I have to tell Sara we have been living in a house with dead bodies buried under it. Who would have thought?"

Chief Wilson shook Doug's hand. "That was good of you to help the Tuttle kid with his bail."

Doug shrugged again. "It was nothing. I feel bad for him and his parents. Has he ever explained how or why he was involved?"

Doug didn't wait for an answer, "And now, with the death of his friend— This is horrible for everyone concerned."

Hank and Chief Wilson followed Doug into a den off the entry-way.

"Do they know how she died?" Doug walked over to the bar, lifted a bottle of whiskey from under the counter, and turned to face the two men. "Drink?"

Hank and Chief Wilson both shook their heads.

"Oh, I guess not. Working, right?" He filled a shot glass, chugged it and placed the glass on the bar.

Doug put the bottle away and motioned for the two men to sit down. "Did the Allen's get moved back in? Oh, I guess they did. Sara told me the kids were in police protection at Rocky's. Probably the best place for them."

"Are you okay, Doug?" asked Hank.

"No. Not really. Dead people under your house is upsetting news on top of everything else. You know Gavin dated that little gal for over a year. She spent a lot of time with us."

Doug sat down with his elbows resting on the arms of his chair, and laced his fingers together.

Hank couldn't help but notice that Doug's hands were shaking.

It was a cold night in Memphis.

Aunt Dana and Mom rode in the front seat of Dad's truck, and the four teenagers squished in the back.

Before they left Sommerville, Mom expressed concern about there not being enough seat belts, but Aunt Dana brushed that aside.

"We'll be fine, Suzann."

"I know we'll be fine. It's *them* I'm worried about."

Aunt Dana glanced over her shoulder and winked at Aspen, "Why don't you two buckle into one seatbelt so your mom can relax."

Aspen and Gavin had been all too willing to obey.

"We're going to eat, right?" Gavin became aware that the other kids were staring at him.

"You know, I mean after the lights."

"Sure you did," said Kiryn.

Dana herded the kids and Suzann toward the park. "We won't let you starve, Gavin. Look at this! It's like a fairyland."

"I wish you and Dad would have invited Grandma to come for Christmas."

Suzann put an arm around her daughter. "It wouldn't be fair, Aspen. This is not a normal Christmas. Maybe we'll bring her out for New Year's Eve."

Aspen shrugged. It made her sad that their Grandma wouldn't be here this Christmas. She was always at their house for the holidays.

Thousands of multi-colored lights expertly laced through the branches of trees and bushes beckoned the group into the festive park.

The metal arch at the entrance had been transformed into a gingerbread house, and just as they walked through it, they were greeted with young girls dressed as elves offering hot chocolate and cider.

They each took a cup as Christmas music filled the air.

Seated on an oversized chair covered by a red cloth with gold braiding, a chubby, red-cheeked, jolly-looking Santa was greeting a long line of excited children.

"I *have* to go see Santa," said Kiryn.

Gavin scowled at his sister, "Are you kidding me?"

"Humph. Well, you had better too. Do you honestly think any-one has had time to think about presents?"

Aspen laughed at Kiryn. She linked arms with her friend and pulled her toward Santa.

She looked up at the star-studded sky.

Just for tonight, I'm going to pretend nothing is wrong in the world.

The tall hedge in front of them twinkled with clear lights, but Aspen noticed an even brighter light on the other side. She let go of Kiryn's arm and climbed onto a small wall. The light was shining on a live nativity.

The young girl who represented Mary looked up, and noticed Aspen.

She smiled.

Aspen smiled back, and her eyes drifted to the sleeping baby Jesus.

It's all going to be okay. It is, right, Jesus?

Grateful to be back in her own bed, Aspen squished her pillow under her head and turned onto her side. The picture of her and Krista sitting on the nightstand stared back at her.

Aspen studied the picture. Tan faces, disheveled hair, wetsuits, and huge grins. The beach, always the beach.

Aspen closed her eyes, and her mind was flooded with memories of her childhood friend.

"Can your little girl come out to play?"

Aspen had bounced out of the house, and the two girls spent the rest of the afternoon in Aspen's sandbox and on the swing set.

Krista's family had moved in just three doors down, and that morning Aspen, Noah, and Mom had dropped some cookies off to welcome the new neighbors.

Krista met them at the door and wanted Aspen to stay and play. Their mothers had agreed this afternoon would be better and right after lunch, Krista and her mother showed up at their door and visited for about an hour.

Krista's mother was happy to let her daughter stay and play while she finished some unpacking.

And so, the friendship began—a friendship which would last a lifetime—unfortunately, a short lifetime in for Krista.

Aspen could almost hear Krista's voice.

"Hey let's get matching suits!"

At ten years old, they begged their mothers for matching red, white, and blue swimsuits. They proudly wore them on the fourth of July and every day afterward until the suits were so thread-bare their mothers insisted they wear other suits, or not go to the beach.

That same year, they got matching wetsuits.

The two girls were inseparable. When Aspen wasn't with Noah, she was with Krista. Many times, it was the three of them. Krista didn't have any siblings until she was eleven and then her mom had two little girls in two years. Aspen and Noah were close, and the three of them often spent their days at the beach together.

"We have to be in the same class. Don't you get it? We are like twins!'

That was the strategy they used to beg Mr. Gilbertson, the elementary school principal, to put Krista in the same class as Aspen every year.

It took three meetings with Krista's parents and Mr. Gilbertson, but the goal was finally accomplished.

In middle school and high school, they made sure when they registered, they got as many classes together as possible.

"I think Noah is so cute."

They were twelve. Aspen couldn't believe her best friend had a crush on her brother. After Krista died, Aspen learned that for years, Noah had felt the same way about her.

Noah and Aspen walked to elementary school with Krista and, along with Derrick, Noah's best friend, they rode their bikes to the middle school that was considerably farther away.

Recess, school lunch, that they all hated but ate anyway, school plays, middle school assemblies, high school football games, dances, and surfing. Always and foremost, surfing.

Aspen rolled onto her back. Surfing took her friends life, although Krista would never say that.

"A stupid mistake was all it was."

Aspen suddenly sat up. "What?"

"A stupid mistake was all it was. I knew better than to go past the breakers that day. The surf was really rough, but I did anyway, and I flipped off my board, and then it bonked me on the head and knocked me out."

Aspen stared in disbelief. Krista was sitting on the edge of Aspen's bay window.

"Maybe if I had been there—"

"Well, that would be dumb. We could both be dead."

"Or maybe we wouldn't have gone out there."

Krista grinned, *"Maybe."*

Aspen reached down and pinched her arm. Yes, she was awake.

"I'm really here."

"But how. Why? Why now?"

Krista shrugged. *"Just time I guess."*

"Time for what?"

"It's great what you did—finding the boys and all. Although it was fun watching you. Ronda practically had to hit you over the head."

"She did?"

"I'm kidding. We are looking at things from a different perspective, so we can see what we want mortals to find, but we can't intervene too much, so it takes a long time. Even though to us, the clues seem to be right in front of your faces.'

"You watch us all the time?"

"Well, not all the time, we can't do that. We have lives too, you know." She giggled. *"So to speak."*

Aspen didn't find that very funny.

Krista smiled. *"We do, Aspen. I'm here, aren't I? We don't disappear. We just go to another place."*

"But where? What about heaven?"

"There are different—places—in heaven. We aren't sitting around playing harps. We have things to do, and sometimes it's helping, or should I say encouraging mortals.'

Aspen suddenly grabbed a bottle of water off her nightstand, opened it, and took a drink.

Krista gave her a puzzled look.

"I'm just making sure I'm awake."

"I promise you are."

"Are you like a guardian angel?"

"More like a helping kind of spirit, for the time being anyway."

"I miss you, Krista."

Krista's expression suddenly looked sad. *"I miss you too, but I wouldn't come back."*

"You wouldn't?"

"Not on your life, no pun intended. I love it here! So peaceful and beautiful and not bogged down by a cumbersome body."

They were both silent for several seconds. Aspen had no idea how to process all of this. Krista, right here in her room, talking to her like it was nothing. Even though she seemed totally awake, she was pretty sure she was dreaming.

Suddenly Aspen realized she was missing a great opportunity.

"Krista, who is Max? Do you know him? Wait, I know you do. On the balcony. I saw you on the—"

Krista smiled. She knew Aspen was remembering.

"Wait! I talked to you on the balcony. I was on the balcony with you both."

Krista nodded.

"Then what— What does Max want from me?"

"Ask them to go under the lake, to the channel, one more time."

"The channel?"

"You and I were in it."

Aspen gasped. "Max! You are real! I knew it!"

It *was* Max, and he was sitting right next to Krista. Red-haired, freckled-face Max and he did look just like Toby.

"What? When?"

"Think." Max touched his temple with his finger. *"Think, Aspen."*

Aspen closed her eyes. Water. She couldn't breathe, and then she could. Loud water. A waterfall. A room. Boys. Flowers, gardens, boys. Grandpa.

Aspen opened her eyes. Krista and Max were still there.

"You were in the water with me! That's why I know you. But wait, was I dead?"

"I told you that you weren't dead. You just couldn't wake up."

"Thank you, Aspen."

Aspen jumped and involuntarily scooted back on her bed.

Behind Krista and Max, Ronda and— Aspen squinted, Thomas?

"Am I dead now, because I am totally talking to dead people, in my own bedroom, like you are alive?"

Krista and Max laughed. Ronda and Thomas didn't. They seemed to not be as *here*, or something. Maybe they were not as talkative as Max and Krista.

"What about my grandpa? I saw him there, in that place. Wherever that place was. What am I supposed to do for Grandpa?"

"Time will take care of that. Just time, and your dad," said Krista. Krista and Max both stood.

"Wait! You're leaving?! Don't leave!" She jumped to her feet. "What about my dad?"

Krista smiled. *"It's okay, Aspen. I promise it's going to be okay."*

"But?"

"The lake. Mystic Lake. The channel." Max grinned at Aspen, and his green eyes sparkled.

Krista and Max turned as if they were going to walk right through the window, but they didn't. They started to fade away instead.

Suddenly Krista turned back, *"Oh, by the way, that girl, Cassie. She has some issues.'*

"Wait! You know Cassie?"

"Well, we don't hang out with her, if that's what you mean. As I said, that girl has issues."

"Wait! Please wait! Are you coming back?!"

"We're burnin' daylight!" Krista's voice was only an echo. They were gone, Aspen was alone again.

65

MOLLY

"You are going on a hunch from a seventeen-year-old girl?"

Hank felt his blood boil. "We would have nothing without this seventeen-year-old-girl, sir!"

Commissioner Thornton was silent. He had returned to Memphis the night before and was most likely not happy that he was being bothered with such a request this early.

When the silence became uncomfortable, Hank said, "I think I can get Kendall Washington to bring his team in. That is if he is in town so close to Christmas."

The Commissioner spoke more calmly now. "That water has to be freezing, Hank, and what about the current they were talking about. I would just as soon not have any more casualties in this case. Especially not this week."

Hank sneered. "Or ever."

"Right, or ever."

Again, the uncomfortable silence hung in the air, but then Commissioner Thornton finally said, "Okay, see if he can get on it today. Push for today. Maybe then we can let things go until after Christmas. At least I am going to try. You shut down that operation under the Mendel house, right?"

"Yes, they will be back on the twenty-sixth."

"And the cellar? The one under the Allen Mansion?"

"Yes. It's the same team."

"Okay. By the way, we got the autopsy report on the girl."

"Cassie?"

"Yes."

"And?"

"Chief Wilson is meeting with her parents this morning. That little girl was chock full of performance-enhancing drugs."

"What? Where would she—"

"Question of the morning, and how could she afford it? This is not going to be good news for her mom and dad."

"They haven't had much good news anyway, sir. Is that what killed her?"

"No. Well, it didn't help that she had so much of that drug in her system, but she was poisoned."

"How, or I guess when? Before she left New York?"

"The autopsy was inconclusive on exactly when, but they think it was within about twelve hours prior to her death. She had a bad bruise and a jagged needle mark in her hip. Somehow the poison was administered through there, but it was like it was jammed into her. The skin was torn, and as I said, she had a nasty bruise."

"I wonder—"

"There is a connection here, Detective. I'm sure of it. We need to get to the Tuttle kid again."

"He is still in protective custody. Should I talk to him today?"

"Yes, and let me know what Kendall says. See if they can get in and out of there. I doubt they will find anything."

"Will do."

Obviously, you don't know these kids as well as I do—especially Aspen.

"Is it okay that we're here?"

Aspen pulled on the sides of her knit hat as if pulling on it would make it come all the way to her chin.

Gavin put his arm around her and pulled her close. "I didn't ask. It is freezing this morning."

"Do we need to ask? I mean it's a free country, right?"

"That it is, Kiryn."

The four kids jumped and whirled around at the sound of Hank's voice.

"Hey, Hank!" Noah laughed. "You scared us."

"Didn't mean to. So, what do you think about this?" Hank directed his question to Aspen.

She twisted her mouth. "I think that I hope this is not a wild goose chase. I guess I think we should at least look."

"For what, exactly? What did—that dead Max guy—what did he say?"

"Are you being sarcastic?"

Kiryn shrugged, "Me?"

They all laughed but were distracted by a loud sound behind them.

"What is that?" asked Noah.

"That is a small submarine. I think it's called a personal sub," said Hank.

"Is it Kendall Washington's?"

"Yes. Well, his company owns it."

Coming down the path from the Mansion house, the bright yellow three-person personal sub was sitting on a flatbed trailer pulled by a diesel pickup.

Aspen's eyes widened. "Did they drive that thing across the grass?"

"Well, they didn't fly across it," said Noah.

Aspen winced, "I'll bet our grandparents are turning in their graves."

Kiryn sighed, "Don't forget the tunnel goes under that grass, to a lot of graves."

"Good point," said Noah. "I guess the time for worrying about our grandparents' feelings is long past."

Rocky had been standing away from them, texting someone. Now he joined the conversation.

"I suspect worrying about feelings and status was the cause of a lot of this whole story."

"Status, political position, money. I'm sure all of it has played a part," said Hank.

"A lot of people died, though," said Kiryn. She directed their attention to the path again. "There's your mom and dad and Dana."

Hank lifted his hand and waved at Jackson, Suzann, and Dana, but then he pulled on Rocky's arm. "May I have a minute with you?"

"Sure." Rocky followed him toward the lake.

They all watched the truck meander along the shore to the side of the lake where Aspen was found. Hank had explained that the water was deepest there closer to shore.

Once it passed them, they all followed.

"I think this is the coldest morning so far this winter," said Mom. "Looks like it might rain."

"I hope not. At least until they get finished with this," said Dad. He turned to Aspen, "I hope you're right about this."

"About what, Dad? I'm not even sure what they are looking for. They just told me—"

"Krista and Max?" asked Aunt Dana.

Aspen rolled her eyes. "I know it sounds crazy, Aunt Dana."

Dana quickly corrected her niece, "No, I did not say that? In this family, I have learned never to underestimate anything. I was simply asking."

Aspen nodded, "Oh, well, yes. At least Max did. He just said 'the channel.' Dad said the day they dived looking for me that they found a channel or something, so I think that was what Max was talking about."

Mom put her arm around her daughter. "Well, you didn't order this. The police did. They must have felt it was important."

"I think that was Hank's doing," said Dad. "He has a lot of faith in you kids."

"Well, he should!" said Dana. "What would they have without you, Aspen, and you, Noah? Without all of you?"

Kiryn giggled. "A quiet, peaceful town."

They all laughed.

"Quiet maybe, but I'm not so sure about the peaceful," said Dad. He glanced at Rocky and Hank as they passed by them. "What are they up to?"

Noah shrugged. "Don't know. Hank just asked Rocky if he could talk to him."

"What time does your plane leave, Aunt Dana?" asked Noah.

"Not until six. It was the only direct flight today, and I didn't want to go by way of San Diego."

"Isn't that kind of out of the way?" asked Gavin.

"Right? That's why I am leaving later. It's so much faster. Are you kids coming with us to the airport?"

"I think we are going to see Cassie's parents," said Noah.

Mom looked surprised. "All of you?"

Aspen knew Mom was referring to her. "Yes, we decided all of us should go."

Mom smiled. "Okay."

They all stopped a few feet from the truck and watched as the sub was unloaded and pushed to the edge of the lake.

Gavin looked back at Rocky and Hank.

Aspen leaned around him to investigate his face. "What's wrong?"

Gavin shook his head. "I don't know. Dad has been acting kind of weird for a couple of days. Something is bothering him, but he won't talk about it."

〰

"So what does she think Doug is doing?"

Rocky sighed. "I don't know if she knows what she thinks. She just said he has become distant. He won't talk to her about any-thing."

"Well, he has had a few upsets in the last week," said Hank. "He was visibly shaken by the news of the bodies under their house."

Rocky shuddered, and they both instinctively looked toward Doug and Sara's house.

"Not just a few either, they uncovered forty-two bodies before the commissioner put the lid on it until after Christmas." Hank brought the subject back to Sara.

"What does she want you to do?"

"I'm not sure, nothing really. Doug and I have never been friends. Cordial yes, but not friends. We are two entirely different people."

"I can see that. Surprises me that you both have been married to Sara."

"I have been, he is."

"Why didn't you ever marry again?"

"Guess I never really tried. I had Gavin and Kiryn, and I just—"

"You still love her."

Rocky's eyebrows shot up. "No, I don't! Well, I do, you know, she *is* Gavin's mom."

"But she isn't really. Sumer is."

Rocky scowled. "That's like saying Juan is his dad, and I'm not." He did not like Hank referring to Gavin's birth parents.

Hank pumped the air with both hands. "Calm down, Rocky. I wasn't taking anything away from you and Sara. I know you have had Gavin since he was what? Two days old?"

"Yeah, I would say that pretty much makes us his parents."

"You're right, I'm sorry. That was a bad way to reference what I was trying to say."

"What were you trying to say?"

Hank turned toward the group of divers. "Nothing. Let's go check this out. I haven't ever seen a small sub like that. Come to think of it; I have never seen a big sub!"

Rocky eyed the detective as he followed him.

Love Sara? That's absurd. I just feel bad for her, that's all.

Kendall Washington introduced everyone and explained that both divers with him, Roger and Les, had been in the search party who looked for her.

"Craziest day ever," said Roger. "We never expected to find you."

Aspen grinned. "Well, I'm glad you did."

Les looked at Roger. "We didn't really find you. You just floated up, somehow."

Kendall's eyes widened, and he raised his eyebrows. "It's a mystery. No one can figure that out."

Kendall went on to explain the reason he called off the search that day. "It was the channel they ran into. My divers are used to going into caves and caverns underwater, but the current was horrendous."

"The whole thing didn't make sense anyway," said Les. "None of us— In fact, I doubt *anyone* had dived in this lake before since it is privately owned, but to find a channel like that in a man-made lake, just didn't make sense."

"And the current had to be coming from somewhere," said Roger.

Kendall clapped his hands together. "Well, let's get to it. We're not finding out anything up here." He climbed aboard the sub and turned to the group.

"The sonar will project onto these screens and let us know when we are coming up on an object. The images from the screen will also be on Roger's computer, so you can all see what we are seeing.

Roger looked around at the group and then at the cab of the truck where his computer was. "I wasn't expecting quite an audience. I'll set it up on the trailer so you can all see. Give me a minute, Kendall."

Les climbed aboard, and the two men buckled into their seats.

"That looks like fun," said Noah.

"Do you like the water? I mean are you okay being in the water?"

A low chuckle rolled through the group at Les's question.

"Uhh, he and she," Kiryn pointed at Aspen, "are surfers, from California."

Les grinned, "Well then maybe you would want to take a ride sometime."

Noah's face lit up. "That would be awesome!" He looked at Aspen.

"Wouldn't mind seeing where my sister spent nearly two days."

Aspen scowled. "Very funny."

Noah shrugged, "I thought so."

"Okay, Kendall, got it. Are you ready to go?" Roger had the computer on a small folding table and sat it on an even smaller folding chair.

"Ready." Kendall pulled the bubble top over them and secured it in place. He appeared to be checking some instruments, and then both he and Les put on headsets.

"Can you hear me?"

Kendall and Les both gave Roger a thumbs up, waved briefly to the crowd and turned away from them. The bright yellow sub with the clear bubble top slowly drifted away from the shore. When they were about twenty feet out, the sub started to submerge. First, there were waves and bubbles, once it disappeared under the water, the waves continued, and gradually, the water was still again.

Aspen shuddered. She was both excited and scared. She wanted them to find something, but at the same time, she didn't know what. She was still trying to process how come Max seemed so familiar. He really hadn't explained much to her. He hadn't explained anything at all! Could she have met this guy while she was in a coma? It seemed so unlikely.

Roger pointed to the computer screen. "We are seeing what they are seeing. The camera is on the front of the sub."

"Looks pretty murky," said Dad.

Roger nodded. "It will be for a few minutes. Molly stirred up the sediment, but it will calm down."

"Molly?"

Roger grinned. "Yep, we call her Molly. Everybody *loves* Molly."

Dad laughed. "Oh."

They all watched the screen: nothing, just dark water.

"Mind if I join you?"

Everyone but Roger whirled around.

Toby stopped by the front of the truck and waited for a response from someone.

Hank was the first to answer. "I don't see why not." He looked around the group. No one had any objections, and he didn't expect them to.

"Toby, these are Aspen and Noah's parents, Jackson and Suzann Allen, and this is Jackson's sister, Dana. Roger here is with the diving team."

"So, you are the one from Australia?" Dad shook his hand.

"Yes, sir. It's nice to meet the two of you."

"How did you know we were out here?" asked Aspen.

"I didn't. I was just taking a walk down to the lake and saw all of you. What are you doing anyway?"

Aspen's eyes pleaded with Hank.

"Did I say something wrong?" asked Toby.

Dad noticed the look on Aspen's face and jumped in. "No. These men are looking under the water to see if they can find any clues about Aspen's disappearance, so to speak."

Toby looked around. "Men?"

Rocky pointed to the water. "They are in a sub."

Toby looked puzzled.

"Marine, a submarine," blurted Kiryn.

"Oh! Well, this is exciting."

Aspen cringed.

Yeah, exciting. I wish you would leave. I would rather you didn't know that I think I know your dead cousin.

"*There isn't much down here.*" Roger had put his headset on speaker, and that was the first they had heard from Molly.

"*A few fish—big fish. They must have escaped the hook for a long time.*"

"Do they still stock this lake?" asked Hank.

Dad shook his head. "I have no idea. I doubt it."

"How long do fish live?"

"Don't know, Kiryn. I haven't really checked into that," said Rocky.

"Hmmm."

"Are you following that fish?" asked Roger.

Les chuckled, *"It's the only thing moving down here."*

"No sign of a cave? A channel of any kind?"

"Not yet, Roger. We are going to circle the entire lake. We are in about fifty feet of water right here. If I remember right, it gets pretty shallow in some spots.'

"It does. Maybe fifteen feet. This side of the lake is, by far, the deepest," said Roger.

Suddenly, the images on the computer screen started bouncing around, and everything went blurry. For a minute, the screen was black.

"Okay! I think we have found it! We are being dragged—fast!— and…w_ha__n_c__nt__r_l." Kendall was breaking up.

"Shutt___ d___ __gi__s." Les's voice was even more garbled than Kendall's.

"They turned off the engine," said Roger.

"Is that a good idea?" asked Suzann.

"Well, if they can't control the sub, it makes sense. Instead of risking damage to the engine, if all they are doing is fighting the current."

Roger studied the screen. "They are moving fast."

"Okay, okay. I think we got this."

"You're loud and clear, boss. What was that?"

"Not sure, it just pulled us along. That was one strong current."

"Looks like it's calmed down."

"Considerably. We are in a dead spot. Like we never came through that channel."

"This is bizarre. Can you see this Roger?"

"Is that a waterfall?" Aspen's eyes widened.

"We have drifted into some kind of a cave. We are surfacing. I have the engine back on," said Kendall.

"Surfacing? What? How?" Roger sounded anxious.

The sub slowly turned a circle. They were looking at the walls of a cave. Right in the middle—or so it appeared—there was what looked like a waterfall.

Aspen's heart was pounding. "I've—I've been there!"

They all turned to look at her. "I have! I was there, and I went through it. I saw a waterfall in the tunnel too, the day you guys left me there."

"We didn't...."

"I know, Kiryn, you know what I mean!"

"Kendall? That looks like a waterfall," said Roger.

"I am taking pictures of it. This is the strangest thing. It's right in the middle of the cave. We can go all the way around it. Strange."

"There are some tunnels that shoot off from this cave. Can you see those?"

The tunnel they saw on the screen didn't appear to be very deep.

"There are five of them," said Roger. *"We are going to check out each one."*

"Is that unusual? To have a cave that is not filled with water at the bottom of a lake?" asked Rocky.

"Well, it's not unheard of. That's how amateurs get killed when they go into underground caves. They come to a place like that, and they think there is oxygen, and there is, but not much. It doesn't take long to use it up. This is pretty big, though. I would say maybe twenty feet across."

"Wait. What is that?" Gavin leaned closer to the screen. "Is that a bone? A foot?"

"Can you see this Roger?" Kendall sounded uneasy.

"We can see it."

"We are going to get a little closer."

The image on the screen got bigger. It was a human foot bone. Two foot bones!

Now, the bright light on Molly beamed right on the object. They were just a few feet away.

"Well, I'll be damned," said Kendall.

"Is that what I think it is?"

Les and Kendall were talking to each other.

"I think so."

"What do you have? You turned the lights off."

"I just— Give us a minute."

Aspen grabbed her dad's arm. "Do you think?"

"I don't know, Aspen, it could be anybody."

Aspen looked over her shoulder. The two FBI agents had wandered over to the group. She could see they were as interested as the rest of them.

"Okay, we have the lights set a little better. Can you all see this?"

"We can see it. Are we looking at two left feet?" asked Roger.

"That you are, but there are three left. No wait that is a right, I think. I am taking pictures. They are lodged in there pretty good."

"This is unbelievable," said Les. *"It's like we are in a liquid time capsule."*

"It will take a few minutes. We are activating the grappling arm and camera. I want to get some closer shots."

"Can they bring them up?"

"Not just yet, Aspen. We need to take some other equipment down. If we disturb them, they will most likely break apart. It's a delicate thing. We would want to keep them as intact as possible."

"Have you ever found anything like this before?" asked Noah.

"Bodies? Oh, sure, but usually entire bodies, drowning victims. Not like this. These have been there for a while."

"Yeah, like fifty years!" said Kiryn

"At least," said Mom quietly.

"We don't know that these are— That they are—" Rocky's voice drifted off. "Yeah, they probably are."

"Well, this would be good then. Maybe we found Ronda and Thomas," said Gavin.

Les was maneuvering the camera. It looked hard. He was trying to get as close as possible, without touching the skeletons.

After almost thirty minutes, he said, *"Okay, I think we got enough. It will be interesting to see what's on that camera."*

A loud roar came through the speakers.

"What's that sound?" Roger looked anxiously at the screen.

"That is water, and it is coming fast," Kendall yelled.

"Camera in!" yelled Les.

Static was all that was coming through the speakers.

"Are you okay? Kendall? Les?"

Static.

"Oh, my gosh! I hope they are okay!" Kiryn looked like she was going to cry.

"They're okay. We just lost contact for a few minutes." Roger sounded like he was trying to convince himself.

Now, complete silence.

"This is like waiting for the astronauts to re-enter the earth's atmosphere," said Toby.

"It really is. I hated that suspense, too," said Dana.

"C'mon guys, where are you?" Roger's elbows rested on his knees, and he leaned closer to the screen.

"Th—is__M—oll—ca—ou—"

"We hear you, Molly!" Roger sat straight up. It wasn't hard to see the relief on his face.

"That was some ride! Are we clear now?"

"Clear as a bell."

"Wait—wait—Kendall, we are still going northeast."

"So— Oh, right. We are going deeper into the channel. We are not coming back out.'

"Can you turn around?" Roger was typing rapidly on his keyboard.

"No. The current is pulling us."

"That is just great! Now they are going to be stuck there!" wailed Aspen.

"I heard that. We are not going to be stuck here. We just need to figure this out," said Kendall.

"This is one smooth ride, though, and we are moving fast," said Les.

"I can see that," said Roger.

"Are those fish? Again?" Noah squinted, trying to see more clearly.

"Yes, but there are a ton of fish. How in the world—" Roger seemed flabbergasted.

"The channel looks like it is getting more narrow," said Jackson. He too, was leaning closer to the computer screen.

"It is," said Roger. "Considerably narrower." He sounded worried.

"Uh, Kendall—"

"Yeah, we know. Can you believe all these fish?"

"Fish, smish! I don't want you guys to crash into the sides of that channel!"

"Whoa! We just stopped—well the current stopped—we are running on our own power," said Les.

"You have just gone from a depth of two hundred and forty-seven feet to seventy-two feet," said Roger.

"We were being pulled up?"

"Seems so."

"But we were at a hundred and five feet when we entered the channel," said Les. *"Where are we?"*

Aspen put her face in her hands. "Lost! And it's all my fault."

Gavin put his arm across her shoulders. "They will be okay."

Aspen didn't think he sounded confident at all.

"We are coming upon some light. What do you make of that, Kendall?" Les's voice seemed quieter.

"Don't go to the light!" yelled Kiryn.

"What? Why?"

"Because Noah! Don't you know when you die, you go to a light? They always say, 'go toward the light'!"

"Kiryn." Aunt Dana suppressed a laugh as she put her arm around Kiryn's waist. "We can still hear them, sweetie, they are not dead."

"Well, they could be. Oh, I hate this."

"Hey, are you surfacing?" Roger stood and scanned the lake. Everyone else did the same.

"We are. We are at ten feet, so we must be," said Les.

"Where? You're not here."

"Yeah, I have been looking at these instruments. Didn't think we were."

"Guess we'll find out," said Kendall. *"The coordinates are— Hold on."*

"I hope they haven't gone into one of those dimension things," Kiryn whispered to Dana. She didn't want Aspen to hear her.

But she did, and she glared at Kiryn.

"Holy smokes! We are at Lake Matthews!" Les yelled.

"What? That's nearly thirty miles away!" Roger stood again. "Are you sure?"

"Pretty sure," said Les, and they heard Kendall laugh. *"I have brought my boat here plenty of times."*

Everyone at Mystic Lake stared at each other. Finally, Roger asked, "Now what?"

They could see Molly moving closer to the shore.

Kendall turned the camera on himself.

"Come and get us!" he laughed.

66

I QUIT

HANK FOLDED HIS ARMS across his chest as he watched Byron and Larry climb out of the car. "And just exactly where have you been? Why are— We were at—" Hank looked up at the sign on the storefront, "A car rental?"

Larry looked pale, and Hank asked if he was still sick.

"I'm feeling a little better."

"Did you have the flu? It's not like you to miss so much work."

"No, not the flu. Just sick. Sick of everything."

Larry was shorter than Hank, and he was looking at the ground, so Hank had to lean down to look up into Larry's eyes. "Problems at home?"

Larry nodded briefly. "Yeah, I need to go home. I think this might be the end of the line for me."

Hank looked over at Byron, who hunched his shoulders and flipped both hands open. He shook his head but didn't say any-thing.

"Look, Larry, I get it if you need some time off. Go home for the holidays. Come back after the New Year. We've got this."

Larry still did not look at Hank. "I don't know. I just need to leave right now."

"Okay, but Larry, you have ten years with the FBI. Whatever it is, we will help you through it."

"Probably not, not this time."

Hank looked at Byron again and then turned back to Larry. "Are you leaving now? *Today?*"

Larry lifted his chin toward the car rental sign. "Yeah, I checked out of the motel. I got a car, so I don't need a ride."

Hank studied Larry, and the three men were silent.

Finally, Hank said, "Okay. Will you let us know that you made it home?"

"Sure." Larry looked up, and his eyes were brimming with tears.

"Larry?" Hank put a hand on his shoulder, but Larry pulled away.

"It's been great, working with you two. Probably the best years of my life."

"Well, don't make it sound so final, Larry. You'll be back in a couple of weeks. We still have a lot to stir up in Sommerville!"

Larry smiled weakly. "Okay, we'll look. I must go. Thanks for meeting with me."

Larry quickly shook each of their hands and walked briskly into the car rental.

Hank turned to Byron.

"I don't know, Hank. I tried to pry it out of him all the way over here. Nothing. He barely talked."

They climbed into Hank's car.

"He called me this morning like I told you and asked if I would pick him up. He asked me to call you to meet us here. That's it."

"And you haven't talked to him for the last couple of days?"

"No, he was supposed to go with me to get the will, but he bailed."

Hank's eyebrows furrowed. "What the—"

"Don't know."

They watched Larry leave the car rental with an agent, signed a paper, took the keys, and in less than ten minutes, he was gone. He didn't look back.

Neither of them said a word for several minutes.

Hank looked over at Byron. His eyes were glistening.

"You okay?"

"Yeah, yeah. I'm good. Just been a damn good partner. Wish I knew what was bothering him." Byron brushed at the corner of his eyes with this fingers. "So, what now? Are we going to see Brandon?"

Hank shook his head. "His dad nixed that."

"What did the Commissioner say?"

"Merry Christmas."

"Huh?"

"That's what he said. "Merry Christmas."

"That guy is as strange as a three-dollar bill."

67

NOSEY NEIGHBOR

NOAH, ASPEN, AND KIRYN stood back a little as Gavin rang the doorbell for the third time. Armed with a huge vase of flowers, a pan of lasagna, and a loaf of garlic bread, they waited.

"Maybe they aren't home," said Aspen.

"Well, there are lights on in almost every window." Kiryn walked back onto the grass to survey the house.

"Hi."

They all turned around to see a woman standing on the sidewalk.

"I'm the Garrett's. I'm Samantha, their neighbor. They aren't at home."

"Oh, should we come back later?" asked Aspen.

Samantha stopped for a second and studied Aspen. "You're, that Allen girl, right?"

Aspen sighed. "Yes."

"Quite an adventure you have had since you moved here." She motioned to the black SUV parked a couple of houses down. "Are they with you? I haven't seen that car around this neighborhood."

Aspen opened her mouth to say something, but Gavin rescued her.

"Uh, yeah, Mrs.— Samantha. "I'm Gavin Fielden. This is my sister, Kiryn, and Aspen and Noah Allen. We wanted to stop by and offer our condolences. Do you know when they will be back?"

Samantha shook her head. "I don't. They didn't say a word. Poor souls, I saw they were putting suitcases in their car early this morning, but they were gone before I got my slippers on and out the door."

I'll bet. This lady seems like the neighborhood busybody. Aspen rolled her eyes, but not so Samantha could see her.

"Well, you know with all that has transpired with little Cassie and all— It's terrible, just terrible."

"It really is," said Kiryn and Aspen noticed Gavin shot Kiryn an annoyed look.

But Kiryn didn't pick up on it.

"So sad that she died. She must have been sick or something."

"Well, we had better get going," said Noah. "Guess we'll have lasagna tonight." He started to walk past Samantha.

"Well, you know it was those drugs. That's what killed her. Such a waste of talent."

Noah stopped short. "What?"

"Oh, yes, her grandmother told me last night. Cassie was full of drugs."

"We really better go." Gavin snatched the flowers from Aspen and thrust them at Samantha. "Here. If they don't come back in the next day or so, Merry Christmas."

He took Aspen and Kiryn each by the arm and followed Noah to the car.

Samantha still rattled on, "Why, thank you!" She waved. "Oh, and Merry Christmas!"

"What a complete moron!" Noah started the Iroc and sped down the street.

"Why would she say that about drugs?" Kiryn was sitting in the front seat.

Gavin had purposely opened the door, pushed the front seat forward, and gently pushed Aspen into the back. Now he pulled her to him, and she snuggled against his side.

"You can't put too much weight in what that woman says," said Gavin. "She was always saying things that weren't true, or at least exaggerated about everyone in the neighborhood."

"She reminds me of that neighbor on that old TV show, *Bewitched*," said Kiryn. "Interesting that her name is Samantha."

"Samantha was the witch," laughed Aspen.

"Well, I know, but still, she does." Kiryn kept talking about the show to Noah, who laughed with her. They were trying to remember the nosey neighbor's name.

Gavin pressed his face into Aspen's hair and whispered in her ear, "I love you, Aspen. You know that, don't you?"

Before she could answer, he took her chin and turned her face to his. "I do, Aspen. I am sorry, and I am sad that Cassie is dead, but I love you."

Aspen peered into his electric green eyes. "I know that," she whispered and her heart pounded.

Gavin cupped her head in his hand and pressed his lips firmly against hers, kissing her with more passion than she would expect with Kiryn and Noah so close by.

He released her and locked his eyes on hers. He kissed her cheeks and then her lips again.

Aspen wrapped her arm around his waist and again snuggled against him, barley hearing Kiryn say to Noah,

"Oh, yeah, it was Mrs. Kravitz!"

68

A BIT OF CLOSURE

"WHAT ARE WE GOING to do with the guns?"

Jackson surveyed the wall-to-wall gun case in the master bedroom of the Mansion House.

"I'm not exactly sure. When we find out what they are worth, we can discuss that, I guess."

Suzann followed him into the hallway, and he locked the door.

"The appraiser is coming on the 27th. I wanted to make sure Dana is here."

The two of them walked down the hall toward the storage.

"It looks so different with all of the paintings off the walls."

"Yes, it does, but it's still better to have all of them safe in one room with all of these people in and out of the house." Suzann looked toward the end of the hall where the FBI had reopened the shaft where Aspen had fallen in shortly after they had arrived in Sommerville.

They weren't supposed to be in the house, but she and Noah and their new friends, Kiryn, and Gavin had decided to explore on their own. When they attempted to move the big potted tree, the wall gave way, and Aspen fell—leading to the discovery of the two rooms below the shaft. Which, in time, eventually led to them finding the statue Jackson's grandfather had buried there in honor of his daughter, Ronda.

Seven doors along the hallway opened each to six bedrooms and the storage room.

The master bedroom was past the staircase at the opposite end, and stood by itself, except for one small bedroom across the hall. Jackson explained that the bedroom was rarely used, even when he lived in the house as a child.

"C'mon, I'll show you my room."

Suzann followed Jackson into one of the rooms.

"Was this furniture here when you lived here?" but then a picture on the wall caught her attention. "There's that picture of you in your football uniform. Jackson, you should take this."

Jackson shrugged. "Why? I have the smaller version already."

"I know you do, but this one is so—"

"Old?" chided Jackson.

She laughed. "Well, yes, but I mean the frame and the picture itself."

Jackson walked across the room and took the large picture off the wall. "Let's put it in the storage room with the paintings."

Suzann nodded. "Perfect."

As they exited the room, she said, "This room is several shades of blue. Did you like blue?"

"Yeah, at the time."

Once in the hallway, Suzann then started toward another room. This was the room where Aspen had tried to show her a small picture that was the same, only opposite, of a picture on the wall of Jackson's grandpa, sister, and brother.

Now the FBI had crews in and out of this room all day long. The closet was where Noah, Aspen, Gavin, Kiryn, and Rocky found the door in the floor with the ladder that took them to the tunnel under the house.

This tunnel was on the opposite side of the upstairs hallway from the shaft and was now being used to gain access to an even longer tunnel which led FBI agents to the room under Doug Mendel's house. The room where they found the remains of what was believed to be the boys that had worked for Allen-Dixon, Inc. in the 1940s.

Suzann walked into the closet. The door in the floor leading to the ladder was closed and padlocked.

Jackson set the picture he was holding on the floor, leaned it against the wall, and followed his wife.

"I'm glad someone is finally working on all of this, aren't you, Jackson?"

He didn't answer, and she turned around.

Jackson was standing by the window so she walked over next to him, and put her arm around his waist.

"You know, Suzann, we never came in this room. We were not forbidden to, like the master bedroom, but we just didn't. We all knew this was kind of a shrine to our grandpa's daughter who had disappeared." He chuckled. "The one that for all these years we thought was Riley."

He turned to look at Suzann. "Now, of course, we know that girl is Ronda." He glanced around the room. "Look at this place. The furniture, the pictures; everything in here was hers."

Suzann noticed the yellowing lace curtains and bedspread, and the sturdy cradle and rocking chair in the corner. She gave Jackson's waist a quick squeeze and then crossed the room to the cradle.

"Why would they have a cradle in Ronda's room?"

Jackson shrugged, "I have no idea."

"Would you or Dana want to keep any of this stuff?"

He shook his head, emphatically. "Definitely not, and I assume if Dana had wanted to, she would have taken it when she moved."

Suzann protested. "Not even this lovely rocker?"

The cradle was positioned just enough in front of the rocker that one was not able to sit in it. Suzann grasped the ends of the cradle and pulled, but it didn't budge.

"Is it that heavy?" teased Jackson and he joined her. He too pulled on the cradle, but it barely moved.

"What is this thing made of?" Jackson lifted the lace skirt to look at the bottom. It looked like a normal cradle on top, but rather than the typical four legs, the bottom was a solid rectangular box. Four metal rods attached to the box, each with a U-shaped holder the cradle rested in allowing it to rock.

He let go of the skirt, and it fell back into place. "Of course, nothing in this house is normal." He motioned to Suzann. "Let's get going. Maybe there is a historical society around here who would be interested in this stuff."

Suzann followed him to the door. "Maybe, but this is a good thing, Jackson. A bit of closure for you." She hesitated and then asked, "Jackson, have you given any thought to going down into the tunnel? I mean, are you curious at all to see it for yourself?"

Jackson stopped and turned to look at his wife. "No. I think what Aspen experienced down there was all that was needed. What possible secrets could this old house hold that would be any more valuable than finding those boys?"

Jackson walked out of the bedroom, picked up the picture, unlocked the storage door, and set the picture just inside without entering the room. He closed the door and locked it, and took Suzann's hand, pulling her along with him toward the staircase.

"Forget I said that."

69

DECEMBER 24TH

"Did they say what they wanted?"

Noah shook his head at his sister. "Nope. Joseph just asked if they could come by this afternoon."

Aspen shrugged. "Just seems kind of strange on Christmas Eve, that's all."

They heard a car in the driveway, and Noah walked to the door. When he pulled it open, he was surprised to see Rocky, Kiryn, and Gavin climbing out of Rocky's truck.

The three got out and walked up to the porch.

Aspen joined Noah at the door and noticed their dad's truck in the driveway. "I thought Mom and Dad went up to the big house."

"They did. Guess they walked."

Aspen rolled her eyes. "Fat chance. I'm not sure Dad should be doing that."

"I think he's doing pretty well, Aspen. We shouldn't discourage him."

She sighed. "You're right. I just worry, and it's cold."

"Hey! Surprised to see us?" Kiryn laughed and threw her arms around Noah, throwing him off balance.

Noah caught himself and leaned back to look directly into Kiryn's face. When he did, he was so surprised that his heart jumped. "Uh, yeah, as a matter of fact, I am—surprised."

They all turned to see Drew's truck roll in and stop behind Rocky's.

Rocky jutted his thumb toward the new arrivals. "Drew called about an hour ago. I was just getting ready to drive Gavin back to Memphis."

Aspen scowled. "Are you spending Christmas Eve with your mom and Doug?"

"Well, that was the plan, but just before Drew called, Mom called and asked Dad if I could stay here. She and Doug want all of us—" Gavin flipped his hand in a circle. "To come over tomorrow afternoon for a Christmas Party."

Aspen's eyebrows shot up. "Really? That would be great, but I wonder if Mom and Dad will want to."

Kiryn had released Noah from her iron grip and now walked past the two of them into the house. "I hope so. Rocky said it sounded pretty important to her."

Rocky nodded. "I will talk to your parents. I hope they will go."

Joseph and Drew had been sitting in the truck, but now both got out and walked up to the group. They were each carrying large baskets spilling over with fruit and several packages wrapped in red, green, and silver foil paper.

The sweet smell of fresh baked goods permeated from the baskets and Aspen could not help but notice how beautifully they were put together.

"What's going on here?"

Everyone whirled to see Jackson and Suzann coming in from the kitchen.

Before anyone could answer, Jackson glanced past them toward Drew and Joseph, who were just now entering the house. He called to them, "Drew and Joseph welcome! Glad you could come over."

Noah was puzzled. "I thought they called to come over."

"They did." Jackson passed his kids and walked directly to Drew, quickly shaking his hand. "Come in. Come in."

Aspen turned to her mother. "Dad's in rare form. What's up?"

Mom laughed. "Nothing. He is just in a good mood."

Aspen became aware of her mother's rosy cheeks and nose. "Did you guys walk to the big house?"

Mom laughed. "Yes, crazy, huh. It is so cold."

"Then why—"

Mom grinned at Noah. "Don't know. Your dad wanted to. We walked up on the road. It's not quite so steep, at least that's what your dad said. I had no idea, but then we walked down the steps. What a beautiful walk! It was so nice, just Dad and me, and he reminisced all the way down. He said he hasn't been on those steps since he was seventeen—just before he left Sommerville."

Noah and Aspen both turned to look at their dad, who was also sporting bright, red cheeks and a red nose.

Noah nudged his sister. "He looks good," he whispered.

Aspen smiled. "Healthy," she whispered back.

The fire that Noah had started was blazing now, and Aspen and Kiryn delivered mugs of hot chocolate topped with marshmallows to everyone in the room.

"This is a nice place you have here, Jackson," Drew said.

"A little bigger than before the fire, but it was nice before. This house was where my grandparents and parents help lived."

Jackson turned to Aspen. "Their servants, not slaves."

That made everyone laugh. Aspen hated the thought of any of her relatives owning slaves.

Aspen studied Drew for a minute. He was a nice-looking man. Tall, muscular, and thick blonde hair which was neatly combed. Not at all like the first day they had met Drew. The big scary gardener with a sweaty bandana around his head, dirty hands, and clothes, who glared at her and Noah through black sunglasses.

"If you go back far enough, you will probably find ancestors who actually did own slaves—especially in this part of the country," said Drew.

Aspen shuddered. "I hope not, but the more I learn about the past, you are probably right."

Drew took a sip of his cocoa and set the mug on a poinsettia coaster on an end table. "We don't want to keep you long." He glanced at Joseph. "This was his idea actually. We just wanted to make amends for those first few weeks you were in Sommerville."

"And to say that we don't care about the money from the will anymore," blurted Joseph.

Drew grinned. "Joseph feels like it has caused a rift in the community and between our two families for a long time—too long."

Drew took a deep breath and slowly let it blow out through his lips. "I'm not sure that I agree."

He quickly looked at Jackson. "But only if it is something we are entitled to. If the will doesn't say anything about us—"

"Dad?" Joseph glared at his father.

Drew laughed. "He's right. Let's just let it go."

Rocky waited for Jackson to say something and when he didn't immediately, he said, "It's none of my business, but I have wondered about this for a long time." He looked at Jackson and waited for his okay to go ahead.

Jackson nodded.

"The note, or letter, the one that Aspen heard you talking about the day she was hiding in the bedroom, and the two of you came into the Mansion House."

Drew shifted in his seat. "Yeah, there is that."

All four kids nodded.

Drew looked at the floor for a few seconds, but then he looked directly at Jackson. "It was a letter that our Aunt, our dad's sister, told us about. She said we needed to find a box. That Grandpa had hidden it in the Mansion House so that, well, I guess, so that no one would find it. No one would think to look there."

"Uh, before we go on, we were sorry to hear about Cassie. Such terrible news anytime, but especially this close to Christmas," said Mom.

Drew nodded. "Yeah, this is not good. Our little sister doesn't even know about it yet. She is in Africa on a tour. We have tried to reach her, but no luck. She will call tomorrow though. Then we will have to tell her."

"Was she close to Cassie?" asked Aspen

"No, she really wasn't. She pretty much stayed away from her so she could have a normal life with Carl and Jan Garrett. They have been wonderful to her—good people."

"It is really a shame. So sad," said Kiryn.

"That it is, and a mystery. I can't figure it out," said Drew.

They were all quiet for a few seconds, but then Dad brought the conversation back to the original subject.

"The box, Drew. What was supposed to be in it?" asked Jackson.

Drew shook his head. "I don't know for sure. Dylan swears Grandpa told him whatever it was, is worth a lot of money and that it belongs to our family."

Drew suddenly looked sad. "Instead of all that has been found though, I really wonder, if it is there, number one, and does it legally belong to the Dixons."

Mom was sitting next to Drew, and she reached over and patted his knee, at the same time speaking to Joseph. "This is very kind of you both to come here. Thank you."

Joseph blushed. "It's just that, well, I have never hated you, Gavin, or you either, Kiryn. I just kind of keep to myself."

"We don't hate you either, Joseph. You are just—"

"Kiryn! Are you kidding me?" Gavin scowled at his sister.

"Nice! I was going to say nice!"

Joseph blushed even more. "Weird, you were going to say weird."

Rocky looked at Gavin, and they both rolled their eyes.

"We try to keep her away from the public," said Gavin.

That made Joseph laugh, and then everyone else laughed too.

Kiryn glanced around the room and quickly stood. "Anyone want some more cocoa? We made plenty!"

"I have a better idea." Mom stood and went into the kitchen, prompting Kiryn to sit back down.

Minutes later, Mom returned with a plate of banana nut bread.

"Homemade?" Aspen's eyes lit up.

Mom nodded and handed the plate to Drew, who took a slice and passed it to Joseph.

"I thought I smelled something good! When did you make this, Mom?" Noah took a huge bite out of his slice.

"Early this morning, before your dad and I left."

"This is so good." Kiryn closed her eyes. "Yummm."

"I have a loaf for you to take home," said Mom.

"Awesome." And Kiryn took another bite.

IT'S AN ALLEN THING

ASPEN, NOAH, MOM, AND Dad sat on the floor in front of the Christmas tree.

The afternoon had been fun having Rocky, Kiryn, and Gavin over, and even with Drew and Joseph. They had stayed longer than they planned. Drew had explained, but it seemed to Aspen the tension between their families had eased, and she felt going forward, there would even be room for friendship.

After all, Drew worked for her dad, and he seemed like a nice man. And Joseph, well, he was a nice guy. He was just painfully shy.

She couldn't help but wonder where Dylan was though, but she didn't ask, and it seemed to her like everyone else was avoiding asking as well.

It was nearly nine o'clock.

For as long as Aspen could remember, Mom had prepared a taco bar for Christmas Eve. She said that way, the ham and au gratin potatoes would taste better on Christmas day.

Mom had delivered a huge plate of tacos, banana bread, and hot cocoa to the two FBI agents holding up in their black SUV in the yard. She was not happy they had to be here on Christmas, but both assured her neither of them was married, so no wives or children would be neglected. They further explained they had both chosen to pull the entire Christmas Eve and Christmas day duty because the money was good.

Satisfied with that explanation, Mom had finally come back in the house.

It had started to rain shortly after Rocky left with Gavin and Kiryn, so now Mom was soaking wet.

While she changed into dry clothes, Dad, Aspen, and Noah finished cleaning up the remnants of dinner. They were all gathered around the tree when Mom joined them.

This was tradition.

Dad read the Christmas story from Luke in the Bible, and Mom read the *Littlest Angel*.

Aspen loved both stories. She always tried to imagine Mary and Joseph traveling all that way just before baby Jesus was born, and she marveled at what a wonderful gift the Son of God was to the world. She couldn't help but admire the brave young couple, and every year, she made a mental note to get to know the Savior better. This year, she resolved she would for sure.

Every year she felt sad for the littlest angel who was trying so desperately to think of a gift to honor the king but seemed to fumble everything he touched.

Even though she knew how the story would end, she longed for his little breaking heart to be happy.

The stories were over now, and the fire hissed and crackled. Aspen loved that sound. She had decided after having a real wood fireplace that when they did return to San Clemente, she was going to ask Dad to replace their gas one.

Aspen looked up at the new Christmas stockings. Each of their names was embroidered into the plush red fabric. Mom had them specially made. On the toe of each stocking was a palm tree for San Clemente, and on the heel, a pine tree for Sommerville.

Aunt Dana's stocking would stay there until she returned on the 27th.

They had all promised not to worry about presents this year. Mom and Dad were grateful they were all healthy and together, and Aspen and Noah agreed. Gifts seemed completely unnecessary this year, but right now, Mom was on her knees, fishing for something behind the tree.

She backed out, turned around and produced two rectangular packages.

"But I thought—"

Mom shushed her daughter. "It wouldn't be Christmas!"

Aspen and Noah glanced at each other, and both started to laugh. Saying nothing more, they tore open the packages, mostly because that is what Mom expected them to do.

Tossing the top of the boxes and the Santa paper to the side—always Santa paper for this gift—they each pulled out solid red Christmas pajamas.

"What? They match!" Noah started to laugh.

"Mom! When was the last time we had matching pajamas?" Aspen was laughing too.

"When you were two and four. They are men's, Aspen. I thought you would look better in those than Noah would in a nightgown."

"Well, at least thanks for that," said Noah.

They both started to pull them out of the boxes, but Mom stopped them. "Wait."

She again scrambled behind the tree and produced two more boxes. She handed one to Dad.

"But—" Dad started to protest.

"Just open it." Mom's voice went up two octaves, and she started opening the fourth gift.

"You bought yourself a present, Mom?" Noah chuckled.

"I did!"

Mom and Dad's boxes were open, and Mom instructed them all to hold them up.

All four pairs of pajamas were identical.

"What does it say?" Noah held his at arms-length and read, "*We are a family of survivors.*" He grinned. "That's cool, Mom."

Mom flipped hers over. "Look at the back."

Aspen smiled, and tears filled her eyes. A wave of happiness washed over her, and she quickly looked at her mom, her dad, and then her brother. She read aloud, *"It's an Allen thing—you wouldn't understand."*

THE END

PREFACE

We need help!

Don't give up!

Please!

You are our last resort!

Trying to escape the voices, Aspen ran as fast as she could, but there was no escape. They were all around her.

She wanted to help, but so much was out of her hands now. How could she tell them? She wanted to explain. Maybe if she could get back to the balcony in the beautiful garden, maybe she would see them there, and she could talk to them. Maybe then they would understand how hard she and her friends were trying.

Suddenly the ground under her feet vanished—

Kendall Washington stood on the driveway of the Allen Mansion House. He had been standing there for nearly an hour. No one had come by. He figured he was safe to come today. It was Christmas, and everyone was with family, and he figured the last place the Allens would want to be right now, was at their family home that had become a crime scene more than anything else.

He had just returned from Nashville and was headed to see his grandfather, but there were so many unanswered questions. He wanted to collect his thoughts. He didn't want to upset his grandfather, but he couldn't keep this inside any longer.

First the dive under Mystic Lake, then finding—miraculously—Aspen Allen's unconscious body. When he took his diving teams back out there that morning, he was positive they were looking for a corpse, but there she was, on the shore, covered in mud and soaking wet, but alive. Barely, but still, she was alive.

The fire at the Allen residence baffled him. There was no question it was arson from the moment he stepped onto the property, and he was not convinced that the teenager, Brandon Tuttle, did this on his own. He was even less convinced that he and Cassie Garret, who herself was now dead, put the whole scheme together out of jealousy.

Kendall had been in and out of this small town all his life. His grandfather lived here, but his mother lived in Nashville. He came here regularly to visit, and he thought he was familiar with the community, but now he was not so sure.

Memphis was his home now, but he was often called to Sommerville for either fire investigation or if someone needed to make use of his diving teams. The latter used the least. Not too many people needed diving teams in Sommerville.

He had been in the lakes in the area, but never Mystic Lake. He had been to Lake Matthews several times, however. Never once had there been any sign of a channel with a current strong enough to pull the divers into it. The fact that he had been in the channel that connected Mystic Lake and Lake Matthews, over thirty miles away, was still something he was trying to wrap his head around.

He hadn't been able to spend much time on any of it, with the holidays upon him, but tomorrow he would. He and his team had already formulated a plan, and it would start with researching past dives, past drownings, past anything that had to do with water in, or near Sommerville.

He looked at the notes he had been keeping in his phone, which related to the Allen case, or cases. One name was highlighted, one name kept jumping out at him, but this man was his friend, and had been a good friend to his grandfather, aunt, and niece. This was a tough call, but he knew he had to do it.

Kendall sighed. Should he involve Detective Hank Cox, or should he first go for it on his own?

Either way, this was going to be a hard week.

1

NOTHING STAYS THE SAME... BUT CHANGE

I'm sorry, I never thought this would ever go so far. When I agreed to help, I was under the impression I was doing something to preserve an important part of history of sorts, although, looking back, that isn't at all true, I used that as an excuse to justify what I was doing. I wanted the money. This was no small sum of cash.

I figured we would drop some hints, scare a few people, maybe even rough some up, but I had no idea anyone would get seriously hurt, let alone die, and definitely—not a kid.

I can't live with myself. I can't go home to my family. Because I know I won't be with them anyway. I am a disgrace, and I will only bring shame to my wife, my kids, and my parents, and I will most likely end up in prison.

I've spent a lot of time in special forces. I know where to go and what to do. I was always a damn good sniper.

I am sending this letter to you, and one to Linda. She will be fine financially. At least I made sure of that.

I can't begin to tell you how sorry I am, but I guess I am also a coward. I just want out—out of this place—out of this life.

I need to disappear.

The holidays will be over, and I will be long gone before you get this.

Happy New Year.

Hands shaking, he folded the letter, carefully placed it in the previously addressed envelope, sealed it, and then tucked it into his coat pocket with the other one.

He grabbed his duffle bag and sauntered over to the locked door. Pulling both letters from his pocket, he slipped them through a thin slot. His face expressionless, he stared at the narrow opening.

No going back now.

Turning slowly, he stared out the window through the pounding rain as the massive transporter rolled up to the gate.

It's done. I'm done.

Aspen reached for her phone and started to push snooze, but then she realized it was a text.

She smiled. It was from Gavin.

She tapped the icon and the text opened to reveal Gavin and Kiryn's faces grinning back at her.

"*MERRY CHRISTMAS!*" was in the text box.

She quickly replied with the same message, attached a picture they had taken last night, of her and Noah in their new pajamas, and then added, "*See you in a while, love you.*"

The next message made Aspen tingle all over, "*I love you too, Aspen Allen.*"

Aspen clasped her phone to her chest and curled under the covers. It was 8:00 am, and the house was quiet.

She rolled over to look outside and was thrilled to see light snowflakes drifting past her window.

What could be better? It's Christmas, and our family is together, Gavin loves me, and—she touched the sleeve of her pajamas—*we have red pajamas!*

She smiled and closed her eyes, but the serenity was short-lived.

The images behind her eyelids caused anxiety to invade this happy moment and the ever-threatening, imposing feeling lodged in the pit of her stomach.

So much was still unsettled.

The Mansion House was slowly being dismantled, at least underneath it. The tunnels leading to Doug and Sara Mendel's house had revealed the remains of nearly fifty bodies, and the files they found in her Great-Grandpa's office positively confirmed that two hundred and eleven boys had worked for Allen-Dixon, Inc.

Jackson Allen Humphrey's last will and testament had finally been located, but not read, and the paintings, all now safely stashed in the storage, were still a mystery.

The bones of three dead people had been found in a channel under Mystic Lake and Kendall Washington had discovered that the channel linked to Lake Matthews. No one, at least to Kendall's knowledge, had ever found that channel before.

Toby Smith had shown up out of nowhere from Australia, revealing that he was the great, great-grandson of Harold Demot, the name on a letter to her grandfather's partner, Lloyd Dixon. The letter gave instructions telling Dixon how to open the secret shelving unit in her grandfather's office at the big house.

There, they had found the files.

A fire had intentionally been set at the little house, forcing her family to move out for several weeks until it was rebuilt.

A classmate, Brandon Tuttle, had confessed to setting the fire and was in police custody for his own safety because of the suspicious death of another of their classmates, Cassie Garret. Brandon had alleged that Cassie had something to do with the fire. Police had planned to question her when she returned from a dance competition trip to New York, but they never had the chance. She died shortly after her parents picked her up from the airport.

And that was just in the last three weeks.

Aspen's head began to spin. A part of her wanted to see Krista's spirit, or even Max, the mysterious red-haired boy, but another part of her wanted that world to go away, at least for today.

She fumbled under her covers until she located Sprinkle. She wrapped both arms around her treasured stuffed animal, hugging it tightly to her chest.

She laughed at herself for sleeping with Sprinkle last night. It had just seemed like the right thing to do. Sprinkle was an important part of her childhood, and last night was, well it was like being home, in San Clemente.

Her eyes slowly closed. *Can it all go away? Just for today, Heavenly Father, please, just for today.*

Aspen laughed at herself when she realized she had uttered that small prayer more than once this past week.

The smell of pancakes and sausage wafted into her room, and Aspen jumped out of bed, abandoning Sprinkle, she retrieved her phone. She knew Mom must already be in the kitchen making their traditional Christmas morning breakfast; pancakes, eggs, hash browns, and a choice of steak or sausage or both.

Aspen loved it.

She hurried out of her room and into the new bathroom at the end of the hall. When she came back, she noticed Noah's door was open. She quickly made her bed, placed Sprinkle on the window seat, facing out, so he could see the snow.

Her thought process made her chuckle, and she all but skipped down the hall. The fire was burning brightly in the fireplace, and the Christmas tree lights were on.

"Morning!" she greeted her parents and Noah—all still in their red pajamas—who were gathered in the kitchen.

Dad placed two more pancakes on an already tall stack, and Mom was turning steaks on a small electric grill.

Seated at the table, Noah was munching on a sausage.

"Morning, Aspen! Merry Christmas!" Mom seemed to literally sing the words.

"Merry Christmas!" Dad chimed in.

Noah looked her up and down, "Nice pajamas."

His offhand comment made all of them laugh, and Aspen took a seat next to him, at the same time reaching for a sausage.

She observed her parents and brother. This was the first time in history the entire family had matching anything, and Mom had chosen red Christmas pajamas.

A feeling of warmth spread over her, and she grinned at her brother. "Merry Christmas, dear brother."

Noah nodded and smiled. "Yep, you too." And he guzzled a glass of orange juice.

"Hank called this morning. He said to wish all of you a Merry Christmas. He said he would be by tomorrow to introduce Byron's new partner."

This news caused Mom, Aspen, and Noah to abruptly stop eating and stare at Dad.

"Why? Where is Larry?" asked Aspen.

"Probably just for a while. Maybe Larry went home from Christmas," said Noah.

"I don't know, sounded pretty permanent to me," said Dad.

"Hmm, that's strange. He didn't even say goodbye," said Mom. "I would never have thought either of them would just leave."

"He does have a young family, Suzann. Maybe this was too much for him."

Mom looked at her husband. "Maybe, but still. We were friends." She looked around at her family. "Weren't we?"

Noah shrugged. "I thought so."

"Yeah, me too," said Aspen.

"Remember, it's a job for them. This is our life, but it is their job. After this case, they move onto the next," said Dad.

Still, Aspen couldn't stop the sadness that tugged at her heart. She really liked Larry, and along with Byron and Hank, he had become an intricate part of their lives in Sommerville.

But Dad was right, the reality of it was that the two FBI agents and the police detective were so heavily involved in their lives only because of the many different issues involving the Allen's. Had none of this happened, they would probably have never met any of them.

Mom and Dad joined their kids at the table, and they all dug in for a filling Christmas breakfast.

"I'm glad we're out of school for a couple of weeks. Maybe life will return back to normal by then."

Noah rolled his eyes. "Are you serious? I think it's just getting going, considering the investigation and all."

"I'm afraid Noah is right," said Dad. "Hank said the police commissioner is biting at the bit to get a full-blown investigation going into every part of this mess."

Mom sighed. "I don't want to think about it right now." She looked at her husband. "Is that okay, if we don't think about it, just for today?"

Aspen smiled. She and Mom were on the same page.

Dad looked at Noah. "Agreed?"

Noah nodded. "Fine by me. We'll get back into all of it soon enough."

⚬

"What time are we supposed to be at the Mendel's?" Dad motioned for Noah to follow him.

"Three, I believe." Mom furrowed her eyebrows. "Where are you two going?"

"Just outside, we'll be right back."

"I know that look, Jackson Allen, and we agreed, no presents."

"We did, so don't get your hopes up. I just want to show Noah something."

Mom heard the front door close, and she turned to Aspen. "Do you believe him?"

Aspen laughed. "Mom, you already broke the rule with these pajamas."

"True, but this is tradition. I couldn't let Christmas eve go by without new pajamas."

Aspen scrolled through her pictures and then held her phone up so Mom could see the one she selected.

"Not a bad selfie, right? I'm going to have it blown it up huge to hang up every Christmas!"

Mom took the phone and studied the picture. The four of them, in front of the Christmas tree and fire, all decked out in red pajamas. "It's perfect!"

She handed the phone back to Aspen.

"Just perfect."

The front door opened, and Dad yelled, "Suzann! Aspen! Could you come out here?"

"I wonder what he is up to." Suzann followed her daughter through the living room.

Dad had left the door open and Aspen walked out onto the porch. She gasped and then whirled around, "Mom!"

"Jackson! When did you— Why did you—"

The surprise on Mom's face was precisely what Jackson had anticipated.

Right in front of the porch, on the grass no less, sat a brand new, shiny white BMW with a huge red Christmas bow plastered across the windshield.

Jackson was like a little kid. He grabbed Suzann's hand and pulled her down the steps.

Noah was standing next to the car, both hands pointing to the gift, as though he was presenting it as a prize on a TV game show.

"This is so cool! Noah, did you know about this?"

Noah shook his head at Aspen. "Had no clue. Dad kept this one a total secret."

They turned to see the two FBI agents standing right behind them. This was the closest proximity any of the agents had come to the kids, except for the day at the Mystic Lake, when Toby Smith showed up.

"Nice car," said the shorter of the two.

"Mom's other BMW was burned to a crisp in the fire," Noah explained. "It was really nice, but I think it was ten years old or something."

Both agents nodded and raised their eyebrows. The same agent grinned, "Well, then, of course, it would need to be replaced," he chided.

Noah smiled and looked over at his mom. "Yeah, she's kind of spoiled."

Aspen knew Noah was feeling the same way she was. Watching their parents together like this—their dad doting over their mother—seemed like old times.

Mom started to climb into the car.

"Wait!" Aspen pulled her phone out of her pocket.

"We need a picture, Mom!"

"I'm in my pajamas!"

Noah laughed, "Exactly!"

Mom stepped back out the car, struck a quick pose, and a grin, and Aspen snapped the picture.

"Now you, Dad. Get in the picture with Mom."

Dad didn't even resist. He stepped right up behind Mom, put both arms around her and leaned his chin on her shoulder.

"That's a cheesy grin, Dad!" said Noah and Aspen snapped the picture.

"It's perfect." She mumbled.

Noah looked at her and winked. "Yeah, it is."

The taller of the two agents reached for Aspen's phone, "Here. Why don't all of you get in? I'll take it."

Aspen and Noah stood by the passenger side, and the agent snapped a picture.

Aspen glanced over at her mother. "Guess I will have to have two pictures blown up!"

⁂

For the next two hours, Mom took everyone for rides in her new car. She even took both agents for a ride. They both resisted, but Jackson assured them he would stay right there until they each got back.

Noah wanted to drive it, but Dad wouldn't let anyone else have a turn.

"You can drive it tomorrow." He said flatly.

Noah reluctantly agreed.

Dad followed up with, "If Mom says you can."

When it came time to leave for Memphis, they were all surprised that Mom didn't want to take the new car.

"We can take the Iroc, Mom."

"It's Christmas, Noah. I want us all to be together."

When they all climbed in the truck, Noah leaned over the seat and patted Mom's shoulder.

"What was that for?"

"Just thanking you for not giving us matching Christmas vests."

Mom whirled around. "When have I ever done that?"

"You haven't, but you were getting a little sentimental about those pajamas."

Mom lifted her chin and turned back around. "Don't be silly."

Noah sat back in the seat and glanced at Aspen. He gave her a "yeah right" look, and she quickly looked out the window so Mom wouldn't see her laugh.

"Of course, when Dana gets back, there will be a fashion show," Mom mumbled, and she threw a side glance at Dad, who pretend not to notice.

"What?" Noah sat up in his seat.

"Nothing, nothing." Mom buckled her seat belt. "Let's go!"

The Allens had never been in Doug and Sara's home in Memphis. In fact, they had never been in their home at Mystic Lake, either.

When they arrived, Aspen noticed Rocky's truck. She was surprised to see Hank's truck there as well. She didn't see Sara's car, but that wasn't surprising. Maybe it was in Sommerville.

When they were climbing out of the truck, Aspen asked, "Who was invited to this shindig?"

"I don't know, Aspen. Sara must not have felt she needed to go over the guest list with us."

Aspen glared at her brother, but she didn't say anything.

He laughed, and lightly punched her shoulder but then he noticed the look on her face.

He put his arm across her shoulders and whispered, "Are you okay?"

She whispered back, "I suddenly feel—I don't know, uncomfortable."

"Why? We know all of these people."

Aspen shrugged, "Doug, I guess. He—"

"He what?"

"I don't trust him. Do you?"

Noah looked straight ahead as they followed their parents up the long sidewalk.

"No, not really, but I don't even know why. After all, he's Gavin's step-dad. He wouldn't do anything weird. You heard Hank; he helps a lot of people in the Sommerville community."

Aspen sighed, "I know." She looked at her brother. "You're right."

"I don't know about that. Guess I just don't want to think about it too much…today."

Aspen nodded in agreement. "Me either."

Dad rang the doorbell, and Kiryn threw the door open.

"Merry Christmas!"

She pulled Mom and Dad inside and then scooted past them, heading right for Aspen and Noah.

She nuzzled between them and then linked arms with each of them.

"So, glad you guys came!"

"We are, too." Aspen laughed with her friend. She leaned over and kissed Kiryn on the cheek. "Merry Christmas!"

Kiryn grinned when she noticed Aspen's eyes dart toward the house. "He's upstairs, wrapping some—Christmas gift—or—something."

Aspen stopped. "*What?* I didn't get him anything!"

"Who said it was for you?" teased Kiryn.

"Yeah," Noah joined in. "It could be for that *other* girl from

California."

"Shut up, you guys."

Aspen's attention was already turned from her brother and best friend. Gavin loped down the steps and walked toward them.

"Merry Christmas!" he scooped her up in a tight hug and then turned to Kiryn, hugged her and bumped knuckles with Noah.

"Did your mom like the BMW?"

"You knew?" Noah couldn't hide his surprise.

"Just since yesterday. Jackson asked Rocky and me to take delivery of it at the Manson House. Then when we left yesterday, we brought it down to the little house and parked it in the driveway—away from the house—so none of you would see it."

"Well, it worked," said Noah. "We had no clue."

"Your two FBI agents noticed us though. They were on us in five seconds. Guess your dad didn't think to tell them."

Noah chuckled. "Wow, they didn't let on either. They acted as surprised as we were this morning."

"Mom took all of us for a ride, including the agents," said Aspen.

"Wow, so they are kind of human," said Kiryn. She glanced in the direction of the black SUV parked under a tree near the entrance to the driveway.

"Apparently." Gavin scanned the cars in the driveway. "Where is it anyway?"

"Mom refused to drive it over here. She wanted us to be together with it being Christmas."

"Well, she is right," said Kiryn. "I totally agree with her. I am sad, however, that you guys aren't wearing those adorable pajamas."

"Are you being sarcastic?" Aspen eyed her friend.

"Absolutely not. I love them. I wish, well, I just mean, it's really cool that your mom—"

Aspen stopped and took her friend by the shoulders. "I'm sorry. I know what you mean, and you're right. It is cool." She hugged Kiryn.

"You can share our mom."

"Yeah, she would love that. Two crazy daughters."

Aspen rolled her eyes at her brother. "Let's go eat. I'm hungry. There is food, right?" She glanced back at Gavin, who was walking with Noah.

"Uh, yeah. You could say that." Gavin chuckled.

Suddenly the front door flew open, and Doug walked briskly past them.

Right on his heels, Sara called from the doorway, "Can't it wait?"

"No. I'll be right back."

Her face flushed, Sara turned to the four teenagers. "I'm, so glad you kids could come."

"Mom, what is that all about?" Gavin took Sara's arm and turned her toward the house.

Sara looked over her shoulder. "Nothing…nothing, Gavin. Don't worry about it. You kids come in. There is a ton of food!"

Still holding his mother's arm, Gavin walked into the house behind her, but he turned and looked in Doug's direction. His green eyes clouded and his mouth twisted, but he didn't say anything.

Kiryn started to follow Gavin, but she stopped and turned around.

Noah and Aspen stopped too, and the three of them looked back at Doug.

He was talking to two men who had pulled up in a silver sedan. They were both standing outside the car, the doors open, each with one foot in the car and the engine was still running. Doug stood next to the man on the passenger side.

From the looks on their faces, it was obvious this was not a friendly conversation.

Aspen could see someone in the back seat, and she squinted to see if she could make out who it was, but she couldn't see clearly.

Suddenly the conversation got more heated, and the man in the back nearly leaped over the seat.

Aspen gasped,

"Dylan?!"

www.ingramcontent.com/pod-product-compliance
Lightning Source LLC
Chambersburg PA
CBHW021951120726
47898CB00001BA/55